Wishing Since Forever

KILTIE JACKSON

ISBN-13: 978 – 1068380501

<u>Also by Kiltie Jackson</u>

A Rock 'n' Roll Lovestyle
An Artisan Lovestyle
An Incidental Lovestyle
A Timeless Lovestyle

Waiting Since Forever
Hoping Since Forever

The Bay of Lost Souls
The Prosecco Pact
A Snowflake in December
Love is on the Air

ACKNOWLEDGEMENTS

As with every book, it takes more than just little old me to get it out into the big, bad world so I give my thanks to the following who are always by my side in these ventures:

John Hudspith – my brilliant and poor, long-suffering editor, who irons out all the wrinkles and crinkles.

Berni Stevens – the most amazing cover designer EVER and who always manages to read my mind and knows exactly what I want.

Mark Fearn – my beta-reader extraordinaire who never says no when I ask him if he's ready to do it all again.

The following Facebook groups are great ambassadors for their author members and worth looking up: The Friendly Book Community which totally lives up to its name… as long as you don't mention brioche! Riveting Reads and Vintage Vibes is a great group run by the wonderful Sue Baker whose support for her author members is second to none and SO deeply appreciated. Thank you so much, Sue, you're a star! Chick Lit and Prosecco is also a fabulous place to hang out if you want to chat about all things romance while Book Mark, and The Fiction Café Book Club are excellent for cross-genre information and discussions.

The members of The Book Club Reviewer Group get a special mention for always grabbing my offerings with gusto and giving up their time to read and review. Thank you very, very much.

Helen Boyce is the fabulous admin who gives up her time to arrange the reviewers in the The Book Club Review Group and li'l ole me appreciates all that she does very much.

Kym Wood – my most wonderful best friend who continues to believe in me after all these years and still reads everything I write.

My Mr Mogs and the Moggy Posse who have to deal with living with a crazy author every day.

And, finally, an extra special "THANK YOU" to everyone who reads my books, leaves reviews – *never* underestimate how important they are – interacts with me on Facebook and who just keeps being there for me every time another novel hits the shelves. Without you, all this would be meaningless. So, again, THANK YOU.

Till the next time,

Kiltie

xx

.

ONE

Flora MacDonald Wainwright sprinkled flour on the wooden kitchen table that had been in her family for over two hundred years and, as she began kneading the dough, she could feel the imprint of the hands which had performed the same task over the decades. The old, solid piece of oak had had many a bread loaf created upon it.

From where she stood, she had a clear view through the bay window opposite and a smile crept over her face as the early morning rays of sun began to sparkle on her loch, suggesting another fresh, glorious day was breaking. She'd always loved the early days of spring – it was still February but the promise of new life and longer days was in the air.

The sight of her two faithful Westies, lying curled up asleep in their bed beneath the smooth seat of the window bay, caught her eye. When they moved their sleeping location from the side of the large, black, kitchen range over to the window, it was a sure sign the coldest nights of winter had finally passed.

Her hands worked while her mind wandered, her gaze returning to the window to soak up the view of the shimmering loch and the steep, black, mountains which rose up behind it, the early morning mist still concealing their peaks. They looked so fierce and brooding at this time of the day, like a big black bear who didn't want to break its slumber, only to transform into shining green and golden pools of beauty when the sun moved round to lay her beams upon them.

As it did every day, the love she felt for this land flowed up through Flora's whole being and she could see it glinting when it teased its way out of her fingers, ready to escape into the atmosphere. Before it could do so, she quickly stuck her hands deep into the dough, allowing the love to permeate through it, for everyone knows that bread loaves infused with love always taste so much better.

All of a sudden, she let out a loud gasp and leant forward, her hands splayed out in front of her on the table, while a sharp pain zipped across her chest. Every muscle from her shoulders to her waist tightened to the point where Flora thought her ribs were about to be crushed into dust.

She couldn't breathe.

She dragged a chair towards her, dropping onto it in a crouched position as silver stars began to dance in front of her eyes, growing larger until all she could see was an expanse of silver which held for a few seconds more before it all turned black and the air around her was filled with nothingness. It was all over.

Several minutes passed before Flora moved again, pulling herself upright. A glance towards the dogs told her they were unaware that everything had just changed. She stood, moved the chair back into place then forced herself to finish making the bread – splitting the dough into the tins and placing them in the oven. The table was cleared, a wet cloth removing the last of the floury motes and as it dried off, the utensils were cleaned and put away. Satisfied that everything was back in its place, Flora pulled the old grandfather chair over from beside the cooking range, placing her crossed arms on the table as she sat down. She then laid her head upon them, drew the curtains closed within her mind and finally let out the tears she'd been holding back since the anchor in her world had crumbled.

She didn't know how long she'd been crying but it was the pressure against the side of each leg that had her looking down to see two small white faces with big black eyes gazing up at her. A whine emitted from Kirsty, and Flora unfolded her arms, shook out the pins and needles then placed a hand gently on the dog's head, while whispering quiet words of endearment to calm her. She looked at Sandy and his wise old eyes told her he knew. She wasn't surprised. Her connection with him had always been stronger.

A gents linen handkerchief was pulled from her pocket to wipe her eyes and face. A tiny glimmer of a smile crept onto her lips as she looked at the initials embroidered in the corner before folding it and putting it away. A couple of deep breaths followed before she was confident she had herself under control, then Flora pulled back the curtains in her mind and sent out a summons. Barely a second later, MacAndrew walked into the kitchen.

'Yer a bit late this morning, Miss Flora, did you sleep in? It's not like you—' He stopped short in his admonition. 'Miss Flora? What's wrong? You've been crying… I didn't sense it. Why didn't I sense your upset?'

'Because I closed my mind, MacAndrew. It was something I couldn't share. You see… I'm afraid to say… Archie has died.'

'But… that means…' His voice tailed off and she knew

he couldn't bring himself to finish the sentence.

'Yes, MacAndrew, it means I must too.'

'Miss Flora, you don't have to go. You have many years left in you, you know that.'

'I do… I do. However, it was the promise I made to the man I love. It's the promise every Flora makes. We promise we will make the final journey together. Archie sacrificed the years we should have shared so I could fulfil my destiny on this land. I have no qualms about sacrificing my later years to give him this. I didn't then, when the promise was made, and I don't now, now that the time has come to honour it.'

'How long do you have?'

'Until midnight. Then I must go.'

'I will begin the preparations.'

'Thank you, MacAndrew. And thank you for the service you have given to me over the years, it has always been appreciated.'

'It has been an honour, Miss Flora.'

'I'll miss you, MacAndrew.'

'I will miss you too.'

Flora gave a small nod of acknowledgement as they moved off in different directions. There was much to be done and little time in which to do it.

Night had fallen when Flora slid into the hand-carved oak bed she'd been born upon many years before. It was fitting that she was about to go out upon it too. The covers were pulled up and carefully arranged. Everything had to be just so for what was about to follow. It was strange that the transition was about to happen with no daughter by her side but her own Flora had died twenty-five years ago in a tragic car accident and despite many attempts to establish contact with her granddaughter, also called Flora as per the family tradition, it had not come to pass. For the first time in history, it was possible the land would no longer have its custodian. She hoped this would not be, but there was no way of knowing what would come to pass once she was gone.

MacAndrew knocked on the door then walked quietly into the room.

'Do you have it?'

'Yes, Miss Flora. I have spent the afternoon performing the cleansing rituals. It is ready for you.'

'Thank you. Please, hand it over.'

MacAndrew stepped across and raised the box he held in his hands, presenting it to her. He stepped back and turned to leave.

'MacAndrew, wait!'

'Yes, Miss Flora?'

He spun around and it saddened her to know she was about to extinguish the hope that had sprung into his eyes.

'If the girl should come… if Flora claims her birthright… promise me you'll help her in every way possible.'

'Miss Flora, I dinnae wish to speak oot o' turn, but she had her chance tae come and learn. It's no my place to be teaching her.'

MacAndrew's slip into his stronger Scottish dialect told her how agitated he was by the request.

'I know, I know. But… things were complicated. Her loyalties were torn. It's not easy trying to please two people at the same time. If there had been more time…'

'There still could be. You don't need to do this now.'

'I do, MacAndrew, I do. I've never broken a promise in my life, and I'm not about to start now, especially not with this one. Please, tell me you'll do as I ask. Teach her what she needs to know, help her to understand.'

The reluctance was clear to see on his face but she held his gaze until finally he mumbled. 'Very well, I'll teach the lassie. If she ever shows up.'

'You promise?'

'Aye, I promise.'

'I mean it, MacAndrew.'

He straightened his shoulders and returned her look.

'Miss Flora, I've never broken a promise in my life. I'm not about to start now.'

She couldn't help but chuckle as he threw her own words back at her.

'Thank you.'

He gave a little bow and walked out of the room, leaving her alone to perform the final ritual.

Flora pulled the black, velvet box towards her, running her hands gently over the soft exterior before opening it to reveal the silver and diamond necklace inside. The silver casing was fine filigree, some of which was twisted into small rosebuds which became two smaller roses and then one large, fully-bloomed, rose in the middle. The middle rose sat over the large, heart-shaped, diamond, its stem buried deep in the centre of the stone. A smaller tear-drop diamond hung an inch below the heart's tip. Her mother had added this before she died, for the main diamond on its own was no longer sufficient.

She sat up, pulled her long red hair forwards and fastened the necklace around her throat. She'd forgotten how heavy it was and knew it was about to become even heavier as she lay back against the pillows, arranging her hair around her so she could see when it was over.

Closing her eyes, she waited for a few minutes, allowing her breathing to become slow and even, then she muttered a few quiet words. It didn't take long for the process to begin after that.

When a short period of time had passed, Flora opened

her eyes to glance at the hair lying over her chest. It was a strange occurrence, watching it change before her very eyes, the colour moving down its length until, after a few more minutes, every strand was completely white. She waited a little longer to ensure the process was complete then removed the necklace which was now twice its original weight. That, however, was not the biggest difference and, as Flora replaced it in the black, velvet box, her fingers gently caressed the heart-shaped diamond which was now a deep shade of red, as was the teardrop beneath it.

She closed the box, placed it on her chest and lay back once more upon the pillows.

The clock in the hallway struck its first chime of midnight as she closed her eyes and let out a long breath. It was time to leave.

TWO

Kenneth MacKenzie sighed, tapping his fingers impatiently on the steering wheel, waiting for the traffic to ease so he could reverse off his driveway.

He glanced at the three-storey town house in front of him and felt nothing but annoyed irritation with it. There was nothing wrong with the house. In fact, it was a rather attractive house, even on a dull February morning. It was well maintained on the outside and renovated to a high spec on the inside. Once upon a time, he'd loved everything about this house along with everything in it – including his wife, Amelia. Or, as she was now, his ex-wife. After ten years together, five of them married, he'd returned home one evening to find a taxi on the driveway and his wife leaving him to "go off and find myself" while clenching a one-way ticket to Kathmandu in her hand. He later learnt from her solicitor that Tibet had been her final destination.

As part of her newfound selflessness, Amelia had signed the house over to him before departing from UK shores but in doing so, had also lumbered him with one-hundred percent of the mortgage. A mortgage which was manageable when his doctor's salary had been added to her six-figures a year for doing something in insurance up in the City, but when that was removed from the picture, it had become an albatross around his neck. His brother, Ross, had shared with him for a time when his work had brought him to London but he was now in Japan and, having been there the best part of four years, was unlikely to move back in again.

A flash of light in his mirror stirred Kenneth from his musing and he saw a car had stopped to allow him out. He quickly made the manoeuvre, acknowledging his saviour's kindness as he drove towards the T-junction where the traffic lights, for once, changed in his favour as he approached and very soon, he was in the nose-to-bumper traffic on the main road, inching his way towards his surgery in Twickenham.

His mind kept wandering back to the housing dilemma he found himself in. He didn't want to get a housemate. Sharing with family was one thing but sharing with a stranger was another. He'd had a stint of house sharing while at uni and had absolutely no desire to do it again. His tidy, orderly demeanour had been able to cope with Amelia's untidiness – love makes you blind to many bad habits – but having to live with a stranger's mess would severely stress him out, of this he was sure. He knew his shortcomings only too well.

Up till now, he'd been disinclined to sell the house because of the fixed-rate mortgage on it and had no wish to pay the extortionate exit fee for ending it early. Thankfully, there was less than two months left until the fixed-rate period ended but that would leave him at the mercy of a housing market which hadn't been stable for over two years and was showing no signs of settling in the foreseeable future.

Another sigh slipped from his lips as he turned into the surgery car park and slid the car into his assigned parking spot. He caught a glimpse of his reflection in the rearview mirror while retrieving his briefcase from the passenger seat footwell and winced at the sight of the black circles under his eyes from yet another restless night.

He slammed the car door in frustration because he knew *exactly* why he was being so indecisive with the house. The crux of the matter was he no longer wanted to be in London. He was homesick and wished to return to Scotland. He'd only moved south to be with Amelia and now she was no longer here… Well, what was the point?

'Good morning, Doctor MacKenzie,' the receptionist greeted him when he walked through the front door.8

'Good morning, Claire, how's it looking today?'

'Full house. Again.'

'Is it ever any different?'

'Not in all the years I've been here, but you never know, one day it might happen.'

'That'll be the same day we see pigs flying over Heathrow.' They shared a smile then he continued, 'Give me five minutes to get settled and we'll be good to go.'

'No problem. And would you like me to ask Susie to make you a coffee?'

'One of these days, Claire, I'm going to marry you.'

'Yeah, yeah. Promises, promises.'

'Oh, we both know your Henry would miss you dearly.'

'Only because he doesn't know how to operate the cooker.'

'He's never going to learn if you keep hiding the instruction book.'

'Good point. Ah well, looks like I'm going be stuck with the daft old git for another twenty-five years. Hey ho!'

Kenneth entered his office with a smile on his face. Claire was always guaranteed to lift his spirits and he did enjoy their morning banter. She'd been sitting behind that reception desk the first day he'd come for his interview and he reckoned she'd still be there long after he'd moved on. Whenever that might be.

'Please, tell me that was the last one for now…'

Kenneth smiled at Susie when she handed him a fresh coffee and removed the old cup from this morning. A cup that was still half full as he'd barely had the chance to drink it before each patient had walked through the door.

'Yep, it was. Well, it's your last face-to-face until this afternoon but you do have the home phone calls to make. I've emailed the list and details to you.'

'And just as I was beginning to like you, Susie.'

'It's a tough job but someone has to do it. I think I'll live.'

She grinned as she closed the door behind her. Kenneth was still grinning himself when he lifted the cup, taking a long drink of the rich coffee. His eye caught the movement of the clock above the door and he decided he could take a few minutes before starting the phone list. A few minutes dedicated to looking for a position nearer his family.

He pulled the keyboard towards him, closed his eyes, and sent out a wish that today would be the day the perfect job would be listed, just waiting for his CV to be sent. Although, as he opened his eyes and typed in the details on the website, it felt like he'd been wishing since forever for this. For the break he so desperately wanted. He entered in his preferred location, Scottish Highlands, and waited for the page to load, holding his breath – as he always did – while the words unfurled before him.

Suddenly, he gave a loud gasp.

Could it be?

Was this it?

Had his wish finally been granted?

He breathed out in a long slow whistle while reading the words in front of him. Could this really be it? Was his mind simply showing him what he wanted to see?

But no! It was all there in blue and white on the screen.

***Rural GP Practice located in Inverness-shire
seeks an enthusiastic and motivated GP
to join our friendly team.***

His heart raced as he read through the listing and saw it was everything he wanted and more. Home visits, weekly clinics, and an Out of Hours requirement. "REAL doctoring" as he thought of it. It was what he'd signed up for when he chose this career. He didn't want to sit behind a desk every day, making telephone calls to people who couldn't get to the surgery. He didn't want faceless, unknown patients whose notes he had to speed-read before they walked through the door. No! He wanted, nay… DESIRED to know every patient by name. To know their ailments by heart and to understand them as people. It seemed that these days, it was all about diagnosing the illness and not the patient yet so much more could be solved from doing the latter.

He continued reading and the more he read, the more excited he became. The area covered couldn't have been more perfect for it was where he'd grown up and he already knew it well. Surely that would go in his favour?

Kenneth breathed in and out slowly, trying to moderate the excitement coursing through his veins. After a moment, he picked up his mobile and hit a number.

'Hi, you've reached Gary Vance. Please leave a message and I'll call you right back.'

'Gary, it's Kenneth. Please call me as soon as you get this message. But not between two and three-thirty as I'll be taking appointments.'

He rang off and stared at the screen, desperately wanting to send his CV right there and then but the common sense he'd spent a lifetime being teased over kicked in. It was best to wait until this evening when he could sit down and go through it all properly.

The computer mouse hovered over the page and he'd just bookmarked it for later when his mobile rang.

'Gary, guess what? The job – it's finally appeared.'

'The job?'

'Yes, the Scottish job I've been hoping to find.'

'Oh! Oh, right, that's… er… great. Brilliant! Well done!'

Kenneth moved the phone from his ear, looked at it and then put it back.

'Are you okay, Gary? You sound… I don't know… a bit strange.'

'No, no, I'm fine. Really pleased for you. It's great news.'

'Are you sure?'

'Of course, I'm just a bit gutted I'm going to lose my best friend. Cherry will be too.'

'Hey, I've not got the job yet. I haven't even sent my CV over.'

'Why not? You've wanted this for so long. Get the info to them NOW! Don't wait.'

'But—'

'Kenneth, don't you DARE say you might not be good enough, or if it's too big a risk to move, or any of the other million excuses you always manage to find when you think something is too good for you.'

'I don't—'

'Yes, you do! Every damn time! Well, this time, I'm

not letting you. You've wanted this for far too long so take that oh-so-sensible head of yours out of your ass and get that CV gone!'

'Are you wanting rid of your best friend that much?'

'No, but knowing that he's happy will make me happy. And right now, he's not happy at all so I'm prepared to make the sacrifice for him. Now, is your CV up to date?'

'It is.'

'Then I want a message from you, by nine o'clock tonight at the latest, telling me you've sent your application.'

'And what if I don't…'

'I'll send Cherry over!'

He thought of Gary's beautiful, sometimes fearsome, wife and knew he was on a hiding to nothing.

'Very well, I'll send it tonight.'

'Promise?'

'I promise!'

'Catch ya later then, gotta go!'

There was a bleep in his ear as Gary hung up, leaving Kenneth looking at his phone in bemusement. It would seem the decision had been made for him. He glanced at the clock again. The next seven hours were going to be the longest of his life, but he'd manage because, and he was thinking as positively as he was able, he was finally going home.

THREE

Flora MacDonald O'Brien was trying to rummage discreetly in her handbag for another tissue when a fresh one appeared underneath her chin. She took it, turning her head to give her dad a watery smile of thanks.

She blew her nose quietly, but when she looked once more at the coffin in front of her, she had to press a fist against her lips to hold in the wail of despair that was trying to force its way out. How was she going to cope? Who was going to be there for her now?

For as long as she could recall, it felt as though there was a hole inside her. A great big piece of emptiness that only ever seemed to cease when she was with her grandfather. She always felt that he'd "got her" – that he understood her without any need for an explanation. When she'd been around him, her world had been just right. She often wondered if this was because he was her mother's father. Her mother who'd died when she was only three and whom Flora had no memory of. When he wasn't around, her world tilted off its axis but now, it was blown apart because Grandfather Archie was dead and she no longer had a hole inside her – it was a gaping wide chasm and she was teetering on the edge.

While she fought to hold it together, she listened to the celebrant speak about her grandfather and the life he'd led. She spoke about how he'd single-handedly brought up two teenagers, her mother, Flora, and her Uncle Craig. About how he'd battled with severe arthritis for such a long time until recent medical developments had given him a semblance of his life back in the last few years. A life which he'd lived to the fullest with his proudest achievement being that he'd ridden "The Big One" – Blackpool's largest rollercoaster – over six times. Unsurprisingly, the mourners gathered in the room laughed at this. A snort behind her had her looking over her shoulder into the faces of his three best friends, Sadie, Bernice, and Rose, who'd taken him under their wings when he'd moved into the retirement village. Another ghost of a smile crossed her lips when she took in Sadie's faded jeans, bright yellow Sex Pistol's T-shirt, which she was sure was an original, and her black leather biker jacket. Always one for being unconventional, Grandfather Archie would have loved her for maintaining it, even now. Mind you, he had specified there was to be no black worn today, but Flora was sure he'd have made an exception for Sadie's jacket.

She turned back as the celebrant began wrapping up her speech, announcing to the room that she was now ready to send Archie off on his final journey. She pressed a button and laughter rocked the room again when the opening chords of Meat Loaf's "Bat Out of Hell" roared from the speakers. During the first verse, the coffin rolled slowly along before coming to a standstill. The curtains had just closed together when the chorus came on and suddenly there was a commotion behind her as Sadie, Bernice and Rose stood up to sing along, clapping their hands as they did so. Before her eyes, everyone around her followed suit and the room was soon rocking along with Mr Loaf's finest. At the end, as the last guitar note faded away, everyone was applauding, whistling, and laughing and Flora knew her grandfather would have loved every minute of his final send-off.

'Uncle Craig, what a funeral. How ever did you manage to keep that quiet?'

Flora gave her uncle a hug as they walked around the garden of remembrance outside the crematorium, looking at the flowers that had been sent. A chilly wind was blowing, forcing her to pull up the hood on her coat. It was the first week of March but some days still felt wintery. Or maybe today just seemed worse because of the circumstances.

'Very easily, I knew nothing about it. It was planned last year when Dad, Sadie, Bernice, and Rose all wrote out their funeral arrangements and shared copies between them. As each one dies, the others sort out the funeral in accordance with the details they hold. The last one standing will pass their final request to Essie who has promised to follow it to the letter, regardless of what is stated.'

'I bet she's looking forward to that,' Flora grinned.

'I think she's dreading Sadie being the last to go because we can't even begin to imagine what her final wishes will be.'

'Hey, she might surprise us all and have something really sedate and normal lined up.'

A raucous cackle made them turn to see the lady in question doubled over in laughter as she shared some story or another with her friends. Flora and Craig looked back at each other while saying in unison, 'Naaaaah!'

'At least Bernice should be something close to normal, her being a refined lady after all.' She looked at the group as she spoke; Sadie – the octogenarian punk rocker with her grey, Sid Vicious, spiky hair, Rose – the tiny, birdlike waif in her long flowery dress, straw boater and Doc Marten boots. Her appearance was deceptive as that sweet little old lady had a stubborn streak that would send any mule green with envy. Finally, there was Bernice, in her demure twin-set and pearls, looking as perfectly groomed as she always did.

'Hah! I won't be betting my house on that one.'

'Surely it'll be some nice orchestral piece.'

'Her favourite tune is the 1812 Overture. If she's got that on her list, the biggest challenge will be preventing Sadie adding real cannons and shooting cannonballs all over the town!'

'Oh, goodness, don't even begin to think that.'

They chuckled together again but when Flora looked closer, her laughter died away as she saw the tension around her uncle's eyes.

'How are you holding up, Uncle Craig?' She laid a hand gently on his arm. 'Are you okay?'

Craig patted her hand. 'Hanging in there, Flora. What else can I do? To lose both parents within less than twenty-four hours… well… I…'

He stopped, the pain of his loss etched on his face. She didn't reply because there were no words she could say to make him feel any better. Instead, she wrapped her arms around him in the tightest of hugs and whispered in his ear, 'I love you, Uncle Craig. I'll always be here for you, whenever you need me.' She kissed his cheek then, stepping back, nodded to his partner, Essie, over his shoulder, who quickly interpreted her glance and came walking over.

'Hey, you,' she said gently, 'we need to start chivvying everyone back to the village and into the pub, otherwise Percy will be sending out a search party. You know what she's like – the landlady with the moistest except when it comes to patience!'

'Yes, you're right.' Craig turned to Flora. 'Do you need a lift to the village?'

'No, thank you, I'll go with Dad and Sally.'

'Okay. We'll see you there.'

'Okay.'

Flora went to walk off but stopped and turned back. 'Uncle Craig?'

'Yes?'

'If I don't get the chance to talk with you again today, have a safe trip up to Scotland. Drive carefully, yeah? I hope it goes okay. Or, as okay as these things can be.'

'Thank you, Flora.'

She watched him walk away, Essie holding his hand as they went. Just then, a movement caught her eye and when she looked closer, a spark of anger buzzed through her. Storming over the paving stones, she walked around the ornamental pillar and grabbed the last person she wanted to see by the arm.

'Joey! What the hell are you doing here?'

'Oh, er… hi, Flora…'

'I asked, what the hell are you doing here?'

She glared into the face of her ex-boyfriend, tapping her foot furiously as she waited for him to speak.

'I saw the obituary for your… er… grandfather in the paper. I came to pay my respects.'

'Pay your respects? You only met him twice!'

'But I liked him. He was nice. And he liked me.'

No, he didn't, she thought. Her grandfather had thought him a useless waste of space, telling her never to bring him again when she visited.

'Well, that was kind of you, Joey, he'd have appreciated it,' she lied.

'Flora, while you're here, can we talk?'

'No, Joey, we can't.'

'But, Flora—'

'Joey, I have made myself perfectly clear to you on numerous occasions – we are NOT getting back together. We are NOT giving it another chance. What we are is OVER! Now, GO HOME!' She threw her arm out and pointed towards the gates of the crematorium.

'Okay. I get it. I'm going.'

Slightly shocked at how quickly Joey had capitulated – it usually took at least ten minutes to get away from him – she watched him leave while seething that he still couldn't get the message. How could he even *think* her grandfather's funeral was an appropriate place to once again plead with her to reconsider?

She drew in several deep breaths, looked about for her father, Matt, and found him waiting by his car. Flora walked over, straight into his arms and gave him the biggest, tightest cuddle she could manage.

'I love you, Dad. I really, really do.'

'I know you do, sweetheart, and I love you too. Very, very much.'

As they held each other tightly, Flora felt a small glimmer of what her uncle must be feeling because even the very thought of losing her father was enough to make her own heart tighten in agony.

FOUR

'Argh! Ouch! Ooooooh!'

After being hunched over her desk for several hours, Flora sat upright, her back muscles complaining at having been cramped in one position for so long. She really should set an alarm reminding her to move more frequently but was concerned that when it went off, the noise would make her jolt and her delicate paintwork would be ruined.

The chair gave a screech on the floor when she pushed it back and stood, stretching her arms high above her head before bending forwards to touch the floorboards beneath her feet, sighing with relief as her body lengthened itself out from the croissant-shaped morsel it had become.

A few side bends and twists later, she returned to her desk and maintaining a standing position, leant forward to peer through the large magnifying lens at the matryoshka doll underneath it. She cast a few glances between it and the photograph she was working from, nodding with satisfaction that the likeness she'd been working to create was accurate.

Despite the pain in her back, she'd have liked to

continue for a while longer but the light outside was gone and while artificial light was okay for certain types of painting, it was no use for the intricacy she was currently attempting so, with a sigh, she carefully moved the doll onto the upper shelf to dry then gathered up her brushes to be cleaned.

Her feet had just hit the hallway floor when there was a knock on the door and upon opening it, Flora was thrilled to see her Uncle Craig standing on the doormat.

'Hey, it's my favourite uncle. Come on in.'

'Hey, it's my favourite niece.'

They exchanged a quick hug while laughing at the silly joke that had begun when Flora was about ten-years-old and had become their standard greeting in the years since.

'Cup of tea?' she asked, walking through to the kitchen.

'Yes, please, if it's not too much trouble.'

'I was about to have one myself so no trouble at all. I need to soak these before I can clean them.' She lifted the hand holding the paint brushes.

'Another commission?'

'Yes, they're coming in faster than I can keep up. I've had to put a disclaimer on my website saying there is now a three-month waiting period.'

'I told you getting mixed up with that Pete Wallace one would only bring you heartache!'

Flora laughed. 'Oh, I don't think I would put it quite like that.'

While sorting out the teapot and cups, she thought about how a small gesture of thanks had given her a new career she certainly hadn't foreseen. Sally, her dad's partner and her friend who ran the local cat-rescue facility, had been brainstorming with her, trying to come up with a unique way to thank Pete Wallace, the world-famous rock star who, as the rescue's patron, had been giving it world-wide publicity which had generated a great number of rehomes and always-welcome donations. The problem had been – what do you give the man who has everything? From somewhere deep in her mind, Flora recalled a stall she'd passed at a Christmas market many moons ago where the man had been painting blank Russian dolls. When she'd asked, he told her that blank dolls were available online so they could be painted in any manner. This had given her the idea to make a doll set featuring Pete and Sukie with their children and animals. Sally had loved the idea as did Pete and Sukie when they were presented with it. In fact, Pete had loved the set so much, he'd posted it all over his social media sites and before she could blink, Flora was receiving requests from every continent of the world asking her to create personal family sets. The demand was such, it had pushed all her other work to one side to become her primary focus and primary source of income. And it was a rather decent income at that. She'd thought that putting a three-figure price tag on the dolls would put people off but there had been no let up on the requests coming in.

'Here you go, help yourself to biscuits.'

Flora put a plate of cookies on the table alongside the teapot, milk jug and sugar bowl. Craig liked a proper cup of tea and she always enjoyed the ritual of making one.

'Thank you.'

'How was the trip to Scotland? Sorry, I haven't had a chance to come round and see you since you returned.'

'I've only been back a few days, Flora, so don't worry about it. The trip was… well... interesting. Difficult. And sad. Very sad.'

'Well, you were burying your mother, it was never going to be anything else.'

'Oh, I didn't have to do that. It was already taken care of before I arrived.'

'Sorry? But… isn't that what you were supposed to do?

Being her son, you know.'

'She'd left strict instructions on what was to be done following her death. As soon as the death certificate was signed off, the body was burned that night by the side of the loch. Her ashes were saved for me to scatter across the loch along with my father's, which the crematorium had couriered up to me. After that, all that was left for me to do was lay a small stone plaque with her name and death year in the family remembrance plot.'

'Family remembrance plot? So why wasn't Grandad put there?'

'Strangely, there are no men in the burial plot, only the women.'

Flora sat back in surprise. 'Hardly a "family" plot then, is it.'

Craig shrugged. 'It's something my mother and I never got around to discussing. Maybe if we hadn't been estranged for so long, we may have done, but we were too busy making up the time we'd lost.'

'I'm sorry.' Flora leant over the table to squeeze his hand. She was deeply fond of her uncle, he was such a kind, gentle man, and she hated to see him upset.

'Anyway! The reason I'm here is to pass on some news to you.'

'Oh! Good news, I hope.'

'I would say so. You are now the proud owner of a cottage in Scotland along with the six acres of land it sits upon. Oh, and a loch!'

'I... I... excuse me? A loch? She left... My grandmother left... she left me her cottage?'

'Yes, she did.'

'But... I don't get it. Why? Surely you should inherit it. You're her son.'

'The cottage is tied to go down through the women of the family. Had your mother still been alive, it would have gone to her. As she's not, that puts you the next in line.'

'But, that's not fair on you.'

'Oh, I'm alright with it. I've known for a long time that it would go to you.'

'But you've never mentioned it.'

'It wasn't my place to tell you. Besides, thinking of my mother dying wasn't something I felt inclined to dwell upon.'

'No, I suppose not.'

Flora went to take a drink of her tea only to find the cup empty. As she poured fresh cups, she pondered over why the cottage had come her way from a woman she'd never met nor had any dealings with.

'So, what happens now?'

Craig bent down, pulling a cardboard folder from the briefcase by his feet. Flora hadn't even noticed he'd brought it with him.

'You need to sign this paperwork which passes the deeds into your name. One copy you keep and the other will go back to Scotland to be lodged with the Land Registry there.'

'So, once I sign these, I become the official owner. What happens if I don't sign?'

'If you decline, it will be held until your daughter is born and passed to her. If she declines, then her daughter, and so on.'

'Seriously?'

Her uncle nodded. 'Seriously. It can only go through the female line.'

'I thought that was illegal these days.'

'Not illegal but could be challenged if there was someone to challenge it, I suppose. However, I'm not going to challenge it and you're an only child so…'

His voice trailed off.

Flora nodded slowly. 'But,' she looked up at her uncle,

'what am I going to do with a cottage in Scotland?'

'Have holidays in it? Go and live there? It's very beautiful.'

'Pfft! I'm not going to live in Scotland! Why would I do that? Everything in my life is here.'

'Well, you don't need to decide what to do right now this minute but at least accept the gift you've been given.'

She stared at the documents her uncle had pushed across the table. They were very official looking and she wasn't good with stuff like that. Her uncle, on the other hand, was and she trusted him implicitly.

'Do you think I should accept it?'

'It's not for me to tell you what to do, Flora. All I can say, is it's a well-maintained, three-bedroomed cottage set in some of the most glorious countryside you'll ever see and I think it would be a crying shame for you to refuse.'

'Ha! So, no pressure then?'

'I'm saying no more.'

For several minutes the only sound in the room was the one Flora kept making as she flicked her thumbnail against her front teeth – a habit as old as her teeth when she was doing serious thinking. Finally, and with an almighty sigh, she picked up the pen, quickly scribbled her name on the documents then threw the pen down again.

'I still don't feel right about this.'

'I understand. It's a surprise and a shock but once you've had some time to get used to the idea, I'm sure you'll feel better.'

'Hmmm, I don't know about that. Let's wait until I've told my father before we make that assumption.'

And, knowing exactly how her father felt about her grandmother, Flora was quite sure this news was not going to go down well at all.

FIVE

'Darling, you're here at last.'

Kenneth found himself pulled into his mother's arms as soon as he arrived on the airport concourse.

'Hey, Mum, been waiting long?'

'No, only about eighteen months!'

Kenneth smiled at the not-so-subtle dig over the length of time since his last visit home as he leant down to place a kiss on her cheek.

'Well, with some luck, that might soon be a thing of the past.'

'Oh, I do hope so. We'd love to have you home again.'

'How are Dad and Fraser? Are they okay?'

'They're both fine. They send their love and luck for your interview. They were busy with "Farming Stuff" so couldn't come along with me to meet you.'

They grinned at each other, as they always did, when his mum mentioned "Farming Stuff" for he'd decided, at eight-years-old, that he wanted to be a doctor and had loudly declared this "farming stuff" wasn't for him! It hadn't interested him up to then and it did so even less afterwards. Talk of crop rotation, seeding, and other such things went over his head so little did he care for it.

'It's not a problem. I'll see them tonight at dinner.'

His mum led the way to the car and he took the opportunity to look her over as he followed behind. There were a few more grey strands in her hair but she was moving with ease, no signs of anything untoward in her gait which might suggest pain being hidden elsewhere in her body, and she spoke and gestured with joy and sparkling eyes. When it came to his mum, every visit saw him give her a quick, doctorly onceover because he knew she'd never think of troubling the local GP with any ailments she might have.

It was no secret in the family that, as much as he loved them all, he had an extra special bond with his mum. Of her three sons, he was the one who looked most like her. All three boys had their father's height, each one coming in between six-foot-five and six-foot-six, but where Fraser and Ross also had their father's solid, burly build, red-gold hair, and deep blue eyes along with their mother's happy, outgoing, personality, he was slim built with his mum's dark brown hair and pale green eyes. Unfortunately, the gene pool selector had also awarded him his dad's quiet, shy, and reserved nature. He was also the only one to inherit her passionate love of the written word and had often been found hidden away somewhere with his nose buried in a book rather than running wild around the farm as his brothers had done. There had been much teasing from them when they were kids but nothing over-the-top and they were close siblings despite their differences. He'd read a few reports on middle-child-syndrome, feeling that being one made him well qualified to form an opinion, but had found, over all, little of it applied to him. His whole family had humoured his need to bandage imaginary wounds and apply salves to sore bits when he was young and this had led to them coming to him in his teenage years with genuine injuries they'd sustained. He'd never felt ignored, under-valued or less important than Fraser or Ross and while he'd been the first to leave home, that was purely logistics. Fraser was always going to follow his farming heritage so no need for him to go anywhere and Kenneth was the next in line so it stood to reason he'd be off to university before Ross.

'What time is your interview?'

His mum's question pulled him away from his memories and back into the present.

'Half-past one. They're doing it in the lunch break because they're so busy and it's the only available time. I believe the other candidate interviews have been before opening and after closing but I was slotted in during the day because of the distance I've travelled.'

'Are you nervous?'

Kenneth felt the butterflies partying on down in his stomach – nervous didn't even begin to describe how he was feeling.

'Yes, I am. Because I want it so much, I suppose, but every job interview does that. No one likes being held up for inspection.'

'You'll be fine, sweetie, I have every faith in you.' His mum took her hand briefly off the steering wheel to pat one of his which was sitting tightly clenched on his thigh.

'Thanks, Mum.'

'Now, how about a coffee and something to eat before you go in. You've got some time and a caffeine blast might help to soothe you.'

'That sounds good to me, but I'll pass on the eating – I don't think throwing up would give a good impression.'

'Perhaps not, dear, but you'd be able to show off your diagnostic skills by explaining how it happened and how to avoid such an occurrence again in the future. Never miss an opportunity to shine, Kenneth, because you shine so beautifully and it doesn't hurt to let others see it. As they say, don't hide your light under a bushel, my darling boy.'

They were both laughing as the car pulled into a parking spot and Kenneth did feel better when he got out. Laughter really was the best medicine.

'Thank you for coming all this way, Doctor MacKenzie. I'm Doctor Cameron – let me show you around the facility.'

'It's no problem at all, Doctor Cameron. Thank you for giving me this opportunity.'

The woman in front of him smiled before turning around and leading him towards a corridor with several brown doors. She was of average height and build, with medium length blonde hair pulled back in a low ponytail. Her makeup was minimal and her attire was a quite sensible polo-neck jumper, tailored trousers, and low-heeled boots. This was a doctor who was all about doing her job efficiently.

'These rooms, Doctor MacKenzie, are our consulting rooms. We have two part-time doctors who also sit with other surgeries in the region and two full-time posts – mine and the one you are here about. We've had a locum for a time and hoped she'd stay on permanently but her sights were always set on the bright lights of the big cities and we couldn't change her mind.'

'Well, it's quite the opposite for me. I'm in the big city and can't wait to move away.'

'Indeed. It's funny how we all yearn for different things, Doctor MacKenzie. The thought of working in London makes me break out in a rash!'

'It does that to me too,' Kenneth said, 'and, please, call me Kenneth, Doctor MacKenzie is a bit of a mouthful.'

'Only if you call me Jennet.'

'I think I can do that.'

Kenneth smiled at Jennet as she held the door open and ushered him into the clinic area of the medical centre. The smaller GP rooms he'd already viewed were pretty much like every other consulting room he'd seen with their examination tables, eye charts on the wall and posters detailing the health benefits of exercise, not drinking excessively, and watching what you eat. He was now being taken around the extension which had been added to the building a mere two years before and it was a rather nifty set-up. They were able to perform minor operations such as a mole removal or setting straight-forward broken bones and he was impressed with what he was seeing. It was better equipped than his current surgery and it made him want the job even more.

'Right then, Kenneth, that's us. You've seen all we have to offer and all that we don't. Does the role still appeal?'

'Yes, Jennet, it certainly does.'

'Even though you will have to do out of hours call-outs and home visits? We're a very hands-on setup here. It doesn't suit everyone.'

'I know we discussed this in our previous Zoom meeting, but it's the very thing that attracted me to this role.'

'May I ask why? It usually has the opposite effect.'

Kenneth smiled as he pulled up the special memory that had led him to this point in his life.

'When I was eight-years-old, I had a nasty dose of chickenpox. I was running a temperature and my mum called for the doctor to come out. A few hours later, she brings this rather severe looking man into my bedroom and

I confess, I was scared but it was all for nothing because he was the kindest, most gentle, man and just by talking to me, I immediately felt soothed and calm. His name was Doctor Carruthers and he explained everything he was doing as he examined me and why he had to do it. His bedside manner was wonderful. When he'd finished, he told me that because I felt so ill now, I knew how horrible it was and it would make me kinder to other sick people when I grew up. After that, he gave my mum a prescription and left. A week later, there was a knock on the kitchen door and when Mum opened it, Doctor Carruthers was standing there. Mum was confused as she hadn't called for a doctor to visit and said as much. Do you know what he replied with? He said, "I was just passing by so thought I'd stop in to see how the little man is doing?" He was just passing by. Such was his dedication to the role he'd made an unscheduled stop simply to see if I was okay. That was the day I decided I wanted to be like him. As he left, he commented on the picture I had been colouring in at the kitchen table. I offered it to him as a gift – you know, the way children do – and he took it. A few years later, I had to attend the surgery for a sprained ankle and saw him again. I can't even begin to describe my surprise when I saw that picture in a frame, hanging on his wall. He really was a wonderful man and if I can be even half the doctor he was, I'll feel I've done well.'

The sound of Jennet blowing her nose returned him to the room and he was astonished to see her crying. Blimey! What was that all about?

Through a rather watery smile, she said, 'Alistair Carruthers was my grandfather. I adored him and hearing you speak so highly of him… well, it brought back all the wonderful memories we shared. Thank you. And I know he would've been over the moon that he inspired you to join the profession he loved so much. Now, I think we're done here, but before you go, there's just one last thing I want you to see.'

She led him up the corridor to the door with her name on it and opened it, standing back to let him enter. He made it a few feet inside then stopped with a gasp for there, on the wall to the side of her desk, hung his old colouring-in picture.

He turned to look at her as, with a smile, she said, 'I think you're going to fit in here just fine.'

SIX

Flora opened the oven door and carefully pulled out the heavy casserole dish. The aromatic smells of the herby gravy floated up in the steam when she took off the lid to give the contents a stir. She did enjoy a good hearty stew and was looking forward to this one as it would be the last one for a few months. The clocks were due to go forward this weekend and it didn't feel right to make stew in the glorious summer months. She picked up the plate sitting on the worktop, carefully dropped in the dumplings she'd made then returned the dish to the oven, after which she went to lay the table in the dining room.

She picked a handful of daffodils from the garden, putting them in a small jug in the centre of the table, while wondering if she'd gone over the top and her father would guess something was going on before she could pluck up the courage to share the news of her inheritance with him. She'd been worrying about telling him for over a week and while she'd finally got her head around it, she knew her dad would not accept the news graciously. He'd spent over twenty-five years blaming her grandmother for the death of her daughter – his wife and Flora's mother – and she knew he'd find this new development a difficult one to accept. She straightened a knife that was barely squint and with a quick glance at her watch, returned to the kitchen to begin boiling the potatoes for the mash. Her dad would be home soon and everything would be ready to eat once he'd had his shower. Knowing she had a few minutes to spare, Flora ran back up the stairs to check the paintwork on her dolls was drying okay.

She'd just returned the smallest doll to the shelf when the sound of wheels on gravel filtered through the window. Flora plastered a smile on her face that she hoped hid her nerves, and headed down the stairs to greet her father, but her heart sank as she reached the bottom step – she'd just heard Sally's voice and laughter as a key was put in the door. *Damn it!* She'd wanted the conversation with her dad to be private. Not sure how much of his, or their, past her dad had shared with Sally meant there was a risk of putting him in an uncomfortable position if she shared her news with them together. Her dad may feel he couldn't properly vent his feelings on the matter and while Flora concluded this would not be a bad thing, it wasn't fair to do that to him. As the door swung open, she made the decision to put off saying anything and didn't miss the sensation of relief that ran through her with knowing she'd got out of it for tonight.

'Hi, Flora, how lovely to see you.'

She found herself swept up in one of Sally's glorious hugs. It could not be denied – you always knew when Sally Edwards gave you a hug. It was an embrace filled with love and care and anyone on the receiving end always felt so much better afterwards.

'Hey, Sally, right back at you.'

'Hi, poppet, how are you tonight? Had a good day?'

'Hi, Dad, all is good, thank you, and yes, my day was productive. I'm close to being finished on this current order.'

'And then it'll be straight on to the next one. I know what you're like.' He ruffled her short pixie-cut locks and laughed as she pulled away from him.

'Oi, give over!'

'I hope you don't mind that I've asked Sally to join us for dinner. I was telling her how fabulous your beef stew is and it seemed daft not to ask her along to try it for herself. We always end up with far too much.'

'Of course I don't mind. There's more than enough for everyone. I'll set another place at the table while you have your shower.'

'Anything I can do to help?'

'There's a bottle of red wine open on the kitchen worktop, Sal. You can pour that out and maybe open another one...'

'I'm on it.' Sally shrugged off her coat, hanging it on the coat rack beside the door before making her way through to the kitchen. Flora smiled to see how relaxed she was in their home – she and her dad had been properly together for almost three years now and as her father had been single since her mother had died, he was long overdue a loving relationship.

She'd just re-laid the dining table to include Sally when the smoke alarm outside the kitchen door suddenly began screeching.

'Nooooooo! The dumplings!'

Flora scurried into the kitchen, desperately thinking, *please don't be burnt, please don't be burnt* as she ran. Smoke was coming from the oven and her spirits dropped as she grabbed the oven gloves to pull out the casserole dish. With a heavy heart, she placed the cast-iron dish on the nearby trivet, lifted the lid slowly off… and then blinked several times with surprise. The dumplings were perfect! Exactly how they should be. Just on the edge of golden brown from absorbing the gravy and ready for the dish to go back into the oven without its lid to allow them to rise and crisp.

'Wha—'

'Oh, they look and smell delicious.'

Sally was peering over her shoulder at the stew and seemed oblivious to the racket still emanating from the smoke alarm. Flora took a slow look around. There was no longer any smoke in the kitchen nor any smell of charring. The alarm stopped as suddenly as it had started and the silence was only broken by the sound of the potatoes bubbling on top of the stove.

With a shake of her head, as though the action might help her make sense of what had just occurred, Flora returned the casserole to the oven for the last time and switched off the heat under the bubbling pan. A popping sound had her pivoting on her heel to see Sally opening the second bottle of wine as she'd requested. Everything was as it should be so why did something feel off kilter?

Just then her dad appeared in the doorway.

'Are we good to go? Anything need doing?'

'Err… only the err… potatoes to be drained and mashed in your superb manner. By the time they're in the serving bowl, the dumplings will be done and we can eat.'

'Fabulous! I'm starving.'

'Dad, you're always starving.'

'It's the manual labour, love, burns off the calories as fast as I can consume them.'

'I know, Dad, I know.'

In the time it took them to sit down at the table, the weird sensation had ebbed away. Common sense had kicked in and Flora surmised that a blob of gravy must have fallen on the bottom of the oven and it was that burning which had caused the smoke alarm to react. After all, what else could it have been?

'Oh, that was all thoroughly delicious. The stew was the tastiest I think I've ever had and I haven't eaten Artic Roll for years. I'd forgotten how much I liked it.'

Sally was rubbing her stomach as she spoke and Flora smiled with a little bit of pride.

'Thank you. I'm glad you enjoyed it. We always have a couple of Artic Rolls in the freezer – they're perfect for when you want a dessert but nothing too heavy. Although, I must confess that on the odd occasion, I've eaten a whole one by myself.' Flora winked at Sally and burst out laughing when she replied, 'Flora, so have I!'

'Let me take these plates out to the kitchen. Flora, why don't you refill the glasses?'

'Okay, Dad. Sally, are you staying over tonight? Can I tempt you with another glass?'

'I am and you can, thank you. Jools is covering the evening feeding shift and Herbert is having a sleepover with her and Peggy tonight.'

'Are he and Peggy still all loved up?'

'Oh, yes.' Sally smiled. 'It's funny seeing them together, especially when they're playing in the garden. Watching a small, ginger cat chasing after a large, golden dog is quite the sight to behold.'

'Try to video it the next time you see it. I can put it up on TikTok – I reckon you'd get a lot of views with that and it would be great publicity for the rescue.'

'Flora, between you and Pete, I don't think the rescue

needs any more publicity.'

'Hey, there's no such thing as too much publicity, trust me. You need to be visible at all times to maintain your following.'

'And that's why I have you as my marketing guru – you're always on the ball with these things. I simply don't have the time.'

'Of course you don't, Sally. Your priority is the cats you take under your wing and look after. I'm more than happy to do what I do if it helps you out. Does it still feel weird when you spend the night away from it?'

Sally ran a local B&B, the profits from which were poured into the cat rescue attached to it. She'd accidentally come across an old, decrepit farmhouse some years ago and had met Flora's dad and, by default, Flora herself, when she'd asked him to quote for the contract of bringing it back to life.

'Yes, it does, if I'm being truly honest. I know Jools is more than capable but I worry that I might miss something important if I'm not around. Even after all this time, I don't like being away for too long.'

'Well, it's a worry you won't have for too much longer, my little control-freak.'

Matt dropped a kiss on Sally's head as he walked back to his chair.

'Flora, I… er… we… the reason Sally is here is… well… not just to savour your fabulous stew… We… um… we have something to tell you.'

'Oh, okay.' Flora sat back in her seat with surprise.

'We've had a long discussion about things and as you've just mentioned, Sally doesn't relax as well as she should when she stays here because of being away from the rescue so, with that in mind, we feel… no, we KNOW, the time is now right for us to take the next step in our relationship.'

'You're getting married?'

'What? Nooooo!'

'Blimey, Flora, no!'

'Then…'

'We've decided to live together and it makes sense for me to move into Bramblebush with Sally given her commitments over there.'

'Right! Wow! I didn't see that coming. Although, maybe I should have. You've been together long enough.'

'It's four years since we first met. That's quite a long time, these days.'

Flora looked at Sally as she spoke. 'I guess it is when you put it like that. Well, Sally, if you're prepared to put up with him leaving wet towels on the bathroom floor every day and snoring like an elephant when he's had a few beers, then I give you both my sincerest congratulations and wish you every possible happiness for the future.'

'Thank you, Flora. I do hope you don't mind.'

'Mind? Why should I mind, Sally?'

'I don't want you to think I'm taking him away from you. You've been such a close unit for so long.'

'Sally, I've been hoping since forever that someone *would* take him away…'

'Hey! How did I manage to raise such a cheeky brat?'

Laughter filled the room before Flora raised her glass in the air.

'I would like to toast you both and say that I hope the happiness you have now is only a fraction of the happiness still to come.'

As they talked about the logistics of how and when her father would move to the other side of the village, Flora waited to ask the one thing not yet discussed – where was she going to live?

'Erm, Dad… I don't want to be a party pooper or anything but… when will you be putting this place on the market? Just so I know how long I've got to find somewhere else.'

Her dad turned to look at her, the surprise clear upon his face.

'Sell this place?'

'Well, yes. Or do you intend to rent it out? Which would be better financially, now I come to think about it.'

'Flora, I'm not doing anything with the house. This is your home. It'll always be your home. If need be, I'll continue to help with the bills although I suspect your new business venture is bringing in nearly as much money as I'm making these days.'

'What? So, I get to live here? On my own?'

'Of course. If you're okay with that?'

'Okay? Darn right it's okay! Wow! Living on my own and having my own space...' She gave a cheeky smile. 'Does that mean I'm finally allowed to redecorate and make the place look like we've stepped into the twenty-first century?'

She laughed as her father rolled his eyes.

'If you must! It'll be your home to decorate as you please. If you can just wait until I've gone before you begin stripping it all down.'

Flora pulled her phone from her pocket and with a laugh, pretended to pull up her calendar. 'What day did you say were leaving?'

SEVEN

'Did they say when they'd let you know if you've been successful, son?'

Kenneth looked over to his father, sitting at the head of the table.

'Doctor Cameron said she hoped to get back to me before I return to London tomorrow.'

'I see. And how long would it be before you took up the post? Assuming you get it, of course.'

'Of course he's going to get it, Dougie. Don't be so negative!'

'Thanks, Mum.'

'Anytime, Kenneth. Your dad's just being an old worrywart.'

'Now then, Mhairi, you know things are just not right at the moment. Everything's all to cock.'

'I know, I know.'

'What's all this?'

Kenneth looked at both his parents before turning his gaze upon his brother, Fraser, who was sitting opposite him.

'It's… well… we no longer have a Flora. For the first time in hundreds of years, there's no Flora in the cottage.'

'Seriously? You're all hung up over some woman?'

'Watch yourself there, son. You know how the community feels about The Flora.'

'What happened to the one we had?'

'She died. Last month.'

'No one told me.'

'Well, bro, you've always had a downer on her and her abilities. We didn't think it would be of interest to you.'

'Look, I know everyone seems to think she has… I mean *had*, some kind of mystical aura but as far as I'm concerned, she simply had an acute ability to read the weather and pass on what she'd gleaned.'

'Is that so? Then fancy explaining why we didn't lose our herd during the foot-and-mouth epidemic when everyone else did?'

'Location, Dad. Nothing more. You had the sense to bring them indoors as soon as you heard the rumours and that's what saved them. Not some witchy potion like you want to believe.'

'I'm not the only one who believes in The Flora. Every farmer in the area trusts her judgement. And almost every household has at least one of her products in their cupboard. She was something to a lot of people and it would be wise of you to keep any other opinion to yourself.'

'Yes, Dad. No problem. But, as a man of science, you'll forgive me for not buying into the whole witchy, magic, fortune-telling malarky. I'm afraid that's asking me to suspend my beliefs just a bit too far.'

'Well, I hope you extend us the same courtesy by accepting that we do believe in The Flora and it's rather disconcerting to be without one.'

'Of course, and with that in mind, if there has always

been one, why isn't there one now?'

'Every Flora had a daughter and the daughter would always move into place when her mother, the previous Flora, moved on. However, on this occasion, the daughter died in a road traffic accident so she's not here to take up her rightful place. That means it moves down to The Flora's granddaughter but she's never been seen. Not even for a single visit. As such, no one knows if she has the powers of her ancestors or if she has any intention of fulfilling her destiny.'

'Hmm, it's more likely she's got the sense to know she's nothing special and is keeping well away from the nutters who think differently.'

'LESS OF THE DISRESPECT, BOY! I'VE TOLD YOU ALREADY!'

'Sorry, Dad. That wasn't intentional. Look, you know how I feel and I know how you feel so let's just agree to disagree and move on. To go back to your earlier question – the medical practice is looking for someone to start as soon as possible. If I got the job, I would need to give three months' notice but I've got eight weeks of holiday accrued – the joys of always being short-staffed – so I'd be able to get away with just one month and take the final months as paid leave. That would get me up here sooner.'

'What about your house, Kenneth, what will you do with that?'

'Sell it. I did think about renting but that suggests I have some intention of returning to London and I can assure you I do not. The fixed-rate mortgage is about to expire so if I'm fortunate enough to get the job, I have absolutely no excuse for dragging my feet on disposing of it.'

'But I thought you loved that house, darling?'

'I did once, Mum, when Amelia was there but since she left, considerably less so. Letting it go will be no hardship.'

'Will you get a good price for it? From what I've seen,

those London houses sell for a lot of money.'

'I don't know, Fraser. The housing market is all over the place right now. Whatever I do get though, should be enough for me to buy a place around Beauly.'

'Would you not stay here, Kenneth?'

'Mum, I might impose upon you for a short time but I'm a bit old to be living at home.'

'What are you saying there, Kenneth?'

Kenneth bit back a sigh. His older brother had always been the one to find a slight where none was intended.

'Fraser, you work on the farm. It makes perfect sense for you to live here. But it won't work for me. I'm used to having my own place. I meant nothing by it.'

'Well, son, I hope you hear good news soon. Now, your brother and I are off to bed. With the clocks going forward this coming weekend, losing that hour will play havoc with our sleep so we're trying to get some extra in now. I'm guessing you'll be gone by the time we come back in tomorrow.'

'Most likely, Dad. I need to be at the airport by lunchtime to catch the afternoon flight.'

His father stood, walked round to his chair and Kenneth got up to accept and return the hug coming his way. His father could be a gruff man but he was a loving man who was always quick to show it.

Fraser and his father were halfway to the door when the sound of his mobile phone's ringtone pierced the air.

Rushing over to his jacket hanging on the back of the kitchen door, Kenneth pulled it out and not recognising the number on the screen, swiped to answer the call. His mum pushed back her chair, went to stand with her husband and he watched his family pull together, all hoping he was about to receive some good news. He instantly recognised the voice in his ear and moved to look out the window, listening with some impatience as Jennet Cameron

45

apologised for calling so late but now that a decision had been made, she didn't feel it was fair to keep people waiting any longer than they had to. It took great willpower not to say just get on with it.

Once she'd finished waffling, it only took a few seconds for her to impart the piece of information he had any interest in hearing. He listened for another minute or two before he was finally able to get a word in and that was only to reply, 'Thank you for letting me know.'

He ended the call then slowly turned to face his family who were standing in such a way you'd be forgiven for thinking they were about to face the hangman's noose.

'Well, son. Was it them? What did they say?'

A smile crept across Kenneth's face as he replied, 'It looks like I'm selling my house!'

EIGHT

Flora pushed the front door closed with her elbow then dropped several heavy shopping bags on the floor beside it, taking care *not* to include the one with her Chinese takeaway and bottle of wine in. Her shoes were kicked off with a groan and she padded down the hallway to the kitchen. A few minutes later, she was on the sofa with a tray on her lap and the TV remote in her hand, looking for something easy to watch.

When she'd made the decision the day before, to move into her father's old bedroom, after several frustrating hours of trying to paint in poor light, she'd realised she'd need to go shopping for some new soft furnishings to make the room more appealing. The built-in wardrobes were more than ample to accommodate all her clothes but the room lacked drawer space. A certain Swedish, build-it-yourself, store, however, had come to the rescue and she'd found the perfect shelving units plus baskets on their website. She'd arrived there just before midday and ended up staying longer than intended, browsing through everything on offer. She'd bought far more than was needed but that was half the fun although her feet were still throbbing as a reminder of how long she'd been on them.

It had been four weeks since her dad had moved in with Sally, and Flora was finally adjusting to living alone. It still felt a little strange getting up in the morning to an empty house but the compensation for that was not having to endure some sports channel on the radio blaring out before she'd had her first coffee. She'd deliberately put off rearranging the bedrooms as it didn't feel right to do it immediately after her dad moved out but yesterday's failure to get any painting done was the last straw. Her bedroom was south-facing, it always had decent light so was the best room to turn into a studio. Furthermore, the bed was a small double which could easily be pushed against the wall to become a sofa where she could chill if she needed to take a break, and the freestanding wardrobes could be shelved, giving her somewhere to stock her art supplies.

With a little happy sigh, Flora gave her now, pain-free, toes a wriggle while pouring out another glass of wine. Only a little one, though, as she wanted to be up bright and early the next day to commence Operation Room Move!

The following morning, Flora was up bright and early. The sun was shining, she'd opened every window in the house to let the fresh, spring air flow through and she could hear the birds chirruping outside. It was the perfect day to wash away cobwebs, hoover up dust bunnies and polish some sparkle into her new sleeping space.

It didn't take long for the bedroom to look like a bomb had hit it as the bed was stripped, the mattress pulled over to the window to be aired while the old curtains were removed and the uplighter ceiling shade with the pearlised seashells that she'd always liked, was taken down to be washed.

With groovy tunes flowing from the radio playing on the internet speaker, Flora worked on making the room gleam and shine. Soon, all that was left to be tackled was the inside of the wardrobes and they'd take no time at all. It was merely a case of polishing the rails, wiping down the old wood panelling along the back and running the vacuum over the carpet fitted inside. When that was done, she could assemble the new shelving units, put them into place and then commence with the task she was least looking forward to – moving her clothes from her old bedroom. Common sense told her that this was the ideal time to do a clear out, there was much she'd never wear again, but her head was also telling her she'd done enough already and to only move in what she'd need in the immediacy, the rest could follow another day.

She stopped to refuel – a cheese sandwich and a cup of tea was more than enough to keep her going – then it was into the wardrobe for the last leg of her cleaning marathon. She carefully positioned the bucket of soapy water to avoid knocking it over and began washing down the long, dark wood, panels. There were three in total along the back of the wardrobe and each featured decorative beading which was rectangular in shape, giving the impression of looking like a door.

'Oh, wouldn't it be fun to find a secret door that led into another land. Just like the wardrobe in the Narnia books,' she said aloud to no one, and her mind went on a jaunt down memory lane as she cleaned.

'Okay, last one and I am done!'

Flora bent down to rinse out her cloth and felt a twinge in the small of her back. She'd spent most of the day bending up and down and her body was letting her know she'd be paying the price in the morning. She was imagining a long soak in the bath when…

'Huh?'

She stopped washing the final panel, standing still to allow her brain to catch up and ascertain the abnormality that had broken into her daydream. She'd been washing the panel… her knuckles had bumped against it… and the reverb from the wood had been different from the others. Hmm!

Slowly, she took the rubber glove off her hand, put her fingers against the wood and trailed them gently across before giving a small rap on the panel. She then rapped on the panel to her left – nope, that did not sound the same as the one in front of her. She tried again. The last panel definitely had a hollow ring to it. It lacked the solid "thunk" of the central panel. For certainty, Flora made her way to the far end of the wardrobe, tapped the panel there and was rewarded with the same deep "thunk" as the one beside it.

She walked back to take a good look at the final panel before reaching out to tap it again. Yup, it absolutely was different from the other two and now she had to find out how or why. A quick step over to the bed had her rummaging underneath the packages lying on top until she located her phone and, switching on the torch, she began inspecting the panel more closely, carefully pressing in the corners and along the edges to see if anything happened.

It was as she was checking the long side of the beading that Flora got a result. Halfway down there was a quiet click and the panel swung inwards ever so slightly.

'Oh, wow! I was only joking when I said I wanted a door into Narnia…'

With a mixture of excitement and curiosity, she pushed the door wide, noting as she did how the hinges had been cleverly hidden under the beading on the opposite side, ensuring the secret space was not easily discovered, and stepping over the wooden frame along the bottom, found herself in a narrow closet. She swung the torch around to see what was there. The beam of light fell upon a switch next to the open panel and when flicked on, the small space was lit up, revealing several rows of shelving, reaching from the ceiling to the floor along with all the boxes stored upon them.

'Oh, poop! No witches with Turkish Delight… Bummer!'

A chuckle of amusement slipped from her as she acknowledged the dipping feeling of disappointment in her stomach. It was good to know her childish belief in all things magical and beyond hadn't fully disappeared with adulthood.

As she moved over to take a closer look at the boxes on the shelves, she wondered if her dad knew about this space. It was dusty and a few cobwebs could be seen in the high corners but it wasn't as bad as she'd have expected it to be if it had been untouched for many decades.

She reached for the first box – an office storage box with a lid on it, as they all were – pulled it towards her and when she peeked in, saw several parcels wrapped in brown paper with lavender coloured handwriting on.

'Okay… how odd…'

Flora reached in, pulling the top parcel out for a closer look. She tilted it towards the light then let out a gasp. Putting it on the shelf, she pulled out the next one, and the next one…

Ten minutes later, she had gone through every box, finding many such packages and a mountain of letters. They all had the same handwriting on the front. They were all written in purple ink.

And they were all addressed to her!

NINE

Kenneth stood with his hands on his hips, looking in dismay at the pile of half empty boxes around him. The problem with book boxes was they couldn't be filled to the top as the removal men would require a crane to lift them. As such, he'd been advised to half fill and top up with soft furnishings or lightweight items. Given how many books were still sitting on the shelves, he didn't think he'd have enough "soft furnishings" to add even if he lived another two lifetimes.

A feeling of sadness came over him as he recalled Amelia teasing him about the number of books he'd contributed when they'd first taken the big step of living together. He'd replied that what he couldn't provide in practical terms, such as the furniture they *actually* needed, he could at least make it up with the sheer number of items.

Amelia hadn't been one for reading. She would read work-related items because she had to and they were beneficial for her career but she'd never been one to read for the pleasure of it. Maybe if she had, he pondered, there might not have been a need to piss off to Tibet.

He, on the other hand, couldn't be without a book. Outside of the medical journals he read to keep up with the progresses constantly being discovered in the world of science and medicine, he loved a good thriller or humour-filled, laugh-out-loud, novel. He also had a little quirk whereby, if he read a book on his e-reader and really enjoyed it, he would purchase a hard copy and this was the reason why he was now standing in a sea of boxes half-full of wonderful words and glorious covers which, he mused with a lifted corner of his mouth, was not a bad place to be. He could think of worse situations to be in.

His eyes swept over the bookcases again, trying to assess how many more boxes he'd need to order from the removal company. His sweeping, however, came to a sudden halt up on the top shelf, for there sat his most treasured books of all – his childhood annuals. The books he, and almost every child in Scotland, would receive from Santa every Christmas – The Broons and Oor Wullie. Oh, how he'd loved those. Back when he was a child, these cartoon-filled delights would alternate each year and he was always happier when it was the turn of Oor Wullie. The mischievous, spikey-haired boy with his great sense of adventure had always managed to make Kenneth laugh with joy and each annual would be read and re-read many times over. He was, in fact, such a fan of the tartan terror, he'd begun collecting copies of the annuals that had been released before he was born and had been surprised to find so many available in the second-hand bookshops he'd visited because he couldn't understand how or why people would get rid of them. Who on earth would give away such a fabulous piece of their childhood? Now that he was an adult, he was able to look back and see he'd been envious of Wullie's ability to just get out there and do things, regardless of the consequences. As a child, Kenneth had always been too serious and it was a trait which had followed him into adulthood. He'd tried so many times to be more outgoing and less buttoned up but it simply didn't suit him. Fraser and Ross had also tried to 'unwind' him but their rambunctious ways just weren't for him. When he'd announced his engagement to the beautiful Amelia, their shock could not be hidden. How on earth had he managed that? Well, it had been more by luck than design. His flatmates had spiked his drinks at a party, with a view to getting him to let his hair down, but their antics backfired terribly when he'd reacted badly to the overdose of alcohol he simply wasn't used to and it had been Amelia who'd come to his aid. She'd stayed with him as he sobered up and had kept up a constant supply of water and fresh orange juice to help him recover. He'd taken her out for dinner as a thank you for her care and they'd become a couple soon after.

Realising he was heading down the memory lanes he'd closed off five years ago, Kenneth gave his head a shake and reached up to pull the annuals down. With great care, he opened one up. This edition was considerably older than he was – its pages were tinged yellow along the edges and the binding creaked if he opened it too wide. He began reading the comic strip in front of him and immediately a smile found its way onto his face. He was almost halfway through the book when he realised what he'd done. Sighing, he looked again at the mess around him and said aloud, 'Oh, sod it! The rest can wait.'

With that, he picked up the rest of the annuals, turned on his heel and walked out of the study, closing the door firmly behind him. Twenty minutes later, he was cosied up in bed with a stack of Nutella-coated toast on a plate beside him, a large mug of hot chocolate on the bedside table, and his pile of books on his lap. He'd done enough adulting for now. It was time to indulge himself in the memories of a life when it had been innocent and simpler.

'Morning, Gary. All set?'

'Hmph! If I must.'

Kenneth grinned as he closed the door behind his friend and followed him through to the kitchen where the coffee mugs and biscuits were already laid out.

'Good to see you're providing sustenance although you may want to open a few more packets of biccies. I'm going to need them!'

'Gary, we're only dismantling some furniture which is considerably easier than putting it together. Besides, if you have too many biscuits, you won't have room for the fry-up later.'

'Hmm, you wanna bet on that?'

'Look, we're not jogging this morning, Cherry won't thank me for sending you back two stone heavier.'

'I suppose. So, have you begun packing up yet or did you save that pleasure for my arrival?'

'I've started on the books...'

'Is that all? It'll take you three weeks just to box them. You might wanna move your removal men back another month.'

'Ha, very funny. No way am I doing that – I'm leaving here as soon as I can. Maybe you should have brought Cherry with you. She'd be through this place like a whirling dervish!'

'She would have come but then Charlotte arrived...'

'Ah! Fair enough!'

Kenneth loathed Charlotte as much as he loved Cherry who was clever, funny, warm, and easy company to be in. Charlotte, her sister, was the total opposite. Shallow, cold, self-centred, and completely obsessed with both him and the Kardashians in equal measure. The latter was enough to ensure he kept well out of her reach. He abhorred reality TV, how it dominated the viewing choices of the public and the influence these programmes had on young girls, making them so fixated on their appearance. He couldn't begin to count how many teenagers had sat in his surgery begging him to put them forward for breast enhancements, nose jobs, stomach stapling or butt reductions. And those were the *normal* requests. He could barely bring himself to think of the more outlandish things he'd had to listen to never mind the number of times he'd had to convince his patients that Cher had NOT had ribs removed to make her waistline smaller.

'Charlotte wants your details when you move.'

Kenneth pointed the screwdriver in his hand at Gary while growling, 'Don't you dare!'

'Don't worry, mate, I wouldn't do that to you. Besides, how's she ever going to reach Scotland – she thinks you need a passport just to go past the M25!'

'Good point. I just don't get why she refuses to accept that I'm not interested. Here, hold this while I unscrew it.' He pointed Gary to the end of the bedstead. 'And, should you really be talking about your sister-in-law like that?'

'The downside of marriage, mate, is sometimes the baggage it brings would be better off left in the lost property office.'

They both grinned in understanding before bending their heads to the task in hand.

'Anyway,' Gary continued, 'It's your own fault for being such a sex-god. I'm forever grateful you were still married when I met Cherry, otherwise, I wouldn't have had a look in. You are the epitome of "Tall, dark and handsome"!'

Kenneth felt his cheeks grow hot at Gary's words but chose to ignore them as he said, 'Can you hold that tighter, this screw won't budge.'

Three hours later, most of the large furniture had been dismantled, including his precious bookcases, the crockery had been boxed, and the dining room was now a storage facility.

'How did you manage it, Kenneth?'

'Manage what?'

'Selling so quickly. It took us months to find a buyer and you get one on the very first viewing. It's not fair!'

'No chain makes a property more appealing. They're first-time buyers – who were also savvy enough to have their mortgage arranged before looking – and I'll be staying with my folks until I get settled. They're as keen to get in as I am to get out which is why I'll be back in Scotland a few days after my last shift. I can't wait.'

'I'll miss you when you go. So will Cherry.'

'I'll be expecting you both to visit.'

'Oh, don't you worry about that, we intend to. We want to see the land that's so awesome, it's taking our best friend away from us. Plus, we also know we don't need passports to get there!'

Kenneth's belly-laugh filled the air as they pulled on their jackets, ready to go and do some serious damage to their appetites in the café around the corner. When he turned from locking the front door, the sight of Gary walking ahead of him brought about a sudden pang of loneliness – he didn't make friends easily and he was about to leave behind the only real friend he had. Suddenly he began to wonder if he was doing the right thing.

TEN

Flora sat on a chair in the dining room, staring at the piles of letters on the table – every one of them addressed to her. After her shocking discovery the night before, she'd carried the boxes, all twelve of them, out of the hidden space and had lined them up in the hallway where she'd picked out envelopes from each one and saw they were all written in the same hand, the same purple ink, and postmarked Inverness. They were from her grandmother – an assumption which was confirmed when she opened one to check. Her legs had given way at that point and she'd slumped back against the wall, sliding down until her bottom hit the floor where she'd remained sitting for some time, trying to comprehend what was in front of her. Eventually, she'd knelt forward to take a closer look at the contents and found the boxes were mostly full of letters although several packages lurked amongst them. In the end, she'd made the difficult decision to place them in the dining room and close the door on them for the night. She was tired after her exertions of the day and common sense told her she was going to need a clear head to deal with what she'd found. Since she'd been almost finished with her task, she completed the cleaning and tidied everything away. There'd been no option but to do this otherwise she'd have been sleeping on the sofa as both beds were still buried underneath the contents of the wardrobes and drawers. All the time, however, her head had been spinning from her discovery and she'd decided to take a sleeping aid when she went to bed to avoid the restless night she knew she'd certainly have. Luckily, her plan worked and Flora was now facing the task of sorting the boxes of correspondence with a fresh head.

'I think,' she murmured aloud, 'the best plan of action is to sort you all into date order. To quote Julie Andrews, "let's start at the very beginning…"! It seems the most sensible approach.'

Two hours later, she was standing staring at twenty-four piles of letters. The first piece of correspondence had been a birthday card on her fourth birthday along with a large, wrapped gift that hadn't yet been opened. The final letter had been sent a few days before her grandmother had died. In between, there had been two letters a month for almost twenty-four years plus birthday, Easter, and Christmas cards along with gifts. In total, that was over six-hundred items waiting to be opened and read.

Last night, her mind had been spinning at her find but now it seemed to have gone into shutdown as it continued with struggling to understand the situation. Maybe another cup of strong coffee would help. She went through to the kitchen, topped up her mug and walked back to the dining room, coming to a stop in the doorway, reluctant to face the questions her brain was now throwing around as she gazed at the piles of purple lined mail.

How?
Why?
How?

Why?

How had this amount of post arrived for her over the years without her knowledge?

Why had her father kept it from her?

Flora turned on her heel and marched into her father's study, where she went to the desk and after rummaging through the drawers, walked out a moment later with a box of rubber bands in one hand, a pad of Post-It notes and a pen in the other. It didn't take long for the loose piles to become dated, secure, bundles.

While returning to the kitchen, she took her phone from her pocket and sent a text message:

Are you at home?

She'd just pulled the large bin bags out from the cupboard underneath the sink when a ping let her know she'd had a reply.

Yes.

I'm on my way over.

A moment later, the bundles had been shoved into several bin bags, Flora had yanked on her jacket and was locking the front door.

Uncle Craig must have been looking out for her because he opened the door when Flora pulled onto his driveway. It was only a short drive from her house to his but it had been long enough for the stopper to come off her temper and she was now fizzing fit to burst. She got out of her little Nissan

Micra, slammed the door closed, opened the back door to retrieve the bags and slammed that one closed too. She pointed her car-key over her shoulder and locked it as she stomped towards her uncle, barging past him when she crossed the threshold.

'Do come in…' he said to her back, but she was already in his lounge by the time he'd closed the door.

'Flora, what's wrong?'

Craig walked in as she was turning the bin bags upside down and emptying the contents onto the floor.

He looked at the pile on the rug before looking back at her, confusion clearly written on his face.

'Did you know?'

'Know what?'

'About these.'

'What are they? Yes,' he held his hand up, 'I can see they're bundles of letters—'

'From my grandmother. YOUR mother.'

'They're what?'

Flora watched his face turn a pasty shade of white as he walked over to the pile. He stopped for a second before bending down and picking up one of the bundles, pulling back the sticky yellow note to stare at the writing on the envelope underneath.

'She always wrote with purple ink…' he said softly, running a finger gently over the neat handwriting. He bent down again to pick up another bundle and Flora noticed the dates were eight years apart. He gazed at the handwriting again before turning the letters over. His eyebrows shot upwards before coming back down to meet in a frown.

'These letters are unopened.' He turned the first bundle over. 'As are these. What's going on, Flora?'

'So, you know nothing about these?'

'I would say the answer to that is pretty self-evident.

No, I don't.'

'I found them last night.'

'*Found* them? Where?'

'In a secret space behind the built-in wardrobe in my dad's bedroom. I was cleaning the room, ready to move into it, and found a concealed door. My excitement was short-lived when this,' she swept her hand over the top of the letter pile, 'is what I found. Or rather, twelve boxes containing the letters… and gifts.'

'Gifts?'

'Yes, gifts. Every birthday, every Easter, and every Christmas since I turned four years-old.'

Craig looked again at the letters on the floor.

'I didn't bring the gifts with me, only the letters. I didn't have enough bags for those.'

'How many letters are there?'

'I've calculated a ballpark of six-hundred and fifty if you include the gifts.'

'And you haven't read them yet?'

Flora let out a bark of a laugh.

'Uncle Craig, I only found them last night. It's going to take a while. Even if I read ten letters a day, it'll still take over two months to get through them. I thought you were the numbers person around here?'

'Of course, of course…' Craig sank down onto the chair behind him and Flora did the same onto the sofa.

'You genuinely knew nothing of the letters? You didn't know your mother was writing to me?'

'No, I didn't.' He shook his head slowly then stopped. 'Actually… hang on… I was aware she'd written to you that one time… if you recall… it was near Christmas. You said you hadn't received the letter and we presumed it had gone AWOL in the Christmas post.'

'Yeah, I do remember now you mention it. How long ago was that?'

'Maybe three years ago? It was the year after our road trip when we'd reconciled our differences.'

Flora knelt on the floor by the letter pile and, rummaging through the bundles, she pulled out the year she was looking for. She flicked through the envelopes until she found what she'd hoped not to see – a letter dated the middle of December.

'Well, it would appear it did go AWOL just not in the manner we'd expected.' She let out a sigh as she handed the bundle to her uncle and returned to sitting on the sofa.

'Why? Why did my father do this?'

'You haven't spoken to him yet?' There was astonishment in his voice.

'No. He's been working over the other side of Oxford for the last few weeks. A company they'd worked with before asked them back for another project. Dad said he'd cover it so Robbie could be closer to Sam and the baby, meaning he won't be home until later this evening. That's why I came to you – I had to speak with someone and you were, if I'm being honest, the better choice because you might help me to make sense of it before I talk to Dad.'

'I see. Well, I don't know how much help I'm going to be there, love, because right now, I would swing for Matt if he was here. He had no right, NO right at all, to keep these from you. My poor mother – writing to you all these years and never getting a single reply. It's a disgrace. A bloody disgrace.'

Flora looked at her uncle in shock. She'd never seen him lose his temper before. She'd never even seen him mildly angry, but there was no missing the fury building up in him now.

'I don't understand why she didn't mention it to you though. Surely something would have been said – if only to ask if I'd received her letters.'

'I hear what you're saying but I think your grandmother

may have worried I'd say something to you that would pressure you, or guilt-trip you, into replying. She'd have wanted your replies to be sent of your own accord.'

Just then, the front door opened and closed and two white West Highland terriers came bounding into the room, coming to a sudden halt when they saw Flora there and the dilemma on their little faces made her chuckle. They didn't know who to run to first – Craig or herself.

'Thanks, guys. Nice to know where your loyalties lie!'

Craig's sardonic words spurred them into action. Heather ran over to him while Rory went to Flora, rising onto his hind legs with his front paws on her knees.

'Hey, gorgeous little man, how's my favourite cousin today, then?'

She bent her head down to nuzzle it against the dog's and allow him to cover her chin with licky kisses. Her uncle's lack of human children meant they always referred to the dogs as his kids and Flora joined in the fun by saying they were her cousins.

'Hi, Flora, I thought that was your car outside. Nice bit of parking.'

'Hi, Essie.' Flora sat up straighter to look out the lounge window and saw how haphazardly she'd parked the car. 'Oh dear, I'm sorry, Essie, I wasn't quite thinking right…'

'Oh?'

Essie looked at Craig and Flora before her eyes came to land on the piles of letters sitting on the floor.

'Let me sort out some drinks, then you can tell me everything.'

'Good idea, Essie. I think your insight will be of great value.'

When Essie left the room, Craig turned back to Flora. 'I hope you're okay with telling Essie about this. She's a mum with far more experience in stuff like this, I believe she'll be more of a help to you than I am.'

Flora didn't reply but just nodded in agreement. She really hoped Essie had some words of wisdom to help her cope with the situation.

'Oh, my goodness, you poor girl. No wonder you're in shock.'

Flora had just filled Essie in on everything and where she'd struggled, Craig had assisted. Between them, they'd brought her up to speed and now she had her arms wrapped around Flora, hugging her for dear life, trying to impart some comfort to her. Flora was extremely fond of her uncle's partner and had no problem accepting the embrace for she surely needed it. Sometimes, you just need someone to wrap their arms around you and tell you that everything will be okay. Essie was doing a grand job of that right now.

'Can you think why my dad didn't give these to me, Essie? Can you shed any light on this?' Flora sat back and looked hopefully at the older woman.

'Now, Flora, I can't tell you *exactly* why Matt kept these hidden from you but I am going to assume it stems from the pain and grief he was going through after the death of your mother. I don't know his side of the story, only what Craig has told me, but I'm aware there was bad feeling between your dad and grandmother since your mum died. When was your fourth birthday, in relation to your mum's car accident?'

'Five months after.'

Essie nodded. 'I see. So, not long at all and most definitely at a time when you'd both still be coming to terms with the changes in your lives. I'd suggest your father was just about coping with things and the questions you'd have asked about the birthday card and your grandmother would have been more that he could have dealt with right then. Hiding the card and gift would have been easier for him.'

'Okay, I can get that but what about the later ones? In the beginning, fair enough but, Essie… this is twenty-four years we're talking about. Why keep hiding them for that long?'

'Maybe once he'd started, there came a point where it would have been difficult to own up to you about what he'd done.'

'Hmm.' Flora wasn't feeling convinced with this explanation.

'Look, you need to speak with your dad. He's the only person who has the answers. Just try to understand how difficult it would have been for him.'

'DIFFICULT? FOR HIM?' Craig's words exploded in the air. 'Did he once stop to think about my mother and the pain he put her through. She had a granddaughter she'd never met and was desperate to communicate with.'

'Desperate?'

'You don't send two letters a month, Essie, when you only want a passing acquaintance. My mother was clearly trying to establish a relationship with Flora and it must have broken her heart every time when no reply came back. How dare he do this to her. And to you, Flora. He was wrong. So wrong. I can see the point you're making about the early days, Ess, I really can, but not to have come clean before now is unforgiveable. My mother went to her grave thinking her only grandchild wanted nothing to do with her when the truth is, her grandchild didn't know she'd been trying to reach out to her for the last twenty-four years. I will never forgive him for this. NEVER!'

Craig stormed out of the room, slamming the door hard behind him. In the ensuing silence, the two women turned to face each other. Essie took a hold of Flora's hands and said quietly, 'I can't disagree with him, Flora. As a mother, I know I would be beside myself if I had a grandchild who was estranged from me. I can't begin to describe how it must have been for your grandmother. I'm afraid that, as of now, your father is no longer welcome in this house.'

'Being honest, Essie, I don't blame you, either of you, for feeling that way. I think your assumption is the correct one but it's not a good enough reason to hide this for all these years.'

'What are you going to do now?'

Flora let out a loud sigh.

'The only thing I can do. Talk to my dad.'

ELEVEN

For the first time since they'd been installed, Flora wasn't cursing the speed bumps on the lane up to Sally's Bed & Breakfast. Even the ten miles per hour speed limit didn't irritate her as it normally would. In fact, the way she was feeling right now, she'd have been more than happy to go at one mile per hour – anything to delay the inevitable showdown she knew was coming.

She'd stayed with Essie and Craig until late afternoon, knowing her father wouldn't be home before six. They'd both understood her fluctuating emotions and while her uncle was furious with her dad, he hadn't influenced her thinking or feelings in any way and had been quite clear that how he felt should not dictate how she should feel.

Eventually, her car came to the small private car park which was strictly for Sally's use. Her dad's van was there and she felt her stomach lurch. She *really* didn't want to do this but that would only be running away from the problem. It had to be faced. Besides, the longer her anger was allowed to ferment, the more ingrained the bitterness would become.

This time, both car doors were closed quietly. The Micra was a little old lady – there was a limit to how often her doors could be slammed. With bin bags in each hand, she walked round to the back door of Sally's basement apartment and tapped on it. A moment later it opened and Sally was greeting her with one of her gorgeous welcoming smiles.

'Flora! What a lovely surprise. Come on in.'

As she stepped into the warm, open-plan room, Flora looked around for her dad.

'Is Dad home? I saw his van outside?'

'Yes, he's just up having a shower. He'll be down in a few minutes. Can I get you a drink? Tea? Coffee? I've even got some bottles of the mixed fruit juice you like…'

'Err, can I just have a glass of water, please?'

'Sure, of course you can. Go and grab a seat. I'll bring it over.'

Sally was eyeing the bin bags in her hand but Flora chose not to say anything. This was one surprise that belonged only for her dad.

She'd just taken a sip from the water glass when she heard footsteps on the spiral staircase. Carefully, she placed the glass on the small table by the side of the sofa and turned towards her dad who was exclaiming his delight at this unscheduled visit.

'Hey, my gorgeous girl, I didn't know you were coming over.' He bent down to kiss the top of her head while giving her shoulders a gentle squeeze. 'To what do we owe the honour? Are you joining us for dinner? You know what Sally's like – she always cooks enough to feed a small army.'

'I don't think I will be, Dad.'

'Oh? Got a hot date lined up?' he grinned.

Flora swallowed deeply. This was it. This was the moment when her life was about to change for the second time in twenty-four hours. Her stomach felt like the bottom of it had fallen out and the palms of her hands were sweaty.

'No, Dad, I don't have a date lined up which is probably a good thing as I wouldn't be very good company right now.'

'What do you mean?'

'I decided yesterday to move into the front bedroom and turn my room into a proper workshop—'

'Well, that makes sense, you get much better light in that room.'

'Indeed. Well, before doing so, I thought it would be the perfect opportunity to give the front bedroom a good spring clean—'

'It probably could have done with it.'

Flora wished her dad would stop injecting his comments, she just wanted to say her piece and get it over with.

'Yes… well… the spring clean included washing down the back panels in the fitted wardrobes.'

She watched her dad carefully as she spoke and knew the exact moment he realised what was coming next. The colour drained right out of his face as she uttered the words, 'And guess what I found—'

'Flora, I can explai—'

'A secret door! That led into a small secret room!'

'My! How exciting! Did you know it was there, Matt?' Sally clasped her hands together in delight, oblivious to her partner's growing discomfort.

'Oh, yes, Sally, my father very MUCH knew it was there, didn't you, *Daddy*?'

Her reply caused Sally to still before turning to look at Matt.

'And do you know what I found in the small secret room behind the secret door, Sally? No? Well, let me show you!'

With a flourish, she upended the bin bags for the second time that day, never taking her eyes off her father.

'What? What are these?'

'These, Sally, are the letters my grandmother sent to me, twice a month, for the best part of twenty-four years. Letters I never received because my father hid them from me.'

'Oh, Matt… you didn't…'

'Oh, Sally, he very much did and now I'm here to find out why, hoping his reasons are good ones because I'm just about managing to hold onto my temper.'

Her dad continued to look at her, not speaking and not looking at the pile of correspondence on the floor in front of them.

'Well, Dad, I'm waiting. Why did I not receive a. Single. One. of the six-hundred plus letters and gifts my grandmother sent to me?'

'I… I… I…'

'Yes?'

'I was trying to protect you.'

'From what?'

'From… From… Look, you were only four and still hadn't come to terms with the fact Mummy was never coming home. Night after night after night, you wanted to know when Mummy would be there to tuck you in and kiss you good night. Every time you asked, my heart broke. You have no idea how difficult it was. When the first card arrived, I knew immediately who it was from – I recognised the ink and handwriting from letters your mum had received. The postmark confirmed it. This was a woman you'd never met but you'd reached the age where you had a better comprehension of the people around you and I didn't give it to you because I didn't know how to explain who it was from. I was also very angry with your grandmother and felt it wasn't the right time for both of us to be trying to deal with her. So, I put it away.'

'Okay, that I can understand. Uncle Craig and Essie said pretty much the same thing.'

'Craig? You've been to see Craig? He knows?'

'Oh, yeah, he knows. And if I were you, I wouldn't think about visiting him for a while because you are far from being his favourite person right now. However, what none of us can understand is why you NEVER told me. Twenty-four years of letters, Dad, how could you have kept them from me?'

'I did mean to tell you at some point but, as time went on, it… it… it became harder to find the right moment to do so. It was easier to say nothing.'

'D'you know, Dad, all that I could have dealt with. I wouldn't have been happy with the secrecy but I'd have understood it. I *do* understand. But what really hurts, what makes this SO difficult to swallow is that you lied to me! You lied to my face and THAT is what I find unforgivable!'

'What? I have never lied to you, Flora. Not ever.'

'Oh, Dad, you did. Three years back at Christmas, Uncle Craig told me his mum had written to me. I hadn't received the letter and I asked you about it. You denied seeing it and mentioned something about Christmas post being unreliable. Except…' Flora bent over and grabbed one of the bundles at her feet. She pulled out an envelope and held it up in from of her. 'This is the letter! We worked it out – Uncle Craig had been up to see Granny Flora—'

'Granny Flora?'

'Yes, that's how she signed her letters. Uncle Craig double-checked his diaries and confirmed the exact dates of his visit. Granny Flora wrote her letters over the weekend and posted them on the following Tuesday. Every two weeks. Without fail. The only time this altered was over Christmas and New Year but they would be posted on the first available day after the holidays.'

'Are you sure?' The desperation in her father's voice couldn't be missed.

'Yes, I am sure. YOU LIED TO ME! You had the chance to come clean but you didn't. YOU LIED TO ME!'

'But it wouldn't have made a difference by then. It was already too late—'

'TOO LATE!' Flora's voice hit octaves she never knew were possible. 'TOO LATE? I WOULD HAVE HAD THREE YEARS TO GET TO KNOW HER! I WOULD HAVE HAD SOMETHING! YOU STOLE THAT FROM ME!'

'YOU KNEW SHE EXISTED, FLORA. THERE WAS NOTHING TO STOP YOU "GETTING TO KNOW HER" IF YOU'D REALLY WANTED TO!'

The shock from her father's words rendered her speechless. Could he really not see it? Was he genuinely oblivious to what he had taken from her?

'Dad, why would I have tried to get to know someone who didn't want to know me? Why would I have wanted to contact a woman who'd never tried to make contact with me? Except... oh, yeah,' the bundle of envelopes was waved in the air again, 'SHE DID! I JUST DIDN'T KNOW! BECAUSE YOU LIED TO ME! YOU STOLE HER FROM ME!'

'Stole her? Now you are being silly!'

These words were her undoing and Flora felt all her anger and frustration burst from her.

'YES! STOLE! MY ONLY LIVING FEMALE RELATIVE AND YOU KEPT HER FROM ME. THE WOMAN WHO COULD HAVE FILLED IN THE GAPS, WHO COULD HAVE TOLD ME MORE ABOUT MY MOTHER, WHO COULD HAVE GIVEN ME THE KIND OF LOVE ONLY A MOTHER CAN! YOU STOLE THAT FROM ME AND I WILL NEVER

FORGIVE YOU FOR THAT. NEVER!'

'Flora—'

'Sally, please… this doesn't involve you…'

'I was able to answer all the questions you asked about your mum, Flora. I never held anything back.'

'No, Dad, you were able to answer questions from the time you knew her but you didn't know her as a child. You don't know what things I did that she may also have done. You tell me I look so much like her but I don't know if I AM like her. There are so many questions you cannot answer and now I will never have those answers – you made damn sure of that, didn't you?'

'You had Craig and your grandfather to tell you those things.'

'They could tell me some stuff but men see things differently from women. They could tell me the man stuff – they couldn't tell me the woman stuff.'

'Flora, I'm sorry…'

'Too little, too late, Dad. You're not the man I thought you were and I want nothing more to do with you. I don't want to see you again. Don't call me because I won't answer.'

As she began piling the letters back into the bags, her father replied, 'Well, Flora, you're still living in our home so I will visit whenever I wish.'

'I wouldn't bother if I were you, I won't be there.'

'What… what do you mean?'

'I'm moving out. I'll be gone by the end of the month.'

'And where are you going to go? Huh? Uncle Craig's? How long do you think he and Essie will want you camping out in their spare room?'

This time, it was Flora's turn to be shocked by the nasty tone behind her father's words. She had never seen him like this before. In the space of a day, the man she'd grown up loving and revering had all but disappeared and it was a stranger who now stood in front of her. She lifted her chin in defiance as she looked him in the eye.

'Granny Flora left her cottage to me. I'm moving to Scotland!'

TWELVE

Flora was busy reassembling the cardboard boxes Jenny from the bookshop had given her when she heard tyres on the gravel outside and, stopping what she was doing, she peered out of the window, a groan escaping her when she saw Sally's car. With a sigh, she dropped the box in her hand and went down the stairs to let Sally in.

'Hi, Sally. Look, I don't want to be rude but if you're here to talk me round, you're wasting your time—'

'I know. Which is why I'm not.'

'You're not?'

'No. I'm here to give you a hand with your packing.'

'But… Dad…'

'Flora,' Sally took hold of her hands, 'Your dad knows he's messed up here. He really does. And while I do NOT condone what he's done, I can understand it. Grief makes us do stupid things and sometimes, the things we do wrong are hard to undo. That said, I DO think it's a great idea for you to go to Scotland. While, sadly, your Granny Flora is no longer there, hopefully there will be people who can tell you more about her and being in what used to be her space might help you to get to know something about the person she was and maybe your mother too. It's nowhere near as good as spending time with her but that horse has bolted and now, we must work with what's left.'

Tears filled Flora's eyes as Sally pulled her into a hug. She'd needed to hear someone else tell her she was doing the right thing. While in her heart she knew she was, it helped to know that this woman whom she so respected, agreed with her.

'Now, is that Vanda I saw sitting outside?'

Flora gave a glimmer of a smile as she pulled a tissue from her pocket.

'It surely is.'

'Craig is letting you have his precious VW camper van?'

'Well, as he rightly pointed out, two boxes and a paintbrush would fill my little Micra right up so he's letting me borrow Vanda – I should be able to get nearly everything I need in her. She's very spacious when you fold everything away, more so when you include her drawers and cupboards. Besides, I don't have that much stuff. My art supplies will take up the most room.'

'So, you plan to continue with your doll business?'

'Absolutely. I may be in Scotland but I'll still need an income.'

'It's lucky it's something you can do anywhere.'

'It is and I'm even more grateful for it now. It's awarded me the freedom to do this.'

'Run away?'

'No, Sally, find myself.'

Three hours later, the last of the boxes were piled into Vanda and she was locked in the garage for safety.

'What time are you setting off?' Sally asked, plugging in the cool box before emptying the contents of the fridge into it.

'Four o'clock in the morning, at the latest. Earlier if I fall asleep as soon as I go to bed.'

'Wow! That's early. How long will it take you?'

'The AA website says just under nine hours so, all being well, about twelve hours by the time I factor in a couple of rest stops along the way and no traffic jams on the A9.'

'But so early…'

'Vanda is an old lady and I've been told that anything over sixty makes her a bit tetchy. I want to be past Preston before the morning rush hour coz if you hit that at the wrong time, it's a nightmare. Plus, I don't want to be driving in the dark at the other end, especially as I don't know where I'm going.'

'I'm guessing there isn't a satnav in Vanda.'

'No, but the route itself is pretty straight forward. It's only the last stretch, the home run, that could be tricky as the road down to the lake, I mean *loch*, is quite well hidden but Uncle Craig has given me rather explicit directions and I've put a Sat Nav app on my phone, so between them, I think I'll find it okay.'

'Right then, I've done all I can for you here so I'm going to go now and yes, before you ask, I will be reporting back to your dad. I know it doesn't feel like it right now but he does truly love you. Go and find yourself but please, Flora, don't forget the man who got you to this point in your life. You need time to heal and when you do, we'll both be here for you.'

The two women hugged again then Sally picked up her handbag. Flora walked her out to her car. As she stood, ready to wave goodbye, the window was wound down and Sally's head popped out.

'Flora, just one small thing to ask – please let me know when you arrive. No need to call, just a quick text or email so we know you're there safely. And, if you want to send messages at any other time, letting us know you're okay, we'd be more than happy to receive them. See you anon, fabulous Flora. Take care. Love you.'

With these parting words, Sally's head disappeared back inside, the horn tooted twice and a hand came out the window to wave before the car turned and disappeared behind the hedge. A moment later, all was silent and Flora stood on the doorstep, taking in the view before her. She'd left home before when she'd gone off to uni but this time it was different. This time, she didn't know when she'd be back... if at all.

Finally, she walked back inside. As she was closing the door, she heard the chimes of the church clock. Six o'clock. Just enough time to have something to eat and a bath before going to bed. After all, three o'clock was the middle of the night so she needed all the sleep she could get before then.

She'd barely walked halfway up the hallway when there was a knock on the door.

'What now?' she grumbled, turning to retrace her steps.

The door was yanked open with no small measure of frustration and the feeling increased tenfold at the sight of her ex-boyfriend standing on the doormat. His bicycle was propped up against the wall which is how he'd arrived so silently.

'For the love of all that's holy, Joey, what are you doing here?'

'I came to tell you not to go to Scotland. Please. You have to stay.'

Flora looked at him in disbelief. 'How... how do you know I'm going to Scotland? Did my dad say something at work?' Even as she asked the question, she knew her dad would never have discussed their argument with Joey, or anyone else for that matter. He wasn't the kind of person to air his dirty linen to all and sundry.

'No, he didn't.'

'Then how—

'I... er... overheard your argument with your dad. I'd dropped by the farm to give him some paperwork he'd asked me to arrange. The window was open... I heard everything...'

'You shouldn't have listened.'

'It was kind of hard not to. You didn't exactly keep your voice down.'

She let out a sigh – in this, Joey was right. She had been shouting rather loudly. She looked at Joey, wondering again how she'd become involved with him. *Because he wouldn't stop asking you out. In the end, it was easier to say yes just to shut him up,* the voice at the back of head said, answering her question for her. And it was right. She'd gone on a pity date with him except the date had turned into six months. The problem was that Joey was a nice person and saying no to him felt like kicking a puppy. He was a tall, gangly man who'd spent most of his life trying to be smaller than he was so as not to be noticed. The only aspect of his rather average looks that could be described as stand-out were his large brown eyes which he managed to use to good effect when he was trying to get his own way. Even his hair was non-descript being sort of brownish in colour with no noticeable style to it – it wasn't long or short or even styled. It was just kind of... well... there.

'Joey, I don't need this right now, I've got enough on my plate so please just go away and leave me alone.'

'But, Flora, I don't want you to go, I need you here. I won't be able to cope without you.'

'For crying out loud, Joey, we broke up over six months

ago. Will you just let it be and accept we are never getting back together.'

'But—'

'ENOUGH, JOEY! ENOUGH! NOT ANOTHER WORD!' She pointed her finger at his bicycle. 'I WANT YOU TO TURN AROUND, GET ON THAT BIKE, CYCLE OUT OF THE DRIVEWAY AND GO HOME! DO YOU HEAR ME? GO AWAY!'

With a look of shock on his face he turned, did exactly as she'd told him and all in complete silence. Once she was sure he'd gone, Flora closed the door behind her again, leaning against it until her heartbeat slowed down to a more normal pace. Honestly, the sooner she got away, the better.

As she strode down the hallway for the second time, she felt a small tingle – like a tiny electric shock – run through her. She walked into the kitchen, picked up the kettle and while waiting for it to fill she muttered to herself, 'And now the excitement begins to kick in…'

THIRTEEN

Kenneth watched as the removal men locked up their van. They gave him a wave before clambering into the cab and making a careful manoeuvre back out onto the street. He closed the door, hearing it echoing around the almost empty house. Everything in the van was being stored in an unused barn on his parents' farm. His clothes were piled neatly in the dining room, ready to go into bin bags in the morning which could be slotted in between the boxes already stashed in the car. His final task for the day was to clean the now-empty rooms – so much quicker and easier with no furniture in the way – then it would be a quick dinner of some beans on toast before hitting the sack which was a blow-up mattress with a sleeping bag. He turned away and his foot had just landed on the first stair tread when there was a knock on the door. Upon opening it, he found Gary and Cherry standing on the step surrounded by bags and a vacuum cleaner in hand.

'What… What are you guys doing here?'

'We're your clean-up crew and sending off party,' replied Cherry, pushing her way past him.

'But we said our goodbyes the other night over that lovely meal you cooked for me, Cherry.'

'I know we did, sweetie,' she reached up to place a peck on his cheek, 'but it wasn't enough for us. We're going to miss you so much and, therefore, we want to grasp every single last minute we can with you. If that means helping you to do housework, then so be it, that's what we will do. I've also,' she held up a cool bag, 'made a chilli which we can warm up later once we're finished.'

'But—'

'You can't travel all that way on a plate of beans and toast.'

'I was planning to stop for breakfast en route, you know.'

Gary shoulder bumped him as he walked past. 'Kenneth, you know there's no point in arguing. Cherry has decided you're having a proper meal so just let it go and help me get this cleaning stuff up the stairs. I'm guessing you're starting from the top and working your way down?'

'Er, yes.'

'Then let's get on with it.'

'Yes, let's!' Cherry came out of the kitchen, picked up a couple of the carrier bags still sitting by the front door and held them up. 'Rubber gloves, kitchen roll, cloths, sprays, and bin bags. We'll have this place shining in no time.'

After two hours of intense cleaning, the three of them were now sitting cross-legged on a picnic rug in the lounge around a low-level, fold-up camping table which was holding bottles of zero-alcohol beer. In their hands were plastic, picnic bowls full of steaming rice and chilli. Cherry hadn't been happy about using microwave rice but as the cooker top had been cleaned, she'd understood the need to compromise. Any splashes in the microwave weren't an issue as that was going to Scotland with him.

'To Kenneth. Here's to a safe, uneventful journey and your good health after that.'

Kenneth clinked his bottle against Gary's and Cherry's but wished inwardly that Gary had kept his toast to himself. He'd been prepared for the goodbyes three nights ago and had coped with them but his friends had caught him off-guard tonight and he was now dreading the moment when they would leave, walking out of his home for the very last time. For him, walking out of their space hadn't been so bad as he knew he'd be back for visits but tonight was going to be a final one – he could already feel the lump growing in his throat just thinking about it.

'What time are you heading off, Kenneth?'

'Five in the morning, Cherry, although earlier if I waken up before my alarm.'

'What time do you expect to be there for?'

'If I can get a clear run, about four o'clock, Gary. That's adding in a few stops along the way, of course.'

His friend took a drink of his beer before replying, 'And how's the new car, or should I should I say *Chelsea tractor*, working out? Is it a good drive?'

'It's a Land Rover and while it might be a "Chelsea tractor" down here, up there, it's an essential requirement. I'll be covering a large part of the farming and rural community and, thankfully, since you ask, it's very comfortable. Once I hit the motorway, I can put on the cruise control and relax. A steady seventy miles per hour all the way, with any luck.'

'Why did you change your car down here? Wouldn't you get a better deal in Scotland?'

'I checked that out, Cherry, the prices were on par but

there were more options to choose from here plus it gives me extra space for my hand luggage.' Kenneth tipped his head towards the dining room pile to which the microwave had now been added.

'What's in the gift bag? I meant to ask…'

'Always were a nosy git, weren't you, Gary?'

'Yup!' His mate grinned at the good-natured jibe.

'It's my leaving gift from the surgery.'

'Ooh, what did they get you?' This time it was Cherry doing the asking.

'A PoCus.'

'A what?' Gary and Cherry looked at each other before turning back to him.

'A Point of Care Ultrasound machine. PoCus for short. It's a portable ultrasound device. Well, it's the scanner handset which I can use with my laptop. They're expensive and I'm really touched by how thoughtful they have been as it will be extremely useful given the remote area I'll be working in.'

'They're sorry to lose you, mate.'

'Yes,' Kenneth stopped to think back to his leaving bash two days earlier where there had been many tears and not just from his work colleagues but also from several of the patients he'd regularly attended to over the years, who'd come along to say their goodbyes, wish him well, and express their sadness at his departure which had touched him more than he'd have expected.

'Kenneth?'

'Sorry, Gary. Yes, they were sorry to see me leave and I'm sad to leave them behind but I know I've made the correct decision. I can't wait to begin this new chapter in my life – this role is all I've dreamed of.'

'D'you know, Kenneth, over the years we've been friends, this is the first time I'd say that you've actually looked properly happy.'

He looked at Cherry in surprise. 'Really?'

'Yeah. Since you came back from Scotland, there's been a sparkle about you. Before, you kinda looked like you were just putting up with life, you know what I mean – kinda sad but not sad – but now you look like you want to embrace it. You look alive and ready to go, like you're full of fizz and pop.'

'I suppose… yes… that is how I feel. It feels good to be going home, it feels great to know I'll finally be the type of doctor I've always wanted to be, so it stands to reason my excitement would be difficult to hide.'

'Kenneth, my friend…'

'Yes, Gary, my friend?'

'No need to always analyse stuff. Sometimes, you just need to let it be. You're excited, just leave it there.'

'Okay, I will take on board your words of wisdom—'

'Oh, blimey, don't say that, Kenneth. I have to live with him, there'll be no shutting him up now.'

All three laughed at Cherry's words as Gary donned an air of gravitas and muttered, 'I speak words of wisdom, take heed. Yes, my words are wise, you would do well to listen to them. I am a wise man—'

'You'll be a dead man soon if you don't button it!' Cherry looked at Kenneth. 'Now see what you've started?'

'It'll be short-lived, Cherry, I wouldn't worry about it too much.'

'Is that a professional diagnosis?'

'It sure is!'

He picked up his beer bottle and drained the last of the contents while his friends continued with their banter.

'Right, guys, I need to get my head down soon and I've got a couple of things to do before I can, so with the greatest of regret, it's time to say goodnight.'

A flurry of activity ensued while their impromptu picnic was packed away and Gary stashed everything back in their car.

Please don't drag it out. Please don't drag it out.

Kenneth repeated these words in his head as Gary and Cherry walked back over his driveway.

'Right then, mate, see you sometime – either at your place or ours. Just don't let it be too long, okay?' Gary stuck his hand out for a shake then pulled him in for a tight hug. After thumping him twice on the back, the way men do, he let go, gave a small cough, and turned towards his car.

'Take care, Kenneth. When you find your new home, be sure to give your clean-up crew a shout. We'll come to help you settle back in again. Love you long time, you lovely man. Be happy. Please. You deserve it.'

Cherry threw her arms around him and hugged as hard as she could making Kenneth wonder if it was the strength of her embrace that was causing him some difficulty in breathing or the emotion of this final parting.

'Cherry, come on. Let the man get to his bed.'

'Okay, okay!' she called over her shoulder before turning back to him. 'See ya, big man. Luvs ya!' Her smile wavered as she turned away and he saw her hand wipe her face as she scurried over to get in the car. A moment later, there was a beep of the horn and a hand in the air as they pulled off the driveway and then gradually silence as the sound of the engine faded into the night.

With a deep and sudden sense of loneliness, Kenneth closed the door as the feeling of being a stranger swept over him. It was no longer his home; it was merely a place to rest his head for one last time. In less than twenty-four hours he'd be home. *Really* home. And he could hardly wait.

FOURTEEN

When the alarm went off at three in the morning, Flora's groan was short-lived as the tingles of excitement ran through her again. For the first time in her life, she bounced out of bed, throwing the quilt back for the bed to air while she was in the shower.

As she blasted the hairdryer over her auburn locks, her eyes ran around the bedroom she'd slept in since she was a baby. Purposely, she pushed her feelings aside – if she began dwelling on the memories the room contained, she'd never leave – and focused solely on ensuring she wasn't forgetting anything that would likely be required. Her holdall was at the foot of the bed with her everyday bits and pieces going into it as she finished using them.

'Oh, bathroom towel.'

Not knowing exactly what she'd find in her grandmother's cottage, Flora was taking all her new purchases, along with her favourite towels. On her way past the bathroom, she stopped to grab the still-damp towel, taking it downstairs to wrap it in a plastic bag before also placing it in the holdall.

She made a large jug of coffee, warmed up the thermal travelling cups while the coffee machine gurgled and did a last check of the cupboards to ensure nothing perishable was lurking within. The fridge had been emptied the night before and all that was left was half a pot of cream and a half pint of milk, both of which would be going in her coffee with any dregs heading down the drain.

For the last time, she checked all the windows and doors and, satisfied they were securely locked, she filled her mugs, washed and dried the jug, then placed it beside the still-warm filter machine. The wet coffee grounds and paper filter were already in the bag of rubbish she was taking to be disposed of at the other end. She didn't want to leave anything nasty in the outside wheelie bins.

The front door had just been unlocked when Flora realised she hadn't made her bed. She hesitated for a moment before running up the stairs. It was only a small task but not doing it would bother her for goodness knows how long. She wanted to leave the house in tip-top condition so when her father came round to check, he wouldn't think she'd stropped off like a petulant teenager. She walked into the bedroom… and stopped dead in her tracks. The bed was already made. She couldn't remember doing it but… she must have done because the pillows were plumped exactly how she did them and the quilt had the quarter fold along the top that she always preferred. The only thing missing was Teddy, her life-long stuffed companion, and that was because he was already packed away in the camper van. She racked her brain for a few more seconds but concluded it must have been done as she'd whirled around the room doing a last check for anything she'd missed. With it being an ingrained habit, maybe she simply hadn't registered what she'd done. With a shrug, she turned and hurried back down the stairs. It was almost four o'clock and she needed to get going.

It didn't take long to get Vanda out of the garage, making sure to lock it behind her, put in her last remaining bags and lock the front door for the last time. Determined not to look back, Flora jumped in behind the wheel, belted herself in and started up the engine. She was doing okay until – while waiting for the electric gates to open – she glanced in the rearview mirror. It suddenly hit her that she didn't know when she'd see her childhood home again and that's when the tears began to well up. So many wonderful memories had been made there alongside so much laughter and so much love. But now it all felt tainted. Her father's deceit had cast a shadow over all she'd believed her little family to be. Grabbing a tissue, she wiped her eyes, blew her nose, and straightened her shoulders. It was time to move forward.

'Onwards and upwards,' she muttered, as the gates closed behind her and she turned into the country lane.

Her next adventure was just beginning.

'Argh! Ooh, ooh, ooh. Ouch!'

After locking Vanda and ensuring the blinds were closed to prevent any nosy parkers peering in while she enjoyed a comfort break, Flora tried to stretch out her cramped muscles.

As she waited for a couple of cars to pass, she was surprised by how busy the Tebay motorway services were. Her Uncle Craig had recommended stopping here, citing the good food available inside and the stunning views outside. Well, he hadn't been wrong on the latter, she just hoped he was right on the former.

Once she'd used the facilities, she wandered into the farm shop for a look around and marvelled at the delicious looking produce on display. The butcher's counter was bursting with fresh cuts of just about every meat you could ask for while the cheese counter appeared to stock almost every variety she knew of and plenty she didn't. And as for the cakes and other baked goods… her stomach rumbled furiously at the sight of them.

Knowing that buying food on an empty stomach was never a good move, Flora headed into the restaurant where she avoided the temptation of a large fry-up – a tummy full of bacon, sausage and eggs would have her falling asleep at the wheel in no time – and chose a rather tasty avocado on toast topped with a couple of poached eggs. She did, however, pop two thick, chunky sausages on her plate as the aroma from the crisp split skins with juice oozing out was simply too mouth-watering to pass by.

When she returned to the farm shop thirty minutes later, it was easier to ignore the gargantuan slices of gateau bursting with fresh cream, ganache, and various jams as she headed straight to the deli counter where she'd previously spotted some huge Scotch eggs which had taken her fancy. The plan was to purchase a few tasty morsels and have a layby picnic lunch somewhere along the A9. An American couple were being served when she returned to the deli counter and she was dismayed to see only two Scotch eggs left from the eight or so she'd spied earlier. Even more dismaying was hearing the gentleman of the party express an interest in them. Just as she used to do when she was a child, she closed her eyes and began whispering furiously inside her head, *Buy the sausage rolls, buy the sausage rolls, buy the sausage rolls. Please, please, please buy the sausage rolls. Or even a pork pie, there's plenty of those.*

A few more agonising seconds passed until, eventually, the couple decided to have some of the "awesome looking" sausage rolls and two of the pork pies. Flora blinked with surprise. Had she inadvertently spoken aloud? The couple gave no indication they'd heard if she had. She was still gathering her thoughts back together when the assistant asked her what she would like.

'I'll have those two Scotch eggs, please,' she replied with a smile.

FIFTEEN

Kenneth was already awake when his phone beeped at four o'clock in the morning. It had been tempting to get up at three, when his body once again skipped with sparks of excitement but knowing the long journey that lay ahead, he'd forced himself to stay in bed for another hour of rest.

It didn't take long to get ready and do a final clean-up of the areas he'd used but when he went out to pack his last few bits into the Land Rover, he saw one of the back doors was slightly ajar while the back door into the garage was wide open. He quickly checked for anything untoward before remembering he'd been in the garage the day before when the removal men had come to say they were leaving. He'd simply forgotten to come back in and close up. A sigh of relief escaped him as his heartbeat moved out of racing mode. A break-in was the last thing he needed.

Soon, he was ready to go. He locked the front door and put his keys through the letterbox. The new owners would get their set of keys from the estate agent when it was time to move in.

Just before getting into the Landy, Kenneth turned to

look at the building he'd called home for ten years, expecting to feel *something* when he looked at it for the last time but there was nothing. Nada! Zilch! He was devoid of any emotion connecting him to it. In the end, it had merely been a place to eat and sleep. With barely a sigh, he got into the car, started up the engine and pulled off the driveway, not even looking in the rearview mirror one last time. This episode of his life was over and he felt only relief.

Less than six hours later, he pulled into the beautiful Tebay services. How, he asked himself, was it possible to get excited about a motorway service area, but when you saw the stunning views – especially from the northbound side – and tasted the delicious food, it was rather easy to see how. On this occasion, however, he was only stopping for a short time. Despite being a doctor who should know better, he'd already sneaked in a cheeky McDonald's breakfast just outside Birmingham. Unfortunately, stopping there had put him in the middle of the rush-hour traffic around Manchester, bringing his cruising speed of seventy down to under forty. But since he wasn't in a hurry, he had every intention of simply enjoying the drive. The less pressure he put himself under, the less stressful it would be.

The, easy to drive while also being quite comfortable, Land Rover was soon parked and Kenneth stepped out, stretching the kinks out of his shoulders before making his way to the entrance and, pausing to let a few vehicles pass, his eye was drawn to a pretty, powder-blue, Volkswagen camper van. He could see it was an older model which had been restored with much love for it was quite beautiful.

Like many people, these little old campers always made him smile. He couldn't put a finger on why but they just seemed to give off a happy vibe.

After a quick stop in the "Room of Comfort" he walked through to the farm shop. They did fabulous Scotch eggs here and he planned to pick some up to keep him going on the journey. He'd driven the stretch of the A9 between Edinburgh and Inverness many times as a student and he knew there was sod all along it when it came to service stations. The few that existed were far from tempting and he definitely wasn't buying anything to eat from them.

He wandered through the shop, coming to a halt by a display of fabulous floral bouquets, and pondered about getting one for his mum but didn't think they'd survive five or so hours in the car. He could, however, if time was on his side, stop off in Beauly and pick up something from the florist there, Oops a Daisy, who made lovely bouquets and he'd be able to choose the flowers to put in it – depending on what they had left, of course.

Satisfied with this decision, he made his way over to the counter and was thrilled to see a fresh tray heaped high with Scotch eggs being put in the display cabinet. His day was just getting better.

Once the friendly, helpful assistant had, at his request, cut his eggs into quarters and placed them in a foil tray, he added two bottles of water to his purchase and returned to the car where he placed the items inside the built-in cool box between the front seats. This added extra detail on this Landy model had been the main selling point for him when he'd been scoping out what was available. Knowing he'd be travelling some distances on his house calls, this facility was a blessing for it would not only keep his lunches fresh but also ensured any medication he had to carry which required refrigeration, would be protected. However, for now, it was perfect for his eggs and water and while belting himself in, he turned on the ignition then scrolled through his musical options until he found what he was looking for.

As The Proclaimers began lamenting about the Sunshine on Leith, Kenneth pulled out of the service area and back on to the motorway, smiling at the fact that one of Scotland's best musical exports were now singing him home.

Two hours later, however, the smile transformed into a scowl when he became stuck in a traffic jam in the roadworks around Hamilton, south of Glasgow. It felt like there had been roadworks on this section of the motorway since forever! As fast as they finished one project, another sprang up. Furthermore, it had just come on the news that there'd been an incident two miles up from where he was sitting, meaning he could easily be looking at a further thirty to forty minutes on his journey. Possibly even more... Ah well, nothing he could do about it. He was stuck here until it got moving again so he sat back, opened the cool-box, and treated himself to a Scotch egg quarter.

It was three forty-five in the afternoon when Kenneth eventually drove into Beauly and the sight of the familiar shops and buildings instantly soothed him. The journey from Edinburgh hadn't been too painful despite a few tractors which had slowed him, and all the rest of the traffic, for several miles but that was part and parcel of driving on that route. The A9 was certainly the slow road but as it was also the only road, you just had to grin and bear it.

It now looked, however, like he might have another issue – Beauly was heaving and it dawned on him that the school had just finished for the day, meaning the town was busier now than it would've been an hour ago. Finding a parking space was going to be a challenge. He drove along the High Street and glanced to his right, hoping there would be a space or two available in The Square. This was his preferred parking spot because it was central for everything and he figured he might as well pick up some groceries from the Co-Op whilst he was here. Finally, spotting a couple of spaces, he drove up to the junction and turned into the parking area but came to an immediate halt as he waited for a rather harassed looking mum to get her two young children plus a pram across the car park and into her car. She mouthed a 'thank you' to him for waiting and he nodded his acknowledgement. As he moved off, he noticed the car which had been in the middle of the two vacant spots was pulling out so he slowed, allowing it time and space to drive out but then, just he was about to reverse into the bay, from nowhere, a powder-blue camper van shot in behind him and parked *across* all three spaces. Kenneth couldn't believe his eyes as a woman with brilliant auburn hair jumped out, locked the door, and then sprinted away towards the main road. She was gone by the time he'd had the thought of opening his window to have a word, but that didn't stop him from being furious at her inconsiderate actions. Who on earth would do such a thing?

SIXTEEN

Flora couldn't believe her luck when she finally found somewhere to park. It was the third time she'd been down the high street looking for a spot. The problem with the camper van was its age and every manoeuvre required great effort which she no longer had the energy for today. She knew the way she'd parked was not acceptable "road etiquette" but she hoped anyone seeing it would understand and be forgiving towards her. There again, tough if they weren't! She'd had no choice.

She scurried up the high street, back towards a small ironmonger she'd passed. Her uncle had advised her to pick up a hot water bottle because the cottage could get cold at night due to being situated on the edge of the loch. The bottle at the cottage had burst when he was last there and he hadn't had time to replace it. Seeing the shop had reminded her so she'd made the impromptu decision to park up and stretch her legs before traversing the last few miles that would take her to her grandmother's loch-side abode.

When she stepped inside, she was immediately taken

back to her childhood and the old ironmongers that had taken up almost one side of the village green in Lower Ditchley. It had been overflowing and cluttered, just like this one, and for a child, it had felt like an Aladdin's cave of treasures. Sadly, it closed some years before and the building now housed a tearoom, a book shop, and an antiques corner which provided an income for some friends of hers while bringing new life to the village from the tourist buses which now stopped there for afternoon teas.

Resisting the urge to have a slow mooch around, Flora soon found what she was looking for and, erring on the side of caution, picked up two hot water bottles with tartan covers – one red and one blue. She was walking towards the counter to pay when she noticed the man and woman behind it looking at her in, what she deemed to be, a strange manner. She'd caught the man nudging the woman just as she'd turned towards them and the woman's mouth had opened in a wide "O" before quickly being snapped closed when their eyes met.

She placed her items on the wooden counter top and pulled her bag round to get her purse out.

'Can… can… can I get you anything else? Do you need a bag?'

'Er, no, thank you. I have a bag and that will be all.'

Flora wondered why the woman seemed so flustered as she served her. Her hand was actually shaking when she handed over her change.

'Thank you.'

Making a point of smiling as charmingly as she could, Flora left the shop while trying to ignore the frantic whispering behind her. She pondered over their behaviour as she walked back towards the car park and hoped this wasn't a town who was resistant to outsiders moving in. Although, technically speaking, she wasn't an "outsider" as such. Okay, maybe neither she nor her mother had been born here but her family roots were buried deep in the soil of this land and that had to count for something.

When she got back to the camper van, she was disappointed to see that both the bakery and the butchers next door had closed for the day. For reasons wholly unknown, she'd developed a notion to have bacon butties for her tea that night. The thought of some thick-sliced bacon on some soft, floury rolls, with a huge dollop of red and brown sauce – because that's how she liked it! – was already making her mouth water. Next to the butcher, however, was a Co-Op supermarket which, she surmised, would have what she wanted plus she could pick up some groceries. Her tummy let out a loud rumble as she walked across the car park and she gave an embarrassed smile to the woman who was passing her with a look of shock on her face.

'Okay, along this road for approximately two miles...' Flora muttered, checking the mileometer on the dashboard, 'and then look for the layby with the "large square stone".'

She drove slowly along the road, keeping her eyes peeled while at the same time hoping no traffic came up behind. Her uncle had, very helpfully, supplied a few extra landmarks she would pass as she grew close to her turning, so she was fully prepared when the layby came up, right around a sharp bend which would have made it easy to miss had she not been concentrating.

She turned into the layby, stopping alongside the strange-looking square stone to read the next part of the instructions she'd been given.

Just past the stone, turn left, driving VERY slowly. It

will look as though you are about to drive straight into the trees but the path makes a sudden left turn. You'll drive only a couple of metres before it veers back to the right. There are several such turns but you'll have no problems provided you don't rush. Once the track straightens out, you'll be close to the cottage and can pick up a little bit of extra speed but Vanda is old so please don't rush down the track as there are several tree roots, many hidden, which may cause her an injury if you go over them too fast.

Flora read the details twice before putting Vanda back into gear and moved at a snail's pace into the trees. True to her uncle's description, the barely visible track went left with such suddenness that had she been doing more speed, she would have careened straight into the vast wooden trunks ahead. The trees towered high above and with the fading daylight, it was dark enough to merit turning on Vanda's headlights as she carefully picked her way forward. Eventually, after one last turn, the overhead canopy cleared and the track finally lay straight ahead of her. She could just about see it as the weeds and grass had already begun to claim back the ground due to the lack of use over the last few months. She put her foot down a little further on the pedal and the extra touch of speed soon had her pulling into a clearance that was, without doubt, her final destination. Directly ahead sat her new home.

She parked next to a tall, dry-stone wall, pausing for a moment to take in her surroundings. A white-painted cottage sat in front of her although partially hidden from view because the wall was so high. Only two upper storey windows were visible.

She drew in a deep breath, murmured, 'Here goes nothing,' and stepped out of the camper. The first thing that hit her was the silence. Total, deep silence. In fact, it was so quiet, she found herself closing the camper door softly so as not to create a disturbance.

Despite knowing the risk of theft in this location was next to non-existent, out of habit, she retrieved her bag and laptop case before locking Vanda up. With a mixture of curiosity and trepidation, she made her way down the narrow path by the side of the cottage and stepped out to a wide view of the loch. To her left, running the width of the cottage was a large slate patio area. Flora placed her bags down upon it and walked slowly forward towards the expanse of water. When she stepped off the grass onto the sandy shore, the clouds above suddenly parted and an array of sunbeams forced their way through to dance upon the surface of the water, turning it from mysteriously dark and brooding into myriad sparkling diamonds. Gentle waves licked the sand as they lazily ebbed back and forth. Across the watery expanse, high mountains loomed, their craggy peaks bold against the clouds that lingered around them. The sunlight, however, came from behind her which lit up the rock and grass undulations, making them less fearsome than they had first seemed in the grey gloom.

A small 'Wow' slipped from her lips as she took in the view. It really was something and she was already looking forward to waking up and seeing this every day. Her inner artist had awoken and she was looking forward to trying to capture it in paint, even though she knew she would never be able to do it justice.

With a soft sigh, she walked back towards the cottage and as she stepped up onto the patio she stopped, casting her eye over the building in front of her. Being her father's daughter – despite the current situation – the first thing she did was assess its condition. The cottage was standard in design – two upper windows, two lower windows and a door in the middle. It had two chimneys, one on each gable end, and from where she was standing, they looked to be in good condition. The pointing appeared sound and there were no gaps she could see from this angle. The roof was grey slate tiles now but had once been thatched, according to her uncle although way before his time. She could just about see the frames of the two skylights embedded up there. Her eyes travelled down – the guttering was secure and the windows were – surprisingly – uPVC double-glazed but then she recalled her uncle saying he'd been helping his mum with some renovations, the windows must have been among them, and the whole cottage was painted bright white which showed off the beautiful lilac composite door to perfection. The small, rectangular pane of stained-glass had a floral design that was clearly influenced by the work of Charles Rennie Mackintosh.

There was no doubt about it – for a building that had been around for a few hundred years, it was looking good. Despite her uncle's assurances that she hadn't inherited some rundown hovel, it had been a concern at the back of her mind. Feeling more enthused, she picked up her bags, dug out the keys she'd been given and stepped across the patio, noting the large tarpaulin-covered mound to her right which she guessed was most likely a table and chair set.

The front door opened with ease and she stepped into a small hallway with two doors, one on either side, and a steep flight of stairs, the stair treads running from wall to wall, lay directly ahead.

She opened the door to her left where her eyes immediately landed upon a large, flat-screened, television and when she popped her head round, she saw it was the lounge, the sofa being the second giveaway after the TV. She pulled the door closed again and opened the one to her right. Stepping into the room, she gasped at the sight of the stunning black range sitting in the chimney space on the far wall. She pulled out one of the chairs around the long, well-scrubbed, table in the middle of the room and placed her bags upon it. At the far end, a solid wooden worktop ran the width of the room and upon it, she spied a kettle. With a huge sigh of relief, Flora walked towards it. She was gasping for a cup of tea.

Her fingers had only just wrapped themselves around the handle when the heavy silence around her was suddenly broken.

'So, you've finally decided to visit. Took yer bloomin' time aboot it!'

SEVENTEEN

A scream flew from Flora's lips and the kettle landed on its side as she spun round. Standing by the table was a man. A rather short man. In fact, he was a very short man. She guessed he was maybe about four feet tall and a good six inches of that belonged to the navy-blue stovepipe hat he was wearing. A sprig of heather was pinned to the hat band.

As she worked on bringing her thundering heartbeat under control, she took in the appearance of this unexpected visitor in her kitchen. He had startling blue eyes that were darkest around the edge of the iris but grew lighter in colour towards the pupil although they were almost hidden beneath the shaggy grey eyebrows that were pulled down in a deep frown. His nose was verging on being bulbous but seemed to have stopped growing just before it could cross that particular line. It was impossible to see his mouth beneath a bushy moustache and a beard which tapered to a small point just above the V of his waistcoat.

He was slim built and wore his dark blue suit well although she did think a frock-coat was perhaps an exaggerated touch in this day and age, but it did set off the tartan waistcoat underneath rather nicely. His trousers were plus-fours and tucked into a pair of long blue socks. On his feet were a pair of sturdy black brogues that had been polished to a perfect shine. All in all, he was perfectly neat, perfectly proportioned and judging from the expression on his face, perfectly angry!

With her!

Some air finally found its way back into her lungs and unsure of what to say, she blurted out, 'Are you a leprechaun?'

She could have kicked herself as soon as the words fell from her lips and, going by the dark puce of the man's face, he probably wanted to do so as well.

'Nay, ah'm no a leprechaun, ya glaikit eejit. How dare ye! Jist how dare ye!' More words rolled off his lips as he stomped and growled but she couldn't make any sense of what he was saying.

Faced with this unintelligible tirade, Flora tried to take a step back only to find herself jammed against the worktop. 'I'm sorry, I'm sorry. I've clearly insulted you – it wasn't my intention. You gave me a fright. I wasn't thinking. And… please… don't think me rude but do you speak English?'

The little man immediately ceased moving, glared at her and then visibly made the effort to calm himself down. She watched as he took several deep breaths and the colour in his face slowly turned back to a normal hue. Through gritted teeth, he very carefully enunciated, 'I *was* speaking English. I was speaking Scottish English, not English English. I will make a point of using the latter going forward.'

'Thank you so much. Would it be too much trouble to repeat what you said – in English English? Please?'

'I said I am not a leprechaun.'

'I kind of got that bit. It was the rest of it I got lost on.'

'I called you a "glaikit eejit" – a stupid idiot.'

'Oh, right. Not very polite of you.'

'You insulted me first.'

'Then I guess that makes us even.'

She didn't miss the small movement within the whiskery face that she decided to attribute to being a small smirk. Had she blinked, however, she would have missed it.

'I suppose! And no, I'm not a leprechaun – they're Irish. I'm a MacAndrew.'

'A what?'

'A MacAndrew.'

'Right.' She dragged the word out slightly while trying to take this in. 'And may I ask your name – if that is permitted?'

'MacAndrew.'

'Yes, I get that bit but what do I call you?'

'MacAndrew. That's what you call me.'

'So… you're a MacAndrew named MacAndrew?'

'No, I'm just a MacAndrew and that's what I answer to.'

It still made no sense to Flora but she decided not to pursue it any further. Her need for tea was greater than trying to decipher what this MacAndrew was trying to say.

'Well, I'm Flora. Would you like a cup of tea?'

'Aye, ah ken who ye are!'

'Sorry?'

'I *know* who you are!' A loud sigh followed his words along with a roll of the eyes.

Before Flora could comment further on his rudeness, she heard voices outside and looked towards the front door which she'd left open behind her. She turned back to speak to the little man again but he'd disappeared. 'What the—'

'Now, I think if we knock the hovel down, this would

be a perfect spot for a lodge. Not too big – exclusivity is key here – then we could charge a decent rate.'

'Would you make it multiple occupancy – like a small hotel – or a facility specifically for renting out? There's a good market for both.'

The voices were drawing closer and she could make out what was being said. One voice was plummy with a Scottish lilt and she knew immediately its owner was someone belonging to the upper classes while the other was most definitely English.

'Oh, look, how convenient, the door is open. We might as well look inside while we're here.'

'Err, are you sure about that? What if someone is in there?'

'Look, the old witch is dead and I have it on good authority the granddaughter has no interest in coming here. We should be able to get the place and, more importantly, the land, for next-to-nothing. She'll be glad to have it taken off her hands, I'm sure.'

As these words were being spoken, two men walked into the kitchen.

'Can I help you?'

They both stopped dead and looked at her. Flora tried to keep her face neutral but inside she was seething.

'Oh, I didn't realise anyone was here.' Plummy voice looked her up and down as he spoke, not even having the good grace to apologise for just walking into her house. Was this typical Scottish behaviour?

'Clearly!'

The word was forced out as the dull throb of a headache began behind her eyes. All she wanted was to sit down with a cup of tea before unpacking her overnight bag, grabbing a shower followed by something to eat and then go to bed. However, for a location that was supposed to be remote and isolated, it was beginning to feel like Piccadilly Circus.

'I'm Jack Arlingh, son of Laird Arlingh.'

Plummy walked towards her with his hand outstretched.

'Flora MacDonald O'Brien. Granddaughter of the "old witch".'

She was astounded when her pointed barb bounced off Jack Arlingh. At least his companion had the good grace to look shamefaced while mumbling something about waiting outside before turning around and leaving the room.

'Pleased to meet you, Flora.'

Her hand was squeezed tightly within his grip while being shaken up and down vigorously then released. She suspected she'd just been the victim of a power move; he seemed the type. Not replying, she looked him up and down instead. Medium height – just under six feet perhaps – and thickly built which was already turning to fat. His blond hair was cut in a standard short back and sides and he was clean-shaven with facial features that weren't unpleasant to look upon – a long, straight nose and brown eyes which were more of a sludgy mud colour than something nice like chocolate or caramel. His mouth, however, was soft and pudgy and she imagined it had spent most of its life pouting with dissatisfaction than smiling with joy and happiness. For some women, Jack Arlingh would perhaps be considered an attractive man but nothing about him was making her bits and pieces react in any way.

'Now, I was hoping we—'

'How did you get here?'

'I'm sorry, what?'

She saw a little spark of annoyance in his eyes as she interrupted him. It would seem the Laird's son didn't like the peasants to challenge him. Well, tough!

'I asked you how you got here as I happen to know the route is not easy.'

'Oh, we came by boat. There's a track on the far side of the loch that's wide enough to get a small motorboat down.'

'I see.' The nipping sensation behind her eyes grew worse. 'Look, I need to make some tea, would you like a cup?'

'Yes, I would, since we're about to talk business.'

She turned to fill the kettle while Jack continued to talk behind her. His loud voice was filling every nook and cranny of the room and the noise was pressing down on her head.

'—and then once the hov... err... I mean cottage has been cleared, we can begin to discuss price—'

'Will you just PLEASE stop talking. Shut your mouth and stand there quietly, for goodness' sake!'

Flora breathed a sigh of relief at the sudden silence behind her. Yes, she'd been rude but this man had bowled into her house and started making noises about clearing it and selling up without so much as a by-your-leave.

A few minutes later, the kettle had boiled, the tea was made – fortunately she'd found some Earl Grey tea leaves as the milk she'd bought was still in the camper van – and she turned around to place the cups on the table. When she looked up at Jack, he was breathing heavily through his nose with a wild look in his eyes.

'Look, I can see I've annoyed you by telling you to be quiet but you were droning on and on without even considering if I wanted to have this conversation. I've had a long day, driving for over twelve hours and I need some time to myself right now. Please send me a letter, with your proposals, and I'll consider whatever it is you want to discuss.'

When Jack didn't reply, she huffed with annoyance. 'For crying out loud – five minutes ago you had verbal diarrhoea and now you've taken a vow of silence! Say something!'

Jack gasped as though drawing in a mouthful of air before turning on his heel and walking swiftly towards the door.

'You… you… I'll… I'll… yes, letter… good idea… will send…'

The front door closed with a bang behind him and when she walked over to the window that faced the loch, it was to see him dragging his unnamed friend by the arm towards a boat moored farther along the loch. A moment later they were skimming their way across the water and were soon out of sight.

As she sat back down at the table to drink her tea, the sound of high-pitched giggling reached her ears.

'Okay, MacAndrew, you can get yourself out here and tell me what on earth that was all about!'

EIGHTEEN

It took Kenneth a further ten minutes to find another parking space and he burst through the door of the florist, having run furiously from his car, worried they'd be closed by the time he arrived.

'Blimey, you're cutting it fine. Another few minutes and the door would have been bolted.'

He held his hand up while he bent over, trying to catch his breath.

'Parking space! Problem,' he gasped.

'Ah, yes, it would be at this time of the day. So, now that you're here, how can I help you?'

'May I have a large hand-tied bouquet, please? Lots of yellow, cream and orange if you can manage it.'

His mother loved bright coloured flowers because the kitchen at the farm was old with dark brown units and not enough light. She'd been hankering after a new one for years but there was never any money. Nor was there ever the time to try painting the units as he'd seen on social media videos but maybe, now he was home, he'd be able to do that for her. For the moment, however, he'd have to make do with the biggest, most colourful, bunch of flowers he could get.

When the florist finished putting together a magnificent floral display for him – she'd thrown in some extra stems due to it being the end of the day – he paid her then walked slowly back to the car to stow it safely behind the passenger seat. After that he walked back to the square, noting when he returned that the camper van was gone. The three spaces it had occupied were now housing three cars parked in the normal fashion. The thought of the driver's ignorance irked him again and he had to force it from his mind as he walked through the doors of the supermarket.

He reached for a basket and did a quick mental run-through of what he needed to buy. First up was a bottle of his dad's favourite whisky – a local brand which was difficult to obtain south of the border. Next, bread, milk, cheese, and baked beans for the nights he couldn't be bothered to cook. He knew his mum would have stocked the fridge and cupboards in the cabin where he'd be living for the next few months but it felt rude to just assume.

As he walked past the meat fridges, he suddenly had a craving for bacon rolls. The very thought had his mouth watering and he veered over to the shelves for a look. While contemplating the low-fat merits of back bacon over the nicer flavour of streaky, he became aware of the chatter around him. He tuned his ears in, trying to make out what the other shoppers were talking about in the cacophony of sound and could just about make out the words "Flora" and "returned" which, if it was what he thought it was, would make his parents very happy. However, as it lacked any meaning for him, he gave a small shrug and returned to filling his shopping basket, having decided to put both bacon cuts in it along with some Lorne sausage and black pudding. Oh aye, it really was grand to be back home!

'Darling, you're here.'

The driver's door was opened before Kenneth even had the chance to turn off the engine.

'Mum!' He got out and gathered his mother into a tight embrace. It was a hug that was returned with equal force and he was reminded again of the strength in his mum's arms from all the work that she did around the farm. While his father and brother maintained the fields, the crops and the machinery, his mum had created her own small businesses in the shape of a farm shop, tearoom and six old outbuildings which had been converted into small cabins or lodges that were rented out as holiday lets.

'Oh, son, it's great to see you. How was the drive up?'

'It's wonderful to see you, Mum, and to finally be home for good. The drive wasn't too bad – I've known it to be worse.'

'The A9 didn't do for you, then?'

'No more than usual.'

'Come on in and have a cup of tea.'

'Mum, would you mind very much if I didn't. It's just—'

'I know. It's been a long drive and you just want to get yourself settled in. I get it. Let me go and grab my jacket.'

'Before you do, I got you these...'

He twisted round and pulled out the bouquet, handing it over with a delighted smile when he saw the joy on his mum's face.

'Oh, Kenneth, you shouldn't have. They're beautiful.'

'I should have and so are you.' He gave her a kiss on the cheek before also handing over the bottle of spirits. 'I got this for Dad. I know it's his favourite.'

'It certainly is. Well, since you're not going to break bread with us tonight, then I insist you join us for dinner tomorrow and we can crack this bottle open to celebrate you returning to the fold.'

'It's for Dad, Mum, I don't think he'll be keen to share it.'

'Oh, he will on this occasion. Now, just give me a minute to pop these inside and I'll show you up to the cabin.'

When they pulled up outside what was to be his home for the next few months, Kenneth's heart sank.

'Oh, Mum, this is the best cabin. Why have you put me in this one? I said to give me one of the small studios.'

'I know you did but they're the most popular and are fully booked until the end of the season. This one doesn't let out so well because of its size.'

'But, it's only a three-bedroom so why not? I could understand the problem if it was bigger than that.'

'We attract ramblers, hill walkers, bird watchers, wildlife enthusiasts, artists, and folks of that ilk – they only need a bed to sleep on, a shower to wash in, and a table for their laptops so they can download and upload. I thought the three-bed would appeal to families but we're not close enough to the kind of amenities they're looking for.'

'Then I'll pay you extra rent for it. I won't have you being out of pocket.'

'You'll pay no rent at all! You're my son – I won't take your money.'

'Yes, you will, Mum, or I'll move out and rent a place in town…'

His mum glared at him in annoyance but knew her boy well enough to know he meant every word. He hid his amusement as he watched the fight leave her.

'Fine! If you're going to insist upon it!'

'I do.'

He turned away as she let out a snort of disgust, thinking it wouldn't go down too well if she knew he was trying hard not to laugh.

'Do you want a hand moving your stuff in?'

'No, Mum, I'll be fine. You get on home – Dad will be in soon looking for his dinner and we both know what a grump he can be when he's hungry.'

That brought a smile to her face and after extracting a promise that he would join them for dinner the following evening, she drove off, leaving him standing in the dusky silence.

He stood for a minute, allowing the glorious fresh air to fill his lungs, before grabbing his laptop and shopping bags from the Land Rover and making his way into the cabin.

The first thing he noticed when he stepped through the door, was the picture window directly across the room. He dropped the bags gently to the floor and walked over to take in the magnificent view ahead of him. The cabin was built on a hill and the valley stretched out beneath him. Glorious swathes of green could be seen in the distance, dotted with specks of white where a few sheep were grazing. The sun had come out and he could see it glinting on a small mirror of water far below. The mountains beyond it glowed brightly against the bluest of skies. Kenneth took some time to savour it for this was Scotland and knowing how quickly the weather could turn, there was no guarantee he'd see it like this again anytime soon.

Once he'd had his fill, he turned back and took the shopping bags into the kitchen off the lounge. It was a decent sized room, big enough to house a table and six chairs without making it feel cramped. It had a set of sliding interior doors to open it up for an open-plan effect if desired.

When he opened the fridge, it was, as he'd expected, already filled with the basics although he was pleased to see his mum had put butter in there for it was the one thing he'd forgotten. He made space on the shelves for his own purchases then went back out to the Landy to bring in the boxes and bags it was loaded with.

An hour later he locked the door behind him while breathing a sigh of relief. He looked at the pile of boxes stashed in the corner and was glad he'd decided to place the bags for the bedroom *in* the bedroom as he'd brought them from the car. All that was left now were the boxes of books which he'd held back from storage and they could be unpacked tomorrow. Now, it was time for the bacon rolls.

He'd barely moved one foot towards the kitchen when suddenly, the peace in the room was disturbed by a rustling sound.

'What the—'

He spun around, cocking his head to the side to hear better while trying to make out where it had come from.

He heard it again, over in the corner where the book boxes were. He stealthily made his way towards them while his heart pounded. He hoped a rat hadn't got in while he'd had the door propped open. He hated rats and growing up on a farm had meant he'd come face-to-face with them on more occasions than he cared to remember. He still had nightmares about the time he was trapped in the corner of a barn by a particularly big fat one. The rustling came again, louder, and he knew he was definitely heading in the right direction. He could also tell it was too big to be a mouse. One of the boxes perched on top gave a small wobble and holding his breath to keep his presence a secret, he put his arms out as far as they could reach and slowly peeled back the dented cardboard flaps on the top. When daylight flooded into the box, there was silence as whatever was inside stopped moving. Slowly, slowly, he edged his way forward until he could just about see inside.

He immediately took in the round, grey body sitting still on top of his books. Another step found himself looking into the biggest black eyes. His breath caught in his throat when a mouth opened wide to display the smallest,

sharpest teeth he'd ever seen and a noise emanated from behind the carnivorous incisors…
'MIAOW!'

NINETEEN

Flora slowly opened her eyes, taking a moment to adjust to her surroundings. She stretched out as long and as wide as she could before turning on her side to look out of the window towards the mountains across the loch.

What a view!

As she took in the tranquillity of the scene in front of her, she considered how easy it would be to get used to that being the first thing you saw every morning when you opened your eyes.

Moving onto her back, her gaze travelled around the room she'd chosen to sleep in. When MacAndrew had reappeared after the departure of Jack Arlingh, he'd been so busy laughing, there had been no chance of getting any sense out of him so she'd taken the moment to find a loo and when she'd returned, he was gone again. She'd decided to explore the rest of the cottage although there hadn't been much to see. Two bedrooms and a bathroom were located on the first floor with a small spiral staircase leading up into the loft. One look had told her it had been, or still was, her Uncle Craig's bedroom. The model airplanes hanging from the rafters were a bit of a giveaway.

Of the two bedrooms on the first floor, one held a large, ornately carved wooden bed, a wooden dressing table and two matching wardrobes. Although the room was tidy and the bed made up with a pretty patchwork quilt, she immediately sensed it had been her grandmother's room. The second bedroom with its twin, white metal bedsteads confirmed it. This room was painted white, with pale floorboards, fitted wardrobes and lavender plants dotted about. The accessories – cushions on the beds and chair, lampshades, and window curtains – were also lavender in colour. She'd immediately felt a calming sense of peace as soon as she'd stepped into it and Flora knew this was the room she would make her own for the time she was here.

After partially emptying Vanda – the art supplies could wait a day or two – she'd taken a quick shower in the surprisingly modern bathroom, made her way back downstairs and had walked in to the kitchen to find two steaming bacon rolls and a large pot of tea sitting on the table. She looked around her in surprise. How on earth…

Just then, MacAndrew had walked in with two West Highland Terriers trailing behind him.

'Oh, hello, aren't you two a pair of beauties.'

She'd forgotten about the food on the table as the dogs had come running over, tails wagging furiously and clambering up at her until MacAndrew called them off and directed them to the large dog bed under the bay window seat.

'Are they your dogs, MacAndrew? They're lovely.'

'No, they're yours.'

'They're what?'

'You heard, they're yours. Sandy is the larger one, Kirsty is smaller. It's easy to know which is which when they're beside each other but may take you a little longer when they're not.'

'But Uncle Craig made no mention—'

'No, he wouldn't because I hid them away when he came.'

'Why?'

'Because the dogs must stay here. He might have wanted to take them away and that would never do. The dogs are a part of the cottage and this land. This is where they belong.'

'Oh, right. And he didn't ask where they were? He must have seen them when he visited his mum…'

'He didn't see me when he came so he couldn't ask any questions.'

'I see.'

But the truth was, Flora didn't see at all. Everything was becoming quite confusing. Putting it down to hunger, she looked back at the bacon rolls, the tantalising smell making her stomach rumble again.

'Did you cook these?'

'Yes, I did. Now eat up, please.'

She considered a few more questions she wanted to ask but hunger got the better of her so she sat down, picked up a roll which was still perfectly warm, and proceeded to eat the tastiest, most delicious meaty delight she could remember. MacAndrew had even added a dollop of both red and brown sauce – exactly how she liked it.

How could he possibly have known? So much of this didn't make any sense.

When she'd consumed both rolls and was on her second mug of tea, MacAndrew had placed a plate of shortbread on the table then clambered onto the chair opposite her. He'd stared hard at her for several seconds before speaking.

'I need to ask, lassie, why did you no come before?'

Even though he'd spoken Scottish English, it had been easy to understand his question.

'Because I didn't know I was invited.'

'Eh? How no? Yer grandmother wrote to ye every other week an' has been askin' ye tae come fir the last seven years.'

As a big sigh left her, Flora tipped her head in the direction of the bay window seat at the front of the kitchen.

'See those bags and boxes – inside, if you care to look, you will find every letter and gift my grandmother sent to me. Nearly all of them are unopened. And the reason they are unopened is because my father hid them from me for all these years. I only found them recently. So, the reason I didn't visit before now was because I didn't know I was invited.'

MacAndrew stared at her, a look of disbelief on his face, before turning his head to look at the bags and boxes she was referring to.

'He didnae tell ye?'

'No.'

A stream of words had fallen from his lips and she didn't need to understand Scottish English to know they were insults of the worse possible kind. In fact, if she didn't know better, she'd have said a few curses were probably uttered as well. Finally, when he'd used up all his steam, MacAndrew's vitriol ground to a halt and he'd sat there panting in front of her. Eventually, his breathing evened out.

'Get yourself aff tae bed and have a good night's sleep because you're going to need it come the morning,' he'd said.

'Urm… okay… but are you leaving now?'

'No, I'll be staying.'

'You… you'll be staying…'

'I come with the house.'

'Oh!'

'Look, we'll talk in the morning when you'll be fresh

after a good night's sleep.'

She'd been hesitant at first but nothing about the little man made her feel uncomfortable and, if the truth be told, she actually felt better knowing she wouldn't be spending her first night completely alone in this isolated location.

'Okay, MacAndrew, we'll talk in the morning.'

Well, now it was morning and time to find out what MacAndrew had to share with her. Flora flung back the quilt, threw open the windows to air the room, and after taking in a deep breath of the finest, fresh air, made her way to the bathroom.

The smell of bacon, sausage and fresh bread assaulted her nostrils when she opened her bedroom door for the second time. She followed the mouth-watering aroma down into the kitchen where, once again, the table was set and a plate of bacon, eggs, some square'ish looking meat and a triangular, squidgy thing was placed in front of the chair she'd sat in the night before. A cafetiere of coffee also awaited her presence.

'Good morning, yer awake, then. Sleep fine?'

'Good morning, MacAndrew, I am and I did. Thank you for asking. How are you this morning?'

'Me? How am I?'

'Er, yes… you.'

'You're asking me how I am?'

'Yes, I am. Why, is that a problem?'

'It's not a problem, not at all. It's just… well… The Flora never asks these things. It's not done.'

'The Flora? I'm sorry? And,' she poked at the food on her plate, 'what is this?'

'Oh, that's a Lorne sausage, more commonly known as square sausage, and the triangle thing you've just desecrated is a tattie scone. I believe they call them potato cakes down your neck of the woods. Go on, try them, they'll no kill ye. Ye might even like them!'

With a look of suspicion at MacAndrew, Flora cut off a small piece of the sausage, dipped it in the yolk of the fried egg and put it tentatively in her mouth. After a couple of chews, she decided it was rather tasty and after doing the same with the tattie scone, concurred that this was a breakfast she'd be happy to feast upon again.

It was as she was mopping up the remains of the egg yolk with a piece of thick sliced, and thickly buttered, bread it occurred to her that MacAndrew hadn't responded her to curiosity over the use of the phrase, "The Flora" – what had he meant by that?

She was about to ask when the empty plate was whisked away, a fresh cup and saucer was placed in front of her along with another cafetiere of coffee, two small shot glasses and a bottle of whisky.

'Whisky? At this time of the day?'

'I reckon you're going to need it.'

'Why?'

'Because of what I'm about to tell you.'

'Which is?'

Flora's curiosity was now on full alert. MacAndrew looked so serious but she couldn't imagine what he could have to say to merit it. Unless… was the cottage sinking and she'd have to pour a ton of cash into it? Or something else like that? It didn't look like it was sinking but she wasn't an expert. Was that why Jack Arlingh thought he could buy it from her cheap – because it was going to need a huge cash investment to keep it going?

'FLORA!'

MacAndrew snapped her name and brought her attention back to him.

'Did you hear any of what I just said?'

'Err… no…' she gave him a sheepish smile to which he rolled his eyes.

'I was telling you that your life is going to be different from now on. Everything is going to change. In fact, it has already begun – the change – although you may not have noticed it just yet.'

'Change? In what way? I haven't noticed anything different. Well, apart from not speaking to my father, that's a blooming big change for me, but—'

'You have gifts and they're starting to develop.'

'Huh?'

'You-have-"gifts",' MacAndrew made a point of making quote marks with his fingers, something Flora found immensely irritating, 'and-they-are-now-beginning-to-develop.'

'I'm not four years old, MacAndrew, no need to speak to me as though I am.'

'Oh, lassie, this would all be so much easier if you were,' he sighed. 'Ye have "gifts"—'

'I know I have gifts – I'll get around to opening them eventually.' Flora's eyes moved over to the boxes still sitting in the bay window.

'Oh, for the love of the goddess…'

'What? For crying out loud, MacAndrew, will you just say what you have to say and stop farting around the houses!'

'Yer a witch! Okay! Is that clear enough for you? You're a witch!'

TWENTY

Flora looked at MacAndrew for a few seconds before she burst out laughing.

'Oh, very good, well done. You almost had me there. I'm a witch. Oh yes, you're very funny. Next, you'll be telling me your first name is Hagrid…'

'Hag-what? What are you talking about?'

'Hagrid. You know, as in Harry Potter. When he tells Harry he's a wizard.'

'Oh, good grief!' MacAndrew dropped his head into his hands and let out a groan of distinctly Hagrid proportions.

'What now?' Flora was just about managing to get her mirth under control but the odd giggle was still escaping.

'Those blooming Potter books, that's what! Everyone who's read them now thinks they're damned experts on magic. They're stories, not bloody encyclopaedias!'

MacAndrew jumped down off the chair and began pacing back and forth across the kitchen. The furious look on his face was enough to quash the last giggle in her throat.

'You… you… you're not being serious, MacAndrew,

you can't be. There's no such thing as witches, wizards, and magic. It's all make-believe. Everyone knows that.'

'Do they? Do they really?'

She recoiled slightly as the little man came to stand in front of her, a scowl so fierce on his face, his eyebrows were almost touching the tip of his nose.

'If I was a witch, I think I'd have noticed it by now. There was more than one boy at school that I wished I could turn into a toad. Funny though, it never kind of happened.'

'It wouldn't back then – you're only just getting your powers now.'

'Why? Why now?'

'Because your grandmother is dead… and so is your mum.' His sentence was spoken so quietly, and so sadly, that Flora knew he was speaking the truth.

'I don't understand.'

'I know you don't, lassie, and I really wish it wasn't me having to tell you. It should have been your grandmother sharing it with you, teaching you, training you, but you didn't come and she ran out of time. Now, it's down to me to help you through all this. Believe me when I say it's not a responsibility I care to have.'

'Okay, let's take it right back to the beginning – how does this happen?'

Before he answered her, MacAndrew opened the bottle of whisky, poured out two shots and handed one over to Flora. With a shaking hand, she took it from him and threw it back, shuddering as the liquid burned its way down her throat and into her stomach but the warming sensation it left behind was strangely soothing.

'Right. In simple terms. There has always been a Flora in these parts for as long as history can remember. Because people, human people that is, can be funny about things referring to magical stuff, she is known as The Flora and the magic is always referred to as her gifts. Hence me trying to tell you, you have "gifts"! The gift comes down through the women and is only passed on fully when the eldest Flora dies. Until recent years, this was never an issue because the daughters of The Flora stayed at home, knew their history, and what to expect upon the death of their parent. Your grandmother broke the mould when she married your grandfather. She was betrothed to a local lad who knew the ways of The Flora but when she fell deeply in love with your grandfather, she moved away to live with him in England. However, when her mother died, she knew where her duty lay and came home. This had always been understood between her and your grandfather.'

MacAndrew paused and poured out another two shots, pushing her glass back across the table towards her.

'Hold that, you're going to need it again in a moment.'

Flora pulled the glass in front of her and steeled herself for whatever was coming next.

'Your grandfather's arthritis had begun to develop by this time and Scotland really isn't the place to be when you have sore bones, so he stayed in England with your mother and uncle. They would visit over the summer holidays but as Craig grew older, he found leaving too distressing and it was causing him problems. Eventually, it was agreed it was better if the children didn't visit again until they were older. The problem is that they never visited at all and so your mum was ignorant of her family heritage. Your grandmother asked her repeatedly to come up to see her – especially after you were born – because she knew the time had come for her daughter to know… but your mother didn't visit.'

'This bit I know. My dad told me this.'

'Finally, after continual requests, your mum came up—

'I'm going to interrupt you there, MacAndrew, because I think I know where this is going. My grandmother informed my mum of this magical stuff, my mother didn't take it very well and in an emotional state, got her in her car to leave only to die from doing so.'

'You're almost right. Strangely, the stuff about the "gifts" she would inherit didn't faze her overly much. Just as you are now, she asked questions and your grandmother answered them all. It was the next piece of information that she couldn't take on board…'

'And that is what?'

'That once you take on the responsibility of becoming The Flora, you are tied to this land until you die.'

'Excuse me? I'm what? Tied to this land? What on earth does that mean?'

'It means you forever become one with this land that you own. You can go on holiday but only for short periods of time. You cannot call any other place home. This becomes your home until you breathe your last breath.'

'I see.'

This time, the shot of whisky went down far easier than the first one.

'From what I heard of the argument that followed, your mum refused to accept what was expected of her. She cited your dad's new business as the reason for not wanting to move up here. There were also words over how your father would never understand all of this and there was no way she was prepared to do anything to lose him. She was very worried about how he would react to this.'

'And with good reason. I can tell you now that he could never have dealt with something like this. I've seen his reaction to the Harry Potter films,' she ignored MacAndrew's eye roll, 'and all of this would have been too much for him. Heck, I'm far more open-minded on these things and I'm struggling with it!'

MacAndrew didn't reply and they sat in silence for several moments. Flora felt a pressure on her legs and looked down to find a dog sitting on either side of her, pressing against her, almost as if they were giving her both comfort and moral support. One of them, she thought it might be Sandy but wasn't sure, looked up at her and there appeared to be a sense of deep wisdom in his dark, brown eyes. Almost as though he was telling her she wasn't alone and they would all be with her on this journey.

She looked back across the table to MacAndrew.

'You said my grandfather knew... Why didn't he say something? Why didn't he tell me what I am?'

'Because he couldn't. Only The Flora can inform others of her status. When you are told the truth of The Flora, a magical charm is immediately cast which makes it impossible to speak of what you know. A person may try to share the secret but they will find themselves unable to speak if they do. Nor can they write of it, in case you were wondering.'

'I see.' Flora paused for a moment. 'So... my grandfather knew what I would become?'

'Yes, he did.'

'Now it makes sense...'

'What does?'

'I only ever felt like I was truly me when I was with my grandfather. The rest of the time I always felt disjointed and alone. Maybe it was his silent understanding that helped me feel... er... as if I was okay as I was.'

'That would make sense. His knowing, and acceptance, of what you are would have eased your psyche even though you were unaware of it.'

There was silence while Flora absorbed this new information. Finally, she said, 'You say my gifts are beginning to develop. What are they and how does it happen?'

'Predominately, your gifts lie with the elements – air, water, earth, etc – but you should also have a reasonable level of what you would call "normal magic stuff"—'

'What? I can cast spells and things? Make magic potions?'

'Well, yes, kind of…'

She watched MacAndrew squirming in his chair as he replied.

'Kind of?'

'In due course, as you learn your craft, you'll have better control but, at the moment, it's little things that are happening without your realisation, such as silencing Jack Arlingh yesterday.'

'*I* did that?'

'You sure did. Why do you think he legged it when you told him he could speak again? It was because you'd rendered him unable to speak in the first place and it freaked him out.'

'Oh!'

Flora sat back in her chair, trying to work out how she felt about this new "gift".

'Urm, could this magic stuff also do housework?'

'What do you mean?'

Flora explained about the made-up bed from the previous morning and how she had no memory of doing it herself.

'Aye, it's possible that was your magic.'

'Wow! I… I…'

Words failed her. She didn't know what she felt right now. It was all so much…

'Look, let's leave it here for now. There's so much more to share with you but I think you need time to let this sink in. We can pick it up again tomorrow morning.'

'But, MacAndrew, you need to tell me everything. You can't just stop now.'

'You will learn everything but it's too much all at once. Here endeth the lesson for today.'

'But—'

'Enough, Flora, enough! Trust me, please. Now, I would suggest you take a drive into Beauly and give yourself some breathing space, away from here, for the rest of the day. We'll talk again tomorrow.'

'Oh, I don't think I can drive anywhere today.'

'Why not?'

'Because my arms and shoulders are aching from driving the camper van yesterday – I really don't think I could face that again – and I've also just had two shots of whisky which may have put me over the legal limit.'

'I'll give you some of your grandmother's lotions for the aches – it'll soon sort them out – and don't worry about the whisky – it doesn't affect you the way it does others,' he gave her a sneaky wink, 'What's more, you can use your grandmother's Land Rover. It's an old beast but not as old as that camper van so should be easier to handle. Come, I'll show you where it's parked.'

He got off the seat and walked over to the door at the top of the kitchen. He opened it and then turned back to her.

'Well, what are you waiting for? You won't find the garage while sitting there!'

Flora rapidly moved from her seat and followed him out into the garden. Maybe MacAndrew was right – it was better that she let the events of the morning sink in before she tried to handle any more.

TWENTY-ONE

Kenneth let out a groan as his body dragged his consciousness out of slumber and into wakefulness. He wasn't ready yet to face the day. His sleep had been hindered by the sight of white road lines running through his head every time he closed his eyes, as he suffered the toll of such a long drive. It had been after three a.m. by the time he finally drifted off.

He rolled onto his side, into the centre of the bed and lay there, taking in the silence around him. No slamming doors from nearby houses, no kids yelling as they ran along the pavement to school. No horns blaring from the main road as impatient drivers cut each other up. All there was, was peaceful, blissful, soothing, silence—

'MIAOW!'

Huh!

His eyes sprang open and found themselves looking into two big, black orbs. Before he could move, the little mouth containing all those sharp little teeth opened wide and let out a yawn of humongous proportions. The smell of stale, fishy, tuna had him recoiling and almost falling out of the bed.

'Urgh! That was revolting! Was it *really* necessary to yawn right in my face? And what are you still doing here? I told you last night – go home. There must be a mother waiting for you somewhere.'

The grey, black and white tabby kitten looked at him before lifting its leg behind its ear and began washing under its tail. Kenneth tried to take a discreet peek to see if it was a boy or a girl but the angle was wrong and he remained none the wiser.

'Right! I'm going to take a shower and then we're going to find out where you came from so I can take you right back!'

The kitten ignored him and he found himself wondering more about it as he headed into the bathroom. Upon finding the kitten the previous night, his initial reaction had been one of relief. Anything that wasn't rodent shaped worked for him. His knowledge of cats was sparse, however, despite growing up around them on the farm. They hadn't been allowed to treat them as pets for feral cats were better hunters and their job was to keep the aforementioned rodents to a minimum.

His relief had been short-lived however when he'd tried to remove the kitten from the box. Every time his hand went anywhere near it, the tiny feline bared its teeth, unsheathed claws sharper than any scalpel, and hissed louder than any snake while backing itself into the corner thus making an approach from the rear impossible. After a few attempts, he'd given up, retreating to the kitchen to make his bacon rolls while hoping that the smell of the meat would entice the furry little heathen out into the open.

One hour, and three bacon rolls later, he surmised the kitten must be vegan as it hadn't moved at all. The other quandary he faced was what exactly to do with it once he got it out of the box. A quick internet search told him it must be about fifteen weeks old as its ears were at the stage of being larger than the rest of the animal's body. As it was clearly still so young, he wouldn't have felt at all comfortable just dumping it on the other side of the door, so in the end, he'd moved the box closer to the window, had put a saucer of tuna and a bowl of water on the window ledge and left the window slightly ajar in the hope that by the time he got up in the morning, the problem would have solved itself by jumping out and going back to wherever it had come from.

'Well, that was clearly wishful thinking,' he muttered, as he lathered soap over his body and pondered on what to do next. After rinsing himself off, he turned off the water, opened the shower door and reached his hand out, groping about for his towel.

'MIAOW!'

'What the—'

The sound made him jump then he saw the kitten sitting on top of the boxer shorts he'd left discarded on the floor.

'Seriously, kid, you want to sit on those?'

'MIAOW!'

'Okay, okay. Maybe you could turn down the volume a bit. There's no need to shout.'

'MIAOW!'

'Look, let me get dried and dressed first and then we can sort out what to do with you.'

'MIAOW!'

'Hi, Mum, how are you this morning?'

'Kenneth, good morning. I'm doing well, thank you for asking, how are you? Did you sleep okay?'

Kenneth took a slurp of his coffee while listening to his mum on the phone.

'It took me a while to drop off – you know that thing when you see all the white lines on the road after a long drive? – yeah, had that going on.'

'Oh, that's rough, darling. There's nothing worse than when your body wants to sleep and your brain won't shut down to let it.'

'Tell me about it! Look, Mum, I'm just calling to ask if you're missing a kitten this morning?'

'A kitten?'

'Yes. A grey tabby, maybe about fifteen weeks old, or thereabouts.'

'No, I'm not.'

'Are you sure? Have any of the cats in the yard had kittens recently?'

'No, they haven't because I now take in feral cats from the animal rescue centre up the road and they always neuter before rehoming. So, definitely no chance of them having babies. Why do you ask?'

'Because I found one in a box last night after I unpacked the car. I thought it must belong to the farm. I mean, how else would it get there?'

'Is it possible it got into the box in London?'

'No, I had the boxes stored in the garage… Oh!'

'What?'

'I forgot to close the car and garage after the removal men left and didn't notice until yesterday morning. I wonder if it snuck in then?'

'Well, there's an easy way to check – are there any little presents in the box?'

'Presents?'

'Poop, darling, poop. There's no way that kitten has gone over twenty-four hours without a pee and a poop.'

'Oh, no, my books!'

Kenneth rushed to the kitten box, and as he bent down for a closer look, the distinct smell of cat pee wafted up towards him. He let out a groan.

'Does that groan mean what I think it does, dear?'

'Yes, Mum, it does.'

'Oh, that's unfortunate.'

'Now what do I do?'

'Well, you could leave a window open and when it grows hungry, it'll toddle off and you can close the window behind it.'

'What? I can't do that!'

No way was he letting on that he'd already tried that move. He looked down at the tiny kitten by his feet as it wolfed down the remains of the tuna from the tin he opened last night, and wondered what on earth had he been thinking.

'I was kidding, Kenneth, I know you couldn't. Besides, if I know you like I believe I do, you've probably already fed it so that wouldn't work anyway. Am I right?'

'Yes, you are.'

'Look, firstly, you need to see if it's been microchipped. If not, you've got two choices – you either hand it over to the animal rescue or…'

'Or what?'

'You keep it!'

'Keep it?'

'Yes, keep it! I think it would do you good. You spend too much time alone – a pet would be good for you – have a think about it. In the meantime, I'll give Morag at the rescue centre a call and ask her to pop in to scan it when she's next passing by. She's very helpful that way.'

'Oh, okay. Thank you.'

'Right, I'd better get on – I've got scones in the oven that should be in the tearoom by now. What are your plans for the day?'

'A spot of unpacking this morning then off to the surgery at lunchtime to meet everyone, do introductions, and sort out my new office.'

'Well, good luck, I hope it goes well. I would suggest that, while you're out, you contain Fluffy in the smallest bedroom – for its safety as well as my furniture's – and that you pop down a small box or container with some shredded paper in it.'

'Why?'

'Because getting cat pee out of the carpet is a darned nightmare!'

When Kenneth pulled into the surgery car park, he was surprised to see it full to the brim. Luckily, there were spaces reserved for the doctors and one already had his name plate on it. He parked up and made his way round to the front entrance as he didn't yet have the code for the keypad that would allow him to use the staff door at the back. Upon opening the door, a cacophony of sound assaulted his ears. Every chair in the waiting room was occupied, several babies were crying loudly, and voices were being raised to be heard over the top of them. He looked over to the reception desk and could see the two women there trying to appear calm in the face of the onslaught of patients.

He made his way across and waited in line, listening to the conversations ahead of him.

'I am very sorry, Mr Donaldson, but please can I rearrange your appointment for another day? Doctor Cameron was called out to an emergency this morning and we're really backed up now.'

He couldn't hear Mr Donaldson's reply but the woman's body language suggested he was not happy with what he was hearing.

'I know you've had to make an effort to travel here today, Mr Donaldson, and that you must have your blood pressure taken each month but you can see how busy it is – we need to rearrange.'

Upon hearing this, Kenneth smiled at the woman in front of him in the queue as he stepped past her and up to the desk.

'Excuse me…'

'Please, sir, I'll be with you when I'm finished with this client.'

'But—'

'Sir, I said I'll be with you when I'm finished with this client.'

The receptionist's tone was polite but firm and he was impressed that despite the situation, there was nothing rude about her manner. He looked at her name tag and spoke again.

'Rhona, I'm Doctor MacKenzie – I might be able to help you.'

The effect of his words on the receptionists were probably the same as someone being told they'd won the lottery. Huge smiles broke out and within minutes he found himself sitting in his new office. His computer access had already been set up so he was good to go but he insisted he'd only see non-urgent or follow-up patients until he'd been properly introduced by Doctor Cameron and that was why he was now taking Mr Donaldson's blood pressure.

'So, you're the new doc then, are you?'

'I am, Mr Donaldson.'

'Did I hear you say yer name was MacKenzie?'

'You did, sir.'

'Would you be Dougie and Mhairi MacKenzie's boy? The one who went off to London?'

'That would be me.'

'Right. Well, nice to see you back.'

'Thank you, Mr Donaldson. Now, is there anything else I can help you with today?'

'No, thank you, I'm good.'

'I see on your notes you sometimes have a problem with eczema – how is that doing?'

'Oh, it's all fine. I got some lotion from The Flora and it cleared it up a treat.'

'Oh, okay. Well, if there's nothing else…'

'No. I'm good. See you next month, doctor, nice to have met you.'

'And you, Mr Donaldson.'

When the gentleman left the room, Kenneth quickly washed his hands then buzzed through that he was ready for the next patient. A moment later, a young woman came in, her right wrist sporting a support bandage.

'Miss Hunt?'

'That's me, doctor.'

'You sprained your wrist three weeks ago, according to the notes here.'

'Yes, doctor. Slipped in the garden after doing a spot of weeding.'

'That's unfortunate. How does it feel?'

He removed the support bandage and gently felt around the wrist while listening closely to the answer from Miss Hunt.

'Well, it all seems to be healing well. You can put the bandage back on now but I'd suggest you begin to take it off when doing light tasks, however, put it on if you're moving or lifting anything a bit heavy. Do that for another two weeks after which, you should be fine again.'

'Thank you, that's good to know. It's been a bother, trying to do things with only one hand.'

'I understand. While you're here, how are you doing with your indigestion? It's highlighted on your file as something you've had issues with?'

'I think you can take that off now, doctor. Ever since I got a tincture from The Flora, I've been as right as rain. It's been a godsend, let me tell you, because I did suffer with it something bad.'

'A tincture from The Flora?'

'Yes. Oh, she's a dab hand with those potions of hers. Anyway, I need to get on, doctor, before the butchers close.'

'Of course, Miss Hunt. Take care and don't hesitate to come back if you have any more trouble with that wrist.'

After an hour, Kenneth had managed to get through several of the patients who'd been filling the waiting room and both receptionists had even been able to grab ten minutes for a cup of tea and a sandwich. While he washed his hands for the umpteenth time, one question was going round and around his head – just how many of the surgery's clients had been seeking additional treatment from the old quack known as The Flora? Nearly everyone he'd seen that afternoon had been singing her praises in one form or another. From anxiety to insomnia, eczema to indigestion, and several other ailments in between, it would seem this woman had a cure for them all. He simply couldn't believe how many gullible people lived in this town. Didn't they understand it was all a load of baloney? How on earth could they be fooled into believing this hocus-pocus charlatan could help them out? He wondered how much she'd charged for her stuff and nonsense. And, more to the point, it now appeared her granddaughter had turned up – did she intend to carry on with the family business?

Well, not on his watch. As soon as he had the chance, he'd be paying a visit to this snake-oil seller and putting her in her place.

He threw the paper towel he'd been vigorously drying his hands upon into the bin and buzzed through that he was ready for the next patient.

The intercom beeped back at him and he held down the button.

'Yes, Rhona?'

'Doctor MacKenzie, would you be okay to register a new patient? Normally the nurse would do it but she's still got a queue of ladies with "specific appointments" if you get my meaning.'

'Ah, yes, I do. Of course, I'd be happy to help. Send them in.'

'Thank you, Doctor. Ms O'Brien is on her way to you now.'

TWENTY-TWO

When Flora first set eyes upon her grandmother's Land Rover, or hers as it technically was now, she burst out laughing.

'Oh aye, you can laugh, but when this old girl is zooming past all the other cars stuck in snow drifts or up to their middles in a puddle, you won't be laughing then. I give you that she's not much to look at but her engine is sound and the suspension will see you over many hills and hillocks with barely a murmur.'

'I'm not sure I'll be able to drive her today, MacAndrew. I'm just not up it.'

'You'll be fine, Miss Flora. You go and rub on that lotion I've put on the bench just inside the door there and by the time you get back here, every ache will have eased away.'

She walked back inside to find a small glass jar sitting on top of the shoe bench by the door. It was clear in colour with a pale purple lid. The same colour of purple was used for the label on the jar which declared the contents to be "Heatherlora Ointment" and, according to the details on the back, eased all manner of aches and pains. When she took the lid off, the creamy contents were a light pink with a soft floral scent. Nothing about it was offensive so she took it up to her room and after removing her top, rubbed it carefully across her shoulders, back and upper arms. By the time she'd put her top back on again, there wasn't an ache left in her. She put the jar down on the bedside table and was walking out the room when she stopped in her tracks, turned around and returned to pick up the jar again, this time giving it a closer look.

"Heatherlora"? Could that be heather and Flora? MacAndrew had said it was her grandmother's ointment – did that mean… had she used… could there be magic in this?

The jar fell from her fingers, landing on the cabinet with a clatter. Magic? How could there possibly be magic? Yet her upper body, which had felt so abused and weary only moments before, was now zinging like it had just received the best of massages. It just… it just…

MacAndrew was right. She needed to go and do something ordinary and normal to distract her while her brain worked in the background, dealing with this new development. She grabbed her handbag, rushed down the stairs and back towards the garage. MacAndrew had brought the Landy out for her and had it facing the opposite direction to the dry-stone wall.

'If you follow that track, it'll lead you up to the one you came down yesterday.'

'Oh, I didn't see a second track yesterday.'

'No, lass, you wouldn't have. But you will. The trees know you're here now. They'll reveal the secrets to you that they hide from others.' He gave her an enigmatic smile while handing over the Landy keys.

She let out a sigh as she climbed up behind the steering wheel.

'I've got a lot to learn, haven't I?'

'Like you wouldn't believe.'

MacAndrew slammed the door closed and stood waving as she set off up the track. When she looked back in her mirror, he'd already disappeared from view.

'Oh, thank goodness.'

Flora heaved a sigh of relief at finding several parking spaces in the same square in Beauly where she'd parked yesterday, although she opted to park at the top end this time, and was even happier to only need one space. MacAndrew was right – the Landy drove like a dream and Flora wondered if her grandmother had bestowed some of her "gifts" upon it to make it so. This train of thought led her to thinking that maybe the powers she would be inheriting weren't such a bad thing. What scared her, however, was how she was using them without her knowledge and the danger this could create for her. In truth, the sooner MacAndrew began to give her proper training, the better.

She jumped down from the driver's seat, locked the door behind her and set off to do some exploring. She'd been tired the day before but now she could take time to stroll leisurely around the town, taking in all it had to offer. One of the first things to grab her attention was the Indian restaurant directly across from where she'd parked. Oh, yum! She did enjoy a good curry and after checking if they did takeaways, she turned to look down through The Square. To her left, on the corner, was a hotel followed by a row of shops beyond it. To her right were parking spaces and then the main road. She stepped over onto the pavement and began walking slowly along, taking in the eclectic mix of retail options on offer. There was a small café, a gift shop, a beautician, and an art gallery, to name but a few, alongside the mini-supermarket that stayed open later in the evening – handy to know – and the butchers and bakery she'd spotted the previous evening brought up the rear. She also meandered a short way down the little side streets, ensuring she didn't miss anything. Flora didn't know how long she would be staying at the cottage so wanted to learn more about the town since it was going to be home for at least the next few months.

On the corner by the bakery, she turned left to see if this little road had anything to offer and found herself passing a medical centre. She paused for a moment, wondering if she should go in and register but decided to leave it for another day. She was never ill but did appreciate that something like this was important. It was added to the to-do list in her head as she carried on walking. She was following the curve in the road that led behind the shops she'd passed when she heard moving water and upon stepping over the grass verge to the metal fencing, found herself gazing down at a river with tree-covered land beyond it. The sky above was a glorious shade of blue and it was all very peaceful. She watched the water flowing past for several moments, finding herself soothed by its presence and, after a few minutes, her scattered mind and scattered emotions regrouped. She turned to retrace her steps back to the main street, realising as she walked, that she felt a little more comfortable within herself.

On the main road, her leisurely stroll continued, taking her past the ironmongers from the day before. The woman who'd served her was changing the window display and gave Flora a tentative smile when she saw her. Flora returned the gesture, adding a small wave which resulted in the woman's smile broadening across her face with a wave in return. This interaction cheered her right up and lightened her step as she continued along the road, observing each shop and building carefully so she would remember them.

Soon the shops petered out and she was walking past pretty houses set back from the road. In the distance, she saw the neon sign for the petrol station and recalled there was a larger supermarket next to it, then the railway station before you were on an open road to the countryside.

Deciding this was as good a place to cross as any, she turned towards the road when her eye was caught by a sign – an arrow pointing down a side street with a large blue and white "P" on it. She walked along the side street then let out an almighty groan when she found, in front of her, a decent sized car park with plenty of spaces including bays large enough to house buses, motorhomes, and even old, VW, camper vans!

Gah! All that bother yesterday could've been saved if she'd known this was here. Oh well, at least she'd know for next time although now she had the Landy at her disposal, it was highly unlikely the camper would be passing this way again.

She turned to resume her walk back into the centre of the little town, passing fewer shops but did note a couple of pubs, another hotel, and an antiques shop. She continued to walk down each side street she passed but they were mostly residential.

As she passed an estate agents, the smell of freshly ground coffee suddenly flew up her nose. Oh, dear goodness, this smell was like nectar from the gods and always guaranteed to make her sit up and notice. She followed the glorious scent and it led her to a small café and delicatessen on the opposite corner which looked very inviting. She sneaked a peek through the doorway and saw an amazing array of cheese displayed in the counter directly ahead of her. However, it was the shelf above that had her sweet tooth groaning with delight for the cakes sitting there were more than worthy of any TV baking show. She took in the carrot cake, the lemon meringue pie, the plate-sized doughnuts with creamy, yellow custard oozing from them.... She almost passed out on the spot with sheer joy.

Unfortunately, or fortunately, depending on how small you wished your waistline to be, all the outside tables were occupied but she could see some of the occupants were close to finishing so figured that by the time she'd walked along the side street and back, a table would be available.

Happy with this, she did a sharp left turn along the pavement although she hadn't gone far when she came to a halt outside the Chinese takeaway. Oh, this town was becoming better by the minute. She may enjoy a curry but she loved her Chinese food more. It was always her first choice. They were currently closed so she took photographs of the menu in the window for future reference.

Once past the Chinese Takeaway, there wasn't much to see – a road sign stating there was a school close by, a red sandstone church standing proudly on the next corner and a squat building on her left with a busy car park which had her wondering if it might be the local library – always a good place for finding ways to join in with the community. She walked up to the door and was surprised to find it was a second doctor's surgery. She wouldn't have expected a town this size to have two. Maybe they also covered the outlying locations. After all, some places in the Highlands must be rather remote.

On impulse, and because it was on her to-do list, she stepped through the door, over to the reception desk and politely advised she was new to the area and would like to register. What Flora hadn't anticipated was the flustered response from the receptionist when she looked up.

'Oh, oh, oh... err... yes, yes, of course. Let me just get

you a registration form.'

A few seconds later, after giving the receptionist her name and date of birth, a clipboard and pen were thrust in her direction and she was guided towards a chair where she sat and filled it in. Well, she tried to fill it in but her first, and albeit only, stumbling block was her current address. She didn't know it! Her uncle's directions had led her to the cottage but she was clueless on its actual address. She desperately tried to remember something from the paperwork she'd signed a few months earlier but… nope… nothing.

'Err, Ms O'Brien, the doctor can see you now.'

'Thank you.' She handed back the semi-complete form. 'I'm so sorry, and I know this probably sounds very strange, but I don't actually know my address. I can describe its location but not the postal details. I'm afraid I'll need to pop back in with the information.'

'Oh, don't you worry about that, Ms O'Brien, everyone knows where The Flora lives. No need to concern yourself over it.'

'I'm sorry…'

'We know who you are and I'm thrilled to have met you. Now, Doctor MacKenzie is ready for you and he's in that room over there.'

TWENTY-THREE

There was a soft knock on the door at the same time as Kenneth's mobile phone pinged.

'Come in,' he called out, his finger quickly swiping the screen to see a text from his mum.

Morag's scanned the kitten – not chipped. It's a girl, approx. 15-16 weeks. No space at the rescue for her right now so she'll come back for her next week. Don't forget you're having dinner with us tonight. Luv u. Mum. Xx

He looked up when the surgery door clicked closed and dropped the phone onto the desk.

'YOU!'

The woman who'd so selfishly parked her vehicle across three parking spaces the day before, causing him no end of stress, was now walking towards him.

'I'm sorry?'

He saw confusion in her silver eyes as she came to stand in front of his desk. Feeling at a disadvantage, he stood and glowered at her.

'YOU! You were the inconsiderate imbecile who thought it acceptable to take up three parking spaces in The Square yesterday afternoon. With absolutely no consideration for others, you merrily parked up and trotted off, not once thinking that at such a busy time of the day, other people may ALSO want to park their vehicles so they TOO can do some shopping before going home!'

As the last syllable spat out through his clenched teeth, he watched the woman transform in front of him. The demure, polite expression flew out the window as shoulders were pulled up, the back straightened, and extreme annoyance settled upon a face which he noticed, much to his annoyance, was most interestingly attractive. It wasn't beautiful in the drop-dead manner pushed upon society by the media but it was a face that immediately caught your attention with its sharp, high, cheekbones, silver eyes that tapered in a feline manner at the corners, a slim nose with a little pert snub on the end, lips redder than he'd ever seen without some cosmetic aid and a chin which came almost to a point beneath them. His first thought was she looked like a pixie in human form although he suspected the vibrant, auburn hair currently cut in a gamine, a-la young Audrey Hepburn, style enhanced that illusion. The same auburn hair also appeared to be shaking with unreleased fury. He, however, was no slouch in the temper department for while he may have inherited his mother's brown locks, his father's sandy colouring with its explosive temper hid inside him and was known to make an occasional appearance. He couldn't recall the last time it had happened but he did know the next time was happening right now.

'For someone who CLAIMS to be a doctor, you're clearly lacking in the basic skill of observation which makes me wonder EXACTLY who the imbecile is around here!'

'What are you implying by that?'

'Oh, I'm IMPLYING nothing. I'm STATING a fact! I thought doctors were supposed to observe and assess their patients before making a diagnosis and I'd have expected the same skill set to be used in day-to-day life.'

'I observed very plainly that YOU chose to park ACROSS three parking spaces, totally at odds with correct car-park protocol and I have therefore assessed you are a selfish woman who only thinks of herself and with no regard for others.'

'Is that so? In which case, maybe I should remove myself from this surgery and register with the other one as you are obviously not up to the job you're employed for.'

'Meaning WHAT exactly?'

The last comment was almost too much for him. He was a darned good doctor and his ability to do his job well was one of the few things in his life that he allowed himself to feel proud of.

'Well, let me spell it out for you. My vehicle was a Volkswagen camper van. They're a bit longer than your average car and certainly bigger than my little Nissan Micra. As the spaces were at the end of the car park, I was worried about it jutting out too far and either causing an obstruction or worse, being hit and damaged. She's on loan and I don't want to return her with half of the back end hanging off. So, THAT is why I parked the way I did. NOT to be a nuisance, not to inconvenience YOU or anyone else but to ensure access was clear for other drivers in the area.'

'Well, apart from the fact that most car park spaces are approximately fifteen feet in length – which would have been long enough to accommodate your fourteen-foot-long van, if you'd been that concerned about being an obstruction, you could have used the much larger parking facility on the edge of the town which happens to have bays specifically for coaches, motorhomes, and even a camper van!'

'And had I known THAT car park existed, I would've happily used it! However, having just arrived in town and realising I had to make an unscheduled stop, I parked in the first available space I could find. The bays looked not only shorter but narrow too and I also didn't want to risk being blocked in. I'd been on the road for the best part of twelve hours by that point, I was tired and I merely parked in the way that seemed best at the time. I am SO sorry I was an inconvenience to you and I will endeavour to do better in the future.'

The sarcasm dripped so heavily from the last part of the sentence Kenneth wouldn't have been surprised to see it pooling on the desk between them. He drew in a deep breath and did the very thing he'd just been accused of not doing – assessing the situation.

As silver eyes continued to glare at him – could they *really* be silver – he went over the information just given to him. The camper was on loan, she normally drove a much smaller car, she'd been driving for most of the day… With all this new data, he could now understand the logic behind her decision. And, if he was being brutally honest with himself, if *he* hadn't been tired from his own long journey, he most likely wouldn't have let the situation rile him as much as it had. Yes, it would've irritated him to see the camper parked as it had been but it wouldn't have got under his skin in such a way it caused him to have an argument with a new patient the minute she walked in the door. THAT was unprofessional and an apology was most definitely required.

'I'm sorry. I shouldn't have spoken to you like that.'

'Pardon?' The silver eyes widened.

'I apologise for speaking to you as I did and for haranguing you in a most unprofessional manner. I shouldn't have done that, it was wrong of me. If you wish to make an official complaint, I can provide you with the paperwork.'

While he was explaining her right to complain, he really hoped she didn't as it wouldn't bode well going forward if he received a complaint before he'd barely warmed the seat of his new chair.

'No, you're fine. Let's just forget it and start again. Flora O'Brien.'

Her hand came across the desk to shake his and as he took it, he noticed a long ginger hair on the sleeve of her jacket.

'Oh,' he pointed to it, 'cat or dog?'

Flora glanced down at her arm then looked back at him with a smile.

'Cat. His name is Herbert.'

'Hmmm, you might just be the person to help me.'

He hoped the change in conversation might clear the air and help to rebuild the patient / doctor relationship which required an element of trust for it to work.

'In what way?'

Kenneth gestured her towards the seat in front of his desk while sitting down in his to explain how he'd just become the owner of a cat.

'While I grew up on a farm with loads of farm cats, they were all feral so owning one as a pet is a whole new ball game to me. I could do with a little input from someone who knows more than I do.'

'I'm afraid my knowledge is quite limited – I know the basics such as the best food to feed, litter trays, neutering, vaccinations and, most importantly, you don't own the cat, the cat owns YOU!' She smiled as she said this. 'My friend Sally is the expert. She runs a cat rescue and is the font of all feline-related knowledge. If you give me an email address, I'll contact her when I get home and ask her to send some further information.'

'Oh, that's very kind of you.'

He quickly scribbled down his email details and passed the slip of paper to Flora, watching as she carefully folded it to place it inside her purse.

'Right, I suppose we should get on with completing your registration.'

He glanced at the computer screen but Rhona hadn't yet sent through Flora's details for him to look through.

'I'm still waiting for your information to come from Rhona so why don't I do the usual checks first then run through your health history. It's a little back-to-front but I'm sure we can muster through.'

He was just writing down the readings from the blood-pressure gauge when his computer screen flashed and he saw he now had all of Flora's medical records in front of him. He read out her date of birth first.

'Yep, that's mine.'

'And your full name is Flora MacDonald O'Brien?'

'Yup, that would be me.'

It took a few seconds for the penny to drop but when it did, Kenneth drew in such a sharp breath, Flora gave him a look of concern.

'Is everything okay?'

'You're... you're Flora *MacDonald* O'Brien?'

'Er, yes. I already told you I was.'

'Flora *MacDonald*... You're... you're... you're The Flora!'

'Um... you know about that?'

'Of course I do! Everyone in the area knows about The Flora.'

'Well, they're better informed than me as I only found out about this barely four hours ago!'

'Do you intend to pick up where your grandmother left off?'

'Well, I'm not sure what you mean—'

'All the mumbo-jumbo she spouted about potions and tinctures and the like.' His thoughts returned to the number of patients he'd seen in the last two hours who'd happily waxed lyrical about the virtues and powers of The Flora and how much *she'd* helped them with their ailments.

'Your grandmother fooled the people in this town into believing she was something special and could heal all their troubles and woes. She drew them into her world of hocus-pocus, letting them think she was a great healer and an all-knowing witch of a woman. If you're planning to carry on her charade, let me tell you tell you now, you'll have a fight on your hands because I won't let you get away with it. I'll stop you and the townspeople will learn the truth about you and your family.'

Flora rose from her chair as he uttered his final sentence.

'You just couldn't help yourself, could you. Once again, you're off making assumptions and not listening to anything I've said. You stupid, stupid man.'

She spun around and walked out the door. He braced himself for the loud bang as it slammed behind her and was more impressed than he really wanted to be when it closed quietly, the catch whispering its way back into its little nook.

He sat back in his seat, feeling as though he'd just done a round with Tyson Fury, and reflected on how badly the whole situation had gone.

'Nice one, MacKenzie,' he muttered, 'nice one, indeed.'

An hour later, he pulled on his jacket, switched off the computer and walked back out into the reception area thinking that, with the exception of Flora MacDonald, the afternoon had gone well.

'Goodnight, Rhona, I'm going to head off now. We can start again and do the formal introductions on Monday.'

The receptionist smiled at him. 'That sounds like a good plan. Thank you for helping today, it really made a difference.'

'No problem at all. See you then.'

'Oh, before you go, Doctor MacKenzie, there's a package here for you.'

She lifted a box up onto the desk and when he looked inside, Kenneth found a litter tray, a couple of bags of litter, tins of cat food and a selection of small toys.'
'What? Who?'
'The Flora left it for you.'

TWENTY-FOUR

'I've put together a box of bits to tide you over with the kitten until Morag comes back next week. She was sorry she couldn't take her this afternoon but she's totally full. There are, however, a few getting rehomed at the weekend, so there'll be space by Wednesday.'

'Actually, Mum, I've decided to keep her.'

'You have?'

Kenneth scooped up the last spoonful of apple crumble with custard and ate it, relishing the texture and flavours of his favourite pudding, before replying.

'Yes, I have.'

'May I ask why? You didn't seem keen this morning.'

'This morning, I was in a state of shock at the idea this kitten had most likely come all the way up from London. She's not what I expected when I opened the box last night, let me tell you.'

'Worried it might have been a rat, eh? Did it have you cornered?'

His older brother chortled at his wit from the other end of the table until his wife, Shona, gave him a dig in the ribs with her elbow.

'Leave him be, Fraser. He's not the only one with a rat phobia so lay off.'

'Cheers, Shona. It's good to have you on my side.' He gave his sister-in-law a smile. 'I was so sorry not to see you on my last visit.'

'Yeah, the kids were gutted they missed you. Couldn't believe I was still making them visit their other grandma when you were coming home.'

'So, what made you decide to keep her?'

'I dunno, Mum, – I suppose when you sent the text saying she wasn't chipped and she'd be going to the rescue. The thought of her sitting in a cage, waiting for someone to choose her, didn't feel right. After I came off the phone this morning, I did as you said – sorted out the box in the spare room for her, gave her some more tuna which she wolfed down but then, when she finished it, she crawled onto my lap and had a wash before curling up to sleep, all the while purring like a wee tiny racing car. She was… well… adorable. So cute.'

'Well, you'll be needing some stuff to get by with until you can make it into Inverness to the big pet shop there.'

'As it happens, I've already got the basics.'

'You have.'

'Yes, The Flora—'

He stopped short. Damn! He hadn't meant to let on he'd met Flora MacDonald already, what with his mother behaving like a crazed, star-struck, fanatic whenever her name was mentioned.

There was total silence around the table as all eyes turned to look his way.

'You've… you've met The Flora?'

'Yes, Mum, she came into the surgery to register this afternoon.'

'The Flora registered with the doctor's surgery?'

This time it was his father who sounded incredulous.

'Yes, what's wrong with that?'

'It's not something they usually do. The Flora is a natural healer, why would she require someone else to do it?'

'Yeah, well, it's what she did, okay?'

'Ken-neth...'

He turned to his mother. The way she'd said his name told him she suspected he'd done something wrong. She'd always had the knack of knowing when her boys needed a cuff around the ear.

'Yes?'

'What did you do?'

'I'm not sure I know what you mean.'

'Oh yes you do! I haven't brought up three boys without learning every expression to cross their faces and what is behind them so, I'll ask again, what did you do?'

'We had a sort of an argument...'

'SORT of an argument? What does that even mean?'

Feeling like he was facing the Spanish Inquisition, he retold the events of the afternoon to his family. Even as he spoke, he could feel the embarrassment at his behaviour flooding his face, although he had no regrets about stating his piece on her supposed remedies – that was one thing he would stand by – although he could probably have put his point across better than he had. When he'd finished, the atmosphere was so thick, you could have cut it with the proverbial knife.

'What?'

He glared back at the eyes looking at him, a mixture of shock, surprise, disappointment, and anger among them all.

'Oh, Kenneth, what on earth did you do that for?'

'I only said how I feel.'

'Maybe so, but if The Flora thinks everyone else feels

the same, she might not stay. We need her to stay.'

'Do we, Mum, do we really?'

'Yes, Kenneth, we do! You haven't lived here for many years so you wouldn't understand the mood of the town these last few months when there's been no Flora in residence—'

'In residence? She's not the Queen. Or the King, as we have now!'

'BE QUIET AND LISTEN TO YOUR MOTHER, BOY!'

He might now be in his thirties, but when his father roared, Kenneth knew to sit back and do as he was told.

'As I was saying, the mood in the town, when there was no Flora in residence, was unpleasant. The uncertainty affected everyone. Since her appearance yesterday, there is already a difference. I went to the supermarket this morning, the big one, and all you could hear was people talking about The Flora being back.'

'But I don't understand why. What makes having this woman here so special? What would happen if she didn't stay?'

'Don't even utter those words, Kenneth, just don't utter them. For as long as anyone knows, there's always been a Flora in this area. She looks out for the local people – she cares for them and she does all she can to help them. In return, the locals look out for her. She's like a talisman to us. When she's here, all is well. No one can say if anything untoward would occur if The Flora was to leave for good but no one is of a mind to find out.'

'But—'

'BUT NOTHING, KENNETH!'

He looked at his father quizzically. Surely this big, solid, hardy man didn't buy into this nonsense.

'Father—'

'Kenneth, since we've gone over to crop farming, the

only reason we've managed to stay afloat is because of The Flora. She lets us know when we need to harvest early or when we can harvest late. In all the years since, The Flora has never once been wrong on when the rain will come or the sun will shine. The few farms who choose to ignore her, do so only the once. She is never wrong. Don't you recall helping when we still had the herd back in the days of the big foot-and-mouth outbreak? Do you not remember mixing the potions she sent into the feed that prevented them contracting the disease?'

'Like I mentioned before, Dad, – we kept them indoors for months. I think you'll find that went a long way towards keeping them safe.'

'It would have helped but I firmly believe it was the assistance given by The Flora that saw us through what was a terrible, terrible time for farmers. I will not hear a single bad word against her and certainly not from the mouth of one of my own. This will be the last time you speak negatively of The Flora under this roof. Do you hear me?'

'Yes, Dad, I hear you.'

'Well, now we have some ground to make up and we need to do it fast. Kenneth, not only do you need to apologise, but you also need to invite her over for dinner—

'I what?'

'You heard. I must undo any damage you may have done.'

At that moment, Kenneth felt his phone vibrating in his pocket. Glad for the distraction, no matter how brief, he took it out and glanced at the screen while his mum carried on.

'You can visit her tomorrow and ask her to join us for Sunday dinner. I'm sure that will appeal.'

'I don't need to visit,' he gave his phone a small wave in the air, 'she's just emailed me so I can email her back to ask the question.'

'You'll do no such thing! You'll make a point of visiting her in person, you will apologise for your bad behaviour today – I didn't bring my sons up to behave like arrogant oafs! – and then you will extend the dinner invitation. Furthermore, you will also be here for that meal.'

'Oh, Mum…'

'It's not a request, Kenneth, it's an order. You will do as you are told.'

'Very well, if you insist.' He felt like a ten-year-old again.

'I do insist.'

Suddenly, he remembered something and he used it like a "Get out of jail free" card.

'I don't know where she lives. There was no address on her registration form.'

'Don't you worry about that. I know where she lives and I'll give you very specific directions so you have no excuse.'

'Okay, what if I do all this and she refuses, what then? Do I bundle her into the boot of the car and drag her here?'

'Less of your cheek, boy,' his father growled.

'She won't refuse. She'll accept.'

'And how do you know that, Mum?'

'Because if she does, you just inform her I was close friends with her mother.'

TWENTY-FIVE

When Flora walked into the kitchen the following morning, having followed the scent of warm pastry down the stairs, it was to see MacAndrew place a plate of HUGE croissants on the table which had been set with a crisp white tablecloth, shining cutlery, dark blue earthenware crockery and a slim vase holding a few sprigs of heather.

'Oh, wow, this all looks lovely, MacAndrew. Thank you.'

'No problem,' he answered, gruffly.

A cafetiere was put in front of her as she pulled out her chair.

'Tuck in, then, don't let them go cold.'

'Aren't you joining me?'

'Um, no. It wouldn't be right.'

'What do you mean by that?'

Flora tore off a piece of croissant and closed her eyes in bliss as a whisp of steam escaped from the pastry. She placed a large knob of butter on her plate and quickly followed it with an even larger dollop of jam. Her dad had often teased that she liked a little bit of croissant with her jam. The thought of her dad pulled her back and for a moment, she felt the sadness in her heart at being estranged from him but when it was rapidly followed by the memory of his betrayal, the sadness was quickly expelled.

'Miss Flora, I'm here to serve you. It's my place. Now, I do agree that circumstances have muddied the waters somewhat but that is by the by. It wouldn't be right for us to break bread together.'

'You're here to serve me?'

'That's correct.'

'So, you have to do as I tell you?'

'In a manner of speaking…'

'Fine. Then I am telling you to sit down there,' she pointed to the chair opposite where MacAndrew had sat the day before, 'and have some breakfast.'

'I… I… I can't.'

'Please, MacAndrew. I'll be honest, I'm not entirely comfortable with the idea of you "serving" me, like I'm your mistress or something. I'd be happier if we both approached all this on a more even footing which also means dropping the "Miss" – Flora is fine.'

With a look that told her in no uncertain terms he wasn't happy with this arrangement, MacAndrew pulled himself onto the chair she'd indicated.

'Now eat. I can't consume all these croissants by myself. Well, *actually*, I could because I love croissants with jam but I'd need to run up and down those mountains for a week to burn off the calories.'

While reaching hesitantly for a croissant, MacAndrew chuckled at her comment before replying, 'As it happens, miss, now that your gifts are coming to the fore, weight gain is something you won't need to worry about. Not for a time anyway. Because of the changes taking place, even though you don't realise it, you are burning through a lot of energy. So, eat away and enjoy some guilt-free noshing!'

The piece of jam-laden croissant stopped halfway to her mouth.

'Calorie-free eating? Are you for real?'

'For now, that's how it is. It's not long-term so you might as well enjoy it while you can.'

'I most certainly will.'

Between the two of them, it didn't take long to demolish the pastry pile and once MacAndrew had cleared the table – Flora tried to assist but received such a scowl for her efforts, she sat back down again – he returned with a black velvet box in one hand and the bottle of whisky and shot glasses in the other.

'Right. Today's lesson,' he began. 'In this box, is an item of great importance and extreme value. When I open it, you CANNOT touch it. You absolutely MUST NOT touch it. Promise me you will keep your fingers to yourself.'

'You know, MacAndrew, considering you're supposed to "serve" me, you're a right bossy wee blighter.'

'Yeah, I know, deal with it!'

Flora laughed as she stuck her tongue out at him. And then laughed even louder when he did the same.

'Right. Are you ready?'

'Yes, I am.'

She leant forward but kept her hands tucked under her thighs, out of the way. MacAndrew opened the lid and turned the box to face her. With a gasp, she stared at the contents and, of its own volition, her right hand escaped, making its way towards the stunning necklace before her.

'NO TOUCHING!'

'Sorry! Sorry! I didn't mean it.' She pushed her hand back under her leg. 'What is it? And don't say "a necklace" because I can see that.'

'The easiest way to describe this is to call it the

"Necklace of Knowledge".'

'Huh?'

'When a new Flora steps up to take her rightful place, she dons this necklace. In doing so, she will be infused with all the knowledge that has been gained by the Floras who have gone before her. As that Flora lives her life, she will gain further knowledge and just before she deigns to move on from her mortal life, she puts the necklace back on and all the knowledge, old and new, returns to fill it. Then, when the next Flora comes along, she puts the necklace on and so the cycle begins again.'

'What are these stones? Are they diamonds? Rubies?'

'They're magical diamonds. When empty of said *knowledge*, they are whiter than any diamond you will ever see, but when full... well, as you can see, they turn the deepest shade of red.'

'Wow! That is rather mind-blowing stuff.'

Flora dragged eyes away from the gorgeous creation to look at MacAndrew.

'So, just to check I'm understanding this correctly – these *magical diamonds* are currently deep red because they're infused with all the magical knowledge of my ancestors but when I put the necklace on, *I* will become infused with the knowledge and the diamonds revert back to their natural white state?'

'Yes, in a nutshell, that is it exactly.'

'Wow! Again!'

Almost against her will, her eyed were pulled back to the box in front of her. The necklace was silver filigree and some of it was twisted into small rosebuds which became two smaller roses and then one large, fully-bloomed, rose in the middle. The stem of the centre rose sat over the large, heart-shaped, diamond, its end buried deep in the middle of the stone. A small tear-drop diamond hung an inch below the heart's tip. The deep red was a colour she had never come across before which was quite something to say given her artistic background.

'Why can't I touch it?'

The urge to do so was so strong, it was taking an immense amount of willpower to keep her hands away.

MacAndrew pushed one of the shot glasses towards her and filled it.

'Oh, one of those moments, is it?'

'Pretty much.'

'Then you'd better get on with it. Spill the beans.'

'You can only touch, hold, put on this necklace once you decide you are staying for good.'

'I'm sorry?'

'Once you put on the necklace, you cannot leave. That is when you become tied to this land until you move over to the other side.'

'You mean, when I die?'

'A coarse way of putting it, but in essence, yes, when you die.'

'And when you say I can never leave…'

'Remember what I told you yesterday – you can't call anywhere else but here home. This cottage, this loch, this earth will be your home. For ever.'

'R-i-g-h-t!'

She stared down at the necklace again, finding the desire to touch it decreasing somewhat.

'Why?'

'Why what?'

'Why do I become tied to this land?'

'Okay, I'm going to use the term "witch" here because it makes explaining easier. Every "witch" has his or her own particular gift which is strong within them. For some it's potions, for others it'll be spells, some are shapeshifters, and for others—'

'Shapeshifters? Seriously?'

'Yes, seriously. And as I was saying, for others it's the ability to commute with nature. You fall into the latter category – you're an Elemental.'

'Excuse me?'

'You commute with the elements. The sky out there,' MacAndrew pointed through the window, 'is your Air. The loch is your Water. The land around you is your Earth.'

'Air. Water. Earth.' Flora counted these out on her fingers. 'Correct me if I'm wrong, MacAndrew, but I'm sure there are four elements. Fire? What about fire?'

'That, Flora, is you.'

'Come again? Me? How am I fire?'

'Your hair, Flora, your red hair. It carries the red of fire. You're the fourth element.'

'Oh!'

'The winds of the Air will bring you knowledge. They will share their secrets with you. Some you can pass on to others and some you must hold firmly in your heart for these are the ones which could endanger you and those around you.'

'Really? Such as?'

'When the time comes, you'll know.'

'I see.'

'The Earth protects and provides for you.'

'Protects?'

'Yes. Anyone with bad energy or impure intentions will not be able to locate your cottage over land. The track from here to the main road can only be traversed by people who mean you no harm.'

'So, what, you're saying the trees move to hide it or something?' Flora giggled as she spoke but it quickly died away when she saw that MacAndrew was serious. 'And the loch? What does it do?'

'The loch is your balance. Being Water, it is your direct opposite element and therefore, the most important. A fiery and passionate nature is not a bad thing but to be most effective, you need to temper how you use it. The loch will help you with this.'

Flora looked at the necklace and as she stared, she felt an almost hypnotic sensation come over her as her hand slowly inched its way towards the black velvet casing again.

'NO!' She pulled herself back, dragging her eyes away to look at MacAndrew. 'I can't. Not yet.'

'It's okay, Flora, I agree the time is not right.'

'I… I… has any other Flora hesitated to put on the necklace? To accept what is stored within it?'

'No, but they were aware of their destiny having grown up on this land. You didn't, which makes you very different.'

'Is that a bad thing?'

MacAndrew looked solemnly at her for several seconds before replying with a gentle sigh, 'I don't know, Miss Flora, I really don't know.'

TWENTY-SIX

Flora sat by the table on the patio, staring out across the loch which was flashing fairy-light twinkles from the sunlight dancing over the gentle waves. MacAndrew was right – she found herself feeling considerably calmer than when she'd come out a few hours earlier, feeling overwhelmed by the information the little man had bestowed upon her. So, her primary gift was communicating with the elements around her – yes, if she didn't like the location of a tree or bush, she had the ability to ask it to move and it would do so. This made her smile with amusement but she was worried over what she would hear when the wind spoke to her. It hadn't happened yet and while part of her hoped it wouldn't, she knew it inevitably would, suspecting it could be soon because she could feel her "witchy powers" gaining strength within her. It was an unusual sensation – she could only describe it as feeling like warm pins and needles that were tickly rather than painful – and she knew the longer she stayed here, the power would continue to grow. And yet… she felt absolutely no desire to leave. In less than forty-eight hours, the sense of belonging she'd craved all her life but never found, was now flourishing. She'd never managed to make close friendships and couldn't understand why, but maybe, she wondered, she'd given off some kind of vibe that had kept people at bay. Something to prevent her getting too close because inside her was a secret she'd never be able to share?

It was also interesting, and daunting, to learn her secondary gifts were healing and potions. For many years, the Floras who'd gone before her had cultivated the heather around them, using it to create various lotions, potions, ointments, and tinctures which they'd once bartered for food and supplies but which were now – oh the joy of technology – sold over the internet. MacAndrew was responsible for fulfilling the orders, all she had to do was make the goods, and learning how would be her first task on Monday. She was looking forward to it and yet dreading it in equal measure.

It was so much to take in – she needed to empty her mind. So, letting her head drop back, she lifted her face up to the sun, taking deep, soothing breaths as the breeze lifted the strands of her hair and let them fall again to tickle the sides of her face. Her fingers played with the crumbs left on the plate from her earlier sandwich. Both dogs were lying by her feet and everything was peaceful until Sandy suddenly stood and let out a sharp woof. Flora jerked upright, her heart racing with both shock and surprise. Just as she was remembering that the land here would protect her, the very last person she'd expected to see again for a while, walked around the corner.

'Doctor MacKenzie?'

'Ms O'Brien.'

'What on earth are you doing here?'

'Well, I—'

'Oh, I'm sorry,' Flora butted into his reply, 'how

extremely rude of me. I'm just surprised to see you here. Please, let me start again. Doctor MacKenzie, what a surprise, how can I help you?'

'Erm, well, firstly, I came to apologise for my behaviour yesterday. I had no right to speak to you as I did. It was wrong of me. While I may have my views on natural remedies and things of that ilk, they should've been kept private.'

As he spoke, Flora found herself becoming aware of an attraction to this man. Physically, he was very much her "type" – tall, dark, and extremely handsome. He made her think of the actor Cary Grant, who she'd always had a little thing for thanks to watching so many of his movies with her grandfather. His tidy hair-cut and smart suit only enhanced the likeness despite his eyes being green and not the chocolate-brown of the famous actor. The Laird's son may not have made her bits and pieces jingle, but this dude definitely did! It's a pity he was her doctor and therefore completely out of bounds, although, that was probably a good thing given everything she was having to deal with right now.

When he finished speaking, she was tart with her reply.

'It may also have boded you well to remember I've only been here two days and am currently on a vast learning curve with regards to the services my grandmother provided.'

'Indeed.'

'Very well, Doctor MacKenzie, your apology is accepted.'

'Thank you. Also, may we dispense with the formalities? You call me Kenneth and I call you Flora? Would that be overly-familiar for you?'

'Is it permitted? Given your professional capacity?'

'You've been assigned to one of the other doctors in the surgery.'

Uh-oh! So much for being able to use the doctor-patient card to restrain her inner jingles and jangles!

'Although, having looked over your almost non-existent medical records after you left, I suspect they'll hardly ever see you.'

'I hope that's the case,' she grinned, hoping she was coming across as normal, 'I seem to have been quite healthy up till now, it would be nice for it to remain that way.'

'Not even a sprain or broken bone – were you rather boring as a child?'

This made her laugh.

'Gosh, no, anything but! I was always the first up the trees, encouraging the other kids to follow, or the first down the potholes or in the river. Come to think of it, I seem to have been the only one NOT to have sustained some kind of injury from my antics.'

'You were clearly very lucky.'

'Indeed, I must've been.' *Or perhaps protected by magic?* The thought flashed into her mind and Flora pushed it away – that was a question to ask MacAndrew later.

'The second reason I'm here is to thank you for the cat gifts you left and for sending on the information your friend emailed to you. I'm both grateful and undeserving of your kindness after the way I behaved.'

'It was done for the cat's benefit – not yours. Why should it suffer over your bad behaviour?'

'Ouch! You pack a verbal punch but as I deserve it…'

'I won't disagree with you there, Kenneth.' She smiled to take the sting out of her words. A truce had been declared – it would be churlish of her to reject it. Besides, she needed to expand the circle of humans in her life up here, MacAndrew on his own was not enough. And she still harboured doubts over him actually being human.

'As a peace-offering, may I offer you a tea or a coffee? I've just been enjoying the solitude of the loch and can highly recommend it.'

'Thank you but I need to get home for the kitten. I daren't leave her too long in case she wrecks the place.'

'So, you're definitely keeping her?'

'I'm afraid so. I just don't have the heart to send something so cute off to a rescue, even though I believe her time there would be minimal. She'd be snapped up very quickly. Talking of snaps, would you like to see a picture of her, even though you're obviously a dog person.' He inclined his head down towards the two Westies sitting by her feet.

'They came with the cottage. I describe myself as simply an animal person and I'd love to see a picture. Have you named her yet?'

'Yeah, Choona.'

'Tuna? Seriously?'

Kenneth laughed and Flora found herself liking the sound of it. Many men – or certainly the ones she'd met – seemed to have quite rough guffaws but Kenneth's laughter had been musical. Masculine but musical. It was a pleasant sound and had surprised her.

'It was all I had to feed her when I found her the other night and she now thinks "tuna" is the word for dinner. I will be spelling it C-H-O-O-N-A though, when she goes to the vet, as calling her directly after a fish is a little cruel.'

Given the serious demeanour Kenneth had portrayed in his surgery yesterday, Flora was surprised to see this lighter side of him. She somehow sensed it was out of the ordinary for him and it gave her a small lift to think he felt comfortable enough to share this part of himself.

'Would you like to come and meet her?'

'I'm sorry?'

She looked at him to see he was as shocked by the

invitation he'd just blurted out as she was to hear it.

'Urm, would you like to come and meet her?'

Flora looked about her, then, realising she'd had enough solitude for one day, quickly accepted.
'Thank you, I'd like that. I'll just put the crockery inside and then I'll be with you.'

TWENTY-SEVEN

Kenneth cast a quick sideways glance at Flora as she fastened her seatbelt. What *was* it about this woman that turned him inside out? For a man who kept his emotions tightly battened down, she managed to unleash them and send them scattering with absolutely no effort. So far, he'd been angry with her, tried to appease her only to lose his temper again, and now he found himself craving her approval. What on earth was going on?

'How did you manage to find me?'

'What do you mean?'

He was driving slowly along the winding track back towards the main road and it wasn't a good moment to take his eyes off the dense foliage in front of him.

'My uncle gave me specific instructions on locating the track to my cottage while informing me that very few people knew of it.'

'My mum told me, and she's the other reason I came to see you. She's invited you to join us for Sunday dinner tomorrow.'

'She has? Why?'

'Because she'd like to meet you.'

His comment was met with silence and as the car emerged from the trees, he looked over to see her brow furrowed with a frown.

'What's the matter?'

'I'm just confused as to why a woman I've never met or spoken with would just invite me to lunch.'

'I wondered the same until she told me she'd been friends with your mum.'

'She what?'

Flora's head whipped round to look at him, her wide silver eyes making him think of shining moons in clear, dark skies.

'She told me she used to hang out with your mum in the summer holidays when she'd visit each year. In between times, they'd write to each other. Mum knew the way to your cottage because she often played there as a kid.'

'I... I see.'

'Look, I don't know any more than that but if you have questions, and I'm sure you probably have many, Mum said she'd be more than happy to try and answer them plus share with you her own memories of those times.'

'I'd... I'd like that very much. Please tell your mum I accept and thank her for the invite.'

'You can tell herself tomorrow. I do need to let her know if you have any special dietary requirements though.'

'No, no, I don't.'

There was silence for a few minutes until Kenneth pointed out the narrow road that led up to the farmhouse.

'I'm guessing it was the proximity of our farm to your grandmother's cottage that lent itself to them becoming friends. Once out of the towns, "close neighbours" can often be several miles apart.'

'Was it your mother's instruction to come and see me that made you apologise?'

'Not as such. I knew I'd been rude and intended to apologise in a reply to your email but my mum was having none of it. She extended the lunch invite then told me how to find you, insisting I apologise in person.'

'And for that, you made a special trip out to see me?'

While slowing the car down to make the turn onto the cabin road, he gave her a quick smile.

'Sort of yes and sort of no.'

'What kind of answer is that?'

'I required time to pluck up the courage to see you again – apologising for bad behaviour is never comfortable and... I was putting it off for as long as I could – so I took myself out on some recce trips.'

'Recce trips?'

'Yes. Oh dear, this is going to make me appear very, very sad...'

'I like the sound of that, keep going.'

'I've spent the morning driving along different routes and timing them.'

'You've done what?'

'You heard.'

'Why would you do that? Apart from being very sad, obviously.'

Her smile as she replied made him smile in return.

'Well, in my capacity for being a truly sad, grumpy, bad-tempered git—'

'Look, stop bigging yourself up here – just tell me why you're timing your driving.'

'—I want to know how long it would take to reach different locations from my home and from the surgery so that, when we get emergency callouts, we can advise the patient on approximately how long it'll take me to reach them. I'd rather tell a worried patient I'll be with them in roughly twenty minutes than just say I'm on my way. Providing a specific time gives them something to focus on when they're panicking.'

'Can't you get that information from online sites?'

'I could but they won't tell me which roads have the potential to flood in the winter or are too steep to use when covered with snow. There are many small, one-track roads which could shorten a journey by ten minutes or increase it by an hour if the conditions are bad. It's far better to learn the local terrain by driving around it than gazing at it from some far-flung satellite.'

'Any other reasons?'

'I'm not sure I know what you mean.'

'How about reconnecting with your homeland? Becoming one again with the land that raised you?'

Her softly spoken comment shot straight through to the heart of him. She was right – he had been doing that. Yes, he stood by the reason he'd stated – he wanted to be as prepared as he could for helping his patients – but his whole being had swelled with joy at the sight of each fresh glorious view while his lungs filled to bursting point with the clean pure air surging through the open windows. He'd been almost giddy with happiness as the car had splashed through small rivers and raced up steep hills with sharp turns that took him through miles of heather-covered land, past fast-flowing waterfalls and looking down over lochs as black as slate. While he may never have wanted to be a farmer, he was deeply rooted in this part of the world he called home and being back here was the best gift he could have given himself.

He pulled up in front of his cabin, switched off the engine and turned to look at her.

'You're very astute. How did you know?'

'An educated guess, if I'm being truthful. While my ancestors grew up and lived here, I didn't but I can already feel the change in me and I've only been here a couple of days. At the core of me, a love is growing along with a pride for this country. If I'm feeling that after barely forty-eight hours, it doesn't take much to guess what it must be like for someone who was born and bred here.'

The silvery eyes crinkled at the corners as her smile spread across her face and Kenneth suddenly wondered what it would be like to spend the rest of his life with this intriguing woman. The randomness of the thought surprised him so much, he took a sharp gulp of air that hit the back of his throat in such a way he found himself suddenly coughing hard with tears streaming down his face.

'S-o-r-r-y…' he croaked, scrabbling around for a tissue and a bottle of water. He'd just found the former in the side pocket of the door when the latter came into blurry view in front of him. 'T-h-a-n-k—' he managed before going into a paroxysm of coughing again.

Finally, after several minutes, he was able to speak normally although still with the need to give a small cough to clear his throat.

'Sorry,' he said again. 'It was one of those moments when the air just hits the back of your throat… do you know what I mean?'

'Oh yes! Been there more than once. In fact, one time, it happened when I was on a date with a bloke I *really* fancied. I was nervous, took a huge glug of red wine along with a vast intake of breath and the resulting coughing fit saw him drenched and his crisp white shirt turned a less becoming shade of pink.'

'Oh no, how embarrassing. What happened next?'

'Let's just say the date was cut rather short as he went home to change and I never heard from him again. I apologised profusely, even offered to buy him another shirt but he muttered something about having bought it from some designer in Milan and that it was irreplaceable.'

'What a twat!'

The sound of Flora's laughter filled the car and, unable to help himself, Kenneth found himself joining in with her. It was another couple of minutes before they pulled themselves together to make their way into the cabin, and when Choona came running towards them, without hesitation, Flora scooped her up into her arms and began cuddling and snuggling her. As he looked on at the two happy ladies, his earlier thought popped up again – what *would* it be like to spend the rest of his life with this woman?

TWENTY-EIGHT

'Oh, my goodness, look at you! Just look at you!'

Flora found herself swept up in a hug that threatened the good health of her ribs as Kenenth's mother held her tightly in her arms. After several seconds of being unable to breathe, she was released when the woman took a step back to stare into her face.

'Oh my, I can't believe it. You're the spit of her, you really are. I... I... Seeing you makes it hard to believe she's really gone.'

'Mum, put Flora down before she jumps back in the car to escape from the mad woman in the kitchen.'

'Oh, I'm sorry, Flora, I didn't mean to... well... you're your mother's double. I wasn't expecting that – it gave me quite the shock.'

'No problem, Mrs MacKenzie, I understand. I know I look like her – I grew up hearing it. I'm only sorry it's upset you.'

'Ah, Flora, what a lovely girl you are. Your mother would be so proud of you. And, please, call me Mhairi. Mrs MacKenzie makes me feel old.'

Flora let out a little chuckle, mostly of relief, that the woman in front of her wasn't about to pass out. Mhairi… It was a nice name although not one she'd heard before. She mentally said it in her head – it sounded like "marry" but with a very soft "h"… M-harry.

'Flora,' Kenneth gently touched her elbow, 'this is my father, Douglas, my brother, Fraser, and his wife, Shona.'

The two men each shook her hand firmly but Shona, following her mother-in-law's example, leant in for a hug which fortunately wasn't quite as rib-cracking as Mhairi's had been.

'It's a pleasure to meet you, Flora.'

'No offspring today either, Shona?'

'I'm afraid not, Kenneth. They're at that awkward teenage stage now when hanging out with the olds is considered lame.' Shona turned back to Flora with a smile. 'I confess I miss the time when they came with me wherever I went, although I'm rather enjoying the freedom of them being old enough to feed and water themselves. Which means,' she gave a cheeky wink, 'I'm all yours anytime you fancy popping into town for a natter over a glass of wine.'

'Now that, Shona, is an offer I can't refuse.'

'Then we must exchange numbers before you leave.'

'Well, that's going to be sooner rather than later if we don't get this roast served up – unless you're all partial to eating shoe leather.'

Everyone sprang into action to assist Mhairi with getting the meal on the long, kitchen table. While they did, Kenneth led Flora to a chair.

'I'm afraid everyone will want to talk to you,' he whispered quietly in her ear, 'which is why I've put you here in the middle. I'll be beside you, so if it feels like it's getting too much or too intense, just tap my leg or nudge me with your foot, and I'll try to push them back.'

'Why would they be so interested in me?'

'You're The Flora, that makes you a celebrity around here. And you know how people behave around celebrities...'

Before she could answer, Mhairi clapped her hands together as everyone, chattering noisily, brought food to the table then took their seats – Douglas and Mhairi at either end with Fraser and Shona opposite her and Kenneth.

'This all looks quite delicious, Mhairi, thank you.'

And she meant it. The bowls of carrots, peas, and Brussel sprouts gleamed under the overhead light as the Ben Nevis sized lump of creamy, yellow, butter melted across them. An equally, cardiac-arrest-inducing buttery dollop, was creating little golden rivers through the mashed potato while the steam rising from the roasties carried their glorious aroma around the room. Yet another bowl was overflowing with perfectly risen Yorkshire puddings and even though it was a golden, crispy-skinned, duck sitting in front of Douglas, waiting to be carved, Flora totally approved of their presence on the table. She loved her Yorkie puddings and would eat them with anything.

'You are very welcome, Flora. Thank you for joining us.'

Once the plates of meat had been passed down and everyone had dived into the veggies and spuds, there was an appreciative silence while they ate which was only broken briefly when Fraser got up to refill the gravy boats.

It was as Fraser and Kenneth were gathering up the dirty crockery and bringing over pudding bowls and spoons that Douglas, whom Flora had already noticed was a man of few words, turned to her to ask, 'So, Flora, will you be staying and taking up your rightful place?'

'Erm... I'm... not decided yet. This is all... erm... everything is quite different.'

'But all the farmers rely on The Flora. You have no idea how valuable you are to us and our livelihoods. We need you.'

'Well, you see, I'm not—'

'Douglas, leave the girl be for now. She needs time to find her feet, to see if this is her calling.'

'But, Mhairi…'

'I know, my darling, I know, but we've all been rather spoilt over the years. Other farmers around the country manage without a Flora and survive – maybe we all need to learn to do the same.'

'Thank you, Mhairi.' She looked up the table to the big man sitting there, 'I'm only just finding out about the position The Flora holds in the community and if I'm being honest, it's rather daunting. Right now, I'm not making any decisions about anything and I won't be rushed into doing so either. I've no fixed date for returning to Oxford – I'm just taking each day as it comes.' She smiled at him as she spoke and was rewarded with a smile and a nod of the head in return.

'Right then, folks, get this syrup pudding down you and, when you're finished, Flora, I have something I think you might like to see.'

With her stomach fit to burst, full of delicious sponge and custard, Flora followed Mhairi along a corridor and into a snug at the end of it. Judging by the soft décor and the sewing materials in the far corner, she guessed this must be Mhairi's own little private domain.

'Did you enjoy your pudding, Flora?'

'Oh, yes, it was lush. It's my favourite.'

'It was your mother's too. She adored anything with custard but syrup pudding was always her first choice. I took a punt on it being yours too.'

'May I ask – how did you know my mum?'

'I lived on this farm as a child – my father was one of the farmhands. While it's not the most remote farm in the area, there weren't many kids my age around. My mother had to take something to The Flora one day during the school holidays and I went with her. It was while your mum and uncle were visiting and being two girls of nearly the same age, we gravitated towards each other. It took only a few hours for us to realise we had quite a lot in common and we spent almost every day of the holidays together after that. We'd become best friends by the time your mum went home and that friendship remained strong all through the years, even after they stopped visiting. Your mum and I wrote to each other regularly and that's what I want to show you – some of the letters she sent.'

Mhairi had picked up a wooden box, passing it across as she spoke. Flora looked down at the solid wood casket she now held in her hands. The top had a simple but quaint design in what she recognised as pokerwork. A little hook swivelled up and down to hold the lid closed.

'You… you don't mind me reading them?'

'Not at all. I thought they might give you some insight into the kind of person your mum was when she was young and how she changed as she grew up. You see, while your dad has probably shared what he knew of her from when they met, and your uncle has most likely told stories of how it was when they were kids together, those memories will be different from mine because women don't share the same things with boys or men that they do with each other. I think you'll find another side to her within these letters. Now, I don't expect you to read them all this afternoon but you're welcome to sit here for a bit to look through a few. You can come back any time, to read the rest.'

'This is so kind and thoughtful of you, Mhairi. It means

a lot to me.'

'You just sit yourself down while I go and get you a coffee. Or, tea, if you prefer.'

'No, coffee, white, no sugar, would be lovely. Thank you again.'

Flora lowered herself into the seat Mhairi had pointed to, placing the box on the coffee table in front of her. She hesitated for a few seconds before carefully turning the hook and folding back the lid.

Inside, the box was crammed full of letters. She would've struggled to get a paperclip between them, so tightly were they wedged in. Carefully, she removed a number of letters, noticing that some of the envelopes were plain white while others were all shades of pinks and blues. She glanced at the dates on the postmarks and saw they weren't arranged in any kind of order so, picking one at random, she took the folded pages from within, opened them up and began to read. Her mum would have been twenty-seven when she wrote it, judging by the date...

My Dearest Mhairi,

Well, it has finally happened! You always said it would one day but I didn't believe you. It would seem you were right, and I was wrong. So, there you go!

What were you so right about, I hear you wonder? I shall keep you in suspense no more – I have met Mr Right! Mr Wonderful! Mr -Pretty-Damn-Amazing! No, they're not three separate blokes, it's one bloke who is all of the above and more.

We met as I was leading a protest on better access rights for disabled people around the university and there was an instant click. I asked him to sign my petition, he asked me out for dinner. We've barely been apart since. His name is Matt, he's very lovely to look at – not "Brad

Pitt" gorgeous but who wants that anyway – and, far more importantly, he's extremely kind. I should also tell you he's seven years younger than me – YES! I have a toy-boy. Or a boy-toy! Hee hee! – but he's mature for his age. Or am I simply immature for mine? Ha! Ha! Whichever it is, we work well together and I can't recall the last time I was this happy. I really hope you are happy for me too. I'll try to sort out a visit so you can meet him but you know how it is with Dad – his health continues to cause us concerns and it doesn't feel fair to leave Gerald to look after him alone while I go off on a jolly with my new amour. Maybe Douglas will be able to manage your boys for a few days and YOU can have a break. After all, when was the last time you left the farm that didn't include a trip to the supermarket or cattle fair?

Thank you so much for your last letter – the boys sound like quite the handful. Kenneth seems very serious for one so young although it sounds like Fraser makes up for him – your story about the puddle did make me laugh.

Anyway, I must go. I can hear Dad trying to move down the hallway. Gerald is currently at work so I need to help him.

Sorry if this letter seems to be all "me, me, me" but you will only be narked if I didn't tell you my news soon as. I promise to be better in my next letter.

With lots of love and joy to you,

Flora.
xxxxxx

Flora sat with the letter in her hand and tears in her eyes. The flowing, curvy, writing on the paper suggested that her mother had been an open, confident woman and her words oozed with happiness. She already knew how her parents had met as her dad had told her many times but it was lovely to read that her mum had been as enamoured with him as he'd been with her. She now felt she'd heard both sides of the story. With a smile on her face, she picked up another envelope and withdrew the letter from within but the smile rapidly disappeared when she saw the date – it had been written just one week before her mother died.

Dear Mhairi,

Great news! I'm finally coming up to see my mum next week – do you think you could manage to squeeze in a visit from me while I'm there? Haha!

As you know, she's been nagging me for ages to come up but I just couldn't leave Flora with Matt as she was too young and he was so busy. Also, can you imagine trying to do a ten-hour journey on your own with a toddler? No! Funny, neither can I! Ha! Ha! However, now that Flora's a little older, Matt feels more comfortable about looking after her on his own and I feel more confident that he'll do a great job in my absence.

I know I've put off my mum's requests for many years but now I'm a mother myself, I have a better understanding of what it must be like to not see your children each day. I'm already dreading leaving Flora behind and it's only going to be for a few days. Mum says she has much to tell me – I hope it includes why she felt she had to return to Scotland while leaving Gerald and myself behind. I could never leave Flora indefinitely; she is my life.

I also have a secret to share with you. I haven't even told Matt yet.

I'M PREGNANT!

Yee-haa! I'm only ten weeks so still have two weeks to go until I hit the "safe zone" but I feel fantastic. I do know, however, that if I were to tell Matt, he'd do everything possible to prevent me driving up. He wouldn't understand I have to do it now because it won't be long until I'm the size of a small house and driving all that way won't be an option. For a start off, there's not enough loos on the A9 for a big, fat, preggie lady – I'd need to tow my own Port-a-loo along behind me!

Anyway, this missive is short and sweet because I want to hear ALL your news in person. Unfortunately, the champagne we've always promised to crack open when we finally met again, face-to-face, is going to have to stay on ice for a while longer. I don't want to risk the Baby Bump getting drunk too early in its development, it'll take all the fun out of it when it becomes a teenager! Ha! Ha!

Right, got to go. Flora got a new tricycle last week and as the rain has just stopped, she'll be champing at the bit to go out on it. I do hope the rain has cleared by next week – any more and Matt will be receiving orders to build arks!

Big massive hugs for now, SO looking forward to seeing you again.

With much love,

Flora
xxxxx

TWENTY-NINE

Kenneth glanced over at Flora, observing her whiter-than-white pinched face and the hands clinging tightly to the seatbelt across her chest, even though he was only doing ten-miles-per-hour down the farm track.

She'd taken everyone by surprise when she'd come flying into the kitchen, tears streaming down her face and demanding he take her home immediately. His mum had gone to comfort her but Flora had grabbed her coat and handbag and rushed out the door before Mhairi had a chance to say anything.

'Stop the car!'

'What?'

'Stop the car, now! Stop!'

As he braked and put the Landy into neutral, Flora fumbled with the seatbelt, finally undoing it, opening the door, and rushing off to the side where she threw up on the grass verge. Kenneth hurried over to help her, grabbing the wet wipes he kept in the car, and gently rubbed her back as the Sunday lunch, so recently consumed, was evacuated. When she reached the point of dry-retching, he took out some of the wipes and handed them to her. While she cleaned her face, he went to the car, and returned with a bottle of water. She spat out a few mouthfuls before taking some tentative sips. Once certain they wouldn't come back up, she took a few more.

'Right, you're coming over to mine,' he said, as they returned to the car.

'No, I'm fine. I just want to go home.'

'I'm sure you do, Flora, but you're as white as the proverbial sheet, you've just yakked up your lunch on my mum's prize begonias—'

'No, tell me I didn't…' Flora's head whipped round to look.

'No, you didn't, I'm messing with you. However, I'm not taking you back to sit alone in this state and while you don't HAVE to give me an explanation as to why you've just run out of my parents' house like all the hounds of hell were after you, it would be nice to hear one.'

When she didn't argue but just gave the smallest of nods, he turned the car around and drove back up the farm track until he came to the fork that took him across the moor to the holiday cabins. By the time he parked in front of his door, a little bit of colour had come back into her cheeks and a tiny smile graced her lips when she saw Choona sitting on the windowsill.

'Hey, pretty girl,' she crooned, as soon as they crossed the threshold.

While Kenneth made his way towards the kitchen to boil the kettle, she wandered over to the kitten and gathered her in her arms. Choona didn't seem to mind as by the time Flora had walked back towards him, the furball was curled up happily against her chest, purring with contentment.

'You definitely have a way with her.'

'As I said yesterday, I've spent a lot of hours at my friend's cat rescue centre. Kitten cuddling was almost mandatory so I've had plenty of practice.' There was another glimmer of a smile as her chin nuzzled against the top of Choona's head.

'I'm making you some peppermint tea to settle your stomach.'

'Thank you.'

'Would you like a bit of toast to go with it? You must be feeling quite empty and it'll ease any cramping you might still be having.'

'That... that would be nice, if it's not too much trouble.'

'No trouble at all.'

He popped a couple of slices of Mother's Pride into the toaster while watching as she wandered over to look out the window. She was holding the kitten so closely to her, he'd almost say she was clinging onto it for dear life.

'This really is the most amazing view. Now that the clouds of yesterday have lifted, I can see my mountains properly, they look so different from up here. And the loch seems much smaller than when you're standing by the edge of it.'

'Your mountains?'

'Apparently so. The sides which face the loch are mine. The opposite sides still belong to the laird.'

'I see.'

'Mind you, the laird's son, Jack Arlingh, is keen to bring the whole of my land back into the family fold again.'

'Oh?'

'He didn't say anything in front of me, but I overheard part of his conversation before he knew I was in the cottage – I think he's considering some kind of luxury shooting facility or game hunting. I wouldn't like to say for certain though as I only heard a snippet and may have misinterpreted it.'

'Actually, I think you've probably got it right. Mum has

mentioned a few times that he seems to think he's another Donald Trump and is keen to develop the land into a high-end resort. The idea of turning the family home into an exclusive hotel hasn't been well received, either by the locals or his family, if the rumours are true. His father's a true gentleman and well liked but the son on the other hand...'

'I see. Well, that's good to know.'

'Do you think you would sell it to him?'

'Honestly? It's highly unlikely.'

'Does that mean you're thinking of staying?'

Kenneth was surprised by the feeling of hope that sprang up as he asked the question.

'I don't know. It's far too soon to say. But even if I don't stay permanently, I'd retain the cottage as a family holiday home.'

'Right.'

'Hey, don't be like that.'

'Like what?'

'Negative. You've just closed down in front of me.'

'Sorry. I... I suppose it's the thought of yet another holiday home up here. Communities are dying because of holiday homes.'

'But surely it's a better option than selling it back to the Arlinghs?'

'I suppose... Anyway, grab a seat and I'll bring your toast over. You might want to put Choona down otherwise she'll be helping you to eat it. I found out this morning she's partial to a bit of toast.'

'Oh, how so?'

'Because I stupidly left two slices on my plate while I went to retrieve my phone from the charger but when I returned, there was only one slice.'

'Oh dear. And where did you find the second slice?'

'I followed the sticky marmalade trail where it had been

dragged along the floor and found both toast and kitten under the sofa. Or rather, I should say, the *remains* of the toast. And this was after she'd been fed!'

The sound of Flora's laughter filled the air and he couldn't help but laugh with her.

'Ah, she's at that age, I'm afraid, where she's growing faster than you can fill her up. She's the cat equivalent of a teenager with hollow legs. Growth spurts right in front of your eyes.'

'So, it would seem,' he replied dryly.

He watched closely as Flora ate the toast. The distraction of the cat and her antics had worked and she seemed to be relaxing after her upset earlier although he was still none the wiser on what had caused it. Reluctant as he was to break her happier mood, anything that caused the reaction he'd witnessed could only be made better by being discussed.

'How are you feeling now?'

She looked down at the crusts on her plate.

'Better, thank you.' She hesitated before continuing. 'I suppose I need to explain...'

'Well, I've always thought of my mother as being a good cook, but...'

'Ha! Trust me, it was absolutely nothing to do with the food.'

'Then what?'

'When your mum took me into her snug, she gave me a box of letters, from my mum, to have a look through. She thought it would help me to see my mum from a different perspective. It was a lovely gesture and I'm very grateful to her for being so considerate.'

'Then... what happened to have you running out of the house as you did?'

'I read the last letter my mum sent to Mhairi. It was written the week before she drove up to see my grandmother. She shared a secret with your mum. She was pregnant. Ten weeks. Which means she was expecting a baby when she died. I didn't just lose my mum, I lost a sibling as well.'

'Oh, Flora.'

Tears began running down her face again and Kenneth quickly took her into his arms, holding her, rocking her gently as she sobbed.

'What I don't understand is why my dad never told me. It's bad enough he kept my grandmother a secret from me all these years but this… Surely, he'd have known about the pregnancy.'

'Post-mortems are nearly always performed on road traffic accidents to properly ascertain the cause of death, so he would have known.'

'Then why didn't he tell me? Why keep it a secret?'

'Did he keep it a secret, though? Maybe it was just too difficult to speak about. And what benefit would it have been to you? Do you feel better now for knowing?'

He paused, waiting for her to reply. It was not a rhetorical question – it was one she needed to think about and answer.

'No, I don't suppose I do. Although that might still be the shock of finding out.'

'Maybe it is. Look, I don't want to sound like I'm taking sides here but I think I understand why your dad didn't tell you – it was to protect you. He didn't know your mum had already told mine and he certainly couldn't have known you would ever find out about it. Ten weeks… women rarely share the good news until after the twelve-week scan.'

'Hmm, perhaps. I just feel… I no longer trust him. Not after what he did with my grandmother.'

'Yeah, you said that already. What's the story there?'

By the time Flora finished telling him, Kenneth was the

one now shocked to his core.

'He never said a word or shared *at all* that your grandmother was trying to communicate with you?'

'Nope! Not a peep!'

'Wow! That's… that's… that's left me rather at a loss for words.'

'Try and guess how I feel. First, I had all that to deal with and now this. Just as I think I'm finding my feet, another punch comes out of nowhere and I'm right back down again.'

'I'm sorry.'

'For what? It's not your fault.'

'I know, but your life has been completely turned upside down and there was me giving you grief over not being able to decide if you want to stay up here for good. With everything else you've got going on right now, that's the last kind of pressure you need.'

'Don't worry about it, Kenneth, it's fine. I'll get there.'

She placed her hand on his, giving it a gentle squeeze. He returned the pressure and, for a time, they just sat, looking out of the window until darkness fell and the soothing view could no longer be seen.

THIRTY

A tiny smile forced its way onto Flora's face as she sat at her kitchen table, eating her delicious door-step slice of toast – she'd been surprised to learn that MacAndrew baked a fresh loaf every morning – and marmalade, while thinking about Choona and her grilled bread thievery. The kitten was a cutie, there was no doubt about that and already had Kenneth wrapped around her little fluffy paws.

A gentle pressure against her legs had her looking down to see both dogs pressing against her, looking up as if to remind her that they were rather cute too.

'Hey, I know you guys are truly lovely. You need to bear with me while I get used to having you around. I know more about cats than I do about dogs, just give me time.'

She was stroking their heads when MacAndrew appeared. He stopped in the doorway to the scullery, took one look at her puffy face with red swollen eyes, turned on his heel and returned a moment later carrying a lilac ring-binder in his hands which he laid on the table and pushed across to her.

'What's this?'

'I was going to show you the stillroom today, where we make the various lotions and potions, but I don't think your head is in the right place for it so I'm giving you homework instead.'

'Homework?'

'Yes, homework. I've put together a file of things you need to be knowledgeable on, including the heather, and you must learn it. It won't be long until the next cutting season – it's imperative you know more than you currently do.'

'I don't know anything.'

'Exactly! It's time you did. The Flora has worked with the heather for centuries and until you decide what you're doing with yourself, you might as well continue the tradition.'

'Right,' she replied faintly. 'Cutting season?'

'We cut on the Solstice and the Equinox. The Summer Solstice is approaching and you need to be up to some sort of speed by then.'

'Why? Why do we cut then?'

'Because that's when the properties of the heather are at their peak. We cut from sundown till sunup.'

'Let me guess – different properties within the heather peak at those times?'

'Now you're getting it. Well deduced. Also, there are different varieties of heather, which flower in different months and each one brings its own unique properties to the table.'

She picked up the binder, opened it and quickly looked at the tabs along the side, trying not to look too impressed at MacAndrew's efficiency.

Skills & Abilities
The Role of The Flora
Heather – The Basics

Some of the tabs contained more sheets of paper than the others.

'I would suggest you make the most of the sunshine this morning and read through this while sitting on the patio. Allow your elements to soothe your turmoil.'

'Thank you, MacAndrew, for your kindness and understanding.'

The little man came to stand beside her chair. She turned to face him and with her being seated, their eyes were level.

'Flora, I understand your world has been tipped upside-down in the last few weeks and you are learning things about yourself that would, honestly, leave a great many people doubting their sanity. I think you're coping really well and I believe you'd make an excellent Flora if you choose to accept your role here. Now, get yourself outside. I'll bring you a fresh pot of coffee along with some miniature pastries I've baked.'

'You've baked pastries?'

'Bread is not my only speciality,' he winked. 'They were one of your grandmother's favourites so I hope you like them too.'

'I'm sure I will. Thank you.'

'It's no problem. Now, go on, shoo!'

Resisting the urge to give MacAndrew a hug – she sensed he probably wouldn't appreciate it – Flora picked up the binder and calling the dogs to join her, stepped out onto the slowly warming patio.

Sandy and Kirsty shuffled along the grey slate tiles, following the movement of the sun and in doing so, broke

Flora's concentration. She sat back in her chair, mulling over what she'd been reading. She was especially interested in the skills and abilities she apparently possessed and had been somewhat bemused by the manner in which MacAndrew had laid them out. They reminded her of her old school reports.

Elemental – *100%. Has the ability to communicate with the three elements of air, earth, and water but no desire to control them.*

Healing – *90%. Strong skills in this area although much practice will be required to obtain the level of previous Floras.*

Potions – *80%. As with healing, good skills that will improve with experience.*

Enchantments & Spells – *50%. Powers are sufficient for small day-to-day tasks and for minor behavioural control in others.*

Shapeshifting – *25%. This ability can only be obtained under great stress, pressure, or upset. Not strong enough to be activated as and when desired.*

All of the above, at the time of writing, are still in the infancy stage but growing stronger each day. To obtain full percentage of powers, however, will require the acceptance of the position of The Flora, donning the Necklace of Knowledge, and absorbing the wisdom it contains.

Flora stared at the last paragraph for some time after reading it. While having these various powers would be quite awesome, she was in no doubt they also carried a wealth of responsibility and when she flicked through to the next tab, she felt more than a little daunted by what the local community seemed to expect of her. Advising them of the various weather conditions that would enable good seed sowing, crop harvests, and lambing safety were the ones which jumped out although the prospect of having to administer midwifery duties if requested to attend either a childbirth or an animal birth, had sent chills of fear down her spine. What on earth could she possibly know about either of those that would be of any use to anyone? In return, the community would provide for her in whatever way she required. If maintenance work was needed upon the cottage, she only had to let it be known and someone would come along and do it while gifts of sustenance were left daily up at the large stone in the layby. Monetary payments were never expected or requested although could be accepted if made voluntarily but *only* if the giver could genuinely afford to give it.

Despite trying to move onto the tabs regarding heather and its uses, she found herself reading and re-reading the first chapters and each time, the words seemed to weigh more and more heavily upon her. It was a blessed relief when the movement of the dogs broke into her thoughts, dragging her eyes away from the pages of mounting obligation and over towards the loch. MacAndrew had said sitting out here would ease her turmoil – who was he kidding? After reading this, she felt even more disturbed than she had before she sat down. Pushing the folder away and her chair back, she stood, walked down to the little sandy shore of the loch, and watched the waves as they gently rolled in and out before calling the dogs to her and turning on her heel towards the path that ran along the side of the water. Maybe a good walk, and some exercise, would help to stop the chaotic thoughts that were tumbling around in her head.

THIRTY-ONE

It took almost forty minutes for Flora to reach the opposite side of the loch. The path she was on came to an end at the foot of a rock outcrop. To carry on walking round the loch, she would need to retrace her steps and take the path that had veered off in an upwards direction approximately ten minutes before. Not feeling inclined towards climbing mountains at this time, she chose instead to clamber up the rocks in front of her, leaving the dogs to sniff around in the gorse and heather below. Soon, she was standing on a wide, flat, plateau that hung over the loch. She walked to the edge, looked down and gave a little squeak of joy when she saw how clear the water was beneath her. She could see all the way down to the loch bed. She lay on her stomach to watch the activities of the fish darting about in between the rocks and stones submerged deep below the surface. After being mesmerised for a short time, she looked across the water to the cottage on the other side. Seeing it from this angle changed her perspective on what she now owned. Her uncle had said this was the best spot to view her land. The whole of the loch belonged to her along with the sides of all the mountains that faced it. The mountains surrounded the water in a loose U-shape and where they gave way to forest and undergrowth, all the trees on either side of the cottage, up to the roadside, fell under her domain. It hadn't looked much when standing on the doorstep of the cottage but from here, it was more than a little overwhelming. Mind you, when she stopped to think about it, she owned less land than Sally and when she went walking through Sally's fields, taking photographs for the B&B website, it didn't seem a lot. Maybe it just felt different because that land was Sally's and this was hers.

She turned away from the stone edge and went to sit at the base of the rockface it was nestled against. The unbidden, and unwanted, thoughts she'd managed to push away, crept back into her head when it occurred to her that she was sitting right in the middle of all her elements, so maybe this was a good time to try channelling her Elemental gift although exactly how she was supposed to do it was anyone's guess. Maybe it was a visualisation thing...

Flora closed her eyes and turned on her "inner eye", trying to visualise herself talking to the wind and the air.

Five minutes later, she let out a deep sigh and a groan. Nothing!

After a few deep breaths, she tried again.

Still nothing.

She'd just closed her eyes for the third time when a voice came out of nowhere, saying, 'You're trying too hard. You need to relax.'

Her eyes quickly opened and there, sitting on the edge of the rock, was a man. A very handsome man. A man so handsome, he was making her breathless. A man who was also half-naked, displaying a chest so fine and muscular, it took all her self-control not to go over and run her hands across it.

'I'm… I'm… I'm sorry, what?'

'I said, you're trying too hard. You need to relax. Let the elements come to you. They need to find you first, to make the connection.'

'Right. I… err… I see. How did you know what I was doing? And, more to the point, where did you come from?'

'I knew what you were doing because you're the new Flora and I sensed you're trying to get to grips with your powers. And, to answer your second question, I came from the loch,' he replied with a smile that reached all the way up to the largest, darkest brown eyes she'd ever seen on another human being. He gave a small shake of his head, sending droplets of water flying from his slicked back hair that looked to be a dark brownish-grey but it was difficult to be sure with it being wet.

'You came from the loch? Were you swimming in it? Isn't it too cold for that? Or are you one of those mad people who likes to go wild swimming? If you are, shouldn't you have someone with you? It's dangerous to go out alone in case you get cramp or something.'

Flora knew she was babbling like a five-year-old with a sugar rush but this was due to realising her new, wet, and shimmering in the sunshine, companion was not half-naked as she'd first thought. No, he was FULLY naked and she was struggling to keep her eyes north of his waistline.

'That is a lot of questions so I'll give you the short, easy, answer. I'm a selkie and I live in the water. I live in the loch.'

'You're a what?'

'A selkie.'

'Which is…'

'A type of seal, who can change into human form.'

'O-K-A-Y.'

She stared hard at him to see if he was kidding her in some way, but his face was completely serious, the easy smile of a few minutes before having disappeared. If he hadn't known of her gifts, and what she was trying to do, she'd have been convinced he was a local lad out to wind her up. But the knowledge he'd shared told her this was not the case.

'Do you have your mobile phone with you? If so, look it up. I'll wait.'

He turned away to look back out across the loch while she fumbled in her pocket for her phone, praying there would be a signal.

A few minutes later, after staring intently at the screen, she let out a large breath and looked up to find him still sitting on the rock edge but twisted round so he could watch her.

'Wow! Urm... I'm not quite sure what to say.'

'Well, I'll start. Hi, I'm Walter, I'm a selkie and I live, with the rest of my bob, in your loch.'

'Bob?'

'Yes, herd... colony...'

'Walter? Seriously?'

'It's my land name. Your grandmother used to call me her water-boy. That became Walter and it kind of stuck. The human voice can't say my selkie name and I wouldn't embarrass you by asking you to try.'

'Thank you... I think.'

'You're welcome. Now it's your turn.'

'My turn?'

'To introduce yourself. It's the polite thing to do.'

'Very well. Even though you already know, I'm Flora, I'm human, maybe a sort of a witch – allegedly – and I live in the cottage over there on the side of the loch.'

Her reply made him smile again and the effect it had on her breathing and heartbeat made her glad she was still sitting down.

'It's a pleasure to meet you, Flora.'

'And you, Walter.'

'So, you're trying to—'

'Sorry, forgive me if I'm being rude, but how are there selkies in my loch? It says here,' she lifted her phone, 'they come from the sea?'

'We can travel, just like humans, although my side of the family have been freshwater for a long time. My uncle fell in love and married a Flora over two-hundred years ago. As it wasn't possible for her to move location to be with him – you do know you're tied to this land, don't you?'

Flora nodded.

'Then he moved here to be with her. His bob, or family if you prefer, wanted to come along too and we've been here ever since.'

'So, we're related?'

'In a long and distant way, yes we are.'

'But… you said your uncle? Followed by "over two-hundred years ago" – how is that possible?'

'Selkies have much longer lifespans than humans. I'm three hundred and twenty-four years old.'

'*How old?*'

'I'm what you humans call a teenager. We can easily see our eight-hundredth birthday.'

'Wow!'

She thought for a moment, her mind going back to what she'd read that morning about her various abilities.

'Apparently I have a mild ability to shape-shift – is that your uncle's input into my gene pool?'

'Yeah, probably.'

'But he didn't pass on the long-life thing though. Kept that one to himself.'

She grinned at Walter to ensure he knew she was speaking in jest.

'Oh no, that got passed on too.'

'It couldn't have. My grandmother was in her seventies when she died. That's normal for us human folks.'

'You need to speak with MacAndrew regarding that. It's his place to educate you on your magical stuff.'

'Oh. Okay.'

Her disappointment at not learning more must have shown because Walter quickly replied, 'I can, however, help you to communicate with the spirits of the Air. They're called sylphs, by the way. I'm guessing that's what you were trying to do earlier. When your face was all scrunched up like a walnut.'

'Oh, gee, thanks for that vivid description,' Flora laughed. 'Now I really feel stupid!'

'Don't be daft. It's not your fault you don't know how to call them.'

'Call them?'

'Yes, they don't just hang around in the hope you might wander along for a conversation. You need to call them.'

'But, you—'

'I've been waiting for you. Your grandmother asked me to help you with this – she said it wasn't fair to expect MacAndrew to do everything. Besides, I'm one of your elements, which he's not, so this will be easier for me.'

'Oaky, what do I do?'

In her excitement, she moved forward on the rock until she was kneeling in the middle of it.

'Ah, see, your natural instincts are already kicking in.'

'They are?'

'Yes. The rock face would've blocked your call. Now it's free to be carried far and wide. Right, please raise your arms in the air, straight up above your head, keep your fingers straight and your palms facing each other.'

Flora carefully followed his instructions.

'Next, you make a figure of eight in the air. Only a small one – the bigger the figure, the louder you are "shouting" – that should only be kept for emergencies.'

It took a couple of attempts to get her arms moving in sync with each other and a couple more to find the rhythm of her movements but soon she was swaying gently from side to side as her arms flowed above her.

'How long do I need to do this for?'

'Oh, you'll know when to stop…' was Walter's cryptic reply.

Another minute or so passed and just as she was beginning to feel an ache in her shoulders, everything around her went still. She glanced at Walter and saw him incline his head ever so slightly. This was it. She had done it.

Suddenly, there was a faint, tickling, sensation by her right ear which felt exactly like Sally's kittens when they crawled on her shoulders and snuffled against her cheeks.

'Hello, Flora, welcome. I am Ahana.'

'Err, hello, Ahana. Thank you for answering my call.' Flora knew instinctively these were the right words to say.

'I'm happy to meet you. I look forward to speaking with you many times but now, you need to return to your cottage. Go! Go now!'

There was a swooshing sensation as though Ahana had rushed around her and then the stillness was gone. She could once again hear the gentle whisper of the water below and the birds calling in the sky.

'Oh, my goodness… I did it. I spoke with the air spirits.'

'Sylphs.'

'A sylph. Yes, a sylph.'

'Who was it?'

'Ahana?'

'Ah, yes, she's one of the younger ones and is very sweet. I'm glad she was your first.'

'Really? Why?'

'Her older sisters, Nasima and Bonaria, have a reputation for being, shall we say, more forthright? Which can sometimes come across the wrong way if you don't know them.'

'I see. Well, she told me I had to return to the cottage right now.'

'Then you had better do as she says.'

Flora was putting her phone back in her pocket when she said, 'So, I've connected with Air and with Water,' she gave Walter a smile, 'I only have Earth to complete the set.'

'That'll be the wood nymphs, although – I think I'm saying this human thing correctly – I wouldn't hold your breath on that happening any time soon.'

'What do you mean?'

'Wood nymphs are incredibly shy. They take their time in getting to know someone. Also, you haven't... you know...'

'What?'

'You know... the power... the knowledge...'

'Oh! You're referring to the acceptance of my situation.'

'Yes.'

'How do you know I haven't?'

'I would be able to feel it. It gives off little pulses and I can't sense them.'

'It does?'

'Yes. But there was another, more obvious, sign that you haven't.'

She raised a questioning eyebrow.

He grinned as he turned to slip back into the water. 'You didn't know how to summon the sylphs.'

Well, he'd got her there. Flora returned his grin.

'Walter.'

He paused at the rock edge to look back at her.

'Thank you so much for helping me today. I really appreciate it.'

'No problem at all. I'm happy to help.'

'Err, is there a way of contacting you?'

She felt a bit shy for asking but knew she was going to need more help in learning to be a magical being.

'Do exactly as you did today but with your hands in the water. I'll feel you calling.'

'Thank you.'

With a small salute, he slipped down into the water and when she moved to look into the loch, a small white wake on the surface was the only indication he'd been there.

Heavy grey clouds began making their way across the sky as she jumped down to the path and called on the dogs. She jogged back the way she'd come and had only just closed the cottage door when the heavens opened.

'Thank you, Ahana,' she whispered, hoping the young sylph could hear her.

THIRTY-TWO

'Hmm, this does sound unusual, Mrs Gray.'

Kenneth was doing all he could to keep a straight face as he listened to the septuagenarian lady in front of him describing her peri-menopausal symptoms to him. A glance at her notes told him she'd gone through the menopause in her early fifties although some additional speed reading told him she'd suffered badly through it. His humour quickly dissolved.

'Mrs Gray, your notes state you've already gone through the menopause so what you're experiencing is post-menopausal symptoms.'

'Oh, when I looked it up on that Shoogle thingy, I'm sure it said peri-menopausal.'

'It probably did because they share many of the symptoms. It's an easy error to make. Now, I see you previously declined HRT but I'm wondering how you'd feel about it now? They've made great advances over the last decade or so and some of the previous concerns people had about it, namely breast cancer, have proven to be false.'

'Would it be safe for me at my age?'

'It's safe although, like everything, it does carry a few risks but from what I can see of your health history, I believe you'd be alright with it. I can prescribe a very low dose transdermal oestradiol which you take in either patch, gel or spray form and is absorbed through your skin. You can choose whichever suits you best and I'll monitor you to ensure we get it right. Here are some leaflets to read for more information. Think about it and if you decide you want to go ahead, come back, we'll do some blood tests and take it from there.'

'Oh, thank you so much, Doctor MacKenzie. I'll read these tonight.'

He watched the leaflets drop into the vast, tartan, shopping bag sitting on her lap before getting up to assist her to the door. When he returned to his desk, Kenneth updated the notes on Mrs Gray's file, managing – just about – to refrain from adding anything untoward over the lack of support given by her previous medics.

Once the file was saved, he leant back in his chair while letting out a long sigh. His morning had been filled with, mostly, non-important appointments. The wheezy cough that had clearly wheezed itself out long before being dragged into the surgery. The sprained ankle that had managed to walk just fine in a pair of three-inch heeled stilettoes. The breathlessness that had turned into girlish giggles each time his stethoscope had come within an inch of the chest.

He swivelled his chair around to look out the window. Rain was lashing against the pane and he'd had to put the light on for his last two patients. He smiled. Of all the things he'd missed about his homeland when he'd moved to London, the rain hadn't been one of them. He appreciated that the glorious Scottish verdancy he loved so dearly was very much down to the amount of rain the country got, but it was easy to forget that when the heavens opened for days at a time.

As his hands came up to rub his eyes, there was a light knock on the door.

'Come in.'

'It's only me, you can relax.' Jennet Cameron walked in holding a ring-binder in her hand, closing the door gently behind her. 'How was your first "official" morning?'

'Err… urm… it was good, thank you.'

When he'd last met Doctor Jennet Cameron, on the day of his interview, her blonde hair had been pulled back in a no-nonsense ponytail and her face makeup barely noticeable. It was, therefore, quite a shock to see her standing in front of him displaying a barely watered-down version of Paul O'Grady in his Lily Savage persona. Her hair was styled in a way he was sure Cherry had referred to as a "blow out" – all loose around her shoulders and face – and the previous minimal makeup had clearly taken a course in self-confidence because it was now out, loud, and proud. Finishing off the ensemble was a lightweight blouse with more than a few buttons undone and as far away from the polo-neck jumper she'd worn previously as it was possible to get. The overall effect, while not unpleasant, wasn't what he'd expected from the down-to-earth woman who'd interviewed him.

'Let me guess – mostly timewasters, just here to ogle the new doctor and size him up for a wedding suit?'

'Yes, there were a few of— Wait! What did you say?'

Jennet burst out laughing. 'Kenneth, single men over thirty are not in large supply around here. Any who look as you do are even rarer. I can assure you that half the women who walk in here today will be determined to get you down the aisle.'

'Oh! Right! Urm…'

He didn't often blush but this was too much and he could feel the heat growing in his cheeks.

'Don't worry, Doctor MacKenzie, we'll protect you if anyone begins to display stalkerish tendencies.' At this, Jennet let out her own version of a girlish giggle.

'Ah, okay. Great. Good to know…'

'Now, I've popped in to go through the rotas with you for the next few weeks. Obviously, we had to put them together in your absence but we're all very flexible and can change anything that doesn't suit. Are you okay to sort them out now?'

'Absolutely. No problem.'

She moved to the opposite side of his desk, placed the ring-binder she was holding on it and leant over to pluck a pen out of the holder. Kenneth, picking up his drink bottle, had just taken a slug of water when he almost choked as Jennet's breasts, encased in a white, lacy, low-cut bra, hit his line of sight.

THIRTY-THREE

Flora yawned as she stretched out in her bed. She turned to look out the window at the newly broken dawn while marvelling at having had yet another great sleep which she was attributing to the clean air and dark night sky – there was no light pollution out here in the middle of nowhere.

Her gaze moved towards the loch, although it was barely visible thanks to the heavy rain that had started on Monday and, four days later, didn't look like stopping any time soon judging by the heavy grey clouds sitting low on the mountains opposite. Was this normal?

Her thoughts returned to Walter and she was wondering what it was like to live permanently in the loch when her stomach let out an almighty grumble. This was another thing which had improved since her arrival last week – her appetite! MacAndrew was an excellent cook whose meals were good and hearty. It was impossible not to clear her plate every time. This morning, however, she suddenly had a desire for fresh croissants. It wasn't that she hadn't been enjoying the delicious fry-ups she'd been served the last few days, it was more she had a craving for something delightfully sweet and the thought of warm croissants, loaded with creamy butter and raspberry jam, was making her mouth water. Hmmm, the day was still very young – maybe she could pop into Beauly where there was a lovely looking bakery which she was keen to try.

With the idea now firmly lodged in her mind, she jumped out of bed and headed to the shower. Within fifteen minutes, she was ready to go but as she walked down the stairs, the glorious scent of fresh, warm, sweet pastry greeted her.

'What on earth?'

She jumped the last few steps, walked into the kitchen and there, on the table, sat a plate heaped high with fat, golden, croissants, fresh out of the oven if the steam rising off them was anything to go by. The table was laid with cups on saucers, side plates with knives and napkins while the dishes in the middle held a selection of jams and the bright yellow butter she was becoming addicted to.

'How… just… how?'

MacAndrew walked in from the scullery carrying a cafetiere in one hand and a jug of warm creamy milk in the other.

'Ah, good morning, Flora, perfect timing. Sit and tuck in while it's all still warm.'

'MacAndrew, how did you know I wanted croissants for breakfast this morning?' she asked, putting one of the crispy treats on her plate as she sat.

'You told me.'

'Err, no, I didn't. I only thought of them myself barely half-an-hour ago.'

'That's right. You had them in your head so I knew to make them for you.'

The bite-size piece of butter and jam laden pastry she'd just prepared came to a halt halfway to her mouth.

'In my… in my head?'

'That's right.'

MacAndrew settled his clear gaze upon her while chewing through his own butter-piled croissant.

Her own morsel was returned to the plate and a large gulp of coffee was consumed instead while her brain tried to reject what was clearly the obvious – but surely not possible – answer.

'MacAndrew... can you read my mind?'

'Well, er, DURRR! Of course I can. I'm your MacAndrew!'

'Wait, wait, wait! You didn't tell me that bit. Why didn't you tell me? And how long have you been doing it? Oh, my goodness, what have you been seeing?'

'Och, calm yourself! It's not that big a deal—'

'NOT THAT BIG A DEAL? Seriously?'

'Look, our minds connected when you arrived. We need to be face-to-face for it to happen. It's just like your modern-day Bluetooth thingy – both objects need to be close-by to pair up.'

'Right...' Flora blinked several times, trying to take in the lunacy that was MacAndrew comparing his mind-reading skills to Bluetooth pairing.

'And, if I'm being honest, what's been going on up here,' MacAndrew tapped the side of his head, 'is no more or less than I was expecting.'

'Why didn't you tell me? Don't you realise this is a big deal – for me? It's an invasion of my privacy.'

'I didn't tell you because I need to know that all this new information isn't overwhelming you. I need to see how you're coping with it, so I know when I can teach you more or when to wait for you to become comfortable with what you've learnt so far. I wasn't invading your privacy. I was looking out for your welfare. Don't underestimate the effect that being overloaded with too much difficult information can have on your mental health.'

She shook her head before dropping it down into her hands. Why was she having a bigger problem hearing MacAndrew talk about Bluetooth and mental health issues than the fact he had access to all her thoughts?

Suddenly, she sat upright, looked at him and said, within her head while keeping her mouth firmly closed, *'You can see / hear / read all this right now, can't you?'*

'Yes, I can,' he replied through the whiskers on his chin. 'If you must know, I can hear your thoughts and I can see anything you picture. I can only "read" your mind if you're envisioning words. Folks don't tend to do that so often.'

'What if I don't want you to hear or see what I'm thinking? Can I "switch you off"?'

'Of course you can. You're The Flora and I do as you bid. All you need to do is picture yourself pulling a thick, black curtain all around the inside of your head. Like, if your head was a round room with walls of glass – imagine you're closing a curtain on the glass walls, going all round the room. I would no longer be able to see or hear anything inside the curtains.'

Flora closed her eyes and drew up a vision of her doing exactly what MacAndrew had described. As soon as the two "ends" of the curtain met up, she immediately felt different. As if she was cocooned in a dark, safe space. She'd never done one of those floatation tank things but she imagined it would feel a little like how she felt now.

Opening her eyes, she looked at MacAndrew.

'Well?'

'Nothing. I can't see or hear anything.'

'How do I know you're telling the truth?'

'You don't. You have to trust me.'

'How do I know that I can?'

'Flora, I'm here to serve you, look after you, and to ensure your wellbeing at all times. I concur our roles are less defined than with the previous Floras I've served but this is due to your lack of knowledge. It's not a role I'm comfortable with, let me tell you, but it's one your grandmother asked me to take on and I will honour her request, no matter how difficult it is. If it makes you feel better, though, I only "listen" when we're together like this and a little before you go to sleep. I switch you off for most of the time but, if you call for me, I will hear you.'

'Can I read your mind? Is it a two-way thing?'

'Yes, you can… when you put on the necklace.'

'Why is so much of what I need to know tied to that darned necklace?'

'Because the knowledge must stay here. While the world might be all gung-ho on the delights of Harry Potter, actually seeing *real* magic truly is more than the general population could comprehend. Sending you back out there,' MacAndrew waved an arm in the direction of the window, 'full of magical powers, would be very harmful for you and those around you.'

'Right.'

The morose tone of her reply fully reflected how she felt inside. She wanted to know more about her capabilities but simply wasn't ready to make the commitment needed for her to gain the information.

There was silence for a time as she made a half-hearted effort at eating the breakfast she no longer desired and MacAndrew topped up her coffee which was going down easier than the croissants.

'Flora,' the little man's voice finally broke into the silence, 'I would ask you to please open the curtains and allow me access to your thoughts. Just to help me to help you. Over time, you'll find you "open and close" as automatically as breathing but as it's still something you need to make a conscious effort with, please could you make the default setting of curtains open.'

She thought over his words for a few seconds before answering, 'Sure, okay' and mentally performing the act of opening them. Immediately, she had the sensation of being naked and exposed but was soothed when MacAndrew's hand came across the table to land on top of hers.

'It'll be okay, Flora, it'll be okay. Trust me.'

And she was comforted by the realisation that she already did.

'Right, then, I think it's time to move on with your education. After meeting Walter and the air sylph, I figured you could use a couple of days off but now we need to get back on it.'

MacAndrew began clearing the breakfast stuff from the table and Flora helped him. He'd finally stopped telling her not to help when she'd persistently ignored him and helped anyway. Whether he was happy about it or not, MacAndrew had realised she considered them to be a team and teams worked together.

'MacAndrew, may I ask you something?'

'Of course you can. Please do. Any time.'

'When I spoke with Walter, he told me about my some of my ancestors and that one of my grandmothers had married a selkie. Is that correct?'

'It is.'

'Is that how I have shape-shifting abilities?'

'Correct. Your abilities, however, are different from Walter's. He can only shift between his seal form and human form. But when the marital bond of selkie and witch came about, the Flora born from *that* union had a greater shifting ability – the magic of the witch enhancing the capabilities.'

'So, when we find ourselves in shape-shifting mode, we can be whatever we want to be?'

'Sort of. Within reason. The ability has weakened through subsequent generations and can no longer be done at will. It'll only manifest itself at times when you are feeling great stress or danger. Adrenaline being the trigger.'

'Okay. The other thing Walter mentioned is that Selkies can live for up to eight-hundred years or so. I suggested the long-life gene didn't pass down through the generations otherwise I'd have a lot of grandmothers dotting around but Walter disagreed...'

'Well, young lady, as it happens, that gene DID come down the line.'

'It did?'

'Yes.'

'But, my grandmother—'

'—chose to die.'

'She did? Why?'

'The Floras are like swans – they mate for life. They will only ever fall in love once and they will love that person with every atom of their being. As such, when their partner dies, it's too painful to go on so they choose to take the next part of the journey with them. In the case of your grandmother, she'd promised your grandfather that even though her responsibilities here prevented her being with him in this life, when his time came to leave this world, she'd walk by his side through the next one.'

'Oh, wow! How... romantic.'

'Aye, maybe it is, but her choice has also left me with the bother of educating you, so if it's all the same, we need to get on. I think you're ready to be introduced to the still room.'

'The still room?'

'Aye, the place where the magic happens.' MacAndrew

let out a mighty chuckle. 'Quite literally!'

'Wait a second… one last question about this eternal life thingy – what happened to the selkie who started it all?'

'When your many-times-great grandmother died – keeping in mind she didn't have the gene, her daughter did – her husband, your long-ago grandfather, returned to the water.'

'Is he still around?'

'He shows up occasionally.'

'So, I… I could get to meet him?'

'More than likely. Speak to Walter about it. But now, it's time for school. Come on!'

THIRTY-FOUR

MacAndrew walked through the scullery, over to the cupboard that was nestled under the slope from the stairs above it and gave it a gentle tap on the left-hand-side. To Flora's surprise, it quietly slid into a concealed recess to her right, revealing a solid wooden door hidden behind it.

A large key was taken from MacAndrew's pocket, inserted into the lock, and turned. A hefty sounding "clunk" echoed around the small space and after a sharp tap to the top and bottom corners, it swung open towards them.

'Follow me, and mind your step, the stairs are a wee bitty steep.'

Flora walked closely behind MacAndrew, finding herself at the top of a cast-iron spiral staircase and when she stepped on it, the door behind her closed with a click followed by a slight scrape which suggested the cupboard had moved back into its original position.

An overhead light gave a clear view as she walked down the staircase which was surprisingly short. For some reason, she'd imagined herself walking down, down, down into the middle of the earth and the room she found herself in was disappointingly ordinary. A large chest freezer sat in the corner beneath the stairs. The wall on the far side, to the left of where she stood, was hidden behind two floor-to-ceiling cupboards. The brick wall directly in front of her had a few shelf racks stacked against it, the shelves themselves holding, what appeared to be everyday detritus; old shoes needing repaired, a teddy bear missing an arm, a broken vase with the pieces stacked next to it in the hope that one day it would be complete again.

'Go on through, I just need to get a joint out to defrost.'

MacAndrew waved towards a section of wall between two of the racking units.

'I'm sorry? Where?'

'Just there. Go through, I'll only be a minute…'

'Go through where, MacAndrew? That's a brick wall!'

'Oh, for the love of the Goddess… The sooner you put that necklace on, the better!'

He grabbed a frozen lump from inside the freezer, dropped it with a thunk onto a plate, slammed the lid shut and sat the plate on top.

'Come on!' he grumbled, stepping across to the bricks and walking right through them.

'What the h—'

Flora didn't get to finish her sentence before his head popped back through saying, 'Well, are you coming or not?'

She walked over to peer at the bricks. They looked, and smelt, as solid as any brick wall she'd ever seen. And with her dad being in the building trade, she'd seen more than a few. Tentatively, she put out her fingers and started with surprise when they went right through the bricks. She quickly pulled her hand back, inspected her digits and saw they were as normal as they'd been a few seconds earlier. She tried again, this time putting her whole hand forward.

There was a cold sensation around the area of her arm that was in the wall but her fingers were now warm. It was very weird.

She was still contemplating on whether to walk herself through when MacAndrew's voice rang out.

'Will you get a bloody move on! We don't have all day!'

With a deep breath and closed eyes, Flora moved through the wall. The cold feeling was akin to stepping through a cold shower but considerably briefer. And drier!

Upon opening her eyes, she found herself in a long, well-lit corridor. Looking over her shoulder, she had a clear view back into the cellar, as though there was nothing there at all.

She hurried along the downward-sloping passageway, coming to a halt in the doorway of a large, round, cavernous room. MacAndrew was just lighting the last of the candles dotted around it which threw light into every space and revealed the very last thing she'd expected to see.

Like most children, Flora had grown up reading various books and stories about witches and wizards, including the famous Harry Potter series, and in almost every case, the impression given was that the rooms where magic and potions were made and concocted were black, dark, musty, and cobwebby. This room couldn't have been as far from that had it tried. The walls were pale-cream and all the cupboards and shelves were painted a soft lilac. The floor was covered with black and white tiles. To her left, was an expanse of solid cream, marble worktop with open shelving underneath housing a range of black, and pewter, cauldrons organised in size order from quite big to incredibly small. At the far end of the worktop, the open shelves stood floor-to-high-ceiling, all filled with jars and bottles in various shapes, sizes, and colours. There were also more cauldrons but these were smaller sets made of gold, silver, and copper. As her eyes carried on round, the shelving gave way to cupboards until finally, on the wall by her right, they came to rest on an array of black, cast-iron objects and racks that looked like implements of torture. She gave an involuntary shudder at the sight of them before turning back to look at MacAndrew standing in the middle of the room beside a huge black cauldron that was nearly as tall as he was.

In her state of almost shock, Flora said the first thing that came into her head.

'Cauldrons? Seriously? Could you be any more cliché?'

'Actually, young lady, we use cauldrons because they're more practical. The heat conduction is better and the iron is thicker which means the contents are less likely to burn and be ruined. The gold, silver, and copper cauldrons are for the more delicate potions. Don't mock what you don't understand.'

Accepting her chastisement, she apologised. 'I'm sorry. I didn't mean to be rude. It's just… this…' she waved her hand towards the room, 'that…' she pointed back down the corridor, 'it's difficult to comprehend when seeing it for real. I just need a moment…'

MacAndrew walked over to stand in front of her.

'NOW do you understand about the necklace? *Now* do you get the conditions set upon it?'

'Yes. Yes, I do. I see it.'

'Good. Then you've already learnt a lesson today.'

'So, the wall back there… is that an enchantment?'

'It is and can only be seen by people who don't have the gift.'

'But I could see it.'

'Because your gift is still young and growing. In a few more weeks, it'll be invisible to you unless you make a point of looking for it. Sooner, though, if you don the jewels.'

'Is there a time limit on how long I can take to decide? Is there an expiration date?'

'No. The power will be held in the necklace for as long as it takes another Flora to put it on. If that's not you, it could be your daughter. Or your granddaughter. Or even great granddaughter.'

'I see. Good to know.'

'Personally, though, I'd like you to be the next to wear it.'

'To relieve you of the burden that I am?'

The wee man chuckled. 'No. Because I think you'll make a good Flora. I was worried that with growing up without the knowledge of who or what you are, you might not be the right kind of woman for the role. But you are. You're very like your grandmother, in many ways. She was a great Flora. You could be too.'

He turned away, leaving Flora with a sizeable lump in her throat. If MacAndrew thought she could do this, then she was going to do her best not to let him down.

She followed him across the room. 'Okay, what's my first lesson for the day?'

MacAndrew was standing in front of a cupboard which he opened when she came to his side.

'First of all, you need to meet the book.'

'Meet the book?'

'Yes. You'll understand in a moment. Now, I need you to put your right hand on here.'

She followed his finger which was pointing at a solid black box about the size of a small industrial safe, except this one appeared to have no door or lid on it. A discreet glance around it revealed no opening of any sort.

'What is it? I want to know first.'

'It's a safe but this one is magical and only responds to the touch of The Flora.'

'I see. So, I have to put my hand on it?'

'Yes. Just there.'

He pointed to the front where a door would normally be found.

'Okay.'

She placed her hand against the cool metal. For a second or two, nothing happened but then she felt her palm begin to prickle and right in front of her eyes, the entire frontage dissolved to reveal two shelves containing books although one book took up an entire shelf by itself.

'Please take that book out, Flora. Carefully. It's several hundreds of years old.'

She gently pulled the tome towards her, noting the plainness of the brown leather cover encasing it.

'Bring it over to the worktop, please.'

With as much care as she could muster, the book was laid on the cool marble. MacAndrew hopped up onto a footstool so he was of an equal height to her.

'Place your hand on the front, just as you did a moment ago.'

This time, Flora obeyed the request without hesitation. Once more, nothing happened for a couple of seconds but then her palm tingled again and the book emitted a gentle sigh.

'Now you can open it.'

Almost reverently, she slowly opened the hard, brown cover. A thick blank page faced her. Before she could turn it, writing began to appear in front of her.

The Book of Knowing welcomes the new Flora.
May your hand always be guided with skill
and your mind guided with care.
You are now the guardian of the knowledge within.
Use it wisely.

'Oh!' Flora jumped back in surprise. 'I wasn't expecting that.'

MacAndrew smiled as he replied, 'I thought it might tickle you. A book that talks to you – now even you can't deny that is something magical.'

'Will it do that every time I open it?' Flora noticed the writing was already fading, returning the page to its previous blank state.

'It will but usually with different messages, depending on what you need from it. So, time to get on with making your first potion.'

She turned over a few of the heavy pages and peered at the small writing, sometimes with diagrams. When she did a quick flick towards the back of the book, she noted those pages were blank.

'I'm surprised, MacAndrew, for a book so many centuries old, I'd have expected almost every page to be written on.'

MacAndrew gave her one of his looks.

'Oh, let me guess… the book will reveal its secret pages once I've put on the necklace…'

'And she gets it! Yay!'

On the back of the smile he threw her way, MacAndrew jumped off his footstool, scurried over to the wall and began to undo a length of rope from a hook on the wall. Looking up, Flora saw a pulley descending into the room with two large lockable hooks on it. In no time at all, her companion had the hooks locked onto the giant, floor-standing cauldron, had pulled it up out of the way, and was gathering a few implements from what Flora had named "the torture corner", placing them over the firepit that was now visible.

'Ah, those are racks for the smaller cauldrons to sit on. That's a relief.'

'Well… most of them are…'

MacAndrew gave a small chuckle as he lit the fire before moving his footstool over in front a shelving unit.

'To begin your training, Flora, we're going to make a simple hand cream. This is purely to get you used to working with a cauldron and open fire. Please read out the requirements on the third page of the book.'

Flora turned the pages as instructed, having a quick read through before looking up at MacAndrew waiting patiently for her.

'Awwww! There's no wing of bat, tooth of dragon or web of spider in this one!'

'All in good time, dearie, all in good time. Now tell me what you *do* need…'

'Wax of bees, essence of heather, extract of almond…'

A moment later, MacAndrew had put the requested bottles and jars on the worktop.

'Next time, Flora, less of the drama, if you don't mind. It's beeswax, heather tincture, and almond oil! Okay?'

THIRTY-FIVE

'When do you think you'll be seeing Flora again?'

Kenneth looked up at his sister-in-law's question. 'I don't know. Why?'

'Because she left so suddenly, we didn't exchange phone numbers. A few of us girls are having a wee get-together on Saturday night and I'd like to invite her along.'

Kenneth peered more closely at Shona. 'What girls?'

'Why? It's none of your business.'

'Shona, I've heard about some of these "Girls Nights" you've had and I don't want Flora being subjected to any of your antics.'

'Well, firstly, it's not for you to make decisions on Flora's behalf and, secondly, Fraser only had to rescue me from the graveyard once.'

'Oh, yes? What about the time you stood outside the Indian takeaway at three in the morning, yelling up to Mr Patel that you weren't leaving until he came down and made you pakora? Or, when you thought it was a good idea to walk along the wall outside the farm shop, fell off and almost broke your neck?'

'I didn't break my neck, just twisted my ankle. Stop exaggerating! Besides, that was a long time ago. I'm far more restrained these days.'

There was a loud snort from the corner where Fraser was sitting doing the monthly accounts on the computer. Kenneth looked over to see his brother's shoulders shaking.

'Are you laughing over there?' he asked his brother's back.

'Nope!' came the strangled reply.

'Where are you planning to go?'

'Again, it's not any of your business, but we're going into Beauly. Catriona Duncan, Angela Johannes, and Sue Baker are coming along.'

Kenneth puckered his brow at the names. Catriona Duncan? She'd been in the surgery just a couple of days ago.

'Catriona Duncan—'

'Yes, yes, she's pregnant! That's why we're going out – a wee celebration for her good news. She won't be drinking so she's our designated driver.'

'You knew what I was going to say?'

Shona stood up, walked over, and dropped a kiss on the top of his head.

'Kenneth, I've known you all my life – I've kinda got you figured out by now. So, will you please send Flora my number and ask her to call me, if she doesn't mind. Thank you.'

With that, she swept out of the room, closing the door behind her.

For a few seconds there was silence until Kenneth said, 'Fraser, could you please tell your wife to stop kissing me on the head. She knows I can't abide it!'

'Kenneth,' came the reply, accompanied by another snort of laughter, 'why do think she does it?'

'Goodnight, Mum, thank you for dinner… again!'

'Always a pleasure to feed my son. Will you be round tomorrow night?'

'No, I've got the late shift at the surgery – I'll head straight back to the cabin after that.'

'Then I'll drop something over tomorrow that you can heat up when you get in.'

'Mum, please, you don't need to keep looking after me. I'm a big boy now.'

Mhari laughed before placing her hand gently on his cheek. 'You might be big in stature but you will always be my little man with his nose buried in a book. Anyway, make the most of it. The novelty of running around after you will wear off soon enough.'

'Cheers, Mum.' He grinned before leaning in to give her a hug. 'And thank you for taking in my delivery tomorrow – it's timer food bowls for Choona.'

'Bowls? How many have you ordered? Do you plan on being out that often?'

'I've got four coming – two spares, just in case. But while she's still young, she needs to be fed about four times a day, hence two bowls in case I'm late getting home.'

'If you're ever stuck, darling, you only need to call and I'll pop over to feed her. Don't worry about that – we won't let her starve to death.'

'You have enough to deal with here but thank you, I'll keep it in mind. Now, I must go.'

He kissed her cheek and with a small wave, made his escape.

As he was driving down the farm lane, he thought about Shona's request to pass her number on to Flora. He wondered how she was doing. He'd sent her a text on

Monday, just to check she was alright and received a reply saying she was fine and thanking him for his understanding the day before. When he reached the fork in the road where he'd normally turn for the cabin, he paused, thought for a few seconds and then, switching off the ignition, he pulled out his phone to call her.

Her phone rang out several times and he felt disappointment creeping in when he realised he'd been looking forward to hearing her voice. After another couple of rings, he cancelled the call as a heavy feeling descended on him. Despite everything she was alleged to be – he just wasn't buying into the witchy / natural healer thing at all – he found he enjoyed her company. For someone who was a natural loner, and more comfortable with his own company than that of others, this was quite a big deal. Flora was sharp and quirky, yet kind and caring and she was the first woman since his wife who he'd considered interesting enough to want to spend more time with.

Just as he was about to re-engage the car, his mobile rang and his cheeky little heart gave a small skip when he saw her name on the screen.

'Hi, Flora, how are you?'

Her breathless voice slipped into his ear.

'Fine, fine. Thank you. Sorry, I missed your call – I was down in the cellar. By the time I got upstairs, you'd rung off.'

'Hey, no problem.'

'How can I help you?'

'I was… erm… just… erm… wondering if you were in the mood for an hour of my company? I've been to Mum's so I'm less than ten minutes away… but only if you're up for it. No pressure or anything…'

'Hey, that would cool. Sure, come on over. I'll see you in less than ten!'

Before he could say goodbye, she'd ended the call.

With a grin on his face and a feeling of joy in his soul, he started the car and carried straight on down the lane.

'Come in, come in.'

Flora's voice rang out when he knocked on the open door of her cottage. The rain had finally ceased but he made sure to give his shoes a good wipe on the mat before following her voice and finding himself in the kitchen.

'It's lovely to see you,' said Flora, dropping a peck on his cheek as she walked past him. 'Would you like a hot drink or a cold one?'

'A coffee would be perfect, thank you.'

'Great, I'll sort out a pot. Now, as you are my first, properly official, visitor, please go through to the lounge and I'll bring it in.'

'Oh, I'm happy to sit at the kitchen table...'

'And any other time, we most likely will but on this occasion, I'd really like to "play with my new house" and use the lounge. Do you mind?'

Kenneth returned her grin. 'Not at all. I'm happy to "play house" with you.'

'Thank you. I'll be with you in a few minutes.'

She pointed to the door across the hall, opposite the kitchen and upon opening it, he found himself in a pleasing room that ran the from the front to the back of the cottage. Decorated in soothing tones of cream and lilac, he noted one end had been designated the dining area with the wooden table and chairs and that he was currently standing in the lounging zone. His eye caught a picture on a wall and when he walked over, he saw it was a young Flora on her graduation day. He guessed the picture must be about six or seven years old but apart from her hair, which was now shorter, she didn't look any different at all.

He looked around and saw an array of photographs dotted about which turned out to be mostly of Flora too, in various stages of growing up. She'd been a cute kid, that was for sure. He also came across a photograph of a man and a woman on their wedding day. The woman was the absolute spit of Flora and he assumed this was her parents. He looked at it for a few more seconds then turned away and found himself standing by the dining table which was covered with piles of letters, envelopes, and packages. This was clearly where Flora had laid out her grandmother's correspondence – the open letters on the side told him she was slowly working her way through it.

He was turning away when he noticed something lying on the edge of the table and had just picked it up for a closer look when Flora walked in.

'Oh, er… I wasn't snooping, honest. I just saw this and I couldn't resist a closer look.'

Flora placed the tray she was carrying on the coffee table in front of the sofa then walked over to him. He handed her the book he was holding.

'Ah, "The Broons",' she read out the title on the front. It sounded funny to hear her very English accent pronounce the very Scottish title.

'I confess to owning a substantial collection of these books which is why I noticed it. The maroon spine is always the giveaway.'

'Then, could you please explain why she'd send this and another one called "Our Willie"? I currently have two of each but looking at the pile of gifts I have still to work my way through, I think I've received one every year.'

Kenneth looked at the annual in his hand and smiled. He remembered this one well. 'These books are printed by a Scottish company in Dundee – D.C. Thomson. The same people who publish The Beano and The Dandy—'

'I've heard of those but never these.'

'The Broons and Oor Wullie, as it's actually pronounced,' he gave her a smile, 'are a Scottish tradition. They're released alternately every year at Christmas and there's barely a kid in Scotland who doesn't get one from Santa. By sending them to you, I'd say your grandmother was trying to pass on something that is pretty much a Scottish heritage. As I said, I love them and have quite a collection but I'd imagine for someone who knows little of them, they probably seem a bit strange.'

'I'll be honest – I've struggled when trying to read them. It really hasn't helped that they appear to be written in broad Scots.'

'No, I imagine it doesn't. But, if you do decide to stick around here for a while, they might help you to learn a bit of the lingo.'

'Fair enough. I'll persevere with them.'

'If there's anything you're struggling to understand, please, don't hesitate to ask. Either text me or send a photograph of the page and I'll "translate" it for you.'

'You're very kind to offer and I'm going to take you up on it right now. What's a "but and ben"? I haven't had time to look it up yet.'

'You've been reading "The Broons" haven't you?' He smiled at her.

'Wow! You really do know your stuff with these. Yes, I have.'

'The Broons are famous for their but and ben. Traditionally, a but and ben is a two-roomed cottage. In the case of The Broons, it's a wee holiday home they own and often visit on weekends. It's supposed to be situated somewhere in the Highlands.'

'I see. Well, thank you for that clear and concise answer. Expect to deal with many more. Now, please, come and have your coffee. I also have fresh cookies, hot from the oven, if you fancy…'

'Oh, please tell me you didn't make them for me coming over. I didn't want you going to any trouble.'

'In less than ten minutes? Hardly!' she laughed. 'They were already baking when you rang. You see, I found one of my grandmother's recipe books this morning and I decided to try a couple of things. The cookies were one…'

'And the other?'

'Hand cream! I *actually* made hand cream! Can you believe it? And, what's more, it turned out not too bad at all.'

It was impossible to ignore the sparkle in her eyes as she spoke of her day and it cheered him to notice the anguish he'd witnessed on Sunday had subsided.

'Hand cream, eh? Well done, you. I bet it wasn't easy.'

'It was easier than I expected.'

'Is this the same recipe your grandmother sold to my patients? I seem to recall seeing one when I first arrived who suffers badly with eczema but was raving on about The Flora's hand cream…'

'Oh, I wouldn't know about that. And I certainly won't be selling this one. Well, not the batch I made today. While I'm pleased with it, I don't think it's to a standard that merits payment. I can do better. Here, let me get you some…'

Before he could reply, Flora had shot out of the room. When she returned, she had some small glass jars in her hand.

'Here, give me your hand – try it.'

'Oh, no, I couldn't…'

'Of course you can.' She opened one of the jars, leant over the table, grabbed his hand, and rubbed some of the cream on the back of it.

Immediately, there was a prickling sensation which, while not unpleasant, made him concerned there could be harmful ingredients within the cream but he'd barely finished the thought when the sensation ceased. He looked down at his hand and noticed a white patch within the redness which was a by-product of the frequent hand-washing his job required.

'Oh! My!' He lifted his hand to his nose and breathed in the light floral tones.

'Heather is the primary ingredient and, as I've recently discovered, it has many medicinal properties. Easing skin problems is just one of them.'

'Ah, right. Erm…' Kenneth didn't know what to say. His head and eyes were in direct conflict with each other. His head was saying that miracle potions or creams don't exist yet his eyes were showing him they did. He'd used various creams over the years to try and combat his washerwoman hands with only a modicum of success. And yet, the first application of Flora's product had worked the wonders other lotions could only dream of.

'Look, here's a few jars for you to take away. You can either use them yourself – I'm guessing you wash your hands a lot with your job so this might help – or you can pass them on to your mum and Shona. I don't mind.'

'Thank you. Oh, and talking about Shona, she's asked me to pass her phone number to you. She, along with her girlfriends, are having a night out in Beauly on Saturday and she hopes you'll join them.'

'Oh!' Flora sat back in surprise.

'She thought you might like to meet some other women from the area since you know barely anyone here. There's no obligation to go along.'

'What are these other women like? Do you know them?'

'Not really. I only know one who is a patient of the surgery. I met her a few days ago and she's nice.'

'Who is she?'

'Sorry, not my place to say. You know that doctor-patient confidentiality thing.'

'Of course. But she's going to be there?'

'Yes.'

'So, there will be two nice people – Shona and A.N. Other.'

'Correct.'

'Hmmm, then I think I might go along. It would be lovely to get out of here and it's been some time since I had a girls' night out. Thank you. Please, send me Shona's number so I can accept. Who knows – I might even meet a nice young man too!'

Kenneth quickly bent his head and pulled out his phone, staring intently at the screen while trying to ignore the sudden lurch in his stomach that had come about at her last words. It was a thought that hadn't occurred to him and one he'd now struggle to get out of his head.

THIRTY-SIX

'I can NOT believe you've talked me into this. I must be mad!'

'Hey, don't you be laying this on me. All I said was it might be worth considering getting Choona a playmate if you're likely to be out and about for most of the day. Kittens get bored, boredom leads to mischief and mischief often turns into destruction. If she has a chum, then your mother's cabin won't require a complete renovation when you move out.'

'It was only one blind she brought down.'

'Today it's one blind, tomorrow... who knows! Why take the risk?'

'And you think a second kitten will prevent that?'

'Sally only allows kittens under twelve months to be rehomed in pairs if there isn't another animal in residence or if the new slaves, like you, are out at work all day. It's not fair on the kitten otherwise.'

Flora hid a smirk when Kenneth let out a sigh of resignation.

'Oh, alright then. You make a valid point. Let's get on with it.'

He stepped out of the car and she rushed to join him as

he strode towards the entrance of the rescue centre. Wait till she shared this with Sal, she'd be so pleased to hear another little fluffy orphan had found a home.

'Kenneth! How are you? You're the last person I expected to see here today – is everything alright with your kitten?'

'Hi, Morag, I'm well, thank you, and Choona is also perfectly well. Probably planning world domination as we speak and beginning her mission with the destruction of Mum's cabin.'

'Ahhhh!' Morag's face split into a wide grin as she gave a wise nod, the news clearly not a surprise to her.

'Flora here says a second kitten may help to avert the world's downfall… Any truth in that? Please say no!'

'I'm sorry, Kenneth, but The Flora is quite correct. How can you even doubt her wisdom? Or feline knowledge. Pleased to meet you, by the way, I'm Morag.'

Flora leant around Kenneth to shake Morag's hand which had been thrust in her direction.

'Nice to meet you too and my feline knowledge is very much second-hand. My friend Sally runs a cat rescue back home and much of what I know is simply from being around her. I'm not an expert by any means.'

'Hey, with so many unknowing idiots out there who think owning a cat is "easy", anyone who has even a modicum of a clue is a godsend. Follow me, I'll take you to the pens.'

Unable to resist, Flora had a good look around as she and Kenneth followed Morag over to a large barn. The yard area was clean and a tractor was parked over to one side.

'You run a farm as well as a rescue?'

'Not really. The farm was my father's and came to me when he died. I had zero interest in running any kind of farm so I rent most of my fields out to the farm on the other side of the valley. We maintain three of the smaller ones –

my husband does canine training – and the main barn was converted into the cat rescue. He's a dog man but I prefer cats myself.'

'I've inherited my grandmother's dogs – two West Highland Terriers. They're quite lovely but I think I might prefer cats.'

'Then maybe we'll find someone in here for you too…' Morag gave her a wink.

'Oh, I don't think so. I don't know how the dogs would react to that.'

'It's easier to take a cat into dog territory than a dog into a cat's territory. They adapt better.'

'Right! However, as it's Kenneth who's in desperate need here, let's get him sorted out first.'

They stepped through the doors of the barn and Flora saw the setup was the standard you'd find in many rescues – long corridors with pens on either side. Sally's method of allowing all the cats to mingle together in one large space was, as far as Flora was aware, quite unusual but it seemed to work because most of her rehomes were a success and she put this down to the sociable atmosphere they came from.

Morag and Kenneth disappeared around a corner and she meandered slowly between the pens, her heart wrenching at the sight of the beautiful but unloved creatures contained in them. How she wished she could take them all home with her.

When she turned the corner at the bottom of the corridor, following the sound of Morag's voice, she came to an abrupt halt. The atmosphere around her had thickened and an intense feeling of despair flowed around her.

'What on earth—'

She looked about her. What was going on? She was alone in another narrow corridor, again with cat pens on either side, but this feeling was… painful. The sensation of sadness was heavy, so incredibly heavy and growing heavier with each step she took. By the time she was halfway along, she was almost struggling to breathe but then, as she moved on, the feeling began to ease.

Flora stopped, turned around and slowly retraced her steps. As she did so, the atmosphere once again grew oppressive then eased. She did this twice more until she came to a stop in front of a cat pen which she'd ascertained to be the epicentre of this desolation. She knelt on the floor and found herself gazing into a pair of lifeless golden eyes that held so much sadness, she nearly cried. She looked at the cat in the pen and it looked right back at her. It was in a sorry state – its right ear was mashed up, there were several scars on its face, and the dirty ginger coat gave up some space for a patch on its chest that looked more grey than white. Everything screamed this was a cat who'd given up and no longer cared enough to groom itself anymore. Its spirit had almost leaked away.

'Oh, baby, look at you. You poor thing. You've been in the wars, haven't you.'

She glanced at the clipboard attached to the pen and saw that "Tyson" had come into the rescue over two years ago.

And now she understood his despair.

Over two years of watching other cats finding new homes, over two years of seeing other cats getting kisses and cuddles from new slaves, over two years of hoping just a little bit less each time that he might be lucky this time around.

Flora could understand why he'd been passed by so often – his large, round body, along with his battle scars, gave him the appearance of being troublesome but she knew this wasn't the case. All her instincts were yelling that this big lump of fur just wanted a slave to call his own. A human to care for him, treat him nice and look after him while he would give them all the love he had in return.

She placed her palm against the wire front of the pen but the cat didn't move. He lay with his head on his paws, his ears at half-mast and a mournful downturn on his mouth, not believing she really wanted to touch him.

Despite being unable to comprehend how she was able to sense this, Flora whispered quiet words of encouragement to him.

'You are a beautiful boy, Tyson, yes, you *are*. Please, come and say hello. Let me stroke your gorgeous ears. Come on, there's a good boy.'

Still, he didn't move. But then, several seconds later, his ears began to twitch as she continued whispering to him and the heavy oppressive atmosphere grew slowly lighter. He'd just dragged himself into a sitting position when, all of a sudden…

'Ah, there you are. We were wondering where you'd got to.'

Morag's voice had her hastily getting to her feet and brushing down her jeans.

'We've found the perfect match for Choona, well, we hope we have, and I'm just about to do the paperwork so Kenneth can take him home with him.'

'Oh! Don't you do home-checks?'

'Normally we do but as I've already seen Kenneth's place, and his mum called to say she's okay with him having another cat, so he can take this little one today.'

'Oh, that's good.'

'I see you've met Tyson. He's our longest resident. Such a gorgeous natured boy but his looks put folks off.' A loud sigh followed Morag's comment. 'Poor fella, I don't think he'll ever leave here.'

'I'll take him!'

The words were out of Flora's mouth before her brain had even realised what she was saying.

'I'm sorry?'

'I'll take him. I want to take him home with me.'

'I think you should take some time to mull this over. I understand how easy it is to be swayed by the sob stories of my residents but animals are not impulse buys who can be returned when the notion wears off.'

'Look, I know it might seem like that but… this cat… he's meant to be with me… Look at him.'

While they'd been talking, Tyson had stood up and was now pushing himself up against the front of the pen.

'I really don't know…'

'I'll prove it to you.'

Flora knelt back down, undid the latch on the pen, opened the gate wide, then sat back and waited. A couple of heartbeats passed before Tyson slowly walked out towards her whereupon he climbed onto her lap, looked into her eyes, then placed his front paws on either side of her neck, raising himself up on his hindquarters to rub his face along her cheek. As she wrapped her arms around his warm, sturdy body, she felt a tiny rumble begin somewhere deep inside and by the time Kenneth had helped her to her feet, the rumble was full-on purring in her ear.

'Well, I never did! I haven't ever seen anything like that. And this cat has never purred in all the time I've known him. Looks like I've got two lots of paperwork to complete.'

'Don't you want to home-check me?'

'You're The Flora – that won't be necessary.'

THIRTY-SEVEN

'Okay, Tyson, I'm just going to put you in here for a few minutes. You're a good boy, yes you really are. I'll be right back.'

Flora put her fingers through the grille of the cat basket and gave Tyson a gentle rub on the nose. Kenneth walked into the lounge just as she turned around.

'I've popped your purchases under the window in the kitchen.'

'Thank you. How lucky was it that Morag also has a shop which sells all the cat requirements one needs?'

Kenneth laughed at her comment.

'I think luck has little to do with it and everything to do with knowing a good opportunity when you see it.'

Flora laughed, 'I think you're right there. And with every penny going towards the rescue, I don't even care that the markup was more than the larger stores.'

'Well, I'd better be getting on – I have my own little bundles of fur to sort out. I just hope Choona doesn't have a hissy fit when she meets him.'

'Oh, she totally will, trust me on that, but they're both

babies – it won't last very long. Get them playing with the toys and she'll soon come round. Thank you for bringing me home. Sorry, "us" home.'

'No problem. I hope he settles down okay and the dogs aren't a problem.'

'Me too.'

What Flora didn't tell him was that the dogs were in fact the least of her problems. It was MacAndrew's reaction she was more concerned about.

'Also, have fun tonight. I know Shona is really looking forward to it.'

Flora's hand flew up to her mouth. 'Oh, blimey! I'd forgotten about that!'

'I'm sure Tyson won't mind you going out.'

'I don't think he will. He'll need time to adjust so some space – without me in his face every few minutes checking he's okay – will be better for him. I'll put him up in my bedroom.'

'Right, then, I'm off. Shall we chat tomorrow and exchange experiences?'

'Sounds like a plan.'

She waved him off then turned towards the kitchen. When she walked through the door, MacAndrew was at the top end of the table.

'Urm…'

'I've put the dogs outside in the yard so bring him in.'

'You know?'

MacAndrew pointed to her head. 'Curtains!'

Of course! She kept forgetting he could hear her thoughts. Not bothering to reply, she returned to the lounge and found Tyson still curled up in his basket, exactly as she'd left him.

'Hey, little man. Time for you to meet… erm… my housemate? I suppose that's the best name for him. MacAndrew. An unusual chap but I hope you like him.'

Tyson gave her a slow blink, almost as though he'd understood every word. She picked up the basket, carried it into the kitchen and placed it carefully on the table. MacAndrew walked round, coming face-to-face with Tyson. They looked at each other for a minute or so until MacAndrew gave a small nod then turned towards her.

'Cup of tea?'

'Err, yes please.'

She continued to stand by the basket, totally surprised by his response.

'That's it? That's all you have to say?'

'Talk me through what happened this morning. From the beginning…'

Flora pulled out a chair, opening Tyson's basket for him to shuffle out into her arms, and told MacAndrew everything.

'R-I-G-H-T!' he said slowly, when she reached the end of her tale.

'I've never felt anything like it before, MacAndrew. And the way Tyson responded to me… It's like he was meant to be with me. Is this… is this… is this anything to do with me being a… with the new powers I seem to have?'

'Oh, yes, it's definitely that. No question about it. The bit I'm trying to understand is how, or why, this cat has connected with you.' He looked closely at her. 'You do know people of your standing can have what are known as "familiars"?'

'Yes, I am aware of that, or those.'

'Traditionally, the dogs,' he jerked his thumb in the direction of the back yard, 'are The Flora's familiars. Always have been. I've noticed, however, that while you get on with them and are nice to them, you haven't "clicked" with each other. I thought it was just a timing thing and it would happen the longer you were here but the fact you've connected with him…' he nodded at Tyson who was softly purring on her lap, 'makes me think that he's your familiar.'

'Is this a bad thing? Have I done something wrong?'

'Oh, no, you've done nothing wrong and its certainly not a bad thing, Just… a different thing.'

'Is different a bad thing?'

'I don't think so. Like I said when you first arrived – because of the circumstances around your life, nothing we do going forward will be as I know it. In many ways, this is a learning curve for me as well as for you. We'll just have to work it out as we go along.'

'Do you think Sandy and Kirsty will be alright with Tyson?'

'They'll be fine.' MacAndrew got down off his chair. 'I'll tell you one thing though –Tyson's not his name.'

'Oh, thank goodness for that. I think it's a terrible name. So, what's he called?'

MacAndrew smiled at her. 'Oh, I'll leave him to tell you that!'

Flora walked into her bedroom, kicked off her high heels and just narrowly missed Tyson's water bowl as she launched them across the floor. She was feeling happy. It had been a great night out and, what's more, she may have made a new friend.

Shona's friends had been very nice and welcoming although a bit older than herself except for one – Catriona. Or Trina, as she preferred. She was only a couple of years older than Flora and had expressed her delight at no longer being the *baby* in the group even if she was the one now *carrying* a baby! It turned out she lived a few miles along the road from the cottage and she'd told Flora she was welcome to visit any time. They'd exchanged phone numbers and Flora was hoping she might now get the best friend she'd always wanted. Time would tell.

'Hey there, Tyson,' she sang, giving his head a gentle scratch as she walked by on the way to the wardrobe.

'Hi.'

'How are doing, little man? Are you feeling settled?'

'Not bad, thank you, although the indignity of being forced to have a bath by your evil troll will not be going down in my personal history as a favourite moment.'

'But you must feel so much bett—'

The lightweight jacket being shrugged off slid to the floor as Flora's movements came to a sudden halt. She stood totally still for a few seconds before turning very slowly to look at the cat lying on her bed.

'Are you… are you… are you talking to me?'

'Well, I can't see anyone else in the room?'

At these words, she spun around, looking to see if MacAndrew was hiding somewhere, winding her up as revenge for bringing Tyson back to the cottage.

'Hey, sweetcheeks, it's me, here on the bed.'

'But… how? I can hear you in my head but you're not talking.'

'Miaoww, mmeww, meww.' This time, she could see Tyson's mouth moving.

'I'm sorry, what?'

*'Exactly! I can only **speak** in cat language but I can transfer my thoughts in human.'*

Not knowing if it was shock or surprise that took the strength out of her legs, Flora landed with a flump on the bed beside him. She immediately noticed the golden eyes which had been so dull this morning, were now shining brightly and twinkling at her. Her gaze drifted south to see the grey patch on his chest was now a gleaming white and the ginger fur was considerably less ginger and a lot more golden in colour. *Rose gold*, her artist's brain whispered.

'I'm sorry you had to suffer the indignity of a bath but surely you must feel better for it? You look very handsome.'

'Thank you. And yes, I suppose I do.'

It took a great deal of willpower for Flora not to laugh at the little hard-done-by sigh that was emitted as he spoke.

'So, this is what MacAndrew meant earlier when he said Tyson wasn't your name and you'd share that information with me yourself.'

'Yeah, that's right. The troll also has the means of being able to communicate with me.'

'He's not a troll, don't call him that.'

'Seriously? With that beard, he looks like he stepped right out from under a bridge. I hope there aren't any goats nearby...'

Unable to help herself this time, Flora burst out laughing.

'You're a sarcastic little sod, aren't you?'

'It's been mentioned before.'

'Would you like to share your chosen name with me along with some of your story? And, if you really like, how on earth we are talking like this?'

'Oh, I suppose. You got me out of that hellhole, I guess it's the least I can do.'

'Was it really that bad?' She stroked his head as he pushed his cheek into her palm.

'I've known worse. Morag is kind but she has a lot on her plate and doesn't have much time to give, although she often took me indoors with her, if her man was away, and we'd watch the boxy thing with pictures in it.'

'The television.'

'Yeah, that's the job. She likes American crime things.'

'Well, that explains a lot...'

'Meaning?'

'Where you got your sassy mouth from.'

'Oh, honey, that only polished up what was already there.'

'You might want to un-polish it a bit,' she muttered.

'I heard that!'

'Good! Anyway, back to my questions…'

Another sigh. *'My name is Friand. It's Norwegian for "Freespirit". It's my family name and we originate from what is now known as Scandy-navia. The colour of my fur represents the colour of my Viking ancestors while my feisty disposition emulates their fearlessness. I am very proud of my bloodline.'*

'It is lovely to meet you, Friand, I hope you'll be happy here. Just promise me you won't terrorise the other creatures who also live around here.'

'Dear Flora, I promise I won't,' he butted his head on her stomach, *'I used to live with a lady who was just like you, with your special gifts. She was kind and we were happy. Sadly, her time came to move onto the next plain and I wasn't ready to make that journey with her. Although, if her sadistic twat of a son had been able to catch me, I wouldn't have been given a choice. Luckily, my paws and claws got some well-aimed swipes in and I was able to escape. I spent many stars and moons on my own after that. Always walking, not knowing where to go. I've always been a hunter so food was not a problem but I got into many scraps with other cats I met along the way.'*

'How did you end up with Morag?'

'I ate a bad rat and it made me sick. The next thing I know, I'm waking up in some bright white, smelly place with a sore paw and even more pain where my bal— err… in my nether-regions.'

'Ah, the vets perhaps.'

'Yeah, that's the one. Then Morag came, took me back to hers where I was caged until you came along. And now

I'm here.'

'And this communicating thing?'

'The troll reckons it's your powers growing.'

'Stop calling him a troll! But I can't communicate like this with the dogs.'

'That's because they were the familiars of the previous witch. There hasn't been enough time for them to move on. It takes time. They like you but they miss her. They're not ready for you yet.'

'Oh!' Flora thought about this for a moment. 'So, does that make you my "familiar" then? Do they really exist?'

'Yes, they exist but not in the evil form that stupid humans like to think. We're companions, we protect our witch from those who would do harm and we help young witches, like yourself, come to terms with the power you now have. It's not an easy path to walk and you need someone who'll always be there by your side. You're very lucky because you also have the troll. Together, we'll look after you. If you want me, that is…'

Flora placed a kiss on his head.

'Friand, I would love to have you by my side. Thank you for choosing me.'

'I think we chose each other, sweetcheeks.'

She laughed again as she stood up from the bed, emitting a wide yawn as she did so.

'Okay, it's been a long day. Definitely time for bed.'

She walked back over to the wardrobe, picked up her jacket and hung it up. She was about to lift off her top when she saw Friand watching her in the mirror.

'Erm… not wanting to be rude but can you turn around, please?'

'Why?'

'I don't feel comfortable undressing in front of you.'

'Hahahahaha! You're cute!'

'Err, thank you?'

257

'It wasn't a compliment! You're too wrong for my tastes.'

'Too wrong?'

'Too tall! Too un-furry! Too HUMAN! Trust me, you have zilch that I wanna see.'

As he replied, however, Friand turned his back on her and lay down in the middle of the bed, placing one of his front paws over his eyes.

Shaking her head in disbelief, but with a smile on her face, Flora quickly changed into her nightshirt, dived to the bathroom to brush her teeth, and then slipped under the duvet, taking care not to disturb Friand who looked to have dozed off.

She curled up on her side, reaching over to put out the bedside light, and just as she was close to dropping off to sleep herself, there was a moment of snuffling by her face on the pillow as Friand crawled under the quilt to curl against her stomach.

Her arm wrapped itself around him and his soft purrs lulled her towards the Land of Nod.

THIRTY-EIGHT

Kenneth woke up when the bright sunlight streaming through the bedroom window poked him in the eye. He let out a lazy yawn as he stretched like a starfish. It was Saturday, it was the longest day of the year and, far more importantly, it was his first proper weekend off since he'd started his new role. He'd been on call for at least one day over the last few weekends which meant it wasn't possible to fully relax but now he could.

As he lay, pondering what to do with the free hours ahead, the sound of thumps and bumps floated up the stairs from the lounge below and he didn't need to be a mind reader to know Choona and Chips were undoubtedly creating havoc whilst waiting for their breakfast. Flora had been so right when she'd said it was worth getting Choona a playmate. Yes, there had been the expected hissing and grumbling at the start but after a few mutual rub-downs with an old sock, lots of crunchy treats, and several games involving a feather on the end of a stick, the kittens had quickly realised there was a lot more fun – and a lot more mischief – to be had if they teamed up. They were utterly adorable when playing together and Kenneth often found himself watching their antics rather than whatever was on the television. He was so glad he'd taken Flora's advice.

Flora...

Although he hadn't seen her since they'd both been mugged at Morag's rescue centre, he thought of her often and there had been a reasonable exchange of texts, mostly concerning how their respective rescues were settling in rather than anything personal. This didn't overly bother him because it was giving him space to think over how he felt about her. Her startling silver eyes, fiery auburn hair, and stubborn chin tilt popped up most nights when he closed his eyes to sleep and he simply couldn't decide if she was just a new, close friend or if something more was brewing. His logic kept being the voice of reason by asking why it couldn't be both—

Suddenly, an almighty crash from below had him bolting upright and swinging his legs out of bed.

'What have you two done now?' he muttered, shoving his feet into his slippers and running down the stairs. The kitchen bin, lying on its side by the kitchen door, answered his question.

'Honestly, you pair are going to be the death of me!'

He righted the bin and scooped up the rubbish that had tried to make a break for freedom.

'Where are you?'

His gaze swept around the room and came to rest on two little noses and four shining eyes peeping out from under the sofa. A soft sigh slipped from his lips as he knelt on the floor.

'Come here, you pair of wee monkeys!'

He patted the floor and two little chunky bodies wriggled out to scamper towards him.

'You'll need to find another hiding place, guys, because your days of getting under there are numbered,' he said, while gathering the wriggling bundles of fur into his arms and smooshing them on the head with his chin.

He popped them back on the floor, picked up their food bowls and quickly sorted out their breakfast. Once they had their teeny snouts in their troughs, he sorted himself out with coffee and toast and sat by the window, looking out across the valley while he ate, admiring the sun glittering on Flora's loch below.

Flora's loch… Why did everything seem to lead back to Flora? Even as the question lit up his brain, he could hear his mother's voice, "Some things are just meant to be…". Hmm, he wasn't one for fanciful thinking and that would *definitely* be fanciful thinking on his mum's part. However, even as these thoughts were going through his head, he found himself picking up his phone and sending Flora a text.

> Hi, how are you? If you're not busy,
> do you fancying going out for the day?
> Ullapool isn't too far and I think you'd like it.

He hit the send button and picked up his second slice of toast while waiting for her reply. The table had been cleared and he was heading towards the shower when his phone pinged. He rushed over to pick it up, surprised at being excited to see what she'd written.

> Hi there, I'm well, thank you, hope you
> are too. Ullapool would be lovely but,
> unfortunately, I already have plans for
> today. Can we arrange for another time?

In an instant, his good mood shrivelled up and crept away and even though he knew it was absolutely none of his business, he found himself pondering what she could be doing and who she was doing it with. He sat back down, wallowing in his disappointment for a few minutes until a glance out the window had him shaking it off.

'No!' he said firmly into thin air. 'No, I'm not doing this again. I will not permit a woman to dictate my frame of mind and wellbeing. Done it once, not doing it again!' and with that he turned on his heel, made his way to the understairs cupboard and pulled out his hiking boots and walking sticks. Once upon a time, he'd known these hills like the back of hand. It was time to get reacquainted and today was the perfect day to do it.

THIRTY-NINE

Flora groaned when she walked into her bedroom and collapsed across the bed. The assurance from MacAndrew that this was the most arduous of all the heather picking duties, did nothing to ease her exhaustion.

At ten-thirty last night, MacAndrew had led her on a hike over to the opposite end of the loch and up to the top of the highest mountain, all the time explaining the heather was collected from a different source on each equinox. The hills and mountains farthest from the cottage were worked in the spring and summer meaning those closer to home were picked in the cooler autumn and winter months.

They'd arrived at their starting location fifteen minutes before midnight and it had been a strange feeling to be up a mountain at that time of night. The air around them was totally still, as though all the sylphs were holding their breath in anticipation of her first night and the stars were the brightest she'd ever seen them. There was little opportunity to fully absorb the magical atmosphere because MacAndrew had been quick to give her a crash course on how to cut the heather although no heather was actually snipped until five minutes after midnight. This was vital to ensure it was fully imbued with the power of the equinox. Flora couldn't see what difference fifteen or twenty minutes could possibly make but MacAndrew was adamant about the timings and she wasn't inclined to argue with him. It had been her job to cut the heather – a task which could ONLY be done by The Flora, she'd been informed – while MacAndrew had the task of bringing the full baskets back to the cottage. She hadn't worked out how he'd managed this and by the time she'd finished cutting at four-thirty – heather gathered on the sunrise was, apparently, just as potent with healing properties as that cut after midnight – she wasn't inclined to question him. All she'd wanted was a long, hot bath to ease the pain in her back, shoulders, arms, and hands. Except, when they'd stumbled through the cottage door, MacAndrew had whisked her down to the still room where they'd proceeded to bottle, bash, grind and mix, along with a plethora of other techniques, that would preserve the product until it was required for her lotions, potions, and tinctures. When everything had been labelled to MacAndrew's satisfaction and the still room had been cleaned, he'd sat her down to eat a massive fry-up before sending her upstairs with a tub of their heather body rub to use after her bath. He'd also left her with the instruction that they'd be going back out at eight-thirty for a second pick as the sun set. Even knowing the second pick wouldn't be as long for they stopped at a minute to midnight, Flora was so thoroughly shattered that she couldn't bear the thought of moving again.

'How did it go?'

A little cold, wet nose pushed against her cheek as Friand butted his head gently against hers.

'I hurt! All over!'

'You knew it wasn't going to be easy.'

'I know but that doesn't mean I don't hurt! Everything aches!'

'Then shift yer butt and get in the bath. It'll help.'

'I don't wanna move…'

'Well, you have to! So, get on with it.'

'Why are you so bossy?'

'Because I'm older than you.'

'But you're a lot smaller. I could just sit on you to shut you up.'

'Well, you could try but you'd fail on two counts.'

'Which are?'

'Firstly, your ass ain't big enough to squash me and, secondly, it would require moving…'

'Okay, you win on point two. I'm incapable of moving.'

'Look, I'll ask the troll to begin running the bath for you. I'll even kick in a couple of the heather bath bombs. Between those and the body rub, they should ease the aches out of you.'

'Yeah, whatever…'

Flora felt her eyelids growing heavy but she also knew that going to sleep before having a soak in the tub would render her almost immobile when she woke up later. It was better to force herself to stay awake just a little longer…

'Wha— Eh? OUCH!'

Flora rolled over on the bed and pulled her foot up to rub her big toe.

'Did you just bite me, you little shit?'

'Yes, I did! Now I need to find some catnip to get the taste of heifer out my mouth. Go and get in that bath NOW!'

Friand was walking down the stairs, his tail stiff and upright as she moaned her way to the bathroom. If this was how the Tin Man in the Wizard of Oz felt, then she had a lot more sympathy for him now than she'd ever had before. With no small amount of difficulty, she managed to ease out of her clothes, and slipped down into the warm, lightly-scented, water. Another groan forced its way from her lips as the heat began to gently work on her poor, taut muscles.

She didn't know how long she'd been soaking but she'd topped the water up twice and was contemplating doing so a third time when her phone grunted at her. She immediately knew it was a text from Kenneth as she'd, rather naughtily, attached the grumpy tone to his name. After drying her hands, she pulled the phone from her jeans pocket and read his message.

'Oh damn!'

Her head dropped back onto the bath cushion as she worked out how to reply. She would've loved to visit Ullapool and, in her tiredness, couldn't fight the admission that she'd have enjoyed it even more by being in his company, but today just wasn't an option. Sadly, she couldn't give him the reason why she was declining his offer because his mind was still closed to what she was and all that it entailed. She knew he wouldn't understand.

After sending back her reply, which she hoped he'd be able to discern her regret at having to refuse, she slipped lower into the water, trying to drown the feeling of disappointment now sitting on her chest.

A few minutes passed until, with a growl of annoyance, Flora got out of the bath and dried herself off. As she worked the heathery body rub into her not-as-sore-as-they-were-but-still-sore-enough muscles, she wondered if there was a recipe in the magical potions book downstairs that could erase people you didn't want to think about from your mind. She didn't want to keep dwelling on Kenneth – she had enough going on with her growing powers and continuing education under MacAndrew's tutelage. The last thing she needed was a man trying to take up space in a head that was already overcrowded.

Somehow, she made it back to her bedroom just before

the enormous wave of exhaustion hit her and she was already asleep when her head dropped onto the pillow. She woke briefly when Friand padded quietly into the bedroom a few minutes later and jumped up onto the bed.

'*Sleep sweet, my Flora,*' he said, nudging the duvet up over her shoulders before turning around to make himself comfortable in the small of her back and joining her as she fell back asleep.

FORTY

Flora scanned the lay of the land as she made her way up the single-track road. She glanced at the written directions on the seat next to her and was sure she'd followed them to the letter. Five minutes after the next bend in the road, she'd be able to see Trina's farmhouse. Well, according to Trina's instructions, that was.

She checked the time and seeing that she was almost twenty-five minutes early, she pulled over and switched off the engine. There was time to enjoy the view through the car window.

It was mid-July and the constant rain from the earlier half of the month had finally given way to sunlit days with brilliant blue skies which were occasionally decorated by a smattering of fluffy clouds meandering by. From her current viewpoint, the brilliance of the sun enhanced the vibrant blues and lilacs of the heather on the surrounding mountains, sporadically interspersed with flashes of green bracken. The blue horizon was broken up by the peaked mountain tops surrounding her and she couldn't remember a time when she'd ever felt so peaceful.

Over two months had passed since she'd arrived at her grandmother's cottage and she was no closer to making a decision on her future. Her days had fallen into a routine where MacAndrew spent the mornings in the still room teaching her the merits of the potions they made, the benefits of the different herbs and flowers they used, and how to mix them "just so" to ensure they blended properly. Who knew that one anticlockwise stir too many could ruin a full batch of hand cream? Or that using a silver ladle instead of a copper one to scoop out the cough tincture would turn it from a light, golden syrup into a congealed, murky brown, lump of jelly? She hadn't... but she did now!

Once all the heather they'd harvested at the Solstice had been utilised and safely stored, they'd moved onto her developing magical powers. This part of her training, however, was hampered by the fact she'd yet to don the necklace and absorb its knowledge. She could perform small acts such as summoning a bottle or container from the opposite side of the room, making her bed in the mornings, and turning the pages of her book without the use of her hands – the latter being especially helpful when working in the still room and both hands were busy with pouring and stirring at the same time.

The afternoons were her own and she spent these working on her matryoshka dolls. Her initial intention had been to clear some space up in the loft, sure her Uncle Craig wouldn't object to his room being taken over for her work, but MacAndrew had come up trumps with a small hut near the cottage that had three sides of glass which gave her excellent lighting. She was sure it had once been a greenhouse of sorts but she wasn't complaining as it was perfect for her requirements. MacAndrew had gone to some effort to make it cosy for her with a deep-piled duck-egg blue rug on the stone floor that matched the blue on the solitary wall. In one corner he'd placed a soft, cosy armchair with a small footstool next to a quaint little wood-burner with a cushion for Friand nearby. Lemon shades adorned the windows so she could pull down or raise up as required. She'd found herself making almost double the number of orders than before she'd moved because there were no distractions. The phone didn't ring as she made a point of leaving her mobile in the cottage and MacAndrew always had dinner ready no matter how late she worked so there was no need to stop in the middle of painting to make something to eat and no father popping his head in telling her not to work too hard. She missed the last one but her heart remained a chunk of stone in her chest when it came to thoughts of her dad. Every time she made a mistake in her training, and MacAndrew let out a tut of disappointment, she was doubly aware of the grandmother she'd lost out on and the pain would stampede through her once again. Interestingly, on these occasions, Friand was the one to bring her comfort. His usual sarcasm was shelved and he'd soothe her until she was ready to continue. He'd become her shadow and she was rarely without him by her side.

Almost, as if by the power of thought, her phone beeped and, turning it over, she saw a text from her dad. A sigh escaped her lips as she dropped the mobile back into the well between the seats. He didn't know the half of it. He didn't know about the bullying she'd endured at school for being the only kid without a mum. Or the fake friends who'd come for sleepovers because their single mothers had forced them just so they could get closer to her widowed father. All her life, she'd felt at odds with people. Her friends had been few and her boyfriends fewer. Even at university, where she'd been included in a small gang of fellow students, the sense of not belonging prevailed. Her father, so caught up in his own deep-seated grief hadn't been aware and she'd never told him. Her Uncle Craig, on the other hand, had understood all too well for he'd been there himself in his younger days although he'd had his sister, her mother, to look out for him. Flora had felt alone all her life and she couldn't help but wonder now if having a relationship with her grandmother could have helped her with that. In the spirit of fairness, she'd acknowledged there had been nothing stopping her contacting her grandmother herself. Well... nothing except the fear of rejection – the one thing all lonely people worry about. A fear that would have been unfounded had her father passed on the correspondence she'd been sent.

After watching a hovering kestrel get beaten to its prey by a swooping hawk of some description, Flora turned the engine back on. If she didn't get a wriggle on, she'd be late and she was so looking forward to spending this time with Trina who was slowly becoming the friend she'd had been yearning for all these years.

While putting the car into gear, she took one last look out of the window – glorious, breath-taking, views were all well and good but they allowed too much headspace for one to think!

FORTY-ONE

'Oh, Trina, that was all delicious. Thank you.'

'You're welcome. I didn't want to overload you with traditional Scottish cuisine, which is why it was a roast chicken for the main course, but I'm glad you liked your starter and dessert.'

'Both were so tasty. The soup, Cullen...?'

'Skink. Cullen Skink. It's a local speciality – well, if you can call seventy-odd miles "local" that is.' Trina grinned as she spoke.

'Given the sparse population in some Scottish regions, Trina, seventy-odd miles is almost "neighbourly"!'

Both Flora and Trina laughed at Bobby's pithy comment.

'That dessert, though. Really was something else.'

'It's only because Trina's pregnant that there was less of a kick to the cranachan than usual.'

'And the fact Flora has to drive home again, my darling husband!' Trina turned to Flora. 'Under normal circumstances, there would've been a lot more whisky in the mix.'

'Right! It's a good thing I'm developing a taste for whisky then…'

'I'd offer you a Scotch coffee to help you with that but you know… driving…'

Flora laughed again. 'Maybe another time after a less boozy pudding.'

Bobby stood and took the plates from the table, asking as he did so, 'Would you ladies like to retire to the lounge or are you okay here?'

Flora looked across at Trina. 'I'm fine here but if you'd like a softer chair to sit on…'

'Actually, I'm better in these chairs. They support my back which is giving me some amount of gyp this time around.' She gave it a rub as though to emphasise her point.

Flora sat back in her own chair with a smile on her face. The kitchen they were sitting in was not dissimilar to Mhari's kitchen and she'd come to the assumption it must be a farmhouse thing. The worktops were cluttered, the shelves on the wall were crammed with all kinds of bric-a-brac while bits of post, flyers, and booklets peeked out around the sides. The terracotta tiles under her feet held the marks and scuffs that came from years of boots and muck being walked across them. Crude, childish, drawings were held on the door of the fridge by whacky magnets, and a large calendar, featuring a big, hairy, Highland cow, was pinned up next to the doorway to the hall. The room had a lovely, lived-in, homely atmosphere and after the painful memories she'd dug up on her way here, it was the soothing balm she needed.

'Here we go then. Tuck in.'

Bobby placed a jug of coffee on the table along with a plate of shortbread. He returned a moment later with a small jug that he placed in front of Trina.

'And a special decaf just for you, my love.' He placed a little kiss on Trina's head before returning to his seat.

'So, Flora,' he said, while pouring cream into his cup, 'have you decided to stay yet?'

Copying his actions, Flora took a few seconds to think about her answer.

'To be honest, I haven't. Now that I'm here, I really don't think I want to leave but at the same time, I'm not sure if it's where I should be. Does that make any sense?'

'It does to me. I'm from Glasgow originally and met Trina at college. We were both on the Aberdeen campus of the SRUC.'

'SRUC?'

'Sorry, that's the Scottish Rural College. The agricultural and organic farming courses are held there. I was doing the agricultural course and Trina was on the organic. After we got together, we'd spend all our holidays here on the farm and I knew I never wanted to return to Glasgow. Something here just made me feel... how can I put it... at peace? Like I'd come home? Where I was meant to be?'

Flora nodded as he spoke. 'Finally in the right place where your soul feels happy.'

'Exactly that!'

'My parents couldn't have been happier when we both said we wanted to live here after we were married. With me being an only child, they'd worried about the farm should anything happen to them. Knowing we'd be here to keep it going was a weight off their minds.' Trina took hold of Bobby's hand as she spoke and seeing the love flowing between them, Flora felt in awe of their closeness.

'So, no siblings, then?'

'No. Mum had a difficult pregnancy with me and the doctors suggested it might be best not to do it again. Which is a shame given she'd wanted a large family. Mind you, she was lucky to be here herself.'

'Oh, how so?'

'As weird as it sounds, the women in my family are blessed with long umbilical cords. You'd think that umbilical cords would be all pretty much the same length but they're not.'

'I have to say,' Flora replied, 'it's not something I've ever thought about.'

'Well, there you go, your something new for today. Anyway, long chords can lead to complications, primarily getting twisted about babies' necks. Which is what happened with my mum. If the chord is twisted once, it's easily remedied but twice – as in the case here – it becomes more complicated.'

'I can well imagine. What happened?'

'Your great-grandmother saved the day.'

'She did? How?'

'We don't rightly know. Back then, home births were quite the norm, especially around here, and The Flora was always in attendance. The doctor was also there, encouraging my granny to push but nothing was happening. No baby was popping out. Suddenly, The Flora stopped him. Somehow, she knew there was a problem and told the doctor to move aside. Whatever she did, it worked. Five minutes later, she asked my granny to push again and no sooner had she done so, when my mum's head popped out.'

'Oh wow!'

'Indeed! And, let me tell you, if I was having a home birth, you'd be the first person on my list to call when labour began.'

'Oh, goodness, please don't do that. I don't know a thing. The doctor would be giving me your gas and air!'

Triana burst out laughing at Flora's mock shudders. 'Oh, you have no need to worry. It's off to the hospital for me at the end of September. I had both my boys in hospital and everything was fine with them. This little lady,' Trina patted her bump, 'will be doing the same, just in case it turns out to be a girl thing.'

'I'm SO glad to hear that. Consider my huge sigh of relief exhaled!'

There was laughter and giggles around the table as Bobby refreshed their drinks.

'Going back to my original question, Flora, there was a reason for asking–'

'No, Bobby, you can't.'

'I have to, Trina.'

'Hey, it's fine, guys. You can ask me anything.'

'I was wondering when you'd be giving us the harvesting dates.'

'The what?'

'The harvesting dates.'

Flora looked from one expectant face to the other. 'I'm really sorry but I don't know what you mean.'

She didn't miss the worried expression that passed between them after her comment.

'Urm, well... The Flora usually tells us, every year, when the rains will be coming and how long we have to get the harvest in.'

'I see. And this is important...?'

'Kind of. The grain must be dry when harvested to ensure it doesn't rot or go mouldy. Ideally, we like a few days after the last rainfall to let the crops dry out before we cut. However, if there is rain coming just as we begin the harvest, that also causes issues. The Flora lets us know what window of time we have before the heavy rain comes again.'

'Right. I see.' Somewhere, in the furthest corner of her brain, a tiny little bell tinkled but she couldn't recall why it would. 'Hmmm... you're... um... going to have to leave that one with me while I investigate further.'

'Sure, okay.'

The look of relief on Triana and Bobby's faces had Flora's insides churning over on a fast spin. What on earth was she supposed to do here? And why hadn't MacAndrew mentioned it to her?

FORTY-TWO

'MacAndrew! Why didn't you tell me?'

'I did! It's in the folder I gave you and told you to learn! You told me you'd read it!'

'Well, clearly, I'd forgotten. You should have reminded me. I felt a right fool yesterday when Bobby brought the subject up and I didn't have a clue what he was talking about.'

'Well, here's a suggestion. Make your mind up that you're staying and put on the bloody necklace. THEN you'll know everything you need to know. I'm not The Flora, you are! I'm supposed to help you deal with the knowledge – not GIVE you the knowledge!'

The little man slipped off his chair, stormed through the door to the scullery and slammed it behind him.

Flora pushed her half-eaten bacon roll away and dropped her head into her hands. She'd expected MacAndrew to tell her what she had to do to obtain this information but now felt it was something she had to solve herself.

A gentle nudge against her leg had her looking down to

see Friand sitting at her feet. She smiled at him even though it was the last thing she felt like doing.

'Hey, where have you been?'

'Talking to the water.'

'You've what?'

'Been talking to the water. Well, the things in the water, to be exact.'

He jumped up on to the table and walked over to sniff at her discarded roll.

'Ah, you've met Walter, then?'

'If that's what you call him. Are you planning to eat this?'

'No, I'm not. So, what do you call him?'

'I can't tell you.' He crunched down on the remains of the crispy bacon.

'Why not?'

'Your useless human ears would burst with the pitch of the sound. Even ones the size of yours.'

'Hey, are you saying I have big ears?'

'Compared to mine they are.'

'It's called proportion, mate! I'd look really silly with tiny ears like yours.'

'Trust me, love, when it comes to looking silly, your ears are the least of your problems!'

'Thank you for that! You do know Morag is only one quick phone call away…'

'Yeah, whatever. Now, have you sorted out what you need to do?'

'Regarding what?'

'Regarding whatever had the troll storming off in a huff.'

'I basically have to get a long-term weather forecast to the local farmers so they can get on with their harvests.'

'Right. Well, that's easy.'

'It is?'

'Duh! How can someone with your gifts be so dense?'

'Again, with the compliments...'

'Think about it, Flora. Think about your gifts. Think about the unusual things you've done since you arrived here. Surely one of them is the answer.'

Flora looked at Friand, mulling over his words as he licked the buttery, bacon residue from the plate. Suddenly, it came to her.

She leapt up, her chair scraping behind her, grasped Friand's furry face in her hands, and plonked a big, fat kiss on his nose.

'Oi! Gerroff, you stinky pink oaf!'

'Friand, I love you. Thank you.'

With that, Flora whirled around and ran out the door. She knew exactly what she had to do.

'Come on, you two, keep up.'

Kirsty and Sandy were busy sniffing around the vegetation on the side of the path while Flora was practically running as she made her way to the rock crop where she'd first spoken with Ahana, the Air Sylph. If anyone was going to have this information, it would be the sylphs, surely...

She clambered onto the overhanging rock and wondered if she should call on Walter. Maybe Ahana only came to her the last time because she saw Walter sitting with her.

'No! I'm doing this myself! It's time to stop relying on everyone else.'

She took another minute to steady herself, taking in deep breaths and holding them while shaking out her arms and legs. Finally, she felt composed enough to try and raised her arms above her head.

With Walter's instructions in mind, she slowly began to weave a figure of eight in the air. At first, nothing happened and she was beginning to think the previous occasion had been a fluke when some instinct seemed to kick in and she "knew" she had to speed up her actions. Another moment passed until suddenly, like before, the atmosphere around her changed and everything grew still and silent. She lowered her arms as she felt the kitten-like tickle in her ears.

'Ah, The Flora has come to call on us again. What do you need to know?'

This was not Ahana. The voice in her ear held a ring of maturity, making Flora gulp with a sense of fear. Was this one of the older sylphs Walter had warned her about?

'Hello, I am The Flora. Who am I speaking with today?'

How she managed to keep her voice from quivering, she didn't know but she was glad she'd managed it. Her earlier instinct was now telling her she mustn't show any weakness.

'I am Nasima.'

'It's an honour to meet you, Nasima. How is Ahana?'

'She is Air, she is as she is. What do you want from us today, The Flora?'

Hmmm, no messing about here, straight to the point…

'The farmers are asking when they can harvest. I need to know when it will rain. Please could you share this information with me?'

For several seconds there was silence and had it not been for the stillness around her, Flora would have thought Nasima had left. Breathing as softly as possible, she waited until, eventually, the tickling sensation returned and Nasima spoke.

'Ten suns will rise and bring rain with them. There will be seven suns with no rain but it will come with the stars. There will finally be eight suns rising which come alone.'

Once again, all went quiet as she absorbed Nasima's words.

'So, you are saying there be will ten days with rain, seven days which are dry but it will rain through the night and then there will be eight days and nights with no rain at all. Is that correct?'

'It is. Well done.'

'Urm, don't want to be rude but couldn't you just have said that in the first place?'

'We like to play with The Flora. We like to test her. We need to know she is worthy.'

'Of what? Worthy of what?'

'Of being, Flora. Worthy of being.'

'But… I…'

The sentence remained unfinished as the stillness dropped away and she was again surrounded by the swoosh of the water in the loch, the chirruping of the birds in the trees and the rustle of the leaves as the gentle breeze skipped through them.

She'd done it.

She'd only gone and done it!

With a whoop and a holler, she jumped down off the rock and, with Kirsty and Sandy bounding in her wake, ran as fast as she could towards the cottage. She had a phone call to make.

FORTY-THREE

'Hey, Mum, how are you?'

Mhari spun round and Kenneth smiled to see the joy in her eyes at his presence.

'Kenneth, oh, what a lovely surprise. Are you staying long? Shall I put the kettle on?'

'If it's not too much trouble, Mum, that would be lovely. Thank you.'

He pulled out his usual chair at the table and sat down, a smile on his face as he watched his mother fussing around, gathering up the ingredients for her tea and his coffee. She paused by the bread board upon which the huge homemade bloomer sat, ready to feed any hungry workers who passed by the farmhouse each day. Raising the knife as well as her eyebrows, he nodded his assent – a buttered doorstep topped with a slab of cheese and his mum's own special chutney, was exactly what this doctor was ordering for himself!

'So, what brings you into my kitchen at this time of the day? It's not even noon yet.'

A quick glance at the clock showed that, in five minutes

time it would be.

'I was over at the Brodies and thought I'd drop in on my way past as my next appointment isn't until two.'

'You can drop in any time you're passing, son.' She patted his shoulder as she put a mug of coffee on the table in front of him. 'Guess what – we got an email from your brother today.'

'Oh, lovely. Did he have good news?'

'Yes. He's confirmed their visit. He and Clarissa are arriving in ten days and staying for a month. I don't think he'll be so happy though when he finds out we'll be starting the harvest the same day. You know the rules – it's all hands on deck.'

'Mum, I don't think Ross will mind at all. He's stuck behind a desk all day so I suspect he'll relish the physical labour. What about Clarissa though?'

'Oh, she'll muck in too. She did the last time she was here and seemed to love it. I'm going to put them in the cabin across from yours – are you okay with that?'

'Er, of course. Why wouldn't I be?'

'Well, you and Ross used to, well… you know… argue a lot… when you were kids.'

'Mum, that was a long time ago. You forget he lived with me in London for a time and we got along just fine. It'll be nice to have him close – we'll have a chance for some proper catchups.'

'Clarissa's mum, Essie, and her partner, Craig, are also visiting for a week. They'll be here for the Harvest Dance.'

'You've met them before, haven't you?'

'Yes, they were staying with Craig's mum – she was The Flora at the time – just before Ross went off to Japan. They helped with the harvest that year too. I like Essie a lot so I'm looking forward to seeing her.'

Kenneth, tackling a large mouthful of bread and cheese, nodded at his mum.

'Talking of The Floras – have you seen our new one recently?'

He took a sip of his coffee before shaking his head. 'No, I haven't. Not for a few weeks. I asked her to come to Ullapool with me but she declined, saying she already had plans. So, I've kind of backed off since. I know where I'm not wanted.'

'When was this? You asking her to Ullapool?'

'June. Mid-summer.'

'The day of the Solstice?'

'Yeah, that's right.'

'Och, ya big daftie! That's when The Flora gathers the heather.'

'Excuse me?'

'You know the heather products she makes – well, the Solstices are the gathering times. Something to do with the potency, I believe. They gather through the night so the lass would have been busy with that.'

'Oh, right. I didn't know. How do you know this?'

His mum shrugged. 'I've always known, since I was a child. I think it's one of those things that just come down through families. I've got a vague memory of my granny talking about it. Anyway, I have a valid excuse for you to visit her.'

'I don't need an excuse.'

'Well, I'm giving you one so you have a good reason to see her sooner rather than later.'

'Fine. What is it? I'll go after work this evening.'

'It's a bit of a strange one and no one knows quite what to do. I got a phone call last night. Some man has been going about enquiring after her around Beauly and Muir of Ord. Asking people if they know of her and where she lives.'

This made Kenneth sit up straighter in his chair.

'In what way is he asking? Threatening? Frightening?'

'No, not that I've been told. He's tall-ish, lanky-like, brown hair that sort of just hangs there, brown eyes. Caucasian. Pretty non-descript from what I can gather.'

'I see.'

'My thinking is that, if it was someone she wanted to keep in touch with, he'd already have her contact details. Has she said anything to you about running away from anyone?'

'No, she hasn't. As far I know, the only person she wants distance from is her dad.'

'Hmmmm, well, it might be nothing but she should know – just in case it is something bigger.'

'Has anyone told this bloke where to find her?'

'Of course not! We're all so thrilled to have our Flora back, there's no way we'd do anything to upset her. You can tell her that everyone is keeping her a secret and this man, whoever he is, knows nothing.'

'Thanks, Mum. I'm sure that'll give her some peace of mind.' He looked up at the clock again. 'Look, I'd planned to stay a little longer, but if I go now, I can do some admin meaning I get to leave the surgery immediately after my last patient this evening.'

'Then, get off with you. And please tell Flora she has an open invite to visit here whenever she likes. We still have things to discuss but I don't want to rush her into anything.'

'I will, Mum.'

He kissed her on the cheek and made a speedy exit to his car. He didn't like the sound of this man trying to locate Flora and the sooner he discussed it with her, the more at ease he would feel.

Or, at least, he hoped so.

FORTY-FOUR

'Oh, you ARROGANT little knobhead! Just you wait till I get my hands on you!'

Kenneth arrived at the open door of Flora's cottage in time to hear a string of expletives that would make a miner blush.

'Err, hello?'

He tapped on the door while stepping over the threshold, hoping he'd arrived in time to prevent Flora from carrying out the threats she was uttering.

'In here,' came her voice from the kitchen and he walked in as a plastic beaker went flying across the room.

'Hey, what's wrong? I could hear you outside.'

'ARGH!'

She let out a growl of frustration before thrusting a letter towards him. As he took it, the first thing he noticed was the quality of the paper. Creamy, thick, and weighty. The good stuff normally used by lawyers and the heading across the top confirmed that.

'You want me to read it?'

'Please. I want to ensure it says exactly what I think it

says.'

Kenneth walked across to the window, reading as he went. By the time he was standing in front of the window seat, the shock from the words in front of him was beginning to mount. When he reached the end of the two pages, he turned back to go through it again from the beginning. Eventually, he looked at Flora who was clearly incandescent with rage and somewhere in the back of his head, a spark of admiration flared up that she'd managed to remain silent while so furious.

'Okay. My take from this,' he lifted the papers in his hand, 'is that you've agreed to sell the cottage and surrounding land back to the Laird for the sum of one-hundred and forty-nine thousand pounds and once a surveyor has visited to confirm he is in agreement with the value, the contracts will be sent out for signature.'

'Thank you, that's how I read it too.'

'I didn't know you were selling. The last time we discussed it, you weren't keen. Said something about keeping the cottage as a holiday home.'

'I'm not selling! I wasn't then but I'm definitely not now! Who the HELL does he think he is?'

'Jack Arlingh is a jumped-up little oik who believes he's more than he really is and always had ideas above his station. He thinks he's some big wheeler-dealer type but he lacks both the intelligence and the desire for the hard work required to become one. I know him from when I was younger and he liked to throw his weight around even then.'

'Well, from what I saw, I reckon he's got some more of that weight now and it's not going to decrease as the years go by.'

'You're probably right. He's always been a bit of a chunker. Anyway, what are you going to do?'

'Many things come to mind but the first one will be to

call this solicitor in the morning, advising them in no uncertain terms that this land is not, and never will be, for sale. Especially not to Jack Arlingh! I'll follow it up with an equally strong email confirming my phone call in writing.'

'Not going to turn him into a frog, I hope?'

'That's not outside the realms of possibility! Cup of tea?'

As Flora spun around and marched over to the sink to fill the kettle, there was something in her tone which sent a shiver up his spine. Kenneth gave his head a shake – it was only the ghost of the stories his mum had shared about The Flora having magical powers. Stories he'd always refused to believe. He wasn't about to start now.

An almighty rumble escaped from Kenneth's stomach as the tantalising aroma of salt and vinegar doused fish and chips from The Friary in Beauly, rose up from the passenger footwell of the car. Despite her anger, he'd seen that Flora was upset by the letter she'd received. And rightly so! To discover someone was trying to take your home out from under your feet like that… Well, it beggared belief! Although, knowing Jack Arlingh as he did, Kenneth wasn't surprised. He'd always been a nasty piece of work. He was a classic example of most bullies – not particularly bright and tried to use his bulk and status to intimidate those around him into doing his bidding. His father, the Laird, was a nice, down-to-earth bloke who'd insisted on sending both of his children to the local schools. He believed it was better for them to be a part of the local community from a young age, enabling them to better serve the area they were the custodians of. Jack's younger sister, Alanna, had been in his year at school although they'd moved in different circles. The few occasions when their paths crossed, Kenneth had always come away with the impression that she was a chip off her father's block – pleasant and amiable to those around her.

Jack, on the other hand, had made the lives of the younger kids quite miserable. Like all bullies, he had the knack for sniffing out the quieter children and Kenneth had been one of his targets. It had been a short-lived experience, however, since it hadn't taken Fraser long to assess the situation and step in. Jack Arlingh may have been bulky but Fraser was as tall as he was broad, even back then, and after he'd finished "having a word" Arlingh had backed right off and never came near him again. A year later, however, he went too far and a boy ended up in hospital. The Laird was furious. He pulled Jack from the school, called in a favour and the last they heard, Jack was off to some military boarding school in the south of England. Everyone pressured Alanna for more information but all she said was her father hoped the strict discipline of the boarding school would sort out Jack and his attitude.

Well, thought Kenneth, as he turned off the main road and began to carefully make his way through the trees, it looked like Daddy had spent all that money for nothing – Jack didn't seem to have changed at all.

He parked alongside the camper van, grabbed the thermal bag containing the goodies, and headed towards the cottage. As he walked down the side path, he heard the tinny sound of bagpipes and drums and when he walked around the corner, it was to see Flora contorting herself into the strangest of shapes while trying to look over her shoulder at the laptop sitting on the patio table. Friand was perched beside it and, if he didn't know better, Kenneth would've sworn the cat was laughing.

'Flora, what the heck are you doing?'

'Oh, you're back. That was quick.'

'I was lucky – there was no queue and they'd just

cooked up a fresh batch. Now stop evading the question…'

Flora closed the laptop, shooed Friand off the table and the dogs out from under it, then gave it a quick wipe down with a germ-killing spray before laying out the plates and cutlery.

She sighed before looking at him. 'I went through the rest of my post after you left and found an invite from your parents to attend their yearly Harvest Dance. Your mum enclosed a note saying it was a ceilidh and to wear appropriate footwear as lots of dancing would be involved. I didn't know what a ceilidh was so I investigated and found it involves a form of dancing which looks about three steps away from an evil kind of torture. I was trying to copy some of the moves when you found me…'

Her voice trailed off as Kenneth found himself trying not to laugh. It was okay for him, and every other kid educated in Scotland, they were taught the moves from a young age and had grown up hating the school Christmas parties because they were expected to do Scottish country dancing which had also included every boy's worst nightmare – dancing with GIRLS! They were also on a par with riding a bike in that, once you learnt, you never forgot. It had been several years since he'd been to his family's annual shindig but he still knew all the fancy footwork.

'Hey, don't worry about it. I'll help you. Let's eat first then we'll begin. The easiest one, in my opinion anyway, is the Gay Gordons. Once you have that under your belt, you'll feel more comfortable with the others.'

'The what? Say that again…'

'The Gay Gordons.'

'Are you winding me up?'

'No.'

'Yes, you are.'

As he placed one of the wrapped bundles on a plate and pushed it towards her, Kenneth knew where Flora was coming from. It was the dance name that had always caused much immature, teenage mirth amongst his fellow classmates.

'It's something to do with the Gordon Highlanders army regiment but I promise you, the name is the real deal.'

'Oh, wow, this fish is delicious.'

Flora blew on a hot chip which caused a little squirmy sensation in his stomach. Realising he'd missed being in her company the last few weeks, he wondered if she'd felt the same.

'So, when you say this dance is easy – how easy?'

'Very. There are only three moves to learn and then it's just repeated until the music stops.'

'And it will definitely be part of the dancing?'

'Oh yes, several times.'

Flora simply nodded, tucking into her fish and chips and there was silence while they both ate.

'They were lush and totally hit the spot. Thank you.' Flora sat back, gently massaging her stomach.

'No problem at all. Do you feel better now?'

'Yes, a little. The initial shock has worn off but I don't think I'll relax until I make that phone call. Anyway,' she smiled brightly at him and the squirmy sensation made another appearance, 'tell me more about this harvest dance. Do your parents always host or does everyone take turns? What's it all about?'

'It's a get-together for all the farmers in the area along with the farmhands, staff, and the local shopkeepers who support the farms by stocking their products. My family have been the hosts for as long as we can recall. Probably because our farm is one of the largest in the area. Although, it's all change this year.'

'Oh, how so?'

'We used to hold the dance in the hay barn near the farmhouse but my mum has completed her events village.

You know the cabins where I'm currently living? Well, Mum has just finished the renovation of an old barn about half a mile along the path from the cabins and the intention is to hire it out for weddings, corporate events and so on. The Harvest Dance will be its inaugural event.'

'Oh wow! How amazing. I bet it all looks fabulous.'

'I don't know. Mum has kept it a closely guarded secret. It's her latest project and she's thrown herself into it. She loves a challenge. Some years ago, it was the farm shop which then grew into a tea-room but now runs so smoothly it's been handed over to Alice to manage. That's when she began developing the village. What started off as old worker's huts became basic cabins to let out over the summer but they're now better-equipped cabins, almost luxury you could say, and the barn is the icing on the cake.'

'How do the local shopkeepers and businesses feel about this? I know my dad had occasions where new developments often faced a barrage of objections due to the threat to businesses in the area.'

'From what I can gather, everyone was on board. It'll bring more people into the area who will, hopefully, spend money while they're here. The catering will be done locally, using local produce and events material requirements will also be sourced – as much as possible – from suppliers in the region.'

'The "green" aspect could be a big vantage point.'

'It certainly will. However, what has my mum in a tizzy is nothing to do with the barn and everything to do with Ross and Clarissa coming home.'

'Wow! I didn't know that. Essie will be thrilled. I expect her and my uncle are already planning to visit.'

'Do you know Clarissa well? I haven't met her personally but we've chatted on FaceTime when I've been talking to Ross.'

'I barely know her. Although we're quite close in age,

her father was a bit of a tyrant who wouldn't allow her to mix with the local kids. Even though they lived in the village, he always thought he was a cut above the rest of us and Clarissa was sent to a private school. He'd have loved to have been our Laird given the opportunity! A few years ago, however, she made a less-than-salubrious discovery about her father which enabled her to break away from his overbearing manner and Essie, her mum, joined her in her escape.'

'I believe that's when she met Ross.'

'And her mum met my uncle. Although, apparently, they knew each other from uni but had lost touch. Anyway, Essie makes my uncle very happy and that's good enough for me. You'll like her when you meet her.'

'I'm sure I will – I look forward to it. Now, shall we move the table and chairs into the corner so you can have a go at some dancing? Once I've gone through the routine with you, we'll put on some hoochta-choochta music and try it out.'

'Some *what*?'

'Hoochta-choochta music.' Kenneth grinned. 'It's an expression we use for Scottish stuff. Bagpipes? Hoochta-choochta music. Scottish dancing? Hoochta-choochta dancing. Ceilidh? Hoochta-choochta party. Its origins lie in the word "hooch" which is a word exclaimed in joyous exaltation while dancing a Scottish reel.'

'I love it. Hooooch-ta choooochta.'

He grinned at Flora's attempt to pronounce the "ch" in the back of her throat, just like in the word loch. Easy for some folks to master, not so easy for others.

'Right then, on your feet. Let's try this…'

Two hours later, while driving home, Kenneth caught a glimpse of himself in the rearview mirror. He was surprised to see eyes full of twinkles looking back at him and a grin still hovering around his lips. Teaching Flora the dance moves had been a lot of fun and, amid much laughter, she was now able to say she could do one Scottish country dance routine. He'd promised to return the day after tomorrow, when the weather would be dry, to teach her another one. For her further amusement, he'd informed her they'd be learning the "Strip the Willow" which had, naturally, caused more hilarity. When he explained he'd only be able to teach her part of it since it was a dance requiring eight people – or four couples – she'd immediately sent a text to Trina who'd replied that she and Bobby would be delighted to join them for the next practise session. Kenneth just hoped Trina wouldn't get too carried away as this particular dance was rather boisterous and not one he'd recommend for pregnant women.

While reminiscing over the evening, he recalled a few occasions which had been a little strange – he'd caught Flora laughing at something over his shoulder but when he'd glanced round there was only the cat sitting by the cottage door. He'd asked why she was laughing and she'd simply replied it was at the hash she was making of the routine but it had still felt odd!

He pushed the thought away and returned to the look of joy on Flora's face when she finally perfected the routine. That had been a worthwhile moment.

Just as he stepped out of the car, Kenneth slapped his hand on his forehead. Damn it! He'd forgotten to tell her of the man asking around the village. He pulled out his phone but then hesitated. Was this the kind of news to impart over the phone? He thought for a moment before putting it back in his pocket. No, this needed to be told face-to-face and she had enough to deal with tomorrow with calling Arlingh's solicitor. It would keep for another couple of days.

FORTY-FIVE

Flora picked at the croissant in front of her. Her stomach was churning and she couldn't ascertain if it was trepidation at having to phone Arlingh's solicitor or anger at having to do so. She was feeling both in equal measure. The anger at the blasé manner of his actions, the trepidation that it may already be too late to stop the sale. She knew in England, it would be difficult to do this but Scottish law was different and her knowledge of it was zero. Kenneth has said she should be alright but until she had the telephone conversation, she wouldn't know.

'Hey, lass, eat up. Fretting won't change anything and you'll shout louder on a full stomach.'

'I'm worried, MacAndrew. What if the process is too far down the line to stop it?'

'You haven't engaged a solicitor and, while some verbal agreements are legally binding in Scotland, luckily it doesn't apply when it comes to land sales.'

'But I didn't agree…'

'You and I know that but you can be sure he's spun a different story to the lawyers. If they try to fob you off and say it is agreed, you reply by saying your solicitor will be in touch with them refuting the agreement, that any such arrangement had been made and that you'll be suing for false allegations if they try to continue. With luck, the threat will be enough to rein them in. If not, we get a solicitor on the case. You're not about to lose the cottage.'

'Thank you, MacAndrew, for that information. It helps.'

'You're welcome. Although,' the little man looked at her from the corner of his eye, 'does this mean you've become attached to your land? Have you decided to stay?'

She laughed. 'Never one to miss an opportunity, are you, MacAndrew? Let's just say I haven't yet decided to leave.'

'Hmph! Worth a try, I suppose…'

'There's one thing I've been meaning to ask you though…'

'What?'

'Am I correct in thinking that while I can see you, other people can't? Am I the only person who can see you?'

'I can be seen by those who have the gift.'

'Can humans ever see you?'

'Humans can see me but only if you introduce me to them. The formality of the introduction serves as a kind of bond of trust which makes me visible to them.'

'Right! So, if I were to introduce you to Kenneth—'

'Not so fast, missy! A couple of things first. It requires a massive belief of trust to make such an introduction. You must be *absolutely* sure the human can cope with the knowledge. Before that can happen, however, you need to—'

'Let me guess… put on the necklace!' she sighed.

'Now you're finally getting it. All the little "added extras" come at a price.'

'So it would seem.'

'Why are you so reluctant? Has being here done nothing to make your mind up?'

'It's not so much reluctance, MacAndrew, but more a case of not feeling up to the task. I don't believe I'm good enough to be The Flora.'

'Oh, lassie, not a single Flora who has gone before you ever felt ready to don the necklace. Do you think you're the only one to have been scared? Let me assure you they all worried about not being good enough and let me also assure you that they always were. You don't only gain powers, you gain knowledge too. Remember that. And, as I've said before, I think you'll be great. Now,' he glanced at the clock on the wall, 'don't you have a phone call to make?'

'Trina! Oh, my goodness, look at you. Where did that bump come from?' Flora had to move to the side to give her friend a welcoming hug.

'Tell me about it! I went to bed one night with a small, elegant protrusion and woke up the next morning looking like I'd eaten all the pies in the county!'

'Well, be sure to take it easy tonight. Babies born six weeks early can do just fine but I'd prefer you to keep it cooking a while longer.'

'Don't worry, Doctor MacKenzie, I only intend to do walk-throughs tonight.'

'Hey, call me Kenneth, please. We're not in the surgery now.'

'Okay. Well, let's get this show on the road while I still have some energy. I seem to have developed the knack of suddenly falling asleep as soon as I sit down.'

Half-an-hour later, Flora dropped down on the chair

beside Trina who'd excused herself after twenty minutes, preferring to watch from the sidelines while issuing instructions on who should be standing or dancing where, while gently stroking Kirsty's head as she and Sandy lay by her chair.

'You know, this one is much easier than the Gay Gordons Kenneth tortured me with the other night.'

Flora glanced around for Friand but he was nowhere to be seen.

'Ah, you say that now but just you wait till you're dancing it at speed and some big bit of brawn in a kilt is birlin you around at eighty miles an hour. We've walked through it tonight. This is as easy as you'll ever get it.'

'Oh, great! That's just boosted my confidence… not!'

Flora stood up. 'I think some cold drinks are called for. Be back shortly.'

When she stepped into the kitchen, she found MacAndrew standing by the pantry, beckoning her over.

'I've put a tray with a jug of fresh lemonade and glasses in there for you,' he pointed over his shoulder, 'but there's something upstairs I want to show you. You need to see it before you go back out.'

He did his little disappearing act before she could say anything and with a slight air of puzzlement, she ascended the stairs and found him waiting outside her bedroom.

'Tell me, MacAndrew,' she sighed, 'if I put on the necklace, will I have the power to jump to places as you do?'

'No, you won't,' he answered bluntly.

'One less reason to put it on then.'

'Clutching at straws there, girlie. Now come on.'

'What is it?'

'You'll need an outfit for the dance and I thought this might appeal.'

He opened the bedroom door and Flora walked in to

find Friand lying on the bed but just as she was about to comment, her attention was caught by one of the most beautiful dresses she'd ever seen hanging on the door of the wardrobe, causing her to let out a gasp of delight.

She walked over and let her hand glide softly across the lace overskirt before sliding underneath to feel the soft satin of the dress itself. The tea length style was perfect for dancing in – the full skirt would allow the freedom of movement she'd need for the Scottish reels and the satin bodice was finished off with lace shoulders and elegant cap sleeves to keep her cool. The colour reminded her of the purple heather that surrounded the cottage and a MacDonald tartan ribbon wound its way around the waist to fasten in a draping bow at the back. On the floor sat a pair of shoes dyed to match the dress. The slightly rounded toe, low heel and silver buckle strap told her they'd be comfortable enough to dance the night away.

'Oh, MacAndrew, this is gorgeous. I love it so much. Thank you. I really hope it fits me okay.'

'Don't you worry about that, it'll fit like a glove. It belonged to your grandmother – she wore it when she was your age. I hope that's alright with you.'

It took a moment for Flora to reply, such was the lump in her throat.

'It's more than alright. Much more than alright. Thank you.'

'Right. Good to know you won't be going to the ball in rags. I suggest you now get back to your friends – you've been gone just long enough to have sorted out a jug of homemade lemonade.'

'Here we go, fresh lemonade and shortbread for anyone who wants to replenish their energy levels.'

Flora, walking out to the patio with the tray in her hands, didn't miss the way the three bodies around the table sat back and stopped talking as she approached.

'Hey, what gives?' she asked, placing the tray down.

'What do you mean?'

'Trina, I can tell from your face that something was being discussed – what is it?'

Trina looked at Kenneth and Bobby before patting the seat beside her. 'Sit, there's something we need to share with you.'

Kenneth poured out the drinks as she sat down, wondering what *this* revelation was going to be.

'Flora,' he began, 'there's no easy way to say this so I'll just come out with it. There's a man been asking around after you down in the town. He's been showing your picture to the shopkeepers, asking if they know you and where to find you.'

'Excuse me? What?'

'I'm sorry. I meant to tell you the other night but I forgot. Mum told me to pass it on to you. She thought it would be better coming from me.'

'Right! I see.'

She took a drink of her lemonade, using the moment to have a think. Could it be her dad looking for her? No, he wouldn't do that. He'd phone and ask her to meet him so it was unlikely to be him.

'Do you have a description?'

'Yes, he stopped me yesterday in Muir of Ord as I was walking back to my truck.' Bobby closed his eyes as he continued, 'He's a tall lad, not old, maybe about the same ages as us. On the skinny side—'

'Oh, let me guess, big puppy brown eyes and brown hair that looks like it doesn't know if it's coming or going…'

'Yes!' Bobby's eyes sprang open. 'That's right! You

301

know him?'

'I do. And I really wish I didn't. His name's Joey. We dated for about six months but I broke it off last year. I never fancied him but he kept asking me out until I gave in and said yes. It was a total mistake – we were never suited but I hung on in the hope something might grow. He's a nice man but just not for me.'

'It would seem he's having a problem accepting that.'

Kenneth took her hand as he spoke, squeezing it gently. Despite her annoyance, Flora noticed how nice it felt as she squeezed his in return and was thrilled when he made no move to break the contact.

'I've told him several times that we're over but the message just won't sink in. He turned up on my doorstep the night before I left, begging me not to come up here. What I don't understand, though, is how he found out where I am. I certainly didn't give him that information.'

'You don't think he'd try anything weird, do you? You hear some terrible stories about rejected lovers taking revenge.'

'Trina, my darling wife, how is it that, even with two boisterous little boys, you still manage to watch so much daytime tripe on the television? Sharing those thoughts isn't going to make Flora feel better, is it?'

'Oh gosh, I'm sorry, I didn't think. I'm sure you'll be fine, Flora.'

Trina patted her shoulder and she put her free hand over it as she sought to reassure her friend she'd be okay.

'Hey, Trina, I'm sure Joey doesn't have any evil intentions towards me but you're right in that I should be careful because situations do change quickly. I do think he'll struggle to find me because, let's be honest, the location of the cottage is not well-known and even if he got as far as the layby, he wouldn't be able to get through the trees. Think of how detailed the instructions were that I gave you. Very few people have that information.'

Flora couldn't share that the trees would protect her but the knowledge was helping her to remain calm.

'Well, from what Mum says,' Kenneth let go of her hand to put his arm around her shoulder, pulling her in close to him, 'no one is telling him anything. Everyone's denying they know who you are.'

'That's right,' Trina agreed, 'we'll always protect our Flora and do all we can to keep her from harm.'

For the second time that night, Flora swallowed down a lump in her throat, deeply grateful to have already made such good friends in the short time she'd been at the cottage. She also couldn't help wondering, sitting this close to Kenneth, so nice and cosy, if there was a chance of something more growing between them.

Before she could dwell on it any further, Trina leant forward.

'Hey, to change the subject completely, have you thought of an outfit yet for the dance? With my choices being limited to either an army surplus parachute or a family-sized tent, I'm hoping you'll wear something sexy enough for the two of us.'

Flora laughed as she replied, 'Trina, you'd look sexy in an old coal sack—'

'Exactly what I keep telling her,' Bobby said, looking at his wife lovingly.

'—but as it happens, I already have my outfit. Would you like to see it?'

'Would I ever! Lead the way, babes!'

Kenneth gave her shoulder a gentle squeeze as she stood up and she could still feel the warmth of his fingers as she led Trina up the stairs to her bedroom.

FORTY-SIX

A glance at the clock on the wall behind Mrs Gordon, told Kenneth he had thirty minutes to go before he could finish up and get out of here. He couldn't wait. Tonight was the Harvest Dance and he was picking Flora up on the way home.

After several days of deliberation, or rather worrying, about how it would be received, he'd finally asked her if she'd like to stay the night at his cabin, after the dance. His reasoning was it would save her having to drive home and she'd be able to relax with a few drinks if she felt like it. With the cabins being just a short distance away from the barn, it made perfect sense to him. Unfortunately, both of his spare bedrooms were full of unpacked boxes but he would sleep on the sofa-bed downstairs and Flora could have his bedroom.

As was usually the case, he'd overthought the issue and Flora had agreed to his suggestion without hesitation. The deal was she'd do her hair and makeup at home then change into her outfit at his place. This way, if he was delayed at the surgery, there'd be no mad rush to get ready.

'Oh, thank you so much for listening, Doctor. I feel better already just for getting that off my chest.'

'Mrs Gordon, it's not easy being the primary care-giver and while I understand your husband's frustration with his reduced capacities, if he's going to vent at you, you need to be able to pass that on. You can't carry the burden on your own. Now, I'm going to get in touch with Social Services—'

'Oh, Doctor MacKenzie, I don't want them involved.'

'It's okay, Mrs Gordon, I understand. We have a social care group with volunteers who visit people such as yourself – primary care-givers. They just pop round a couple of times a week and you can talk about the weather, a TV programme you've watched, or anything that might be troubling you. They simply listen and if you ask for help, but ONLY if you ask, then they will assist in getting it for you. Think of them as being friends you've not yet met.'

'Well... it would be nice to have a wee blether, I suppose. It's good to lay your worries down for a time.'

'That's a good way of looking at it. When I have details of time slots available, I'll call to discuss which are convenient for you.'

'Thank you again, Doctor.'

'No problem, Mrs Gordon, it's what I'm here for. Now, let me get the door for you.'

He'd barely saved the update on Mrs Gordon's notes when there was a firm knock on the door and Jennet Cameron strode in. Other than the weekly meeting, he hadn't seen much of her recently. On each occasion, however, her attire usually merited a double-look and today was no different. Her blouse was fastened demurely up to the neck but was so tight, every small detail beneath it was visible. Or *not* so small, for that matter... It accompanied a black skirt that was so short, it would have to email her knees if they wanted to chat! The skirt too was on the tight side – so much so, he could see the outline of a suspender belt, and her high-heeled shoes were so high, he was in awe of her ability to walk in them. Under normal circumstances, he wouldn't notice a woman's clothing in such detail but as Jennet had perched herself on his desk next to his chair, it was rather difficult not to.

'Hey, stranger, I've hardly seen you these last few weeks so thought I'd stop by to see how you're getting along. Are you feeling settled in now?'

If asked, Kenneth would've sworn she'd almost purred at him. Her voice had definitely taken on a sultry tone.

'Hi, Jennet, you're looking well. Yes, we've been like ships passing in the night – the downside of being the senior doctors, I suppose, we work opposite shifts to each other. And I'm quite settled, thank you. To be honest, I feel as though I've worked here all my days. London is a distant memory and there's no desire to return there.'

'Well, that's good to hear because I'd be sorry to see you go. Patient feedback has been most favourable and everyone now considers you a valued member of our team.'

'Thank you, that's nice to know. It's a great team to be a part of.'

There was silence for several seconds broken only by the rustle of paper as Jennet slid along the desk, closer to him. The smell of her musky perfume enveloped him and he swallowed hard, hoping beyond hope that he was reading the situation wrong and she really *wasn't* coming on to him. But when she unclipped the clasp in her hair and shook her blonde locks free, he guessed she really *was*.

'Err, how are the kids? I'm guessing they must be back at school now?'

'Yes, they are. They spent all summer moaning about being bored and now they're moaning about being back at school. You can't win!'

'Ah, I doubt we were any different at their age. And your husband, is he glad they're back?'

He knew little about Mr Cameron because Jennet never mentioned him. All he'd gleaned, from little bits of chatter around the kettle in the kitchen, was that he was super clever and wrote books about history.

'I suppose he's enjoying the peace to stick his nose back in his fusty old research books.'

'That must be rather interesting—'

'Not as interesting as you, Kenneth.'

'Ah… err… right… well, I… I…' he looked at the wall clock again. There were still ten minutes to go but sod it, he had to get out of here right now. 'I really need to get off, Jennet. It's the Harvest Dance tonight and I promised my parents I'd help.'

Her hand landed on his arm when he leant over to switch off his monitor.

'Do you need a partner?' She *definitely* purred this time. 'I'm rather nimble on my feet… In fact, I'm pretty nimble all over.'

'No, thank you, I already have one.'

'You do?'

Ah-ha! A lot less purring in that comment, he noted. A quick look at her face showed him eyes which had narrowed with annoyance and lips pouting in displeasure.

'Yes, I do. And if I don't get a move on, I'll be late.'

'May I ask who?'

'Sorry, go to go. Take care.'

He grabbed his briefcase with one hand, yanked his jacket off the hook by the door with the other and legged it as quickly as he could while trying to display decorum. It wouldn't look good if it appeared he was running out of the building to escape the arms of an amorous colleague, even if that was *exactly* what he was doing.

'Hey, I managed to get away a little early. Are you ready to go?'

'I sure am. Let me just put my stuff in the car and lock up.'

'Here, I'll take those.'

Kenneth picked up the overnight bags just inside the front door as Flora collected her dress bag from where it was hanging on the lounge door.

'Is it okay for me to say you look stunning?'

Flora laughed. 'Of course it is! No girl objects to being told she looks stunning. Although I think my dungaree shorts and old T-shirt might be spoiling the look a little.'

'You mean you're NOT wearing those to the dance? What a disappointment...'

Although he was joking, the sight of Flora's long, slim, tanned legs was playing merry-hell with his innards. The squeezy sensation in his stomach was occurring more frequently whenever he was in Flora's presence and quite a few times when he wasn't but she was in his thoughts.

'I do recall your mum's invite saying it was a dressy affair. I don't believe these qualify.'

'I can have a word with my mother on that. Being her son does come with some perks.'

'You're good but thank you. I'll suffer the indignities of wearing a dress to keep her happy.'

'Well, if you change your mind...'

Laughter filled the car as they set off and Kenneth realised just how often he smiled and laughed when in Flora's company. He wondered if she'd noticed it too. And, more to the point, was it as important to her as it was to him?

An hour later, Kenneth found himself hoping Flora was feeling what he was feeling as he watched her walk down the stairs of the cabin, looking beyond beautiful in the heather-coloured dress which set off the red of her hair perfectly. It had grown considerably since the day he'd first seen her and she'd left it hanging loose across her shoulders, allowing the soft curls to frame her face with her barely-there makeup, letting her natural beauty shine through.

When she looked up and saw him waiting at the foot of the stairs, her face lit up with a brilliant smile and as his heart seemed to bloom inside his chest, that was the moment he realised he'd fallen in love.

FORTY-SEVEN

Flora shoved her lipstick, face powder and some tissues into the tiny drawstring bag she could wear on her wrist. When she looked up, it was to see Kenneth standing at the bottom of the stairs and the sight of him took her breath away. He was dressed in the formal evening attire of a short, black jacket with a crisp white shirt and bow tie. She presumed his kilt was MacKenzie tartan and it was the first time she'd seen his legs albeit they were mostly encased in the traditional thick black socks with little side flashes that matched the tartan of his kilt. She also noticed the little dagger which, she recalled, was named something like "Skeen Doo". Even though he was tall and slim built, he carried the outfit exceptionally well. In fact, she'd go as far as to say, it was the probably the most relaxed she'd ever seen him.

'Wow, look at you, young sir. You look absolutely amazing. I love that you're in full Highland dress. Will all the men be wearing kilts tonight?'

'Most will be although not so many in formal dress. Mum likes us to dress formally as we're the hosts.'

'Well, if you don't mind me saying, I love it. I really do. And you look comfortable in it. Not many men could wear that and look so relaxed.'

'Strangely, I've always been happy to wear my kilt, even when I was a kid. Ross and Fraser would grumble and groan but I never did. Maybe my inner Scotsman is prouder than I realise. And, while we're handing out the compliments, may I say you look divine. Your dress is beautiful and so are you.'

'Oh, err… thank you.' The heat rushed to her cheeks from the compliment and she welcomed the distraction of Choona and Chips chasing each other around the room.

'It looks like they're the best of chums now.'

'They most certainly are. I'm also sure they gang up on me which is why I think we should make a move before they decide to run up my legs again. It'll be considerably more painful in a kilt than when wearing jeans.'

'Oooh, ouch! Yes, let's go.'

After locking the cabin door, Kenneth turned to offer her his arm. When she placed her hand upon it, she could feel his warmth seeping through the jacket sleeve and into her fingers, sending little tingles up her arm and into her heart. The evening sun shone above them as they walked along the path to the barn, other couples ahead and behind them, and Flora realised that this was the happiest she'd ever felt in her life.

'Uncle Craig! Essie! Oh, how wonderful to see you. When did you get here?'

Flora pulled her uncle into a massive bear hug, becoming aware in that moment of just how much she'd missed him.

'Late last night. The roads were a nightmare – all the

311

holiday traffic meant we arrived later than intended. I didn't get the opportunity to text you today because Mhari has kept us busy in here.'

She followed her uncle's hand to look around the barn. It was beautifully decorated and while it still retained its original barn-like structure, the walls had been painted a pale cream colour, making it light and airy, and hundreds of twinkling fairy-lights hung from the ceiling. At the far end was a stage which had been decorated with flower covered hay-bales and tartan ribbons. She hoped none of the band, whose instruments and equipment were already set up, suffered from hay-fever. Bunches of heather and purple thistles were dotted around the room, the tablecloths had tartan edging, and the chairs looked quite regal with tartan sashes tied across the back. The whole room was an elegant explosion of Scottishness and it sang to the Scottish blood running through her veins. Kenneth had mentioned his inner pride earlier and she could now feel it in herself. This was a part of her. This was her heritage. *This* was how it felt to belong. Tears crept into her eyes and she had to blink hard to keep them at bay.

Her uncle put his arm around her shoulder and pulled her in for another hug.

'Hey, it's okay,' he whispered in her ear. 'I totally get it too.'

'Flora, come here, you gorgeous girl. Oh, look at your hair – how has it grown so long already? I can see the clean Highland air is working for you.' Essie landed a kiss on her cheek.

Flora smiled but didn't reply to Essie's comment on her hair. How could she explain that it would be back down to her waist by the end of the year? MacAndrew had told her that much of The Flora's powers lay in the fire of her hair and its fast-growing length was a major part of that.

'Flora, please meet Clarissa. I wish you could've been

friends growing up but my pig of an ex-husband put the kybosh on that. However, since we're almost family, I hope you can be now.' Essie pulled her daughter forward.

The two girls smiled as they shook hands and Flora could see Essie in her daughter. If Clarissa also had Essie's delightful personality, then she was sure they could be great friends.

'So nice to meet you, Flora, I've heard a lot about you. Craig talks of you fondly.'

'Thank you, Clarissa. How are you liking Japan? Kenneth mentioned you and Ross both live there now.'

'You know Kenneth?'

'Yes, we're friends. We both drove into town on the same day which caused a little… shall we say… discontent to begin with but we got past it and now we're friends.'

'Just friends?' Clarissa's right eyebrow lifted in curiosity.

'Err, yes. *Just* friends.' Flora desperately wanted to add "for now" but refrained from doing so. While she might be having "all the feels" for Kenneth, she couldn't say for sure that they were reciprocated.

'Okay. Well, I'm off to find my beloved because I think the dancing's about to begin and I don't want to miss a moment of it. It's such fun. I look forward to catching up with you, Flora.'

She spun off and, sure enough, just as she turned into the crowd, the musicians appeared on the stage. A few seconds later, after fiddling around with the mike-stand, the lead player declared that everyone should take their partners for the Gay Gordons. Before she could move, Kenneth spoke softly in her ear.

'I believe this is our dance.'

'Oh, no more, no more! Time out! Please!'

With her hands on her hips, Flora leant forward, trying to drag some air back in to her aching lungs. Between twirling around like a whirling dervish and laughing her socks off with joy, she was exhausted and the night was still young. If she didn't pace herself, she'd be asleep in a corner before long. A peaceful sit down was top of her agenda right now.

'Oh, if you insist, you lightweight.'

'Lightweight? I've danced about three times with you alone. Add in Fraser, Ross, your father, Bobby, my Uncle Craig, and then Ross again – I'd say I've done alright for a beginner! How come you're still so fresh?'

She mock-glared at Kenneth who grinned back.

'I grew up on all this. I was conditioned and brain-washed from an early age. You'll get the hang of it although you might need a few more dance nights. Anyway, I'll let you rest as I need to go and do hosting duties. I'll come and find you as soon as I can.'

To her delight, he kissed her on the cheek before disappearing into the crowd. Her delight was short-lived as she saw Fraser coming her way. With a shake of her head, she turned from the dancefloor and, spying her uncle over by the bar, pushed her way through the hot, sweaty, bodies towards him.

'Hey, need a hand with those?' She looked at the four drinks in front of him.

'That would be good, thank you.'

She took the wine glasses and followed Craig back to his table. Essie was sitting alone but the empty glasses in front of her suggested she'd recently had company.

'Is Clarissa back on the dancefloor again?'

'No, she's gone off to the buffet. Flora, you look like you need a break. Please, join us.'

'Cheers, Essie. It's been so much fun but it's a lot

livelier than I'm used to.'

'Tell me about it. Who needs a gym after all this?'

They sat watching the dancers spinning around in front of them and she grinned to see Trina among them. So much for her promise to take it easy this evening. If she carried on like this, her bump would be coming out dancing a jig. Her friend caught her watching and threw a big smile at her as an arm came around her waist – well, in the area where her waist would be – and whisked her away again. Everywhere she looked, all Flora could see were happy, smiling, laughing faces. Everyone was having fun.

'So, Flora, how are you liking it up here? Craig says you seem to be settling in.'

'Honestly, Essie, I wasn't at all sure at first but now, I love it. People have been so kind and accepting of me. I've made friends and tonight I feel like I've found the place where I belong.'

'Do you think you'll come back to Oxfordshire?'

It was the question which still hovered in her own mind and the one she still had no answer to.

'I really don't know, Essie. I'm finally finding the person I should be and I think going back home might not be the right thing to do.'

'Have you spoken with your father? Have you told him this?'

'Essie Walton – don't you try that one on me. I know how friendly you are with Sally and I'm sure she's kept you well up to date on the state of relations between us.'

The older lady grinned unrepentantly. 'Of course. But I'm curious as to how you feel now. Has the distance eased your anger?'

'Uncle Craig, have you spoken to my father recently?'

'No, I haven't. I've seen him around the village a few times and it's taken all of my self-control not to walk over and punch him. He inflicted hurt upon my mother by keeping you from her. I know, and acknowledge, that I wasn't the best son over the years but we made our peace with that and I did all I could to make it up to her once we were reconciled. It hurts me you never got to meet your grandmother and I don't think I'll ever be able to forgive him for that. Rightly or wrongly, it's how I feel.'

There was silence between them as Flora let her uncle's words sink in. She understood how he felt because it was what she felt too. At the same time, however, she had to consider that her father and her uncle were the only true family she had. When you've only got two people who've been with you all your life, the last thing you want to do is lose one.

Just as she was about to reply, a waiter appeared by their table and placed slim flutes containing fizzy wine in front of them.

'What are these for?' asked Essie.

'I believe there's to be a toast, ma'am.'

'Oh, okay.'

Sure enough, five minutes later, Mhari and Douglas took to the stage to thank everyone for coming along, for participating so wholeheartedly and for making the night yet another success. They were just about to ask everyone to raise their glasses when Ross jumped up onto the stage beside them and took the microphone.

'Ladies and gentlemen, I would like to echo my parents' sentiments. It's been four years since I was here last and let me tell you, I have missed you all. But I'm here tonight and before we raise our glasses, there's something I must do first.'

He turned towards the side of the stage and gave a small nod which was the cue for his two nephews to walk onto the stage, holding a small tartan cushion between them. Flora was close enough to see it carried a single red rose with a MacKenzie tartan ribbon tied around it, surrounded by white heather and… Polo mints? Her witchy sense went into overdrive and she instantly knew what was coming next. She glanced at Essie to see if she'd worked it out yet but the expression of interest on her face suggested she hadn't.

Ross looked back across the crowd below him before speaking again.

'As some of you know, four years ago, I went off to Japan to further my career. Before I left, however, I was fortunate enough to meet the most beautiful girl in the world and even more fortunate that she liked me enough to come and live with me away across the other side of the world. Clarissa, where are you?'

Everyone turned to look around and the room bellowed with laughter when they saw Clarissa standing beside the buffet, munching down on a sausage roll.

'Erm, I'm here…' she replied in a muffled, meat and pastry-filled voice.

'Would you come up to the stage, please?'

While Clarissa wiped her hands and walked forward, Flora looked at Essie again and saw the penny had dropped. Her eyes were shining as she clutched Craig's arm with both hands.

Upon arriving at the foot of the stage, Kenneth and Fraser materialised from the crowd to lift her up beside Ross who proceeded to take the rose from the boys and hand it carefully to her.

'Clarissa, I am presenting this to you as a thank you for being by my side for the last four years. You have made being away from home so much easier to bear. The rose signifies my love for you which will never die. The Polo Mints are there to tell you that while not everything in life is perfect, everything in my life is perfect when you're with me. And white heather is for wishes coming true.'

At this, he went down on one knee, took a small box

317

from his sporran and a great collective sigh filled the room.

'Clarissa Walton, you will make all my wishes come true tonight if you'll agree to let me be your husband. Will you marry me?'

FORTY-EIGHT

'Did you know Ross was planning to propose tonight?'

Kenneth grinned at Flora as they danced sedately around the floor. The night was drawing to a close and everyone was done in. A slow waltz was all they were capable of.

'Yes, but only about thirty minutes beforehand. While he may have had it planned for several weeks, he only shared it with us this evening. Our parents knew nothing until he went down on his knee. Mother, as you can imagine, is thrilled as she now has her first wedding booking for the barn.'

'Have they already set a date?'

'September next year, exact date to be confirmed.'

'That's lovely. An autumn wedding.'

'Do you think you'll still be here then?'

He watched her face as he asked his question. Would she guess the reason behind it?

'Er... urm... I don't know. That's a long way from now... Why?'

'Because I'd love for you to be my date.'

Surprise made her eyes open wider but the smile that immediately followed made him feel so much better.

'I would be delighted to accompany you although a year is a long time to wait for a first date.'

'Who said it would be our first date?'

'Well, we currently have no other dates planned so, until we do, that'll be our first.'

He tightened his arm around her waist, pulling her closer to him. 'Then we need to work on that. What are you doing tomorrow? Or is that too soon?'

Flora giggled and he couldn't believe he was being this forthright; it was so out of character. When he was with Flora, however, he felt he could conquer the world. She brought out a side of him that even he hadn't known existed. His usual shyness slipped away and he could feel the confidence surging through him.

'I don't think I can wait till then. What are you doing tonight…'

She looked up at him coquettishly, her eyelashes making little flutters in his direction.

'Well, when we've finished here, I'll return to the cabin— Oh!'

Suddenly, realising the meaning behind her words, he looked into her eyes and saw every emotion he felt for her, flowing back at him.

'I believe,' he whispered, 'it's time to say our goodbyes. I didn't think to use their timer bowls so Choona and Chips require feeding…'

'Then we cannot tarry a moment longer. Let us depart into the night.'

When Flora took his hand and began making her way to the door, Kenneth realised that he and Ross were, for once, on the same page at the same time because he too, had found the woman he wanted to spend the rest of his life with.

'Here you go, you two. Honestly, you'd think you hadn't been fed for four weeks, never mind four hours!'

Kenneth chuckled as he placed the food bowls down for Choona and Chips. He glanced at Flora and the sight of her standing in front of the picture window, bathed in moonlight, sent every part of his being into overdrive. After quickly refreshing the water bowl, he went to stand beside her, tentatively putting his arm around her shoulders, and gave a tiny sigh of relief when she snuggled in closer to him.

'I was admiring my loch – it looks so stunning under the moon and stars. It's a delight to view it from this angle, to see the ripples of light floating across it.'

She turned in to him and her silver eyes shone as the moonbeams flitted over her face. He had never seen her look as beautiful as she did right now and unable to hold back any longer, he lowered his head to place his lips upon hers. The initial touch sent a sharp bolt of electricity through him and every nerve danced with joy. His entire body felt as though it had just woken from the deepest of sleeps as it revelled in each new sensation. He pulled her closer to him, tighter, trying to absorb the very essence of her into his soul. The pressure of his lips grew stronger and she matched him with her fervour. His hand moved up from her shoulder to lose itself in her thick, auburn hair and it felt as though the tresses were winding themselves around his fingers. His other arm captured her waist while her palms crept up and across his back, as though she was trying to touch every part of him as he was trying to touch her. In the distance, his mind was yelling this was too good to be true, he should pull himself away, but his body was under the enchantment of these feelings; he was already lost in her and never wanted to find his way out.

'Do you have to sleep on the sofa-bed?' she whispered, her breath hot against his ear.

'No, if you'd rather I didn't…'

She raised her face to him and he fell deep into her silver-pooled eyes as she replied, 'I'd rather you didn't…'

'Did you know I hate spiders? And you walking your fingers up my chest like that is what I think a spider on my chest would feel like… One day, I'll end up slapping your hand which will be painful,' Kenneth murmured sleepily, pulling Flora tighter into his side and smiling when she giggled in his ear.

It had been one week since the dance. One glorious, fabulous, wonderful week. A week since every fibre of his being had exploded with happiness. One week since every nerve ending quivered with joy. One week since his sepia life had been flooded with colour. He hadn't known it was possible to feel so alive and he was loving every moment of it.

'I suppose we should get up and have dinner…'

'Hmmmmm, I suppose…'

The rain was lashing against the windows of the cottage, the wind was howling around the gable ends and it was nice and cosy here in Flora's bed. He really didn't want to move.

'Come on, up you get. Even doctors need to eat.' Flora flung the duvet back. 'I'll race you to the shower…'

The look she threw over her shoulder was enough to get him moving. There was a promise he wasn't about to miss out on.

'Is this rain ever going to stop?' he asked a short while later as Flora dished up the stew that had been slowly cooking. 'I had three patients cancel today because the roads are too treacherous to drive on.'

'Urgh. I hope they weren't urgent cases.'

'No, thankfully, just routine checkups but they're still checkups that are important long term. Anyway, to change the subject, this stew is delicious.'

'Thank you. It's a recipe I found in one of my grandmother's books – it looked quite straightforward so I thought I'd give it a try.'

'Well, it's excellent. After this though, and as much as I hate to leave you, I need to get home to feed the furry monsters—'

Just then, his mobile phone began to ring and a mere second later, Flora's did too. He didn't recognise the number which meant it could be a call forwarded from the surgery so he answered immediately.

'Hello? Doctor MacKenzie speaking.'

As a voice spoke rapidly in his ear, Flora turned towards him, her phone pressed close to her head, a look of horror on her face. He knew instantly what was happening.

'Bobby, is that you? Yes, okay, okay, calm down. I'm here with Flora – I'm guessing it's Trina on the phone with her?'

Flora nodded he'd guessed correctly.

'Bobby, keep Trina as comfortable as possible, I'm on my way.'

The kitchen chair scraped along the floor when he stood.

'I need to go now – Trina's gone into labour, there's been a landslide just outside the town on the main road meaning they can't pass to get to the hospital and the ambulance can't get through to them.'

'Yes, Trina said.' Flora was already heading towards the door, 'I'm coming with you.'

'You can't. I'm attending in my professional capacity as her doctor. I can't be seen to be bringing my girlfriend along.'

Flora, sitting on the bottom step of the stairs, stopped tying the laces of her boots to look up at him.

'Trina has asked ME to go to her in MY capacity as The Flora. Now I agree I'll be as much use as a fart in a windstorm but my FRIEND has asked me to be by her side and that's where I intend to be. So, you can either take your *girlfriend* in your car with you or she travels in her own car. Either way, she WILL be there!'

They glared at each other for a few seconds until he relented.

'Fine! Fine! Come on, then!'

They grabbed their jackets and ran out into the night. As the sharp needles of the driving rain stung his face, Kenneth hoped the roads between here and the Duncans' farm were still clear because there was going to be even greater problems if they weren't.

FORTY-NINE

Flora looked through the windscreen into the wet, dark night. Despite having the full beams on, they couldn't see more than three feet ahead. Kenneth was crawling along the road at barely twenty miles an hour, worried about coming upon another landslide. The tension was thick in the car and neither spoke, their heads too full over what could be happening at the Duncan place. As she peered into the darkness, she rubbed her hand along her sternum, trying to ease the itching sensation deep in her chest.

It took twenty-five minutes to pull into the yard in front of Trina and Bobby's farmhouse but it had felt much longer. By the time they'd opened the doors and dragged themselves out into the pouring rain, Bobby was at the farmhouse door with a large torch in his hand, lighting the way.

'Quick, get in,' he beckoned, pushing the door closed behind them as he fought against the gusty wind.

'How's Trina doing?' Flora asked, getting her question in ahead of Kenneth. She tried to appear calm on the outside, hoping to hide how terrified she was inside. What on earth did she know about childbirth? Apart from hot water and towels, her knowledge on the issue was a big fat zero. She'd told Trina this and couldn't believe she still wanted her by her side.

'Trina's doing just fine but would like someone in here with her!' came a voice from the lounge.

'She's in the lounge?' Kenneth raised his eyebrows at Bobby.

'Yes. There's a log-burner in there. The electric has gone off meaning we're on the emergency generator so I'm trying to ration how much electricity we use. I got the guest air-mattress ready when the weather turned bad, just in case. I honestly didn't think we'd need to use it though.' Bobby talked as they walked into the lounge and Flora had to admit it was nice and toasty.

'That's my husband for you – a regular little boy scout.' Trina grinned up at them from where she was lying on the floor. All the furniture had been pushed against the wall to provide more space. 'Would either of you like a drink? We've got hot water going on the Aga, ready for whatever you require, Doc.'

'Some tea would be good, to help us thaw out, and then I'll do an examination.'

'Thank you, Doctor MacKenzie.'

'Please, call me Kenneth. After all, this could be a long night. Now, Trina, I need to ask a few questions, just to see where we're at.'

'Hey, Bobby, I'll give you a hand with the drinks.'

Flora followed Bobby into the kitchen and started in surprise to see a chair in the middle of the floor surrounded by water.

'What the…' she pointed.

'We called you when Trina's waters broke. I haven't had time to clean it up yet.'

'Well, where's your mop? I'll do it.'

'You can't be doing that, you're The Flora. You need to be in with Trina.'

A cold sweat trickled its way down her spine. Sure, she wanted to be here for her friend but she honestly didn't know what she could do to help if she got into difficulties. The tale Trina had shared regarding her great-grandmother saving the day all those years before was playing on her mind and the thought of being in a similar position was filling her with dread. Perhaps, by staying busy, it would keep her thoughts from going where she didn't want them to go.

'Please, Bobby, let me help. Lead me to your mop and bucket. I'll clean this up while you make the drinks and check the boys are okay. I'm guessing they're up in their beds? Then we can tell Trina everything is good and she'll have less worries playing on her mind.'

The smile she received back from Bobby was enough to let her know he appreciated her assistance. She just hoped it was the only assistance she'd need to provide before the night was over.

'Right, Trina, I'm going to perform an examination of your cervix and then I'll do a scan to ensure your little lady is doing okay.'

They'd been at the Duncans' for just under three hours and Trina's contractions were now coming closer together.

Trina looked at Flora in confusion before replying, 'Kenneth, how can you do a scan? You need a scanning machine and your case doesn't look big enough to be hiding one of those in there.'

'Ah, well that's where you're wrong, it does!' And with a flourish worthy of any magician, he produced a small case from within the big case. 'Thanks to the wonderful progression of technology in the twenty-first century, Mrs

Duncan, we now have portable scanners and I just so happen to have one here. In a few minutes, it'll be all powered up and ready to go.'

'Blimey! They really do think of everything these days.'

The sigh of relief Trina let out was matched quietly by Flora. If Kenneth had the means to do a scan, then she didn't need to worry about being called on to help with the birth if there were complications. Kenneth would be able to sort them out. Despite all her self-assurances, however, the itchy sensation deep within her chest, that had manifested itself when she'd taken Trina's call at the cottage, was growing heavier as the hours passed. With Trina's contractions now just over two minutes apart, Kenneth had explained she'd soon be ready to push.

'Oooh, that's cold!' Trina squeaked, as the ultrasound gel was squirted onto her stomach.

'Sorry, needs must though. It helps me to see more clearly what's going on.'

As Kenneth brushed the ultrasound probe around, Trina grabbed her hand again and held it tightly.

'Thank you for being here, Flora, I feel so much better knowing you're close by.'

'Hey, you're doing great, you don't need me.'

'Hmmm, I think that looks okay. Your baby's lying at an awkward angle, I can't see her as well as I'd like but the head is in position so we're almost there now.'

Flora suddenly let out a sharp gasp and three pairs of eyes turned towards her.

'Are you okay, Flora?'

She held up her hand in a stop position while trying to get air into her lungs. The itching sensation had ceased and her chest now felt as though a ten-ton boulder had been dropped on it.

'Kenneth, look again at the scan. Check the neck area,

please,' she panted, 'can you zoom in…'

By now, she was almost doubled over with the pain and while her brain was shouting *Please be wrong…* her body was telling her she was right…

'Oh, hell! Nooooooo! Trina, whatever you do, DO NOT push!'

Kenneth turned from the small screen in front of him to look at Flora.

'How… how did you know?'

'Trina told me the female births in her family were problematic. I haven't been able to stop thinking about it all night. I don't know… some sixth sense has been nagging me since we arrived.'

'Is it… is it the cord? Is it double-wrapped around her neck?'

'I'm sorry, Trina, yes, it is.'

'Then fix it. Do something.'

'I… I'm not sure what I can do. If it was sitting loose, I could try a few manoeuvres but it looks tight and I'm worried that moving her will make it worse. If we were at the hospital, you'd have experts in the field who'd know exactly what to do but…'

'Don't you have a tool that can… well… hook it up or something…'

Flora saw the concern on Kenneth's face as he shook his head and her heart sank. This was it. She could no longer put off her decision. In a way, it had already been made for her. Her great-grandmother had saved Trina's mum, it was now up to her to do the same for Trina. And there was only one way she could do it.

'Excuse me,' she got up from the floor, 'I need to… to… I'll be back shortly.'

FIFTY

Flora walked out the lounge, aware that all eyes were upon her as she left. She offered no explanation because what could she say – *excuse me a minute, just off to pass Go and collect my magical powers…*

She walked into the kitchen and through a door she knew led to a small pantry at the back. Ensuring the door was closed tightly behind her, she took a deep breath, closed her eyes, and called for MacAndrew, hoping with all her heart she could do this.

'MacAndrew, please come to me and bring the necklace…'

She opened her eyes and seeing, to her dismay, that she was still alone, she took another breath to try again.

'MACANDREW, PLEASE COME TO ME—'

'Okay, okay, I'm here. No need to shout, for goodness' sake!'

'MacAndrew. Thank you, thank you. Did you bring the necklace?'

'Aye, I did but I need to ask if you're *absolutely* sure you're ready to do this. There's no going back once it's done. You can't shed it like an old coat you no longer want.'

'I'm sure, MacAndrew. For the first time in my life, I have a best friend and she needs me to save her and her baby. If I don't do it, then no matter where I go in this world, I will carry the weight of their loss with me for ever. I can't let her down. If this is what I'm meant to be, then it's time to get on with it.'

The little man stared hard at her for a few seconds before pulling the box out from behind him and, upon opening it, held it up to her.

'Does it hurt?' she asked, reaching down to remove the necklace from its velvet bed and surprised to find it warm to the touch.

'I don't know. I'm not usually in the room when the exchange happens. It's supposed to be a ceremony between The Floras.'

She held the red heart in the palm of her hand but apart from being warm, she felt nothing more and was a little disappointed there was no pulsing or throbbing sensation. Hmph! What kind of a magical necklace was this?

'Right, well, here goes nothing…'

She fastened the clip behind her neck… and waited.

At first, nothing seemed to happen but then a tingling sensation began to slowly move down through her body. It wasn't unpleasant – in fact, it was exactly like the feeling you get when you're cold and step into a hot bath; like pins and needles but not in a bad way. And, instead of coming up from her feet, it was slipping down towards them. She closed her eyes but where there should have been darkness, flashes of light flew around her head. All the colours of the rainbow darted in front of her eyes until suddenly… they stopped.

Everything in her body seemed to come to a standstill until a wave of peace and serenity washed over her. She stood silently for another few seconds before opening her eyes.

'I know what I need to do.'

She opened the door, rushed out, then rushed back in again while removing the necklace and handing it back to MacAndrew.

'Thank you for coming, MacAndrew,' she said, before rushing out again.

A second later, she was back for a third time. 'MacAndrew, would you be kind enough to feed Choona and Chips for Kenneth. We're going to be here a while yet. Thank you so much.'

This time, Flora spun on her heel and quickstepped it back into the lounge, issuing orders as she approached Trina who was now sobbing on the airbed.

'Bobby, can you sit with Trina over there and hold her hand because there will likely be some discomfort. Kenneth, you need to move out the way. I'm going in the business end but you'll have to watch the screen so you can guide me on where to go. I also need a dollop of your micro gel – germs and all that.'

Whether it was the tone of her voice or the air of authority she was now exuding, but no one argued with her and both men did as she asked.

'Okay, Trina, try to relax. I know it'll be difficult but you need to work with me here…'

Flora positioned herself between Trina's knees and closed her eyes, focusing all her energy down her arms and into her hands. She really hoped she could do this. If this wasn't a moment of extreme pressure, she didn't want to know what was.

When her hands grew cold and tight, she opened her eyes a little to peer down and saw, to her amazement, that they were beginning to shrink and lengthen, just as she was willing them to do. Once they looked small enough, she moved forward to help Trina.

'Kenneth, I'm going in now – tell me where I need to be.'

She eased her way inside, slowly and carefully, listening to Kenneth whispering directions. With her eyes closed again, she let her sense of touch take over.

'You're passing the head, keep going, that's it, almost there now. Okay, stop, you're touching the cord…'

Her fingers moved gently over the obstruction around the baby's neck as she tried to find the outer wrap. A slight tug which provided some give told her she'd found the one she needed. With the utmost care and delicacy, she pulled it up and back until Kenneth whispered that she'd cleared it past the head. She moved her hands forward again until they came to the second wrap. Once again, she pulled it gently until it was lying loose on the baby's shoulders. There was no need to slip this one off, it would do so itself as the baby came out.

She sat back on her heels, removing her arms and hands from Trina's undercarriage and watched in total wonder as they instantly returned to their normal shape and size. The desire to let out a yell of delight bubbled up inside her but she managed to hold it back as she said, 'Trina, I think you can begin pushing now.'

FIFTY-ONE

Kenneth looked up when Flora walked, nay… *strode*, back into the room. He immediately noticed there was something different about her. She suddenly had a sense of absolute purpose around her; an aura that ensured people would do as she said.

When she voiced her requests for him and Bobby to move positions while stating she was taking over with the delivery, no one batted an eyelid. No one argued with her – they just did as she asked. He busied himself with adjusting his scanning equipment, ready for her to proceed.

'Kenneth, I'm going in now – tell me where I need to be.'

Her words had him focusing on the small screen in front of him. For a few seconds, nothing bar the baby could be seen but then…

No!

NO!

What on earth?

He glanced up at Flora but her eyes were closed and her face was scrunched up tight in concentration.

He looked again at the screen. He could now see Flora's hands but… they weren't her hands! These hands were tiny! Her arms were so thin. While his voice whispered directions, he was enthralled, watching the teeny fingers and arms move around. His eyes were awe-struck by what they were witnessing. At the same time, his brain was yelling this was wrong. It was all wrong. He was struggling to compute the images flowing into it but for now, he had to force himself to ignore it. Two lives were at stake here – there would be time for reasoning later.

Now… it was later!

When his phone pinged, letting him know a text message had arrived – or rather, *another* text message had arrived – Kenneth felt a sharp pain in his lower lip as he bit it while exhaling from the corner of his mouth. He didn't need to look to know it was from Flora. Nearly every text he'd received in the last three days had been from Flora and he hadn't replied to a single one.

How could he? What on earth could he possibly say? He thought over all the tales he'd heard while growing up, of the special powers The Flora possessed and he'd always regarded them as codswallop – local myths told again and again to give some mysticism to the area. After all, who doesn't love a good old witchy story or two. His logical, science-and-facts focused brain had given them zero-credibility which was why it now felt like it was about to spontaneously combust. It… he… just couldn't handle the fact that not everything in life comes down to logic. And this was the conundrum he was now facing – could he possibly change the beliefs he'd held for over thirty years?

He'd been asking himself the question, over and over, and still didn't have an answer but he knew he'd have to find one and find it soon because he couldn't avoid Flora any longer.

With another sigh, this one of resignation, he sent a text back saying he'd be round to see her later today after surgery had finished.

Once he'd navigated his way through the trees surrounding Flora's cottage, Kenneth sat for a while longer in the car, trying to force his brain to come up with something… anything… for right now, he still had no idea of what to do.

It was the snuffling outside that brought him back into the present and he looked through the window to see the two Westies sitting there, tongues hanging out and tails wagging.

'Hey, guys,' he greeted them as they rushed across to rub against his legs when he swung them out of the car door. He wasted another minute petting them before standing upright, pulling his shoulders back and willing his feet to move.

Flora was sitting at the table on the patio, gently stroking Friand who was lying on her lap, when he walked round. A tartan throw was across her shoulders for although the sun was shining, the breeze off the loch mitigated what little warmth there was in it. When she looked up from the drawing pad in front of her, the smile he received was reserved and mingled with sadness. His heart ached from knowing he'd hurt her. That hadn't been his intention.

'Hi,' he said, taking the seat opposite her.

'Hi yourself.'

'How are you?'

'I'm not sure yet – it depends on what you have to say.'

'Meaning?'

'Well, the fact you've ignored my texts for the last three days.'

He leant forward, placing his elbows on his knees and clasped his hands. He only realised how tightly when he saw his knuckles whiten.

'I… I don't know what to say, Flora.'

'About what?'

'About what?' He looked at her incredulously. 'About *what*?' he repeated. 'About what I saw the other night. About the means you used to help Trina deliver her baby. That's what!'

'I only did some gentle manoeuvring. Nothing more.'

'Flora,' he sighed, 'I saw everything on the scanner. Your hands had shrunk to a fraction of their actual size, not to mention your arms growing about three times longer and ten times skinnier.'

'Oh, right. I never thought of that.'

'It's put me in a terrible, ethical, situation.'

'In what way?'

'All scans are recorded, even mobile ones, and have to be uploaded to the patient's record. They can be viewed by anyone, at any time, and due to the nature of Trina's delivery issues, will most likely be reviewed as a matter of caution against any future complications.'

'Ah! Hmm, yes, I can see how that could be a problem.'

There was silence as they stared across the table at each other, broken only by the sound of the waves from the loch creeping up and down the small sandy inlet.

'Is there any way that you *can't* upload the recording? Or that particular recording as, I'm going to guess here, there were a number of recordings over the course of the night… you know, given that you weren't scanning Trina the whole time.'

'But how would I explain the missing time?'

'It would involve a small bending of the truth, I suppose, which I don't like to ask as I know it won't sit easy with you. You are a man of morals and scruples which is rare these days but sometimes our morals and scruples can choke us if we hold on to them too tightly. Everything, or everyone, requires a little bending on occasion otherwise we break.'

'And how do you propose I "bend" this truth?'

'Perhaps you could say a friend of Mrs Duncan's, with some midwifery experience, was present and you were helping her perform some manipulations of the baby in the hope it would move the cord from around the neck... In essence, this would be true as you *were* assisting me...'

Flora let the rest of the sentence hang in the air and he mulled over what she'd suggested. The phrasing was loose enough to let people draw their own conclusions so long as he kept it brief and avoided providing unnecessary detail.

'Okay. Yes, I believe I could make that work. I'll delete the recording because we certainly can't let that go out into the world.'

'Thank you. And I am sorry to ask this of you.'

'Can you tell me how you did it? I mean... what are you? I could tell you were different the instant you walked back into the room – how did that happen?'

For the next twenty minutes, Flora spoke words he never thought he'd hear. Words that made sense but didn't. Words that so many gullible people would chew a limb off to be allowed to hear. Words he really didn't want to listen to.

'That's a much-abridged version but you get the gist of it,' she finished. 'Would you like some tea to help you digest it all?'

She stood and as he looked up at her, he blurted out, 'Is it normal tea or a magic potion?'

Disappointment came to rest on her face at his lack of

trust.

'It would be norma— *What* in the name of the Goddess?'

Suddenly, a loud roar filled the air and he turned in his seat to see a small motorboat powering across the loch. Flora was already marching towards the larger beaching spot at the top end of the loch where the boat was clearly headed and he jumped to his feet, following quickly behind. He caught up with her just as two men stepped out. One he recognised immediately – Jack Arlingh – but the other was a new face although he matched the description of the man who'd been asking around about Flora.

'What *the hell* do you think you are doing here?'

The tone of her voice was one Kenneth had never heard before and it chilled him right through. He detected the anger hovering just under the surface and knowing what he did now, hoped it wouldn't lead to something else he couldn't explain.

'I'm here to see you, you double-crossing bitch.'

As always, Jack Arlingh was the epitome of good manners and politeness… not!

'I beg your pardon?'

'You heard me. What do you think you're playing at, telling my solicitor you're not selling to me when you told me you were?'

'I never said I would sell to you. I told you to send your proposal to me in writing and I would have a look at it.'

'No, you didn't and now it has cost me a fortune in legal fees so I suggest you call my solicitor back and tell him you WILL be selling to me.'

Uh oh, that was not a good move on Jack's part, he thought, as he watched Flora draw herself up, pull back her shoulders and step closer to Jack.

'Let me try to make this perfectly clear to you, Mr Arlingh. I WILL NOT be selling my land. Not to you and not to anyone else but ESPECIALLY not to you. Now I suggest that YOU get back in your boat, go back the way you came and NEVER, EVER, again set foot on a single blade of grass that belongs to me.'

'I will not—'

'Oh, I think you will, Mr Arlingh, if you know what's good for you. And you can take this lanky piece of nothing with you.'

She turned to the man standing a little way off from Jack.

'Joey, I don't know how you found me or what you hoped to gain by following me here, but I will try to put this into language simple enough for your small brain to understand – I do not want to be with you. I do not love you and right now, I do not like you. I will not be returning to Oxford. I have moved on, quite literally, and my life is here now.'

She twisted round to give Kenneth a small smile of hope as she said this before looking back at her ex-boyfriend.

'I don't know how you managed to get mixed up with this slimy worm but I suspect that between you, you hoped you could persuade me to sell up and return to England with you.'

The look of surprise on Joey's face told Kenneth that *that* was exactly what the plan had been.

'Joey,' Flora's voice softened, 'Go home. Find a nice girl who you can love and who will love you back. You deserve it. I'm sorry I'm not that girl but you will find her, I'm sure of it. And try to avoid hanging out with lowlifes like this,' she thumbed towards Jack, 'they're not worthy of you and they'll only drag you down to their level. Now leave.' She pointed to the boat.

'You haven't heard the end of this, you slaggy cow. You WILL sell to me or, mark my words, you'll regret it.'

Flora spun around and growled right into his face.

'If YOU ever come near me or my land again, YOU will regret it. And that's a promise I will keep! Leave! NOW!'

The two men returned to the boat, moving it back into the water to turn it around, and as they got in, Jack Arlingh called out, 'This isn't the end of it! I will have this land!' before the vessel began to speed across the loch.

'Oh, you think so, do you,' she muttered.

To Kenneth's amazement, Flora lowered herself down onto her knees, dropped her hands into the water and began quickly moving them around. A few seconds later, his jaw dropped when a seal's head popped up in front of her.

'Intruders, Walter. Intruders in the boat. Please, teach them a lesson BUT DO NO HARM! Frighten them enough that they won't return.'

Kenneth barely had time to comprehend the instruction she'd given, never mind that she'd been talking to a seal, when the water in the loch began to grow choppy. The waves grew larger and the small boat was suddenly being thrown hither and thither, water splashing into it as it rocked from side to side. Even from this distance, he could see the fear on the faces of the two men sitting in it, as they clung on for dear life.

Their torment lasted for the best part of five minutes until they rounded the bend at the far end and were lost from sight. A moment later, the previous calm waters returned and it was as though nothing had happened. The seal reappeared in front of them.

'Thank you, Walter, and please thank your people for their help, I am appreciative of it.'

The seal made a few high-pitched squeals and squeaks before disappearing once more.

Flora turned and began walking back towards the cottage.

'Right, I think I was about to make some tea before we were rudely interrupted.'

With feet that felt like concrete, Kenneth followed her but not with the intention of drinking tea. He had to get away from here as quickly as possible.

What he'd just witnessed was a step too far.

What she'd told him was too much for him to deal with.

He couldn't be here. He had to get away!

Now!

Far away!

Panic rose up within him and he thought he would vomit; such was the intensity of his alarm and fear. The woman he thought he loved was not the woman he'd fallen in love with. She was something much more and he couldn't be around her.

Flora had reached the doorway of the cottage when he called out to her, his feet already scurrying across the patio, rushing towards his car.

'Flora, I can't... I can't... I can't do this,' he gasped, 'I can't be with you, you're... you're...'

'I'm The Flora, Kenneth.'

He stopped to look at her.

'Yes, Flora, you are. And I can't cope with that. I'm sorry.'

He ran to his Landy, jumped in, started it up and with a roar of the engine while the tyres kicked up the loose pebbles, he spun around, then drove as fast as he could towards the main road.

The enormity of what he'd learnt was so overwhelming, he didn't realise the usual winding track through the trees had become a straight, short path until he was flying along the smooth tarmac of the main road and almost halfway home.

FIFTY-TWO

After standing stock still on the doorstep for the best part of five minutes, waiting and hoping that Kenneth would return, Flora felt MacAndrew take her hand, gently pulling her inside and closing the door.

'Come on, lassie, in ye come. Sit yerself down.'

The part of her mind which was now occupied by her ancestors, reared up at the audacity of his familiarity. The greater part of her, however, was grateful for his tenderness.

A moment later, a cup of tea was pushed in front of her along with a plate of biscuits. The biscuits were ignored but she wrapped her hands around the cup, letting it thaw out her frozen thoughts.

What had gone wrong? When had it gone wrong? She understood that what she was would be difficult for some people to contend with but Kenneth had grown up knowing about her family. Surely it couldn't have been that much of a shock to him? Okay, compared to the other members of his family he was rather uptight and, to be blunt, often behaved as though he had a stick up his ass – Fraser's words, not hers – but there was an element of truth in them. She, however, loved this aspect of his character – it gave him a strength which other people recognised and knew he was a person they could rely upon. It was the reason why he was a good doctor.

She let out a mirthless bark of a laugh. Oh, the irony – for when she'd needed him to be strong for her, he'd let her down in the worst possible way.

Her mind wandered off for a minute or two and when she reined it back, it was to perform a post-mortem on the events of the afternoon. While she'd been explaining why she'd left the Duncans' a different woman to the one who'd arrived there some hours earlier (although not *how* – that was very much a secret between the Floras), Kenneth had appeared receptive to what she was telling him. Sure, he'd been surprised and a little confused but, on the whole, had been taking it quite well. His question regarding the tea being normal had disappointed her but it would be unreasonable to expect him to just accept her as she was now and carry on as they had before.

Suddenly, she jumped up from her chair.

Jack Arlingh!

Jack bloody Arlingh.

His arrival had tipped the scales against her. They'd been so delicately balanced up to that point and his unwanted appearance, along with her subsequent actions, had swayed Kenneth to turn and run.

Jack bloody Arlingh!

The very thought of the damage he'd caused sent a tsunami of rage through her and, spinning on her heel, she marched out the back door, across the yard to her studio where she fired up her laptop and proceeded to write a very strongly worded email to the Laird's estate in which the full level of her annoyance was laid out.

Finally, after jabbing the "send" button several times in

anger, she slammed the laptop closed and let out a loud scream of frustration before bursting into tears.

'Hey, Flora, it's time to get up now. The troll says dinner will be ready in twenty minutes.'

Flora felt Friand headbutting the back of her shoulder but she maintained her position of facing the window, looking out over the loch although dusk was now falling and she could barely see it.

She'd lost count of the days since Kenneth had driven out of her life. At first, she'd waited to see if he would get in touch but when two days of radio silence had passed, she caved and sent him a text, asking him how he was doing. She then sent a second text, then a third before trying to phone him. The call had gone to his voicemail while the texts received no response.

'Flora, come on. Move. NOW!'

This time, Friand jumped up onto her shoulder and began to softly bite her earlobe.

'Friand, just bugger off, will you.'

'No! You must get ready for you leave in an hour. You can return to be being a woman who mopes tomorrow but for now, you have a responsibility to your position.'

A large sigh accompanied her action of sitting up and throwing back the bed covers. The cat was right. Today was the Autumn Equinox, or Mabon as it was known in the circles of those who acknowledged it. The day in which the last harvests are celebrated before moving into winter and thanks is given to the Goddess for the sustenance she has provided. Tonight, she would be out again to cut the autumn heathers. MacAndrew assured her this would be a less arduous task than the mid-summer cutting as the beneficial properties within the autumn heathers are richer and therefore used more sparingly.

In truth, she could really have done without the gathering but the wisdom she'd recently acquired told her it was a blessing that she must go out otherwise her inertia would only become longer and more severe. It also reminded her that she was not the first Flora to have sacrificed love to fulfil her duty.

'Please tell MacAndrew I'll be down shortly – I want to shower first. And STOP calling him a troll. He is not a troll. How many times do I need to tell you?'

'But it's fun. Besides, he calls me fleabag. They're our pet names for each other.'

'You have pet names?'

'Sure we do.'

'Do you have one for me?'

'Sure we do!'

'What is it?'

'Pfft! Yeah, right. Like I'm gonna tell you that... Now shift your butt, time is moving and you're not.'

And with those words, he jumped off the bed to trot out of her bedroom with his tail high and straight behind him.

It was four-thirty in the morning when Flora arrived home with MacAndrew and the dark cloud of despondency settled on her shoulders once more. Surprisingly, the strenuous activity of cutting the heather had put the state of her love-life, or non-existent love-life, to the back of her mind but returning to the cottage brought it to the fore again.

'Right, I'll put this lot in the still room, then we can have some sleep and after a late breakfast, we'll get to work.'

'Thank you, MacAndrew, for your help with this harvest. Mabon blessings to you and your family. I will see you in a few hours.'

'Mabon blessings to you, Flora. I've left a small potion by the side of your bed – I suggest you drink it. You need to be fully refreshed later and it'll help you sleep.'

'Thank you. As a rule, I don't like to take such things but I bow to your knowledge on this occasion. Good night.'

'Good night, Flora.'

When she entered her bedroom, she spotted the bottle on the bedside table and upon closer inspection, saw it was a sleep enhancement tincture she'd created from the summer cuttings. She put a few drops in her water glass, drank it, changed into her pyjamas then slipped under the duvet. A moment later, Friand jumped up and curled up against her back, for once keeping his thoughts to himself.

As she waited for sleep to come, Flora thought of the changes within her since she'd finally donned the necklace. The initial frenzy of saving Trina and the baby, followed by the fallout with Kenneth and subsequent upset meant there hadn't really been a proper opportunity to reflect fully on what she'd done. It was very strange to find she now had memories that weren't hers – the experiences of her ancestors lived on in her and, although not present every minute of the day, it still threw her when they popped up. For example, tonight, while cutting the heather, she'd seen herself doing the same task in previous lives, and it had been the clothing she was wearing which had made her realise what was happening.

There was also the night at the Duncans' – the memory she'd needed had come to her immediately and had guided her safely through saving the baby. When she'd discussed this with MacAndrew the next morning over breakfast, he'd told her the relevant memories would rise-up when she called upon them. Although, she didn't think there had been any calling with her actions on the side of the loch – that had occurred without any thought and it was the following day when she caught a memory of a previous Flora doing the same.

Her eyes began to grow heavy but before she gave in to her sleepiness, it dawned on her that she should now have full access to all her powers but she hadn't noticed any difference. Her last thought was to ask MacAndrew about it in the morning.

FIFTY-THREE

'If you're not down at the kitchen table within the next ten minutes, I'm eating your breakfast! So, I suggest you move your skinny ass.'

'And a good morning to you, Friand.'

Flora opened her eyes and blinked, dazzled by the sun outside her window. She turned over and came nose-to-nose with a furry ginger face but where she stifled her yawn, he was less polite meaning she was treated to a full view of his tiny teeth while being blasted with cat breath. The latter, she was sure, smelt worse than a rotting dung heap and she told him as such.

'Hmmm, looks like some sleep has done you the power of good.'

She didn't reply, just pushed him off the bed and got up. The pain of loss was still rampant inside her, it would take more than a few hours' sleep to sort that out.

MacAndrew was clearly still in tune with her feelings as the breakfast that greeted her was a simple mug of coffee and an almond croissant. She was grateful for his understanding as a full-blown fry-up would've been more than she could cope with. A coffee and croissant, however, was manageable.

The last of the pastry had been forced down, helped along with a large gulp of coffee, when she pushed the plate away and stood up.

'Right, MacAndrew, let's get this show on the road. Still room, here we come.'

'You go on, I'll clear the table before I join you.'

Flora made her way down the stairs and through the doorway. She hadn't been in the still room for over a month so when she first walked into the room, she didn't immediately notice the change in her surroundings, being too busy thinking about the past lives inside her, and it was only when she reached the large cauldron in the middle of the floor that she suddenly halted to look around.

'What on earth?'

All the walls in the room, that had previously been a pleasing, pale-cream were now a dark, glittering, charcoal and almost appeared to be throbbing.

She heard MacAndrew coming down the stairs and called out to him.

'Hey, MacAndrew, when did you redecorate in here? And why?'

'Ah, now then—' he burst through the door and stopped in his tracks. 'Oh no, oh no, this will never do. This will not do at all!'

'What's wrong?'

The little man turned to look at her. 'The still room is also a mood room. It senses your feelings and changes colour to reflect them. It's a power only a true Flora can see.'

'You mean, it changed every time I was in here and I didn't notice?'

'Yes, but you need the power to see it. It's another safety measure that's in place.'

'Okay, I understand. But why are you so dismayed now?'

'The room senses your mood because your head and heart must be in the right place when you make the potions. Your very essence is part of the creation process and if your essence is wrong, the potions will be wrong.'

'And charcoal means bad essence?'

'Yes, very bad. Black is the worst but this shade of charcoal means your essence is too sad and damaged right now. You can't do potions today. You can't do anything today, or any day, until your colours change.'

'Surely there's something I can do?'

'No. If you try to pick up a vessel or jar right now, you'll be unable to do so. Go on, try it – see for yourself.'

She walked over to the nearest shelf, placed her hand upon a small copper cauldron and tried lifting it up. As MacAndrew had said, it couldn't be done. She pushed and pulled but the small pot wouldn't budge. Walking over to a different shelf, she tried again but to no avail – the instruments in the room remained stubbornly unresponsive.

'What do we do now? Will the heather go to waste?'

'Oh no, definitely not. There are means of preserving it but you can't touch it now for risk of tainting it. I must do it alone.'

'But I touched the heather last night when I was cutting it.'

'That's different. It's what we do in here that matters. However, I need to tell you, if the heather is in a preserved state for too long, it begins to lose its potency. I know your heart and soul are in a bad way right now but, somehow, you need to find a way to overcome it. And soon!'

'In others words, pull myself together.'

'I wouldn't be that blunt, Flora, a broken heart is a terrible thing but you do need to move past it.'

'I see. Well, I'll get out of your way and leave you to get on with it. Trina was allowed to bring the baby home yesterday – maybe a visit to see them will help.'

'A new wee bairn – how could that fail to lift your spirits? Go, have a lovely day with your friend and we'll try again tomorrow.'

Having been effectively dismissed, Flora wandered slowly up the stairs, filled with disappointment that she was unable to put her newly acquired skills to the test. It was the one thing she'd been looking forward to. She really hoped that, somewhere, Jack Arlingh was being made to pay for what he'd done.

When she finally found her phone – Friand was sleeping on it! – she sent Trina a text, asking if she fancied having a visitor and was delighted when a speedy reply came back saying she definitely did.

Flora replied to say she'd be with her in a few hours. She felt the need for a walk around the loch with the dogs - a habit she'd developed when the whole magic thing became too overwhelming - and then she had to go shopping to buy both mother and baby a gift. It would never do to turn up empty-handed. That would never do at all.

'Oh, Trina, she's adorable! And what a head of hair she has.'

'Hasn't she just! That explains the chronic heartburn I had. But she was worth every second of it.'

'And she's been given a clean bill of health? No concerns about anything?'

'None at all. Now that she's put on weight, they're very happy with her.'

Flora looked down at the little snuffling bundle in her arms. She was gorgeous and the adorable baby smell was helping to ease some of the pain in her heart. She may have lost the man she loved over her decision to save the life of this child but she would never regret it – not for a moment. How could she? Her one sacrifice gave a whole lot more happiness to other people. Maybe that's what it meant to be The Flora. Her grandmother sacrificed living with the man she loved to serve this community. Her mother sacrificed her life – albeit not by choice – so her family wouldn't be uprooted. Letting go of the man she loved would have to be hers.

'Does she have a name yet? We can't keep calling her "Bumpie" – that would be very unfair when she goes to school.'

Trina laughed before replying, 'That is kind of tempting but we've decided to call her Florrie. Not Florrie shortened from Florence but actually Florrie. Being honest, we wanted to call her Flora but it didn't feel right, given your position, so this was the next best option. I hope you don't mind.'

'Mind? Why should I mind? It's a gorgeous name and I can already see that she suits it. I feel immensely flattered that you even considered Flora.'

Before Trina could say anything more, the kitchen door flew open, slamming against the wall as two small boys came bouncing in and ran over to Flora. The noise caused a small mew to slip from Florrie's lips but she soon settled back into her sleep.

'Boys! How many times have you been told not to throw the door open?' Trina hissed at them.

Callum and Finlay ignored their mother and squeezed in close to Flora, one on either side.

'Auntie Flora, is it true you saved Florrie from dying?'

Flora's head shot up in surprise to look at Trina and

witnessed a look of chagrin on her face.

'I'm sorry. Bobby was so excited and impressed that he's been unable to stop talking about how you saved his daughter's life. I'm afraid the whole town knows.'

'Well, that explains all the smiles, grins, and waves I received as I drove through earlier. I also hope he's been sharing Doctor MacKenzie's part in it all. It was a joint effort and I couldn't have done my bit without his help.'

'I believe he gets a mention but I'm afraid Bobby's been raining most of the glory down upon your head. The town is very excited to know their Flora has returned to them. I'm sure everything will calm down soon.'

'I hope it does. Thank goodness I chose to go to Inverness this morning otherwise I may never have made it here today. I fear the townsfolk would all have found an excuse to talk to me and I'd still be there now.'

'I think you may be right. Why did you go to Inverness?'

'In order to buy these gifts for Florrie.'

She passed over one of the bags she'd brought in with her. Turning to the boys, she picked up two smaller bags.

'I've brought each of you a gift too because it's not fair that the new baby gets all the attention. You are both special big brothers now and will require sustenance to do your job.'

'Susty nance? What's that?'

'Biscuits, young Callum! Biscuits. Very special, homemade, chocolate shortbread to keep you strong to protect your sister while she's still little.'

'Oh, wow!'

The boys set about opening the bags and were thrilled to find the HGV toy trucks inside had been packed full of chocolatey-shortbread goodness.

'Don't eat them now…' gasped Trina, quickly confiscating the sugar-filled treats.

'Aw, Mum!'

'You can both have one now with a glass of milk and another before bed. Okay? It'll be tea-time soon so this is a treat. And, what do you say to Auntie Flora?'

'Thank you, Auntie Flora.'

Two pairs of little arms hugged her tightly before the allure of chocolate dragged them over to the kitchen table. The small gestures chipped away some more of her heartache which allowed a tiny sliver of pleasure to slip in.

'And, finally, because a certain baby momma did all the hard work, she should not be left out, this is for you.'

Handing over the last bag, Flora watched the joy on Trina's face as she opened it to find all manner of assorted goodies within.

'Oh my, these are posh chocolates! I'll never get rid of my baby fat eating these. And this candle smells divine. Jo Malone? Are you sure?'

'Of course I'm sure. You deserve something nice.'

'Aw, Flora, you shouldn't have – this is too much.'

Trina had just pulled out the gift basket she'd made for her, full of all the heather-based products which she'd thought were appropriate.

'Hardly too much, Trina. They're just homemade gifts.'

'They're gifts from The Flora, don't underestimate how special that makes them.'

'Whatever.' She waved her hand in the air. 'You are worth all of it. You and Bobby have been so welcoming and have shown me nothing but kindness and friendship since we've met. This is the least I can do to say thank you.'

'Flora! You saved our baby's life, I don't think "thank yous" come much bigger than that!'

She was saved from having to reply by Bobby walking through from the scullery.

'Bobby! At last! I thought you'd got lost. I've been

biting my tongue for an hour now!'

Trina gave her husband a play-punch on the arm before turning back to face Flora.

'Flora, now that my husband has FINALLY arrived, we have something we'd like to ask.' Bobby gave her a small nod before she carried on. 'Flora… would you be Florrie's godmother?'

The following morning, Flora made her way down to the still room again. She felt better within herself although only if she made a point of not thinking about Kenneth. Her visit to see her friends and the new baby the previous day had been so full of positivity, it was impossible to maintain the bleakness she'd been drowning in. There was a place for her in this community and it was where she belonged. Sure, she'd have preferred to belong with Kenneth by her side but if she was more than he could deal with, then she had to move on. She couldn't change who or what she was and she had to accept that.

She paused in the doorway and took a deep breath before walking in. For a few seconds nothing happened then the walls around the room began changing colour. Soon she was surround by warm yellows and deep purples. One wall, however, while not as darkly charcoal as it had been, was still dark enough. This was her "Kenneth" wall. She knew it would be a while yet before it changed colour.

She sensed MacAndrew walking in and turned towards him.

'Ah, this is better. Not perfect,' he said, catching sight of the wall behind her, 'but better. Now, come on, let's get to work!'

FIFTY-FOUR

The brash overhead lighting in his office was beginning to give Kenneth a headache. At least, that's what he was blaming and not the weeks of restless sleep he'd been going through since driving away from Flora.

The November rain outside was torrential, he could hear it battering down on the roof of the surgery and he was trying to stifle a yawn when there was a knock on the door. Surgery hadn't been as manic as usual this morning, the bad weather resulting in a few cancellations when some patients decided their illnesses were not sufficient to merit getting soaked for.

'Come in.'

His yawn was not the only thing he found himself stifling when Jennet Cameron's head peered round the door. He hoped she hadn't heard the start of his groan before he'd quashed it. The friendly, professional, woman he'd met in March had become a far-flung memory as he faced the under-dressed, over-made-up, femme fatale standing in front of him. If her skirts got any shorter, he'd be able to see the label on the neck of her blouse when she

357

bent over! The expertly made-up face was very lovely but it was far too much for working in the surgery. Neither of these, however, discomfited him as much as the flirting which was no longer subtle and had become quite overt. He'd seen other staff members giggling when Jennet started on him and it felt like a daily chore he tried to avoid. The problem lay in maintaining a professional distance from her behaviour without causing offence or upset. He'd mentioned he didn't feel it was appropriate on several occasions but his objections seemed to fall on deaf ears.

'Well, good morning there, handsome man, aren't you a sight for sore eyes on this dull and dreary day!'

She sashayed over to him and, horror of horrors, perched herself on the desk next to him. The already short skirt rode up her thighs and his eyes caught sight of lace stocking tops before he could turn them away.

'Good morning, Jennet. It is rather hideous out there. Have you had many cancellations this morning? I think about twenty percent of my appointments realised they weren't ill after all.' He pulled a pile of files towards him. 'Since it's quiet, I'll go and put these back in the filing room.'

This would normally be a job for the surgery administrator but he'd grasp any excuse to leave the room. He pushed his chair back but as he stood up, Jennet did too and with a quick twist of her body, she was standing in front of him. One hand sent his chair rolling off to the side while the other began to trail itself up the buttons on his shirt.

'Oh, Kenneth, now we're alone with no patients, it seems a shame to waste the free time. I'm sure we can find a way of keeping each other entertained...'

He stepped back, trying to escape her advances but with each step back, she took one forward until he was against the wall with Jennet pressing hard into his body. Her hands were roaming over places they had no right to be and moved with a speed that made grabbing hold of them impossible.

'Jennet, this is too much. Please step away. Someone might come in…'

'Oh, but they won't,' she purred, 'I dropped the snib on the lock when I came in.'

She'd what? The woman must have had ninja training at some time in her life because he hadn't heard her do that. Now he was trapped in a rapidly compromising situation.

Her lips were against his neck, scattering butterfly kisses up towards his ear. The sensation made his stomach churn and somewhere in the back of his mind, he was aware that when Flora used to do the same, his stomach skittered with joy.

The smell of her heavy, musky perfume revolted him to the point of nausea. His irrational logic whispered he'd need to get his suit dry-cleaned if there was to be any chance of getting rid of it.

With her lips getting ever closer to his, Kenneth realised the time for diplomacy had passed. It was more luck than judgement that helped him find her hands and grab her wrists, pushing her away to hold her at arm's length while she squirmed like an octopus, trying to get close to him again.

'Jennet, stop. Stop this now.'

'Oh, Kenneth, don't be such a prude. You know you want to.'

'No, I don't.'

'You do… you do. I've seen you looking at me—'

'You've seen no such thing. You couldn't be more wrong.'

'Don't try to hide it from me, there's no need. I'm all yours—'

'JENNET! THAT'S ENOUGH! NOW STOP!'

Kenneth glared at her as he repeated his words.

'ENOUGH! STOP IT THIS MINUTE!'

As he ceased roaring at her, the woman in front of him stopped her wriggling and became totally still. After a few seconds, he released her arms and walked around to the other side of the desk, ensuring there was some safe space between them.

She turned round, a dazed and shocked look on her face as she lifted her eyes to his. 'But... but you want me too. I know you do...'

'No, Jennet, I don't. I never have.'

'But... I felt the attraction.'

'Not from me you didn't. I have great admiration for you in a professional capacity but not in a personal one. There *is* no personal capacity between us.' He spoke softly for he didn't want to hurt her but he had to be certain she fully understood the situation.

'I thought... I was sure...' Her voice was a mere whisper and, looking like she was about to keel over, he rushed to push his chair towards her. She sank down slowly onto it as he quickly returned to the safe space across the desk to perch on the edge of the seat there.

'Jennet, I cannot think of an occasion where I could've behaved in such a manner as to give you the idea that we could be anything more than colleagues but if I did, I am very sorry.'

There was silence in the room for several moments and Kenneth sat back, waiting for her to respond. He didn't know what else he could say.

Finally, just as he was beginning to grow concerned, her ramrod straight body slumped forward onto the desk, her head landing with a thump upon her arms and her shoulders began to move up and down, in rhythm with the sobs now filling the room. He plucked a tissue from the box on his desk, pushed it between her fingers, then moved the box closer to her. Once again, he sat back and waited.

A few minutes later, the torrent of crying eased and a few small hiccups took their place. The tissue disappeared into the cocoon between arms and head and he heard her nose being blown. Eventually, Jennet pushed herself back to sit upright in the chair and slowly raised her eyes to look at him.

'I've been a fool. A complete and total fool.'

'That's too harsh. I'd say more that you've made a small mistake.'

'A small mistake? I've been a right bloody idiot! Look at me, for goodness' sake! What on earth was I thinking? I haven't worn outfits like this since I had the kids!'

'Maybe that's partly why this has come about.'

'What do you mean?'

'When was the last time – before I came here – that you allowed yourself to be a woman? To be Jennet? Not a mum. Or a wife. Or a doctor. Just Jennet, the woman inside you. The woman who doesn't get much attention anymore.'

'I… I… I don't know,' she whispered.

'Has your husband said anything to you about your appearance? Don't you think he might have noticed the extra efforts you've been making?'

'Oh, crap!' Her head dropped back down onto her hands. 'What must he be thinking? Or feeling?'

'Perhaps a bit confused?'

'But he's always so wrapped up in his history and research, I don't think he notices me at all anymore.'

'Do you notice him? It works both ways. And it can be difficult to stop being "mum and dad" all the time. It takes extra effort to remember the two individuals you once were.'

'I know this. I've told this to more than one patient over the years. Why can I see this in other people and miss it for myself?'

'I think it's well known that doctors make the worst patients.' He gave her a small smile.

'You must think I'm absolutely horrific. You've barely been here five minutes and I'm throwing myself all over you. I feel so bloody stupid.'

'In a way, it's a little flattering but I think that, for you, it was better it was me than anyone else.'

'You do? Why?'

'Because I didn't take advantage. I stopped you taking it any further. Someone else may not have been so scrupulous and that really would've caused you problems.'

'Oh blimey, you're right there.'

'May I ask – do you love your husband?'

'Yes, yes, I do. I really do. I just feel that we've become strangers of late.'

'What would you say to a patient sitting in front of you telling you this?'

'To find ways to reconnect. Arrange a date night or weekend away to sit and talk things through and for both parties to work on making an effort to "see" each other again.'

'So, you already know what you need to do.'

'I do. Thank you, Kenneth, for your kindness and understanding.'

He shrugged as he stood and walked over to the cupboard in the corner.

'Here, use that to tidy your face before you go back out. We don't want the staff talking now, do we?' He handed her a bottle of baby lotion, picked up the paperwork from earlier and took it out to the front desk. When he returned, Jennet looked more like the woman he'd first met several months before.

'Better?' she asked.

'Better,' he smiled, 'although maybe your buttons…'

He moved his finger up and down his own chest and was relieved when she burst out laughing.

'Hmm, yes, perhaps a good idea.'

A minute later, Jennet got up and walked towards the door. Kenneth followed behind her. It was lunchtime and he'd had a sudden desire for a crusty cheese roll and a cup of hot tomato soup. As they stepped out into the reception area, he heard Rhona speaking urgently on the phone.

'Yes, yes, I've got the details. Doctor Cameron is here now. I'll pass on the information. Sorry, what? Err, yes, Doctor MacKenzie is here but he's not on call today. I see… err… let me ask, one moment please…'

She tapped the mute button and looked over.

'Doctor MacKenzie, there's been an accident up at the big house. Something to do with a shooting party and they've asked if you could please attend.'

'Is there a reason why I've been requested over Doctor Cameron?'

If this was some sexist "we don't want a woman doctor" load of tripe, he was not buying into it.

'A member of the shooting party has been injured while out on the far side of the grounds. They're worried about moving him and will need extra assistance to carry him back over the rough terrain.'

'I see.' He turned to Jennet. 'Doctor Cameron, are you okay with this request?'

'Doctor MacKenzie, I think – in the circumstances – that you would be better placed to attend this one.'

She gave a discreet nod down towards her short skirt and high heels.

'Very well. Rhona, please let them know I'm on my way and will be there shortly.'

FIFTY-FIVE

Flora sat quietly in the still room, her hand resting on top of one of the books she'd found in the magical safe. Prior to donning the necklace, she'd felt slightly uncomfortable around the old, worn tomes but now it was the opposite. She could feel them vibrating gently in her hands and when they were opened, a sense of joy would go through her to see the handwriting of her ancestors. If she let her fingers slide across the words, she could hear their voices in her head, reading out what they'd written.

Contrary to what she'd expected, not all the books contained spells and charms – many were diaries from the Floras who gone before her. Notes and observations along with things they'd experienced. Experiences she could now call upon should similar events ever arise again. Such as delivering little Florrie.

It had been a strange seven weeks. Since putting on the necklace, unusual feelings and emotions had been going through her. MacAndrew had explained this was simply her body and soul adjusting to the changes although, he'd said, it would've been easier had Kenneth not broken her heart. That was an obstacle she could have done without. Friand, on the other hand, had just said she was now officially a weirdo and should deal with it! Sometimes, she wondered why she kept that cat!

The sound of rain splashing against the skylight window had her raising her eyes towards it. It was such a small window; she'd originally wondered why it was even there but now she knew that at certain times of the year, the sun and moon would be at the right angle to shine through and there were rare potions to be made which required the essence of sunlight or moonbeam.

On a good day, however, she could see the tops of her mountains across the loch and they *were* her mountains now. Further to the angry email she'd sent to the Arlingh estate after Jack Arlingh's last visit, she'd received a long, hand-written, letter from the Laird apologising for his son's behaviour. He'd explained that Jack had behaved outside of the orders given which were that no country club or exclusive leisure establishment was to be built. The Laird had been against the idea from the start, when Jack had first brought it up, and had believed the matter to be closed. Finding out otherwise had displeased him greatly. As such, measures had been put in place to ensure no such venture could be carried out at a later date and these included extending her land to include both sides of the mountains around her loch plus a further two acres around the perimeter of what she already owned. He was aware that her land held important ecological sites for the area and he knew The Flora could be trusted to look after them both now and in the future. He hadn't expanded on what the other measures were that had been taken.

'Ruminating again, are we?'

MacAndrew walked in, carrying a tray of beakers he'd just cleaned.

'Hmm, sort of. Just learning to listen to what is around

me and how I should or shouldn't respond to it.'

'And how's it going?'

'It's... unusual. I don't seem to "hear" in the conventional manner, it's more that I sense things. There's a mouse under the shelves in the far corner. I haven't seen it but I can sense it being there. I felt small vibrations on the air from its whiskers. There was a very soft throbbing inside me that matched its heartbeat. I could see myself through its eyes. For the first few seconds, I felt panic but then realised that was me, not it. Once I'd calmed myself and went with it, the whole experience was not... unpleasant.' She turned to face him. 'Is it always like that? Will I feel everyone and everything around me?'

'No. You learn to filter out what's not important. It'll come as your gifts settle.'

'The connection with you is different, though. You said we'd be able to do the mind thing once I'd accepted the job.'

'We will – eventually. Just be patient.' MacAndrew inclined his head towards the book she was caressing lightly with her fingertips. 'The more you read of those, the more answers you'll get. Unfortunately, there will be questions I can't answer and without your grandmother's guidance, you're going to have to muddle through the best you can.'

'She's left a very detailed memoir and even went as far as to create a reference table should I need to obtain information in a hurry. But...' she paused for a moment, 'it's not the same as having her instruct me herself. I really do wish I could have had that.'

'Unless I'm mistaken, you haven't spoken to your father since you arrived here. Is that correct?'

'Yes. I just don't know where to start. I still feel angry and resentful towards him for keeping us apart but I now also know, within me, that my grandmother wouldn't approve of it. She understood his feelings and she expects me to do the same.'

'Then perhaps your next piece of "homework" should be to work on tapping into how he feels. Maybe that'll help you find a way to a reconciliation.'

'I can do that?'

'Yes, you can. If you really want to. Read some more of the memoir, I'm sure you'll find what you require in there.'

'Very well. I'll try. By the way, what's for dinner tonight? I'm in the mood for—'

'Cottage pie – I know. It's already in the oven.'

'MacAndrew, you truly are amazing. Thank you. What would I do without you?'

'Starve!'

Flora laughed as he walked out of the room before settling down again, focusing her mind inward to access the knowledge of how to connect with those she loved. She'd just reached a point of calm and peace, ready to step into the memories when MacAndrew suddenly reappeared by her side.

'Flora, come quickly. The trees need to speak with you urgently.'

Her eyes flew open.

'The trees? Are you sure?'

'Of course I'm bloody sure! Come on.'

Confused, Flora hurried up the cellar stairs behind him. She hadn't yet made contact with the tree nymphs, understanding more now of their shy nature, and had been intending to wait a little longer for them to accept her as The Flora, just as the knowledge inside her had advised. For them to come to her was quite out of the ordinary.

She followed MacAndrew out the front door and round to the side of the cottage to see a tree standing where no trees usually stood. When she drew closer, it swayed and she found herself looking into the face of a man as he emerged from within it.

'I am Choilleich, the guardian of the forest.'

She bowed her head. 'I am The Flora.'

'I bring news to you. Your heart is in grave danger. You must hurry to save it.'

'I'm sorry? I don't understand.'

'Your heart is about to die.'

Suddenly, there was a crackling sound as a vision poured into her head.

Jack Arlingh was standing above her… pointing a double-barrelled shotgun right between her eyes!

FIFTY-SIX

Kenneth pulled off the main road, through the imposing red stone gate posts marking the entrance to the Arlingh estate and followed the smooth tarmac road towards the main house. He drove around the second bend and ground to a halt when Jack Arlingh came running towards him. He wound down his window.

'Jack, what's happening? Where's the casualty?'

'Oh, Doctor MacKenzie, thank you very much for coming out. The patient is through the woods there, on the far side of the estate. I believe I told your receptionist this.'

'Yes, you did. Do you want to drive and I'll follow?'

'The track is not clearly marked, Doctor, and there are some hidden, treacherous ditches which can catch you unawares if you don't mind where you're going. It's better to go in my vehicle.'

'Very well. Let me pull over behind you and get my bag.'

Kenneth sighed as he manoeuvred his Land Rover onto the edge of the small layby. He didn't relish being in the enclosed space of a vehicle with Jack Arlingh and would've preferred to have taken his chances with the ditches.

'So, care to fill me in on what happened?' he asked, once he and his bag were ensconced in Jack's four-by-four and they were bouncing across the uneven terrain.

'Shooting party. Some stupid fool ignored the rule to put the safety catch on when his gun wasn't in use and ended up shooting one of his colleagues. I think it may have been the boss so I don't fancy his chances of being employed for much longer.'

'Where was he shot? And did you call for an ambulance?'

'I don't know exactly but there was a lot of blood around his...' Jack pointed down towards his groin.

'Right!'

He turned from Jack to look through the windscreen at the expanse of trees, noticing they'd driven deep into the forest. So deep, there was no longer any need for the windscreen wipers to swipe as so little rain was penetrating through the tall, green, foliage.

'Okay, this is as far as we can go in the car. The rest of the way is on foot, I'm afraid.'

They got out and when Kenneth retrieved his medical case from the back seat, he was shocked to see Jack taking out his rifle.

'Err, do you really think you need that? Is one gun injury today not enough for you?'

'I never walk through the woods without it. Don't know when you might need it.'

'You expecting to meet lions, tigers or bears, perchance?'

Jack grinned. 'No, but a Scottish wildcat may not be out of the question.'

'Excuse me?'

'Ha, ha! Just messing with you. They're more

frightened of us but it's always worth having something that makes a big, bangy, noise to scare them off.'

'I see. Thanks for clarifying.' Kenneth breathed out slowly in relief. He didn't know Jack well enough to tell if he was joking and really hoped he was. He knew there were Scottish wildcats in the area but in all his years, he'd never seen one. He didn't fancy today being the day for that to change.

'Is it much farther now?' he asked, thinking of the injured victim.

'About ten minutes or so. Luckily, there was a barn close by that we were able to take Mr Montagu to. At least he's out of the cold and wet.'

'There's not a lot of wet to worry about, Jack. It's almost as dry as a bone in here.' He gestured around and above him.

'Ah, we were on the edge of the treeline – safer to shoot there, more space – but also less sheltered so we were getting wet.'

'Fair enough.'

A few moments later, they crested a small hill and he saw a barn a short distance away. As they began descending towards it, something began to niggle at the back of his mind. He tried to grasp it but it skittered around the edges of his brain, elusive and avoiding his efforts for clarity. At the same time, he was having to concentrate on his footing as there were many hidden tree trunks and holes which would be painful if he were to fall over, or into, so he could only pay half attention to whatever his head was trying to tell him.

Within a few minutes, they were crossing the clearing in front of the barn.

'Here we go, back into the dry again. After you, Doctor.'

Jack opened the barn door and stepped back to allow

Kenneth to precede him. He'd just crossed the threshold when the veil lifted and the memory he'd been chasing reared up in full technicolour, but before he had a chance to say or do anything, something solid slammed against the side of his face and everything went black.

'Ooooowww!'

A groan slipped from Kenneth's lips as he slowly regained consciousness. His face, above his right ear and around his jaw, was throbbing. There was also an ache above his left temple. He sat for a few moments, trying to gather his thoughts then remembered the sudden jolt of pain against his face and suspected the ache by his temple was from hitting the stone cobbled floor. The same stone cobbled floor he was now sitting on and from which a freezing chill was oozing up into his buttocks and lower back. He moved and realised his hands were tied behind him with a solid pillar in between. His legs were positioned straight out in front of him and he could feel something binding his ankles.

'What? What's going on? Jack? Jack, are you there?'

'Oh, yes, I'm here!'

'Why, am I...' he paused to lick his dry lips, wincing when his tongue touched the wound on the lower one, and tried again. 'Why am I tied up like this? What... what's going on? Are you okay?'

'I'm fine. Well, as fine as can be expected.'

'I don't... I don't understand? What do you mean?'

Annoyed with his groggy lack of comprehension, Kenneth lifted his head but instantly regretted the move as shards of pain shot through him. He managed to prise his eyes open a fraction but the light around him was poor and he couldn't see beyond the gloom. He could hear Jack's voice but couldn't see him.

'I mean that, thanks to your bloody girlfriend, I have lost everything! EVERYTHING! And she's about to pay for that!'

Suddenly, the elusive memory bounced back into his brain.

That was it!

He'd overheard a conversation in the surgery last week where Jack Arlingh and his father had been the hot topic of conversation. Further to his aborted attempts to take the land back from Flora, she'd complained to the Laird who'd been absolutely livid. So much so, he'd immediately set about disinheriting Jack – something to do with him going against his wishes once too often – and had moved the line of succession to his daughter, Alanna. Jack had been ostracised from the family and all their businesses with immediate effect.

Damn!

Damn!

Damn!

This was all an elaborate setup. A trap to lure Flora away from the protection her land gave her so Jack could exact his revenge.

'I don't have a girlfriend, Jack. I don't know what's happening here.'

That's it, try to act like you don't know what's going on. Good move. His brain had decided to join the party and he was beginning to feel a little more alert.

'Don't try to kid me. The photograph of you and The Flora dancing at your wee annual shindig was in all the local papers. You'd have to be blind to miss that you're a couple. And I'm not blind!'

'I'm telling you, Jack, she's not my girlfriend. I hoped she might be but it didn't work out. We're not together.'

'I saw you both that day at her cottage. Don't you tell

373

me there's nothing between you. You don't fool me.'

'That's the last time I saw her. I broke it off just after you left. If you're thinking of using me as bait to bring her here, then you may want to come up with an alternative plan because you'll be waiting a long time.'

'You think so? We'll soon see, won't we?'

His eyes slammed themselves closed as the barn was abruptly filled with light. When he opened them again, it was to see the double-barrel of the shotgun sitting barely three centimetres in front of his face.

FIFTY-SEVEN

Flora drove through the lashing rain as fast as she dared. The windscreen wipers were flashing in front of her eyes as they swiped back and forth at top speed, giving their best efforts to keeping the window clear.

The imposing red gate posts of the Arlingh estate had just come into view when her phone pinged. She lifted a hand from the steering wheel long enough to jab the screen quickly with her finger and was turning through the gates when a message from Kenneth appeared.

Hi Flora, I've had a terrible accident.
Come and help me. Kenneth.

She read it twice and was about to pull over to reply when she turned a bend and saw Kenneth's Land Rover parked up ahead. She drove past and pulled into the vacant spot in front of it. The ignition was turned off as she grabbed her phone.

Of course I'll come. What's happened? Where are you?

She knew from the tone of the text that it hadn't come from Kenneth. Even by his standards, it was far too formal which meant Jack Arlingh must have his phone.

Thank you. I'll drop you a pin.

Thanks to her surprisingly helpful wood nymph and his forest of trees, she already knew Kenneth was somewhere on the Arlingh estate and Choilleich had promised her the trees would guide her to him but she was wary of her ability to "read" them just yet. She was, after all, still rather new to this "gifted" stuff.

Almost immediately, the GPS information appeared on her phone and, from what she could make out, he was right in the middle of nowhere. It looked like she was going to have to trust the trees after all.

Before re-starting the engine, she jumped out, ran back to Kenneth's car, and placed her hand on the bonnet. The stone-cold engine told her he'd parked up at least an hour before. The rain suddenly stopped and she wondered if the sylphs had also come to her aid.

She was getting back into her Landy when she spotted some wheel tracks on the gravel ahead of her and grabbing a torch from the back seat saw, upon closer inspection, tracks veering off to the left of the layby then disappearing into the thick expanse of trees.

'Okay, nymphs,' she murmured, as she turned on the engine, 'time to show me what you can do.'

With great care, she slowly turned and drove towards the trees. At first, the track between them was visible but as darkness began to fall, her visibility lessened by the minute. She was just beginning to despair of being able to find the path through the forest when, quite suddenly, the trees moved, creating a clear route in front of her.

As she drove, the dark brown, woody curtain ahead

would open wide enough to let her pass, then close tightly again behind her. Only darkness could be seen in the rearview mirror.

Finally, after what felt like hours but was less than twenty minutes, she drove over the crest of a hill and the headlights picked out a barn-like structure in a clearing below. The pin on her phone showed she had reached her destination and she quickly switched off the car lights.

'At last,' she whispered, putting the car into neutral and taking a moment to survey the area.

The barn was surrounded on three sides by trees and a single light high up in the eaves picked out the small patch of gravel in front – just large enough for her to turn the Landy around, ready for a quick getaway. She picked up her phone, switched it to camera night mode and used it to zoom in closer on the barn doors. It wasn't perfect but given her lack of binoculars, it was the best she could do.

The doors were nothing spectacular – standard wood with a wicket gate in one. She'd seen plenty of those when out and about with her dad. Unless the Arlinghs had put some kind of internal reinforcements on them, they shouldn't be a problem to breach. She looked at the small array of tools lying on the passenger seat beside her. She hadn't quite brought a knife to a gunfight but she wasn't sure that a pin hammer, a long screwdriver, and a torch were any better. They'd have to do, however, as they were all she'd had time to grab before leaving in a frenzied rush.

She looked about, trying to locate another vehicle as she didn't think for a moment that Jack and Kenneth had walked all this distance. How Jack had lured Kenneth here was a question she'd pushed to the back of her mind – that one could be answered once Kenneth was safe and out of harm's way. However, despite scanning the area the best she could and peering into the trees, there was no sign of a car or truck. Maybe Jack had gone, thinking he had more time before she arrived, wholly unaware that she was already on the estate when he'd sent his text. Whatever the case, she was here now and going in.

Flora took her foot off the brake but kept the Landy out of gear, rolling silently down the incline and using the power of gravity to bring her closer to the barn. If Jack was close-by, she wanted the element of surprise to be on her side.

The Landy rolled to a standstill and she watched in awe as the trees moved around her, hiding the vehicle from the barn but still giving her enough space to turn around and flee when the time came.

And it would – of that she was certain.

One way or another, she'd be leaving here with Kenneth by her side.

Not allowing herself to dwell on what lay ahead, she slipped the hammer and screwdriver into the long pockets of the workman's trousers she was wearing. All the better to hide them from Jack. Let him think she was a defenceless wee woman – it would work in her favour.

She slipped out of the car, pushed the door to, and made her way over to the barn as stealthily as she could. The earlier rain clouds from the day had moved on and the black sky above was speckled with just a few pricks of starlight. The darkness swallowed her up as she relied upon her memory to bring her to the side of the barn.

The change in the air let her know she'd reached the building and she flattened herself against it while edging towards the gable end where the barn doors were located. When she reached the corner she stopped, listening to the silence. It was so quiet she almost believed the forest was holding its breath on her behalf.

Inching slowly around the corner, she reached the wicket gate and let out a sigh of relief when it moved beneath her touch, opening slowly while permitting the light from inside to fly out. She quickly moved back into the shadows but when a few seconds passed with nothing happening, she braved peeping around the gap into the space beyond.

Several bales of hay were dotted about alongside large chunks of farm machinery, a number of wooden barrels which looked rotten around the top, and – seriously? – a husk of a sailing boat in one corner. She didn't even want to think how that had gotten there!

There was, however, no sign of Jack although there were plenty of nooks and crannies where he could hide in among the junk. Her breath caught in her throat though when her eyes finally fell upon Kenneth, sitting on the floor, his arms pinned behind the pillar he was leaning against.

While her first instinct was to rush to his side, after years of shouting at film characters who did exactly that before checking what they were rushing into, she exercised caution and, instead, put her eye to the gap where the hinges sat on the small wooden door, trying to see if Jack was standing behind it or waiting along that side of the barn but, once again, there was no sign of him.

A groan made its way across the room towards her and she knew she had no choice, she had to go in.

Kenneth needed her.

FIFTY-EIGHT

Flora drew in a deep breath, pushed the wicket gate open and stepped through, closing it behind her. If Jack Arlingh was elsewhere, she wasn't giving him any warning of her arrival.

Feeling like her head was on a swivel, she slowly made her way across to Kenneth, checking every space she could see into as she passed.

When she reached him, she knelt and placed her fingers under his chin, lifting his head gently while trying not to hurt him further. The blood on the side of his head told her he'd already suffered at the hands of Jack Arlingh.

'Hey, sleepyhead, time to wake up and get out of here.'

'Flora?'

'Yes, babes, it's me. Come on, I'm here to take you home.'

'Flora… shouldn't have come. Trap.'

'Trap?'

Kenneth's eyelids fluttered upwards and she caught a quick glimpse of his gentle green eyes before they closed again.

'Trap. Shouldn't have come. Not good.'

Before she could say anything else, there was a noise behind her then something cold and hard was pushed against the back of her skull.

'Don't move! Don't even breathe or I'll shoot!'

She took a shallow breath and stilled her movements.

'Get up!'

'You told me not to move…'

'Don't get smart with me!'

Her head jerked forward as Jack jabbed the gun against it. Carefully, she inched herself up to her feet, the barrel of the gun rising with her.

'Put your hands up and turn around. SLOWLY!'

She did as she was told and came face to ugly face with Jack Arlingh. His eyes held a cold, vengeful look and an icy chip of fear lodged itself in her stomach.

Up till now, Flora's thoughts had all been focused on saving Kenneth, she hadn't stopped to think of what could happen to her.

'What do you want, Jack? What's this all about?' She forced herself to speak calmly to him.

'I want revenge, you bitch! I want REVENGE!'

Spittle from his wet thick lips landed on her face and it took all that she had not to give in to the urge to wipe it off in disgust.

'Revenge for what, Jack? You'll need to fill me in here.'

'My father has taken everything away from me. EVERYTHING! Because of you, I no longer inherit the title. I no longer have a position on the estate. I no longer have a HOME! He's taken it all from me and given it to my sister. I have nothing! NOTHING! If you'd just sold me the land as I'd asked, I could have done my deal and shown him that I DO have what it takes to be a success.'

'Would that be the deal your father told you to abandon

and not pursue?'

'He'd have changed his mind. I know it. My plan would've brought prosperity to the area. It would have provided jobs and security for the people in the town.'

'No, it wouldn't, Jack, as well you know.'

Jack's eyes swept behind her at the sound of Kenneth's voice. 'It's no secret that you didn't think the townspeople good enough for your exclusive resort and were planning to ship workers in from elsewhere.'

'The visitors would have spent money in the town. Everyone would have benefitted.'

'Also not true. The clientele you planned to target are the kind who fly in and fly out in their helicopters. They're not going to spend ten hours driving up from London. The town would've gained nothing from it. Nothing!'

'Why you…'

Jack pushed Flora roughly away, causing her to stumble over a coil of rope on the floor. When she'd regained her balance and spun around, he was looming over Kenneth.

'SHUT YOUR MOUTH! SHUT YOUR STUPID DUMB MOUTH!'

She watched in horror as he raised the gun high. The butt was millimetres from Kenneth's head when a long, thick, tentacle swiftly wrapped itself around Jack's waist, lifting him high up in the air. A second tentacle wound around the shotgun, yanking it from his grasp and chucking it across the barn.

'What the— What on—?'

He dangled for a couple of seconds before Flora realised she was the one holding him up there. Seeing the man she loved about to be assaulted by this sad apology for a human being was more than she could bear. The power within her had taken over, causing her to shape-shift to save him.

Fury like she'd never known before swept through her.

Jack Arlingh intended to take the life of someone so precious and for what? A deal over some land? A chance to make more money when he already had everything he needed? His sense of entitlement would never fade; he would never change. He needed to learn the universe didn't revolve around him—

'Flora! Flora! Stop! He's not worth it! Stop!'

Kenneth's voice penetrated her anger and she saw she'd been squeezing Jack tighter and tighter. His face was now bright red and his bulbous eyes looked ready to pop right out of his head.

Some seconds passed while she breathed deeply, forcing the rage out from her body, before she replied, 'Kenneth's right, you are SO not worth it.'

As she released him from her grip, she swung the tentacle around so that Jack flew across the barn, coming to a stop against the far wall, which just so happened to be solid brick. He slid down and came to a stop on the floor behind the hay bales.

Flora ran to Kenneth, wrapped her now-back-to-normal arms around him and kissed him on the forehead – the only part of his face that didn't seem to have any bruising.

'Are you okay? Here, let's get you out of these things.'

She tried to pull the cable ties but they were too thick for her.

'My medicine bag, over by the door. It has scissors in it.'

It took a few minutes for the feeling to come back into Kenneth's legs after sitting on the stone floor for so long but when he was finally able to stand, the first thing he did was check Jack's vitals.

'Is he alive?' Flora asked.

'Yes, he is. Just out cold.'

'Good! Although he deserves worse. Anyway, it's you I'm here for. Come on, let's get you home.'

'What about—'

'He can stay there! We'll notify the estate later where they can find him.'

With those words, Flora put her hand out to Kenneth, picking up the medicine case with the other, and led him out to her car. After helping him into the passenger seat and closing the door, she turned to face the trees around her.

'Thank you,' she whispered to them, 'thank you so very, very much.'

The leaves over her head rustled and swayed and she smiled as she stepped into the Landy and turned the engine on.

FIFTY-NINE

Kenneth tried not to grimace as the Land Rover jolted his sore, bruised body over the hillocks and hollows underneath. The bruising was beginning to come out on one eye and the swelling was causing it to close up. He could still see enough, however, to know the route they were leaving the forest by was not the one he'd gone in on with Jack.

'Are we going the right way? This isn't way I came in.'

'Are you sure?'

'Yes. Jack was all over the place, turning this way and that to avoid the trees.'

'Hmmm, well, if you look closely, you'll see the trees are now avoiding us…'

'What?'

He leant forward to watch the trees, picked out ahead of them in the beams from the headlights. Sure enough, they were moving aside as Flora drove slowly towards them.

'Oh, my…'

'Yes?' Flora gave him a side-glance.

'Nothing!' he sighed. 'Nothing at all.'

He closed his eyes, his head falling back against the headrest, and hoped it wouldn't be long till they reached the smooth tarmac of the road.

His wish was granted five minutes later and when he felt the car turn, he opened his eyes to see his own vehicle still sitting where he'd parked it a lifetime before.

'My car?'

Flora slowed to a stop alongside it. 'Do you need anything from it right now?'

He thought for a few seconds.

'No, I have everything important. I've got my bag and my phone – there's nothing urgent in there.'

'Okay. We'll call Fraser and ask if he and your dad would mind coming to pick it up. We'll do it when we get back to the cottage.'

'They'll ask questions and I'm not sure I can even begin to explain.'

'Leave it to me. I don't think they'll question The Flora so intently.'

She turned to look at him and he caught her wink in the light from the dashboard.

'Yeah, you're right! I don't think they will.'

'Ooh, ooh, ouch!'

'I'm sorry, I'm trying to be as gentle as I can.'

'I know you are but we doctors are a sad bunch–'

'Yeah, I've heard it before… great at patching everyone else up, not so good at looking after yourselves. Well, you need to sit still otherwise this is going to end up in your eye and I'm sure you don't want to add blindness to your list of injuries.'

'Fine. I won't move again.'

They were sitting at the table in the warm kitchen of Flora's cottage. The two dogs were by his feet and Friand was sitting at the end of the table, his leg in the air as he groomed himself. Kenneth smirked at the sight of it. Cats really didn't care, did they?

'I told you not to move.'

'Sorry. I was just smiling at Friand and how little cats care about social situations – if they want to groom, they will groom. No human would ever get away with licking their ass in front of everyone.'

'He says you're just jealous because you can't get your legs behind your head.'

'Excuse me?'

'You heard.'

'He didn't say that…'

'Didn't he?'

He looked at the cat again who, with his leg still stuck in an upright position, had stopped licking to look right at him. And then, bold as brass, stuck his tongue out before resuming with his ablutions.

'Did he… did he just do that?'

'Yup! He says you've to stop being a big baby and just deal with it.'

'Are you telling me you can communicate with him?'

'Sadly, yes I can and it's a right pain in the ass at times – as is he!'

He watched Flora and Friand pull faces at each other before she resumed tending to his wounds.

'And what is it I have to deal with?'

'He says, everything. It's time to accept things for what they are so suck it up and move on.'

He swivelled his good eye back to the cat who now gave him a long, hard look before nodding its head and jumping from the table.

'Tilt your head up a bit more, please.'

He did as he was asked and finally let himself think over the afternoon's events. When Arlingh had taken his phone and ordered him to dictate a message to send to Flora, he'd initially refused. This had resulted in repeated kicks and punches in the face and ribs until he relented. He'd then made the message as cold and unfeeling as possible in the hope she'd refuse to come. He'd been horrified when she'd replied she would but shouting at Jack to leave her alone had only resulted in another punch which knocked him out cold again. He'd just begun to come round when Flora arrived and was too groggy to give her any kind of warning that Arlingh was behind her with his gun.

His thoughts came to a grinding halt. What came next… was… was… was more than he could ever have believed possible.

Yet… it *was* possible.

He'd seen it with his own two eyes.

As he'd mouthed off at Arlingh, refuting his plans for his leisure resort, he hadn't anticipated his reaction and he most certainly hadn't anticipated it angering Jack enough for him to storm forwards with his gun at the ready. He'd closed his eyes tight, expecting the worst, but when it didn't happen, he opened them to see Flora suspending Arlingh in the air, her arms having morphed into long tentacles that were strong enough to hold the fat git up high.

The bigger surprise, however, was the pride he'd felt in that moment. His heart was so proud as he'd watched her grow into herself in front of him. Her hair had risen upwards, swirling around her head, vibrantly red and fiery fierce, while her magic was saving him. She'd looked utterly majestic and he'd known then that he would never leave her side again. She was the woman that she was and he loved every last particle of her being – magical or not.

The very essence of her was made up of things he didn't believe in but he believed in her and she was everything that he needed.

'Thank you, MacAndrew.'

Huh? MacAndrew? Who? What?

He opened his good eye to see her silver ones looking right back at him.

'Well?'

'Well, what?'

'Have you heeded Friand's advice? Have you sucked it up? Are we moving on?'

'Yes, yes, and yes.'

He took hold of the hand that was still dabbing goodness knows what lotions and potions on his face and pulled it close to his heart.

'Flora, I'm desperately sorry for how I behaved and how I treated you. I could give you a million excuses but that's all they'd be – excuses. I shouldn't have left you and if you'll let me, I will spend a lifetime making it up to you. I love you. I have done from that first day when you nicked my parking space and it's only grown stronger. I will never let you down again. I promise.'

She looked at him for several seconds before replying, 'I know you won't. Because you now know what I am capable of!'

She stared at him a second longer before bursting into laughter.

'You know, saying stuff like that really *doesn't* help…'

Flora leant forward and murmured against his sore, bruised, mouth, 'I know, but it's so much fun,' before kissing him gently.

When she pulled away, she looked over his shoulder.

'Is this a good time?' she asked.

Kenneth half-turned to see who was there but it was only empty space between him and the kitchen sink.

'Who are you talking to?'

'MacAndrew, I'd like to introduce you to Doctor Kenneth MacKenzie.'

As she spoke, a man appeared in front of his eyes – a small man wearing a tall blue hat, a blue coat, a tartan waistcoat, and blue plus-four trousers.

'And, Kenneth, I'd like you to meet MacAndrew.'

He felt the pressure as five pairs of eyes came to rest upon him. Two dogs, one cat, Flora, and this strange little man all waited to see what he would say or do next.

And, really, there was only one thing he could do.

'Delighted to meet you, MacAndrew,' he said, holding out his hand.

SIXTY

Flora picked up her coffee mug and smiled as she looked over the rim, watching Kenneth absorb whatever new medical advancement was currently on his tablet while his breakfast grew cold on the plate beside him.

It was almost a month since their "adventure" as they referred to it and his bruising had all but disappeared. The cut above his eye had been deep and would almost certainly leave a scar. She had a potion to prevent that but Kenneth had declined, saying the scar would be a reminder of what he'd almost lost and would ensure he never did in the future.

Friand strolled into the kitchen, sprang up onto the table and cast his eye in Kenneth's direction.

'Hey, sweetcheeks, tell your man over there he's got five minutes to eat the bacon roll or he'll be going to work on a bread bap!'

With a snort of laughter, she relayed the message. Kenneth looked from her to the cat.

'You know, I was wondering, is there any way I could learn how to converse with the animals the way you do?'

Friand's head spun round to face her, his eyes wide with pupils dilated.

'Noooooo! Don't you bloody dare! Can you even begin to imagine the things he sees and has in his head? I'd be scarred for life! And we both know that's gonna be a very long time!'

Unable to help herself, she broke into laughter again.

'What? What did he say?'

'My darling, the polite version is that Friand feels it would not be appropriate given your current employment position. I believe he's worried the doctor-patient confidentiality thing may be compromised.'

'Hmmm, I didn't think of that. Fair enough. I'll just need to rely on you to be my translator.'

'Anytime, my love.'

'Good save, honeybun, I owe you one!'

When Kenneth slid a rasher from his roll over to Friand before hastily consuming the rest, clearly not trusting the cat to wrestle him for it, she hid her grin as a lazy, contended sigh slipped from her. These last few weeks had been the best she'd ever known. She and Kenneth spent a lot of time together but they also agreed that time apart was good for them.

'How can you miss someone if they're always there?' had been his words of wisdom. 'Missing the one you love is actually part of the joy of being in love.'

It was a lovely sentiment and she did enjoy missing him. For now. Her heart, however, was hoping they would move on from this stage of the relationship towards something more solid, sooner rather than later.

McAndrew had just begun to clear the table when there was a knock on the front door.

'Huh?'

Flora looked around in surprise. The dogs hadn't barked any warning and unexpected visitors just didn't happen. Now that she'd gained her knowledge, she'd understood the need to redo the protection ward on the loch which had broken down in her absence and was why Jack Arlingh had been able to cross it.

'Aye, I wondered how long it would take them tae visit!'

She looked at McAndrew. 'Who's visiting? What do you mean?'

'You'd best just go and get that, Flora.'

When she opened the door, a sharp gust of wind blew in followed by a man and a woman, both dressed in sharply tailored, dark mauve suits.

The woman looked at a clipboard in her hand.

'Ms Flora MacDonald O'Brien?'

'Yes, that's me.'

A hand was thrust out towards her.

'I'm Donaghue and this is Krichen. We're from M.A.G.I.C.'

As she shook the hands held out, Flora replied, 'Magic?'

'Magical And Gifted Incidents Committee.'

'Oh, right.'

'We're here about an incident involving a Mr...' Donaghue checked her clipboard again, 'Jack Arlingh, which occurred three weeks and five days hence.'

'Ah, right. Well, if you'd like to come in and take a seat, I'd be happy to answer any questions you may have.'

'You might want to ask your Natural to join us.'

'My WHAT?'

Donaghue looked at her clipboard for the third time.

'A Doctor Kenneth MacKenzie. He's your Natural, yes?' Flora's look of confusion led her to explain. 'He's your non-gifted partner? Is that correct?'

'Oh, you mean he's a Muggle? Yes, that's right. I'll ask him to come through.'

393

She led the two visitors into the lounge and swore she heard Donaghue mutter, 'If I EVER get my hands on that bloody J.K. Rowling…'

A few minutes later, they were all seated and MacAndrew brought in a tray of refreshments.

'Abbygale,' he nodded at Donaghue.

'MacAndrew,' she nodded back.

'You guys know each other?'

Donaghue smiled. 'We do. The realm of the magical and gifted is not as extensive as some would think. It's a small *other-world*, as we say. Now, please tell me about the events of three weeks and five days ago…'

Between them, Flora and Kenneth described what had occurred with Jack Arlingh and the reason behind his behaviour. They also presented the photographs Flora had taken as proof in the event the police may come calling. They just hadn't expected the policing to be in magical form.

'Thank you both for your honesty. I'm happy that your gift was used correctly, Flora. Protection of self and loved ones is permitted within acceptable guidelines.'

'May I ask what brought you here now? It's been almost a month.'

'You haven't heard? Jack Arlingh was babbling his mouth off about The Flora stealing his voice, growing tentacles, and throwing him against the wall. Now, while *we* know that to be the truth, it's not beneficial for others to know it. A suggestion was made that being disinherited has tipped his already delicate mental state over into irrationality and his obsession with trying to obtain The Flora's land is the core of the issue. He's currently residing in an establishment with many locked doors and is likely to remain there for some time.'

'Oh, right. Well, it's good to know he won't be troubling us again.'

'You're welcome. It was nice to meet you both.' Donaghue smiled, gripped the sleeve of her rather silent partner, Krichen, and they both vanished into thin air.

There was a moment of silence until Kenneth cleared his throat and asked, 'Can *you* do that?'

'No,' Flora replied wistfully, 'not one of my gifts.'

She was in the middle of replacing the teacups on the tray when her phone beeped in her pocket and, after stopping to read it, she let out a loud groan.

'What now?'

Flora turned the screen around so Kenneth could see it.

'It's from Sally, informing me that she and my father are coming up for Christmas, they've already booked a room at a hotel in Beauly and she is *not* taking no for an answer!'

SIXTY-ONE

Christmas Eve

'Can I tempt you with another mince pie, Sally?' Flora picked up the plate and held it over the table.

'Oh, gosh, no. Thank you. Another crumb and I will surely burst. It was all quite delicious but I'm full to the brim.'

Just then, Sally's phone beeped. She took it from her pocket and quickly read the message. 'Jools has locked up for the day and is looking forward to her time off. She sends her love.'

'How is she? Any updates regarding her and Nick? Wedding bells, perhaps…' Flora liked Sally's friend and colleague, Juliet, a lot. She was funny, down to earth and was as passionate about animals as Sally was and the two of them were as thick as thieves.

'No wedding bells yet but the latest is that Nick is moving into the cottage with her.'

'Oh, wow! That's brilliant news.'

'It's all worked out rather well, to be honest. With his

father retiring, and moving out of the flat above their surgery, Nick can now include the accommodation as a sweetener to attract staff. The last I heard was he'd offered it to a husband-and-wife team who are both vets and keen to bring their young family to live in the country.'

'That sounds perfect. And quite advantageous for everyone.'

'It will be.'

There was silence for a moment and then Sally leant over the table towards Flora,

'Flora, you need to forgive him. It's time.'

Flora hesitated for a moment before replying.

'I know… and I want to… but… I just don't know how. He broke my trust. He hurt me.'

'Oh, Flora,' Sally's hand came to sit on hers, 'people are always going to hurt you because that's what human beings do. No one is perfect and you shouldn't expect them to be. Nobody can live up to such high demands.'

'But… what he did…'

'All too often, good people do bad things but for good reasons.'

'Has it ever happened to you?'

'Yes. Jools and I had an incident about four years ago, give or take. She did something which was very difficult for me to deal with. I won't say what because you don't need to know but I had to decide if I was going to let one bad decision mar what was becoming a good friendship. Everyone makes mistakes, some bigger than others, but if people are essentially good, those mistakes shouldn't define the rest of their lives. I made the decision to put the incident behind me, move forward with my friendship and I don't regret it at all. Jools is wonderful, my trust in her is fully restored and I would've been the loser if I'd walked away. Don't walk away from your father, Flora. He's a good man who loves you very much. You can't change your past but you can change your future. And now, at the risk of being rude, I'm going to take a stroll around this gorgeous loch and would love if your delightful Westies came with me.'

Flora looked down at the two dogs lying at her feet.

'Well, do you want to go with Sally for a walk?'

'Of course we do!' Kirsty wagged her tail.

Sandy grunted. *'When have we ever refused a walk? We'll show her all the good sniffing spots.'*

She turned back to Sally with a smile. 'They'd love to join you.'

Sally's brief look of confusion caused her to chuckle inwardly. It still gave her a thrill to finally be able to communicate with the dogs on this level and she hoped she'd never take such a special gift for granted.

Once she was alone, Flora cleared the crockery from the table, walking into the kitchen in time to see her dad placing the cutlery in the dishwasher – just as he always had – and she knew the moment had come for her to take the next step into her future.

'If I grab some throws, would you like to sit outside on the patio with me?'

He looked at her tenderly for a few seconds before replying, 'I would like that very much.'

As she settled herself down on the bench she'd placed in the sheltered corner beneath the kitchen window, Flora swept her gaze over her small domain. The patio table and chairs had been stored away for the winter, giving her a perfect, unbroken view of the loch and mountains before her. When it was dry, which wasn't as often as she'd like, she would sit here, allowing the peace and solitude to flood through her. Kenneth joined her whenever he could and they'd sit side-by-side in silence, holding hands, enjoying the simple pleasure of being together.

'It's very beautiful. I can understand why you don't want to leave.'

'Yes, it is. I've come to love being here more than I could ever have imagined.'

'You're wearing your locket! I didn't know you still had it, you haven't worn it for so long.'

She looked down to see she was fidgeting with the small silver locket her dad had given her on her tenth birthday. It had a picture of her mum and dad inside and he'd told her at the time it was to let her know she'd always be loved by them no matter what. They would never stop being a family.

'I stopped wearing it because the chain became too small. I always meant to buy a new one but only recently got around to it.'

The real reason she was wearing the locket was because it enabled her to connect to her dad. Her grandmother had described the process in one of her journals. The best way to keep the link between her and her loved ones was through a personal item they'd given to her in love. For her grandmother, it had been the wedding ring Grandfather Archie had placed on her finger all those years ago. When Flora was looking for something to help her reach her father, she'd found the locket and knew it was the perfect token. Not that she could tell her father any of this. If he were to ever hear any of the stories the local community liked to tell, she'd have to laugh and wave them away as folklore and speculation. Only the life-partner of The Flora could ever know the truth.

They sat quietly again for a bit, watching Sally and the dogs making their way over to the other side of the loch, when her father suddenly blurted out, 'I'm so sorry, Flora, for keeping you away from here and the heritage that is rightfully yours. It was wrong of me, I know that. I thought I was protecting you but I now realise I was protecting myself. I feared losing you. I'd already lost your mother. I couldn't have gone through that again.'

She took his hand and squeezed it gently. She could feel the turmoil within him and it was up to her to help him work through it.

'It's okay.'

'But it's not! Craig is right – I was unnecessarily cruel to his mother by keeping you away from her.'

'She understood and she didn't hold it against you. She wrote about it in her journals, specifically for me to see when the time was right for me to read them. She wanted me to know that she never held your choices against you and she didn't want me to do so either.'

'She said that? Really?'

'Yes, she said that.'

Her dad sighed and she felt the darkness of his guilt through his hand. 'I feel so bad that I stopped you from enjoying all this,' he swept his other hand out towards the loch, 'when you were a kid. Holidays here would have been wonderful for you – all these trees to run around in. I stopped you having that freedom of adventure.'

'Dad, stop.' She took his hand in both of hers. 'I've come to realise that everything happens for a reason and everything has its own special moment. Kenneth and I shared with you last night how we first met. I firmly believe that had I visited when I was a kid, we'd most likely have known each other back then because of the friendship between his mother and mine, meaning our meeting earlier this year wouldn't have had the impact it did. I could be wrong – maybe we would have still fallen in love, but then… maybe we wouldn't have. If changing the past meant losing the man I love now, then I'm happy to let it be as it is.'

'You've grown rather wise since moving up here.'

Flora smirked to herself. He didn't know the half of it!

'Well, Pops,' she grinned, 'it had to happen sometime.'

He pulled his hand away to wrap his arms around her in a warm bear hug which she submitted herself to quite happily – it had been a long time since she'd had one. As they sat together in their embrace, she felt the trust she'd had before return to her. Sally was right – he was a good man who'd made a bad decision for a good reason. She squeezed him tightly, letting him know they were good again.

'While I've got you like this,' he murmured against her ear, 'there's something I need to tell you. And then ask you.'

'Oh, yes?'

She leant back and twisted round on the bench to look at him.

'I've… errr… I've asked Sally to marry me. And she said yes.'

'Well, I'd damn well hope so! She'd be a fool to let a fine specimen like you slip away. That's wonderful. I'm so happy for you. For you both.'

'You really don't mind?'

'Mind? Why on earth would I mind? I've been wanting you to get hitched again for years!'

'Sally's hoping you'll agree to be one of her bridesmaids along with Jools.'

'I'd be thrilled to be a bridesmaid but what about Karen? She's Sal's best mate.'

'Karen was a bridesmaid when Sally married Steve. She thinks it would feel weird having her do it again and Karen agrees. This is a new beginning for us all. Sally will formally ask you herself but she wanted me to test the waters first to avoid any upset.'

'Then please tell her I can't wait to be formally asked,'

she smiled, 'although, if she's thinking of big, pink, meringue dresses, I may well change my mind.'

'I'll pass on your concern but I suspect you'll be safe there. She's not a pink frills kinda gal.'

'I reckon you've got that one right.'

They shared a snigger before Matt drew in a deep breath.

'There's one more thing we need to discuss.'

'Which is?'

'The house. I'm guessing you won't be returning to Lower Ditchley.'

'That would be accurate.'

'And so, I'm wondering what to do. I'm not of a mind to sell the house, it has too many memories I don't want to lose, but renting it out feels all wrong too. However, leaving it lying empty…'

'Well, old man, I might just have a solution for you AND it'll help you to mend those broken bridges with Uncle Craig.'

'Really? I'm listening…'

'Clarissa and Ross are returning to the UK permanently in February. Ross will be UK based and only needs to go into the London office once a week so the rest of the time, he'll be working from home. I know Clarissa would like to be close to her mum, having been away all these years, so why not rent the house to them. After all, one way or another, they're practically family. That might be less traumatic for you…'

Flora let her fingers stray up to her locket. Her dad was battling again with his emotions, she could feel them, but as she waited quietly beside him, she felt them settle and a wave of peace flowed through her fingertips.

'That is a very good suggestion. Yes, that would work. Do you think Craig and Essie will go along with it? I know Craig's still angry with me.'

'I think it's a good olive branch to hold out. Essie's desire to have Clarissa close-by may just be enough to soothe the waters. If Uncle Craig still digs his heels in, she'll talk him round – of that I am sure.'

She turned back to look at the loch, smiling when she saw the tip of a tail break the surface of the water just as a gentle breeze blew and the trees swayed, all telling her in their own special way that they belonged with her.

And she belonged with them.

SIXTY-TWO

Harvest Ceilidh – 9 months later.

'Mum's done herself proud here, wouldn't you say?'

Kenneth followed Ross's eyes around the barn, taking in the stunning décor. Their mother had finally found her niche – event planning was her thing. She loved it and the success of her venture was a testament to that. The venue and cabins were fully booked for the rest of the year and well into the following one too. Traditional Scottish weddings had proved to be exceptionally popular along with writing retreats and numerous kinds of conferences. It had been a relief for Kenneth when he'd moved into the cottage with Flora because being in the middle of a party atmosphere every night was more than he could cope with. He was a man who enjoyed his solitude.

Although, on saying that, while the cottage sat in an area of outstanding beauty and peacefulness, solitude within its walls was in rather short supply when you lived with three cats, two dogs, one Flora and a MacAndrew!

Choona and Chips had bonded wonderfully with Sandy

and Kirsty – the two young felines followed their doggy companions everywhere and it was rather cute to see. Friand, however, preferred to hang back, rarely venturing far from the cottage. He adored Flora despite, according to Flora, being a sarky little brat towards her most of the time. But she didn't see what he did – that Friand was never far from her and always watched over her fiercely.

'Yes, she sure has,' he answered his brother's question, 'but then, she was always going to pull out all the stops for a family wedding.'

Every bouquet in the room had been tied with MacKenzie ribbons while the beams overhead were adorned with tartan swags, hanging ivy interspersed with bunches of heather and twinkling fairy lights. The gilt chairs on either side of the aisle were decorated with large tartan bows and tall, free-standing cast iron candle holders were dotted all around the room. It really did feel very special.

He glanced at Ross tugging on the sleeves of his jacket and shuffling with the chain on his sporran.

'Feeling nervous, little brother?'

'Of course I am – I'm getting married! What man doesn't?'

'Good point.'

'But,' Ross grinned at him, 'I *am* about to marry the most wonderful woman I have ever met. I fell in love with Clarissa the very first instant I set eyes on her. She took my breath away with her smile and still does every day. I didn't know it was possible to love someone this much.'

Kenneth smiled at his brother's words for they echoed his own feelings for Flora. She was his sun, his moon and everything in between. Her gifts no longer bothered him and he'd come to learn that they did not define her as the wonderful woman she was, they merely enhanced someone who was already special in her own true way. She was the person that she was and nothing on this planet or in this universe would ever take him away from her side.

They both checked the time on their watches while acknowledging their friends and neighbours as they traipsed in to take their seats, many sending waves and smiles in their direction.

'Not long now, little bro.'

'No, big bro, not long at all.'

Flora looked into the vast mirror in front of her and caught the eye of Clarissa sitting close by. Essie was putting the final pins in her hair, piling her curls into a glorious up-do and not being too gentle about it.

'Ow, Mum, don't be so rough. I'm not the one marrying a doctor here!'

Essie laughed along with Clarissa and Flora as she slid the last hairgrip into place.

'I'm sorry, darling, I just want to be sure it all stays in place.'

'Essie, with the amount of lacquer you've sprayed on it, it'll still be in place when poor Clarissa celebrates her fiftieth wedding anniversary. Here, sit down, relax, and drink this.'

Sally passed round the glasses of champagne she'd just poured, laughing as she spoke.

'We've got a few minutes to spare before these two need to get into their dresses – let's make the most of them.'

Flora exchanged another smile with Clarissa before sipping on the glass of fizzy bubbles in her hand. As the kick from the alcohol ran through her, it was immediately followed by a burst of immense happiness that had every nerve ending in Flora's body tingling with joy. At long last, after all these years, she finally had friends and, even more important, she had the family she'd grown up craving. She now had a mother in Sally although they were friends, first and foremost.

Through marriage, Clarissa was about to become her sister-in-law but, to the surprise of them both, they'd bonded so well over the last year, sharing many long internet calls and weekends together, they'd mutually agreed to drop the "in-law" from the title and call themselves sisters – the sibling they'd both spent a lifetime wishing they had. When Kenneth and Flora had announced their engagement at the beginning of the year, Clarissa had jumped straight in and begged them to get married alongside her and Ross. As it was, the request couldn't have been more generous because she and Kenneth would've had to wait another twelve months for not only was Mhari's venue fully booked up but getting all the neighbours together again would have been almost impossible due to their work commitments. The Harvest ceilidh was always the first booking put into the calendars each year so was the perfect time for a wedding. Once Clarissa had convinced her she genuinely would be delighted to share her wedding day with them, Flora was fully on board and they'd all had so much fun planning the day with Mhari who was, naturally, over the moon and beyond that one of her boys was marrying The Flora. Their family had just gone up a little more in the estimation of the townsfolk.

'Okay, girls, time to get your posh frocks on.'

They stood, slipping off their cosy bathrobes, while Essie and Sally bustled across the room, each with a hanger held high in their hands.

Stepping into their wedding dresses, Flora and Clarissa turned to face each other while the older women fastened, laced, and buttoned them up.

'Your dress is stunning, Clarrie. You look amazing.'

And she did. The elegant, long, pale cream silk sheath fitted her lovely curves while the delicate lace across the bodice and cap-sleeves matched the fishtail train behind her.

Flora, on the other hand, had always dreamt of a frothy, frilly, creation and while not the full "toilet roll doll" style, her soft lilac A-line dress had enough lace and beading to satisfy her inner five-year-old Disney princess while still managing to be classy and understated.

'Stand still, Flora, these buttons are fiddley!'

Sally reprimanded her as she cast a glimpse over her shoulder to view the long satin train trailing on the floor. *That* had been the one thing she'd refused to compromise on and seeing it now made her five-year-old self jump up and down with glee.

'Honestly, whoever thought of the idea of tiny buttons on a lace bodice needs shooting,' grumbled Sally, stepping back to arrange the train just as the photographer knocked and called through the door, asking if it was all clear for her to come in.

She posed Clarissa and Essie first then stepped back to take her shots.

'Oh, Clarissa, I feel like I've been waiting since forever for this day to come. I'm so proud and happy for you.' Essie dabbed her eyes carefully once the photographer said they could move.

'I'm proud and happy for us both, Mum. George did his best to quash our spirit but we conquered all. Waiting *since forever* made us into the women we are today and I'd say we're pretty damn awesome.'

'I'd agree with that!' Sally smiled. 'You know, I always felt there was something missing from my life,' she continued, 'but I could never say what it was. In some ways, you could say I've been hoping *since forever,'* they grinned at her words, 'to find contentment and now I have it. A husband I love dearly, a daughter I adore, a business that fulfils me, and a friend,' she smiled broadly at Essie, 'who makes me laugh every day. I really couldn't ask for anything more.'

The three women turned to face Flora.

'Oh, my turn, is it?'

She looked at them and saw the love they all shared for each other shining on their faces. She could *feel* it pulsating around the room, intermingled with their joy and happiness. Each of them had fought their own demons, in whatever form those had taken, and come out the other side all the better for it. Better yet, they were now all bonded together through love and as family. Individually, they were strong but united… they were formidable!

Flora picked up her abandoned champagne glass and nodded to the others to do the same.

'I love my dad, more than anything, but all I ever desired was a mother,' she tilted her glass towards Sally, 'a sister,' she did the same to Clarissa, 'and an aunt who was slightly naughty and would lead me astray.' Everyone laughed when she looked at Essie. 'You could say I've been wishing *since forever* for a proper family. And now I not only have that, but so, so, much more. I feel very blessed every day for the life I now live and never want to change.'

She raised her glass in the air.

'To our lives, our blessings and our family.'

They chinked their glasses together while the photographer snapped her camera all around them.

'Can we come in now?'

Matt's voice came through the door and Essie rushed over to let him and Craig in.

'Oh, my goodness, Flora…'

His voice thickened as he strode towards her, hugging her tightly.

'Hey, only happy vibes in here, old man!'

'You look so beautiful. Your mother would've been immensely proud of the woman you've become.'

'I'm sure she would've been. Just as the mother I have now, is.'

She watched Sally blink away tears as she joined their little group hug before turning to Essie who was doing the same with Craig and Clarissa.

'Okay, Essie, time we were out of here, I think.'

When they'd gone, the photographer pushed and pulled them all into their respective poses before finally allowing them to head out to the two horse-drawn carriages waiting outside.

Flora stood calmly in the outer entrance of the barn, waiting for her turn to enter while her Maid of Honour, Trina, who'd asked to meet her at the barn because she hadn't wanted to leave Bobby trying to look after three small children for too long, fussed with the long train of her dress. Flora had wanted all of her new family with her on this special day so Essie had been given charge of Kirsty and Sandy who were now inside sitting with her. Friand, however, had insisted on walking down the aisle in front of her and he now stood quietly by her side, looking quite handsome in his MacDonald bandana. His silence was short-lived, however, when he looked up at her and said, *'Scrubbed up not bad there, Sweetcheeks. If I didn't know better, I'd think it was a special occasion!'*

Unable to talk aloud because of her dad's presence, she mentally replied, *'Right back at ya, fleabag!'*

She grinned down at him and he winked back in return.

A second later, MacAndrew appeared in front of her.

'Only a minute or two now, Flora. Clarissa and Ross are just getting into position.'

She smiled at the little man who'd come to mean so much to her and who still guided her each day. While Friand had insisted on being here today, she'd had to insist that MacAndrew also be with her. He'd argued against it, saying it wasn't the done thing in their community, until, left with no choice, she'd made it an order and that was the moment when they finally connected and she'd felt his joy at being included.

Lifting her head to face straight ahead, she drew in a deep breath as she waited. She'd insisted Clarissa should walk down the aisle before her as this had been her wedding day first and it was only right that she got the initial blaze of bridal glory. The other reason for her going in first was that the length of Flora's train meant it was almost in a different postcode!

Soon, the signal came that it was now her time to join her groom. The vast doors slid open and she walked in, her dad counting his steps quietly under his breath while the sound of stifled laughter rolled around the room at the sight of Friand walking so proudly in front of her. She glanced down at her bouquet – a simple concoction of heather and lily-of-the-valley tied with MacDonald and MacKenzie tartan ribbons – and when she looked back up, she met Kenneth's eyes. The smile on his face radiated immense happiness and reflected her own feelings. She sent out a quick probe and felt only joy and love within him. A joy and love that matched her own.

As she came to stand beside him, he leant slightly towards her and whispered out the side of his mouth, 'Are you ready for this?'

She thought back to the earlier sentiments shared in the dressing room and her answer sprang to her lips.

'Oh, yes, my darling man, I'm ready. I've been ready… *since forever*!'

ABOUT THE AUTHOR

Kiltie Jackson spent her childhood years growing up in Scotland. Most of these early years were spent in and around Glasgow although for a short period of time, she wreaked havoc at a boarding school in the Highlands.

By the age of seventeen, she had her own flat which she shared with a couple of cats for a few years while working as a waitress in a cocktail bar (she's sure there's a song in there somewhere!) and serving customers in a fashionable clothing outlet before moving down to London to chalk up a plethora of experience which is now finding its way into her writing.

Once she'd wrung the last bit of fun out of the smoky capital, she moved up to the Midlands and now lives in Staffordshire with one grumpy husband and another six feisty felines.

Her little home is known as Moggy Towers even though, despite having plenty of moggies, there are no towers! The cats kindly allow her and Mr Mogs to share their home as long as the mortgage continues to be paid.

Since the age of three, Kiltie has been an avid reader although it was many years later before she decided to put pen to paper – or fingers to keyboard – to begin giving life to the stories in her head. Her debut novel was released in September 2017 and her fourth book was a US Amazon bestseller in Time Travel Romance.

Kiltie loves to write fiery and feisty female characters and puts the blame for this firmly on the doorsteps of Anne

Shirley from Anne of Green Gables and George Kirrin from The Famous Five.

When asked what her best memories are, Kiltie will tell you:

1. Queuing up overnight outside the Glasgow Apollo to buy her Live-Aid ticket.
2. Being at Live-Aid.
3. Winning an MTV competition to meet Bon Jovi in Sweden.

(Although, if Mr Mogs is in earshot, the latter is changed to her wedding day.)

Her main motto in life used to be "Old enough to know better, young enough not to care!" but that has since been replaced with "Too many stories, not a fast enough typist!"

You can follow Kiltie on the following platforms:

www.kiltiejackson.com

www.facebook.com/kiltiejackson

www.instagram.com/kiltiejackson